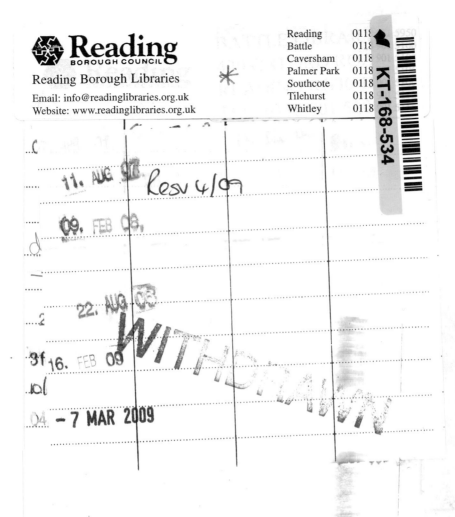

Reading
BOROUGH COUNCIL

Reading Borough Libraries

Email: info@readinglibraries.org.uk
Website: www.readinglibraries.org.uk

Reading	0118
Battle	0118
Caversham	0118
Palmer Park	0118
Southcote	0118
Tilehurst	0118
Whitley	0118

KT-168-534

11. AUG   Resv 4/09

09. FEB 08.

22. AUG 08

3f 16. FEB 09

04. -7 MAR 2009

WITHDRAWN

CLASS NO.

TO AVOID OVERDUE CHARGES THIS BOOK SHOULD BE
RETURNED ON OR BEFORE THE LAST DATE STAMPED
ABOVE. IF NOT REQUIRED BY ANOTHER READER IT MAY
BE RENEWED BY PERSONAL CALL, TELEPHONE OR POST.

0333 713 060 1 549 E4

The Rich
and the
Profane

By the same author

Firefly Gadroon
Gold from Gemini
The Gondola Scam
The Great California Game
Jade Woman
The Judas Pair
Moonspender
Pearlhanger
The Sleepers of Erin
The Tartan Ringers
The Vatican Rip
The Very Last Gambado
The Lies of Fair Ladies
The Grail Tree
Spend Game
Paid and Loving Eyes
The Sin Within Her Smile
The Grace in Older Women
The Possessions of a Lady
Different Women Dancing

Omnibus editions
Lovejoy
Lovejoy at Large
Lovejoy at Large Again

As Jonathan Grant
Mehala, Lady of Sealandings
Storms at Sealandings
The Shores of Sealandings

JONATHAN GASH

The Rich
and the
Profane

A Lovejoy Novel

MACMILLAN

First published 1998 by Macmillan

an imprint of Macmillan Publishers Ltd
25 Eccleston Place, London SW1W 9NF
and Basingstoke

Associated companies throughout the world

ISBN 0 333 71306 0

Copyright © Jonathan Gash 1998

The right of Jonathan Gash to be identified as the
author of this work has been asserted by him in accordance
with the Copyright, Designs and Patents Act 1988.

All rights reserved. No part of this publication may be
reproduced, stored in or introduced into a retrieval system, or
transmitted, in any form, or by any means (electronic, mechanical,
photocopying, recording or otherwise) without the prior written
permission of the publisher. Any person who does any unauthorized
act in relation to this publication may be liable to criminal
prosecution and civil claims for damages.

9 8 7 6 5 4 3 2 1

A CIP catalogue record for this book is available from
the British Library.

Phototypeset by Intype London Ltd
Printed by Mackays of Chatham plc, Chatham, Kent

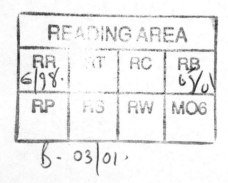

READING AREA

| RR 6/98. | KT | RC | RB 6/01 |
| RP | RS | RW | MO6 |

b - 03/01.

To the Chinese God Wei D'To,
protector of books from the ungodly,
this book is humbly dedicated

Lovejoy

For

Jackie and Bill

Thanks

Susan

1

S EEING A WOMAN get arrested makes you relieved it's not you. Except this time I'd really relied on Irma for today's dinner. The antiques game is the pits.

Irma had found me feeding my robin, a creature of psychotic jealousy. It flirted its beak, its tail, stood truculently four-square and made its kick-kick-kick sound. I told it to shut up. It took no notice, which is typical. Women, infants and animals treat me like a serf.

'Are you Lovejoy?' She gave me a photo of a necklace. 'I need your help.'

She looked beautiful and rich. I'd never seen her before. 'You want me to find an antique necklace like this? Easy. They're pretty common. Late Edwardian, semi-precious stones. Tourmaline's bonny, but these small malachite greens are horrible.' I pointed to them. 'A lady's beautiful swan neck can only take so many absolute primary colours.' But you couldn't tell the Edwardians that.

A cool lass, dressed for visiting a maiden aunt. Celtic, my old Gran would have said, black hair, radiant blue eyes, pale skin. Twenty, give or take.

'I don't want to buy, Lovejoy. I want to steal it.'

'Why steal something so ordinary?'

'This necklace is mine.' She said it with fervour, caught herself and read my tatty sign, LOVEJOY ANTIQUES, INC. 'I expected you to be quite grand.'

I admit I don't impress. Crumbling thatched cottage, rickety porch, windows partly boarded from recent bailiff trouble, my old Austin Ruby rusting among weeds, and a workshop with rotting doors agape.

'It's in Gimbert's Auction. My aunt won't give it back.'

'Tomorrow's sale?' I tried to judge her. 'Why not bid for it? It'll only be a few quid.'

Angrily she erupted, 'And give her the satisfaction? They said at the Antiques Arcade that you knew how to steal things.'

I sighed. East Anglia's famed reticence was in action. What with that and this girl's hate, they'd have the TV news cameras waiting. I felt uncomfortable.

'Look, love. Once upon a time, a bloke in our next village got left his grandad's old motorbike. It was a 1954 AJS Porcupine – banned in its day for being too fast. He sold it for quarter of a million. Same day, a vicar in the next county sold a Thackeray chamber pot and went on a Mediterranean holiday from the proceeds. That famed author criticized the city of Cork, whose Victorian citizens put his face in their utensils. See? There's legit money in antiques, if you only look. But not with necklaces like this.'

'Teach – me – to – steal,' she said, as if to an infant.

Three things exist in the world of antiques, and only three. They're antiques, women and money. The trouble is, everybody knows – they say – everything about all three, when they know nothing. In fact, knowledge is pretty useless. Give you an instance:

Last year, a famous university (Southampton; don't tell) spent up psychoanalysing dogs. Their project: which dog is man's best pal? Their conclusion was (1) greyhound, (2) whippet, (3) the basset hound. So let's all rush to friendly neighbourhood kennels and buy, because now we know. Except there's one hitch. What if you prefer Buster, your lovable spaniel, instead? See what I mean? All that magnificent research can take a running jump. Knowledge is useful, up to a point. But it's what you *want* that matters. That dog info, so expensively bought, is on a par with all sorts of other 'essential facts'. Like, the Indian elephant has a hell of a temper in the morning. So? And, the world's first recorded tornado occurred, guess when, in AD 1410, in – guess where? – Venice. So? And intrepid polar flyer Commander Richard E. Byrd, first human to fly over the North Pole, er, faked it. Didn't get within a hundred miles of the Pole. The Norwegian Amundsen *really* did it in an airship less than a week later. I explained all this.

'Knowledge only goes so far, love.'

'Get on with it,' she said, lips tight.

'It's nothing to do with me, OK?' I couldn't afford another brush with the law. I'd not long squared Dunko for my last bail.

'Thank you, Lovejoy. I'll pay.' She held out a hand. 'Irma Dominick.' We shook politely. 'One thing, please.' She hesitated. 'Is it true? And can you tell from a photo?'

They all ask this.

'Being a divvy? Yes.' Before she could start I went on, 'Genuine antiques – *genuine*, mind – make me feel odd. It's a rare gift.' That was a laugh. Gift? My 'gift' has caused me more trouble than any number of friends, police, fakers and dealers. 'Forgeries don't. And no, I can't tell from photographs.'

The answer seemed to be what she hoped for.

'How much will the lesson be, please?'

'I'll teach you how to steal free of charge.' I like to spread culture.

In less than an hour I showed her how to confuse whifflers – auctioneers' grotty assisants. I explained how to obfuscate, distract, deflect, shuff – i.e. switch – items.

'Whatever you do, never protest, hit, scratch,' I warned. 'Theft is simply nicking something. Robbery is different. Robbery is stealing with force or fear. Law hates both, but robbery most. Got it?'

'No violence,' she said.

'And don't carry a coat over your arm,' I told her. 'Everybody'll just laugh at that old shoplifter's trick.'

'What's the quickest?' she demanded.

'It's called the plop. Carry a plastic bag with shopping in it.' I hadn't got one, so pretended. 'Hold it down, at arm's length, but not with your elbow flexed – that's another giveaway. Examine some trinket. Check there's nobody watching – pretend to tilt it, to scrutinize. Then you *seem* to replace it on the display trestle, but keep hold of it with your forefinger and middle fingers.'

'And then leave?'

'No.' I struggled for patience. 'You let it slide into your bag. The plop.'

She was slow picking it up, but I drilled her.

'If anybody challenges you, go all flustered and say it must have fallen in accidentally. Don't, for God's sake, try to look cool. Shed tears, apologize until they're sick to death of you. They'll let you go. Suspicions don't count.'

'But then I'll not have the necklace, Lovejoy, so then what'll I do?'

She had really bonny eyes. 'Send for me, love, and I'll do it.'

I saw her into Gimbert's – auctioneers of no renown – and went to look around the shops bordering the town square. Pleasant, with colourful stalls and barrows, a fountain, children playing, a little band parping away. I'd only been there five minutes when I heard the rumpus, the shouts, and saw a constable extending his stride – bobbies are taught never to run, in case we realize they ought to move about more often. My heart sank. I listened to the hubbub, the excited chatter of shoppers. She'd done it wrong and got caught.

Sad, I sat at a café table.

'No, ta, Ellie,' I said when the waitress came pestering.

'It looked like that Irma you were with, Lovejoy.'

You have to put serfs down. 'I don't know the woman.' No cocks crowed.

'She shouted, "Tell Lovejoy." She was wrestling to get away.'

So much for my advice. 'Mine's a common name. Any tea?'

She glanced about. Porridge, her stout boss, a man of calamitous greed, glared because I wasn't throwing money at his dingy business.

'Sorry, Lovejoy,' she said, and went on her way. Ellie's nice, but too mean to risk her livelihood for nothing, selfish cow.

Freddy Foxheath found me. He was red-faced and flopped down breathless. The police van was just leaving, watched by gloaters rejoicing it wasn't them.

'Near thing, Lovejoy,' he puffed, like he'd been under

shellfire. 'She'd almost got it in her handbag when that whiffler saw.'

'Saw?' I was appalled. She'd done the plop really quite well in my garden. 'What was she playing at?'

'Don't start, Lovejoy. You sent her in, not me.'

This is the thanks you get.

'For God's sake, Freddy, it was a tiny necklace, not a Rolls.'

I seethed at my wasted effort. It's not like shoplifting, when you can be in and out like a fiddler's elbow. Antiques are different.

'She shouted to get you to help her.'

Thank you, Irma. 'Ellie told me.'

See what you get for being kind? Choosing Freddy Foxheath as Irma's cullet had been no great stroke of genius. A cullet's a lookout man while you're thieving. But standards are falling. Once, cullets were ten a penny. Now, you search all morning and get a deadleg like Freddy Foxheath. He's a horse-jawed dapper little bloke, lazy but with a knack of looking keen.

'What'll you do, Lovejoy?'

'Me?' I said, offended. 'For her? Nowt. Why should I?'

'You two want serving?' Porridge's bulbous belly ballooned a yard ahead of his glare.

'Your coffee improved, has it?'

So I went to see Michaelis Singleton, a lawyer who was nearly struck off for putting sex and greed ahead of legal principles. As if everybody doesn't do that.

2

NEEDLES CAUGHT ME as I crossed near the Arcade. He was agog.

'Did you see it, Lovejoy? A posh bird got done for nicking a bit of purple pottery! Can you imagine? Rich crumpet.'

We common folk are in awe of the rich. Our fascination makes the rich become even more important than their millions, truth to tell. Clark Gable, driving home, once ran over some pedestrian and killed him stone dead. Studio executives quickly dragged C.G. out of the driving seat and replaced him with some other poor bloke before the cops arrived. The substitute got arrested and did a year in prison. He was *very* well paid, but Clark Gable was in the clear. See? We serfs know our place. We aid and abet the posh and the mighty. It's the aura of money.

'Ta, Needles.' He's called Needles because knitting is his pastime, not from anything more sinister. He carries messages between antique dealers.

'It looked like that rich tart who's been hanging about the Antiques Arcade asking after you.'

'Aye,' I growled. 'She found me.'

Wary, I entered the august chambers of Michaelis Singleton, lawyer. These are the cellars of Vaunce & Playfair, wine merchants, where Michaelis spends hours sampling the wares. When the Law Lords almost disbarred him, he bought this ancient family firm of wine importers. It's now his niche.

'Mikko?' I kept my head low. 'It's me, Lovejoy.'

'What now, Lovejoy?'

'Charming.' I'd done him favours in the past, and he speaks like I was nothing but trouble. The musty place was unlit but for one candle on an upturned barrel, amid racks of gleaming bottles.

There he was, scion of a once-great family, swaying. It was a scene from *Kidnapped*.

'You're a metabolic miracle, Mikko. Do you never eat?'

Chin to my chest, the vault scraping my head, cobwebs on my ears, I kept wafting my hands, scared of spiders. 'How do I spring a bird? She's been arrested.'

'What's she in for?'

'She tried to steal from Gimbert's Auction.'

He darted me a shrewd look. 'What's your interest, Lovejoy?'

Michaelis affects straggly hair, wispy beard, tatty long coat almost to the flagstones. What with his gear and the candle, he'd do Scrooge without make-up.

Nothing for it but to come clean.

'Irma Dominick's her name. Her folks died, left her this ordinary necklace. She showed me a picture. It's hardly old at all, barely Edwardian. Her auntie's an old bitch, took it and wouldn't give it back.' I shrugged. 'A women's row. I showed her how to nick it, but some whiffler called the Plod.'

'Who was the whiffler?'

I was surprised I hadn't thought of that. Michaelis had a point. Whifflers don't usually scream blue murder. When spotting a thief, whifflers slide up and let on. If the thief has any sense he slips them a few zlotniks, whereupon the whiffler turns Nelson's eye and lets the robbery go ahead. It's a very ancient crime in itself, properly called theftboot, but only crooks know these points of law. Whifflers in antiques auctions will always help you steal this way, unless it's an especially valuable antique, of course, in which case they take the bribe and *then* blow the whistle and call the Old Bill. That way, they convince the auctioneers of loyalty and honesty.

'Dunno, but I saw Daffo smirking his head off as the Plod loaded Irma in.'

'Daffo's a wino,' said this model of sobriety. He belched, poured a refill, offered me none. He hates friends who interrupt life.

'Can you spring her, Mikko?'

'Any flaw in the tale?'

'No.' Then I thought, hang on. Needles said it was a pot thing. But Irma had definitely gone in to steal a necklace. Discrepancy, or not? 'Except Needles said she tried to nick some porcelain – "purple pottery", is how he described it. She told me she wanted a necklace. Does it matter?'

'Theft is theft,' he said, sighing. 'But I'll tilt at your windmill, Lovejoy. It'll cost you.'

Which astonished me. Lawyers never do favours, but we were friends.

I said, gingerly, 'I thought you'd do it for friendship's sake, Michaelis. You and me being pals.'

We *did* go back. Once, he'd been hired to defend Saint Floosie, a lady of sour fame. Saint Floosie – no saint, but definitely the latter – ran a 'house of comfort' in Frinton-on-Sea. Her main attractions were a dozen ladies in perfumed bedrooms and bathing pools. Her gimmick was a plaster saint that wept holy tears of blood, because the world will always flock to see a holy con. Floosie charged visitors to see it do its holy stuff. The council alleged deception, and Saint Floosie was had up. Michaelis called me as a witness. I saved his bacon. With 10 grams of calcium carbonate and a 25 gram solution of ferric chloride, dialysed, and 1.7 grams of salt chucked in, you get a gel. It's not firm, but it doesn't have to be. When vibrated or shaken it liquidizes and turns the colour of blood – as when folk make the floorboards quiver, parading past a holy alcove. In the witness box I learnt the word thixotropic. I've been dying to use it ever since, so there it is. The chemicals are common enough ingredients in plaster modelling, and for setting small objects – like doll's eyes into plaster. So Floosie was sprung, back to being the holiest purveyor of sex in the Eastern Hundreds. Michaelis became my greatest fan, because he owned St Floosie's bawdy house for services rendered. In return, he got me off two charges of burglary, by legal technicalities I still don't comprehend.

'Tit for tat, Lovejoy. Scan me a wine lake?'

'Eh?' He'd gone barmy, all alone swigging wine among the rodents and bottles in his ancient vaults. 'You're off your frigging . . . er, sure, Mikko,' I ended lamely. 'Anything for a pal.'

And went my way rejoicing. But scan a *lake*? I scan antiques, more antiques, and nothing but antiques, so help me. Still, the thing about promises is they needn't be kept. Any antiques dealer will tell you that.

Putting on a grave face, I strolled into Gimbert's Auction Rooms. It's no good beating about the bush. I sought out Daffo. He looked shifty, tried to edge away.

'How do, Daffo. All quiet since the Plod took that Irma girl?'

'Excuse me, mate. I've a job on.'

'For the moment, Daffo.' My angelic smile would have lit lamps. I looked round. It seemed full of tat, clothes, wobbly furniture, trinkets, Old Masters turned out by forgers – which included me. It's the usual dross that litters the Eastern Hundreds. Gimbert's catalogue would describe the mounds of gunge in glowing terms, but beware. Auctioneers invent lies.

A few people were in. I waved to Stylish, a new dealer in from the West Country with, it was said, heavy gelt, though we'd seen precious little evidence of it. Alisa was chatting to Gimbert. Gimbert's a skeletal bald man who is ageless. He's lately had GIMBERT'S AUCTION ROOMS ESTD 1739 painted in rococo lettering over his door. The lads joke that he's certain of the date because he remembers that far back. He looks made of dry brown paper dressed in black, not quite an undertaker. Gimbert wears squinty specs, has flattened oily black hair and considers himself a cut above us hoi polloi. Incredibly, he has a son who is a sports broadcaster. The lads all speculate about Gimbert's sexual ability. They say he got his son in a job lot. It's a joke. Maybe not.

Alisa rushed across, full of exciting news.

'Oh, Lovejoy! You missed it! There's been an arrest!'

'No!' I looked shocked.

Daffo was talking urgently with a lady near the office, one wary eye on the aloof Gimbert. Reporting to her, doubtless about me. Why?

'This woman tried to steal a porcelain!' Alisa said.

'Not a – not a mistake?' Not a necklace?

Alisa squeaked, thrilled. 'It was there one minute and gone the next!'

'So you reported her?'

'Certainly not, Lovejoy!' Alisa can be trusted. Her voice sank to a whisper. 'Daffo did it. *Told* on her. I think he's a rotten sneak!'

Alisa is from some exotic young ladies' finishing school, hence the 1880 vernacular. She has languages, and rides horses in pursuit of innocent creatures. Her husband owns motorbikes. In spite of all, I like Alisa. We made smiles once, but she took up with a Hatton Garden jeweller. I quickly shelved her fourth-form slang. I had to find out what Irma had done, as Michaelis sobered up to gallop to the rescue.

'Funny,' I ruminated. 'Ellie at Porridge's caff said Irma tried to steal a necklace. Which was it, necklace or porcelain?'

'Irma?' Alisa purred, eyes dancing. 'You know her name!'

'Ellie said it. No, never met her in my life.'

'It's still here. The police are sending a photographer.'

'They usually leave some cretin on guard.' I said it outright before realizing there was somebody behind me.

'Hello, Lovejoy. Inspector Cretin, at your service.' There he stood, thin and intense, hating my every breath. Malice personified. 'On guard,' he added pointedly, 'against criminals.'

'Wotcher, Mr Summer.' I smiled ingratiatingly. 'I was just passing.'

'The perpetrator called out your name, Lovejoy. Why?'

'Maybe she was hoping to sell me the . . . item.' I always find it hard to keep a lie simple, one of my faults. 'Not that I'd ever buy anything stolen.'

'Of course not, Lovejoy. Yet she's asked for you to come to the police station and make a statement.'

'Me? About a cheap necklace?'

'No. About this.'

It wasn't a necklace at all. It was a small jug. My knees went funny. I had to steady myself on the edge of the table. Inside me a deep chime resonated. Alisa looked hard at me, took my arm.

'Are you going giddy, Lovejoy?'

'Moi?' I laughed a swaggering denial. It came out falsetto.

'Why did you think it was a necklace, Lovejoy?' Summer wouldn't give up.

I looked away to get my breath. 'How should I know?' I felt rotten, moved away. The rare antique beamed after me. I wanted to have a word with it, see how it felt, being so valuable among this load of crud.

'Soon as the photographer comes, Lovejoy, I'm taking you in.'

Alisa leant me against a tatty wardrobe and wafted me with her auction catalogue. I stared over her at the beautiful, exquisite, lovely Rockingham jug. You can't help it. It stood there proudly radiating perfection.

Some two and a half centuries ago, a bloke called Edward Butler was wandering Yorkshire. A vigilant lad, he came across a bed of high-quality clay of a rather odd yellow hue. Instantly he set up a pottery at Swinton, up Rotherham way. His pots weren't remarkable, merely 'household browns', as trade slang has it. When he popped his clogs in 1765, a friend called Malpass carried on. Here's an interesting thing, though: no original Swinton pieces have yet been confirmed. So somewhere Out There, in some junk shop, in some boot fair or street market, a common-as-muck piece of brown Butler or Malpass domestic pottery is waiting, screaming, to make you a fortune. Find one, you'll never see so many noughts this side of the National Lottery.

Well, time passed at the little factory. Then, enter the

great Thomas Bingley, bringing the Brameld brothers. It was evolution time in the old Swinton pottery. Fashions, and partnership, changed over the years, but those ancient old craftsmen were equal to it all, being nothing less than slogging geniuses. You've only to see the Rockingham glaze's purplish-russet colour to fall in love with it.

Except this little thing wasn't *it* at all.

For the descendants of the Bramelds went from strength to strength, and from strength to bankruptcy, since those youths were great experimenters. While great savants were discussing the number of angels dancing on pin heads, or the ability of the stars to think, the young Bramelds did solid experiments, testing the effects of kiln heat on metals and clays. In early 1826 they went for it, and started producing bone china so superb that it melts your heart. The Bramelds' bone china was so light and delectable, and their brilliant high-quality standards were so impeccable, that they went bust. The Swinton pottery was done for. Gloom abounded.

At the last minute, an astonishing white knight arrived, none other than creaking old Earl Fitzwilliam. He put up a fortune and fired the kilns, on condition that the Swinton factory was called the Rockingham Works. The old gent also wanted his own crest on the china. It's not much to look at, actually, a somewhat cocksure griffin, with *Rockingham Works* and the name *Brameld* underneath.

There are forgeries, of course, but one tip I've found reliable when trying to find a path through the minefield of Rockingham-type antiques is this: as rival potteries flourished, the Bramelds developed superb enamels of unequalled colour from the 1830s on. To me, the giveaway isn't their dazzling ground colours or their famous 'Rockingham blue'. It's that they went ape on gilding, lashings of it. But sometimes, just sometimes, one or two items crept out with a curious delicate, lacey gilding. One glance takes your breath away. With the passage of time, the Brameld gilding in surviving pieces has gone dark, maybe even golderer, if there is such a word. It's like the gold is trying to become copper, exactly like new pennies used to be before the Great Decimal Trick made us paupers.

This little jug in Gimbert's Auction was genuine lacey-gilded Rockingham. That alone would have made me faint, but it was also the most special colour of all, the ultra-rare light peach. OK, some would see only an ornate little milk jug, and dealers would only see a ton of money – if they spotted it. To me it was pure magic, shaped by wonderful people of the dim past who laboured in hell, and who created a radiant gift for all generations.

Summer saw my gape. 'That jug's evidence, Lovejoy. Keep your thieving hands off.'

See what I mean? Silently I apologized to the antique for the company it had to keep. Alisa took me to a chair, sat me down.

'Are you all right, Lovejoy?'

'Course.' I felt clammy. The Rockingham jug was sad, hating all this. 'Sorry, love,' I called over to it.

'Oh, don't worry, Lovejoy,' Alisa said, thinking I meant her.

She went to the office. I heard Summer interrogating some whiffler. When I'd recovered enough to take notice, the lady who'd been talking to Daffo had gone. I beckoned him over.

'That lady. She dash you?' Dash is bribe. He glanced around, edgier still. 'I'm serious, Daffo.'

'She dropped me a tenner to blow the whistle if that Irma lifted anything.'

'Okay, Daffo, no harm. What did Irma try nicking?'

'That Rockingham fake jug.'

Fake? It was as genuine as breath. 'Who put it in?'

'Entered it in the sale? That lady, Mrs Crucifex.'

Wobbly, I stood and beckoned him with a jerk of my chin to where the necklace lay on phoney velvet. I examined it in case I'd missed anything from its photograph. Still Edwardian, still mediocre, nothing more than dress jewellery, tourmaline, miniature malachite greens not even worth counting. Now, I really like semi-precious stones, as people cruelly call them, but this wouldn't break anybody's bank. What, eight quid in wet weather? Not a farthing more.

'Who entered that necklace?' It was what light-fingered Irma had really wanted to steal.

Daffo riffled through his catalogue. 'A Miss Dominick.'

'You sure, Daffo?' Irma had entered it herself?

He saw Gimbert peering from the auctioneer's office and firmly folded his catalogue away.

'That's confidential, Lovejoy!' he said in a voice like a thunderclap.

Which ended my involvement, because the police photographer came just then, and two newspaper stringers bawling idiot questions. I slipped out.

Why did Irma Dominick enter a cheap necklace in a country auction, come to me for lessons on how to steal it, then get herself arrested trying to steal something totally different, namely a Rockingham bone china jug of outstanding richness and quality, wrongly described as a fake and belonging to her aunt Mrs Crucifex? I went to stave off a migraine in the Welcome Sailor.

There was one local Crucifex, the tavern's phone book told me, a Mrs J. She didn't answer when I rang. No

Dominicks. I sat among antique dealers and heard the saga of Irma's arrest a thousand times more I thought of Florida, queen of hearsay, tittle tattle and fable. As soon as her flower arranging class ended, I'd ask her what was going on. She'd know. Florida's a gossip frenzy.

3

IT'S A SAD truth that housewives murder antique silver. They will pay a fortune for a lovely Regency silver salver or be delirious with delight that they've inherited Auntie Elsie's valuable Georgian mint Paul Storr silver candelabrum, then fall on it like vandals, polishing the poor antique as if desperate to wear it away. I can't understand it.

'Lovejoy,' Arty greeted me. 'This is genuine, right?'

I looked at the poor thing, a sugar crusher. It doesn't look much, nothing more than a silver rod with a rounded end. The capital Roman-style A silver mark came in during 1796, lasted until 1816. It is, believe me, a precious clue, but housemaids had all but worn away the sugar crusher maker's mark and the date letter – they used rouge to scrub their mistress's silverware. Life's less risky for silver now, but try telling this lovely little damaged antique that.

'Aye, Arty.' It rang my chimes, but was having a hard time.

Why don't people simply wash silver in baby soap, followed by a hearty rinse? It's the best way. *Never* use scrubbers, scourers, vicious detergents. Antique silver deserves care. Think of a three-month-old baby's skin, and you have it.

'Why aren't you glad, Lovejoy?'

Arty finances his gambling by dealing in antiques, if you can imagine anything more cock-eyed. One activity would ruin Midas, but Arty does the two together. I explained about not wearing away silver treasures.

'Modern polishes often incorporate tarnish-retarders, Arty.'

'Must I clean it, then?'

'No!' I bawled, then muttered, shamefaced, as everybody looked, 'It's clean enough.'

Sugar crushers, oddly, are rather rare, perhaps because they look ordinary. Loaf sugar, usual in Georgian times, was cut by the maid and served in a sugar basket. The pieces were gracefully broken by the hostess with a silver crusher at tea, her skill impressing gentlemen callers.

Which genuine antique had now come down in the world, to end up being bartered in a low-life tavern. I almost had tears in my eyes. We discussed the price. I gave him an IOU.

'I'll redeem it tomorrow at noon, Arty,' I lied.

'Earlier, Lovejoy. There's racing at York.'

'Right, right.' I was peeved. Now I'd have to evade the blighter all morning, in case he wanted me to pay my debts. Is life unfair, or what?

The sugar crusher I wrapped in my grotty hanky. I only had a few quid, so I got hold of Liz Sandwell, a lovely dealer, but whose bloke is a rugby player of frightening size. She was talking to Maureen Jolly. This luscious lass doesn't belie her name and is given to displaying her long legs to impress any passing impressario, she being a songstress/actress of burning ambition. Her doting husband believes in her, which only goes to show.

'Lovejoy!' Liz purred. 'That miniature. Better cough up.'

'Honest, Liz, I'll have the dosh any sec.'

'Buyers are queuing up, Lovejoy. I'll give you till tomorrow.'

Some days are nothing but bother. A couple of days previously I'd IOU'd a miniature painting from Liz. It was quite good, done in pewter as a plain brooch. What interested me had been that the lady in the portrait had been wearing stomacher jewellery. This has nothing to do with the padding that ancient ladies used to bulge them-selves out front as if they were pregnant. In jewellery a stomacher is a large – *large* – triangular setting of pearls and gems to adorn her bodice, often to hang as low as the waistline, or down from the décolletage. Sometimes, as in the miniature portrait I'd conned off Liz, the stomacher can even be in two separate pieces of similar design. They are rare. And I was almost sure I'd seen it before somewhere, hence my eagerness. Trouble was, Jessica from Norwich had conned it off me – women have ways – 'to show a friend'. Once a duckegg, as they say. Now I was in a real mess.

'Ta, love. Do us a favour, Liz? Please?'

Her lovely eyes fixed on me. The non-laughing laugh is a woman's trick men can't do. She did it now. I shrank.

'Your favours always cost me, Lovejoy.'

'No, honest, love. Just go to Gimbert's and write me a bid for a fake Rockingham jug. Number 152.'

'Fake? You? Bidding for a *fake*?' Now they both did laugh, Maureen so much she had to put her drink down in case it spilt. 'I thought only genuine antiques clanged your bell!'

'Among other things, Liz!' Maureen fell about.

'Very droll,' I said gravely. 'Will you?'

Liz sobered, appraised me, slid from her stool and collected her handbag.

'This once, Lovejoy, and that's final. I can't go on subbing you.'

'Ta, Liz. I owe you.'

She left, ignoring invitations, in various grades of eloquence, called after her by the mob of dealers lusting in the taproom. Which left Maureen.

'Maur, love. Look. I've no barker – you know Tinker got gaoled?'

'Yes.' Maureen smokes long cigarettes that must be specially made. Sit near, you've to watch your eyes for burning fag ash. 'What's that to do with me?'

'I need a barker.'

Her eyes widened in astonishment. 'Me? To be your—?'

'Shhh!' I said, showing my teeth in a jovial grin to prove we were only chatting. 'On the sly. Nobody'd know. OK?'

She looked about the tavern, checking the mirrors. 'Why, Lovejoy?'

'I couldn't pay much, love.' I lowered my eyes, inventing shyness. 'And, well, Maur, you know how I feel about you.'

'You, Lovejoy?' She was surprised and wary. 'Are you saying—?'

'No,' I denied nobly. 'I'm honestly sincere.'

'I thought you had that horrid Florida.'

'She's only learning the antiques trade, Maur. I can pay you in kind.'

'In kind of what?' she asked shrewdly, narrowing her pretty eyes.

'I know this bloke.' I made sure nobody was earwigging, this being one of my ultra-special fables. 'He puts on shows and that.' I petered out, not knowing anything about the stage.

'You do?' she breathed. Her eyes uncrinkled, revealing undiluted faith.

'His agency's big.' I invented, rollercoasting recklessly on. 'Jonno Rant and me played football together.'

'Jonno Rant?' she whispered in awe. 'I've heard of him!'

'Shhh, love. I don't want every tinpot actress in East Anglia asking me to put in a word.'

'When do you see him next?' she demanded. 'He's stupendous!'

'Soon. Jonno always pops in from the Hook of Holland.'

'Oh, Lovejoy! You darling!' She was almost beside herself. She bought me a white wine and told me of her outstanding performing abilities. I didn't listen. Acting is endless infancy, just as politics is endless bullying. Crime is endless barbarity. The antiques game on the other hand is perpetual lust.

Which was how Liz Sandwell found us, me trying not to nod off while Maureen bashed my earhole with how superbly she could play every female part in Shakespeare given half a chance, and sing better than anyone on earth.

'Hello, Liz,' I said, relieved at the rescue.

'No go, Lovejoy.' She drained my wine, settling on my stool. 'The Rockingham fake's gone. Withdrawn from sale by a Mrs Crucifex. And Gimbert's withdrawn the charges against that Irma.'

'Great,' I cried gladly, because in the antiques game the last thing you must do is show dismay.

'Shouldn't you offer me a drink, Lovejoy?' Liz asked petulantly.

'Er, another time, love. A friend's due off the ferry soon.'

'Yes, let him go, Liz!' Maureen cried with a meaningful look.

'Summer's mad at you, Lovejoy! He wants to see you.'

'Right, right. I'm going past the police station. I'll call in.'

I weaved into the High Street traffic, where it was safer. Tomorrow dawn, I'd do the boot fair on Roman Meadow by the river. I forgot the Irma problem for ever. I thought.

4

NEXT MORNING WAS my kind of day: fresh wind, light rain, grey as a goose. I fried my last chunk of bread in my last scrap of margarine, brewed my last tea leaves. I had to do it on a paraffin lamp, because the electricity barons had gone fascist again and wanted money. All the while the hedgehog was trundling and snuffling underfoot for its grub, and bluetits were hammering on the windows. The robin even had the frigging nerve to come in and cheep his silly head off. Narked, I shooed them all out in a temper. I had to bring a bucket of rainwater in for a bath, because our water barons – who sell us our own God-given rainwater – had also gone ape. I had a soak, yelping at the cold. Yet another of life's mysteries: why do we shout when dunked into a cold splodge? Shouting doesn't warm the water, that's for sure.

Dressed, I shredded a ton of cheddar cheese for the birds, and filled their feeders with a bushel of peanuts.

'Right,' I called from the gate into the garden at Mother Nature. 'Can I go now?' Not so much as a ta. The ungrateful little swine live better than me, and that's a fact. Another mystery: who fried hedgehogs their morning bread before I came along? Did bounteous Mother Nature? Did she hell as like. She just lets them all get on with it, the idle cow.

To the boot fair.

The boot fair is our creaking old kingdom's best ever modern invention. Get all that old tat from your attic, the clag of years you keep meaning to chuck away. Heap it in the boot of your motor. Next morning before cockshout, drive to the boggy field that's advertised on every telegraph pole. You'll find hundreds of cars and vans, people everywhere. Rickety tables are set out. Yawning girls collect your gate penny in their buckets. It's usually raining. And here's the miracle: unbelievably, other people actually buy your gunge, and cart it off in triumph.

It's the boot fair, the ultimate in conservation. Nothing is ever destroyed. Buy something and find you hate it, why, just take it back next week and sell it, and life's cruddy pageant rolls on. It's every garage sale, jumble rumble, flea market gathered and dumped in a truly rural morass.

I arrived without a motor or possessions, wheedled my way past Gloria and her voracious bucket by promising to take her to the pictures to see that new action-packer, then went to the nosh van. (This saves you hours of muddy blundering, but be careful. You'll see why in a sec.) Arold – his spelling – serves gangrenous fry-ups on chipped plates and makes a killing, if not several. I cadged some swill in a cup big enough to fall in. It had a floating pubic hair.

'Here he comes, lads,' Barko said. 'Watch your women and your wallets.'

'Which from you, Barko . . .'

Barko had been in the Plod. He'd arrested me back in the days when I'd been a pickpocket. I wasn't very good, not like Dosker in Southminster or that sickly specky-eyes they call Deli (short for Delivery) from Romford, who can filch your fillings while you yawn.

His face darkened. 'Watch it, Lovejoy,' he growled. 'I'll send my pals to visit your patch.'

'Don't, Barko. They'd get lost.'

My cottage was only three miles off as the drunkard limps. Some of the blokes standing about gulping Arold's enteric gave outright guffaws, for Barko once became famous. He'd mistaken Southwold for Southminster in a police night raid, thereby earning the undying gratitude of antique smugglers from King's Lynn to Kirby Le Soken. Hence Barko's resignation. Now, he tries to be a freelance antiques barker. He pretends to be good at it, which is like pretending to be fluent in Swahili – it cons everybody except the Swahili. Here in East Anglia, Barko is utterly useless, for we have the world's best barkers. Like, Tinker can be drunk in a police cell for days, then emerge saying, 'Here, Lovejoy. That Harrison fake clock just sold for nigh on eight thousand an hour ago. Good, eh?', making you wonder if he's got a carrier pigeon secretly kipping in some voluminous pocket.

No, Barko's a nasty piece of work. He scares me. I spoke to Arold.

'Any sign of Rupert, Arold?' That's my code, Rupert being fictional. Normally Tinker changes my code names every day, but in view of his absence I was stuck in a Rupert groove.

'Nar, Lovejoy.' Arold spat expertly out from his serving hatch, spittle frosting his rock cakes. 'But I'd visit the far end if I wus you.'

'Ta.'

This astonished me, though I just grinned and went on. The opposite side of the field, rapidly filling with cars and bargain hunters, was usually reserved for amateur flower growers, vendors of pot plants. I only rarely meander among foliage because flowers are pretty famous for not being antiques, though geriatric aspidistras have notched up handy prices lately, the same as ancient bonsai trees – their poor feet, though, cramped in those bowls.

'How it comes, Lovejoy?' somebody said close to me.

Like a fool I turned and said hello. I should have taken to the hills.

'Wotcher, Prince.' I did my heartiest beam, ready to flee.

Prince cracks on he's from Eastern Europe, and that he's ultra noble. But Pollack, who really is from there, says that anybody with a hundred goats was titled Prince This, Duke That, when they were really only smallholders. The Swahili syndrome again. Don't misunderstand me. Prince dresses the part, even down – up? – to the monocle and deerstalker, but the whole effect is of something got up to seem. In a word, fraudulent. The feeling would persist even if you discovered he honestly was the Czar of All the Russias, God of Danzig, whoever.

'It's coming along fine, Prince, ta for asking.' I drew apart from the bell-like shell-likes of the craning listeners, all dealers or barkers. I didn't want them overhearing my latest fraud.

'Really?' His thin features glowed with the antique dealer's fervour that only greed can bring. 'How soon, Lovejoy?'

'The porcelain,' I intoned loudly for everyone else's benefit, 'will be ready in two weeks, Prince.' I stepped into another puddle inches further away. It was still raining.

'Ha! I see, Lovejoy!' Prince boomed. 'You seem secret, yes?'

People snickered. He has gelt, but lacks brains.

'It'd help, Prince,' I whispered. 'Those blokes by Arold's van are rivals. They might steal your porcelain.'

He glared at them. 'We deceive them, yes?'

Not any more we don't. Blokes like Prince wear you out before coffee.

'That's it, Prince. We—'

He winked through his monocle. 'We not reveal it is furniture, yes?'

'No, yes. Er, aye, we don't.' My mind was going ????? I clung to my point of lying reference. 'Fortnight, Prince. I promise. I'll bring it round in a bag.'

'Bag! Ha ha ha!' thundered Prince, yet more secrecy. 'That is good yoke, hey? I send lorry, Lovejoy!'

So now the world knew it was a monster piece of furniture requiring a pantechnicon. I tried to escape. 'Sorry, Prince. I'm meeting somebody at the daffodils.'

'Daffodils!' the nerk announced to the world, nudging me. 'You give red herrings, yes? Oh, Lovejoy. You get varnish I send?'

'Er, yes. All in hand.'

I escaped down a row of sodden trestle tables where people milled and rain did its little thunders on plastic awnings erected over heaps of saleable rubbishy crud. It was quite an interesting walk.

Don't be deterred. There's always something worth finding at a boot fair. There were the inevitable record and CD stalls, collectors' tables of toys and comics, the inevitable car maniacs' arrays of bits from obsolesent motors, boxes of books, clothes in stacks, racks, packs, and umpteen stalls of pottery, brasses, ornaments and plastic everythings. Cover the field in volcanic lava, and just think what a tourist exhibit it would make in two or three millennia. For now, though, an expanse of garbage.

A few folk called hello. I waved, trudged on through the damp dross, thinking of the world's costliest piece of furniture that I was faking. It was the reason I'd installed locks and bolts. It was also partly paid for by Prince. I'd taken only a small advance – he's not as dumb as all that – to buy materials, but I'd had a bit of a mishap. Broke, creativity had to halt. I was too scared to tell Prince because he's volatile and has vile connections in Austria. Until I scraped some groats together, I was stymied.

Fakers of antiques these days don't do right. Their shoddy workmanship's enough to drive you to drink. Typical instance? There's a young bloke called Toggle near Long Melford. He's a near genius with inlays, veneers and the like. You'd think he'd do fakes of, say, Boule the Frenchman's beautiful cabinet fronts, which are sheer furniture magic. Toggle could make an absolute fortune. (Toggle badly needs fortunes, because he has this lust for a parson's wife, lavishes his all on her to impress. She accepts everything with disdain. Dealers swear blind that the nearest Toggle's got to her is in the third pew of a Sunday evensong.) Question: so does Toggle make worthwhile fakes, which he's good at, and earn a life of luxury? Not on your nelly. He wastes his time rattling off bits of decorations on modern sideboards for a few zlotniks, to please a tease.

Not me. I'm a genius at forgery, when I've the time. OK, I'm always broke, but that's because women have barmy schemes I can't get shut of. I make gorgeous fakes. Only the best is good enough to be bad enough. When Prince called on me to make a 'jig', I thought long and hard, then decided on the ultimate, the world's most pricey piece of antiquery. It's in America. It's also American.

'Jig' is any replica of an antique that really existed but which is now missing. To clarify: if you sculpted the

Colossus from Rhodes, of the same original stone, using the same tools, the same size, and make it look, test as, the original, then as far as most people were concerned it would actually *be* the Colossus of the Ancient World. Right? That's a 'jig'. I've done several jigs. The immortal Turner's missing painting of the Grand Canal in Venice, the missing Monet scene of the side canal, the Italian waterfall by Richard Wilson, others. Jigs are always worth doing, very satisfying to the dedicated forger. They aren't easy, but perfection never is.

Furniture, in particular, is hard to fake well. There comes a time when the faker – the buyer too, come to that – simply has to place all his trust, not in money or analytical spectroscopes, or in complicated electron spin resistance tests, but in something called love. And who has enough of that? Not your investor, not your greedy bankers.

The answer is me.

I chose to do the Brown desk.

This glorious bookcase-desk wasn't made by anybody called Brown. It's actually the handiwork of one John Goddard, who in the 1760s slogged with his gnarled hands in Newport, in Rhode Island, in the American colonies.

Every so often, there arises some bloke who is sheer dynamite. King or clerk, sooner or later his fame spreads. People start flocking to see him. If he's a poet, folk suddenly take interest, and before long your quiet scribbler is having tea with the Queen Empress and everybody's calling him Lord Tennyson.

Cut to the neophyte colonies of the Americas. One day, this John Goddard got an order for four – repeat *four* – bookcase-desks. (Mr Brown, merchant of Rhode Island, had four sons, so it was logical.) They were to be the very best. Old John Goddard was equal to the task. He produced four staggering wonders, all similar. The eldest son, Nicholas Brown, passed away in 1791. Luckily, his bookcase-desk was detailed in his will. Down the decades, its course was charted by meticulous Browns into modern times. Arriving as pristine now as when the immortal John made it, it was auctioned by Christie's for a cool umpteen million zlotniks, setting a craze for Goddard furniture. Fakers everywhere gasped. We all set to. The reason wasn't so much the sale at Christie's, but a linked tragedy. Remember that I said a jig was a faithful repro of a named *missing* antique? Well, then.

On a truly terrible day in the nineteenth century, one of the four miracle bookcase-desks burnt to cinders in a fire at Moses Brown's place. Forgers rejoiced, for who's to say that a lovely Goddard desk of Brown pattern isn't the one so tragically lost to history? In other words, enter the jig.

They're all there in history, the great makers. Here, we are within each of their wonders: Sheraton, Chippendale, Hepplewhite, John Goddard, Vile of Yorkshire, Ince, Mayhew, the rest of the immortals. Their furniture is in museums and the great collections.

And also in smaller country auctions, if you're lucky. But beware. Unscrupulous forgers will, I've heard, actually make superb fakes. Luckily, too, auctioneers and museums and galleries are so keen to show their wares that they will provide catalogues, plus photographs, measurements, and even identify the original wood used.

Prince got me all the details of the Brown bookcase-desk. I started two months ago.

'Good day,' a man said, smiling. 'Might I enquire if you are Lovejoy?'

'No,' I said airily. 'He's at the nosh van. You want him?'

He was sparse, with a grey intense smile. Wan, I think

the word is. My height, but older. He wore a homburg, rare at boot fairs, and spectacles made for peering over instead of through. Neat, he wore button boots. I hadn't seen those since I was a little lad. A beautiful woman stood by him, hating me. I'd never even seen her before, but I recognize hatred.

'If you would, please.' He twinkled over his glasses. 'I'm on the pot stall.'

'Who shall I say wants him?'

'Prior George Metivier.' He was really friendly. 'Please do impress on him that I aim to make his trouble worthwhile.'

'Worthwhile?' My tongue licked my lips. 'You mean . . . ?'

'Money.' He sounded so sad. 'Please give him my apologies, introducing the subject of filthy lucre before I've a proper introduction. I'm afraid I'm compelled to move rather quickly into disposing of certain antiques.'

The beautiful woman upped her hate quotient. I looked round. It really *was* me she hated.

'You are?' Metivier? I'd heard the name. Wasn't a prior some sort of priest? 'Money *and* antiques?' My feet wouldn't budge.

'Yes.' He was anxious to get back to his hyacinths or whatever.

Finally I managed, 'Got any nice hydrangeas?'

Lucre's not as filthy as all that.

5

THE MAN'S STALL was a trestle table creaking under the weight of greenery. He smiled apologetically.

'My idea of the hard sell, I'm afraid.'

Go for honesty, if all else fails. '*I'm* actually Lovejoy. I thought you, er . . .'

Honesty tends to run out. I was stuck. Truth does that.

'I quite understand, Lovejoy.' He was anxious to put me at ease. 'Not another word. I might,' he added magnanimously, 'have been anyone, mightn't I?'

True. I decided to forgive. Meanwhile, his bonny lady hated me with a fulsome loathing even I don't often come across. She wore a shaped fawn coat with a wide collar. I suppose it's imperialist, chauvinist or some other -ist to say she was attractive. Her high heels were incongruous. She stood sheltering under a gaudy table umbrella, the sort you see on sunny seaside posters. Women detest rain.

He said with mock grandeur, 'My first excursion into the market economy.'

'It's fine,' I said, a toad to the last. This geezer was up to something. Dunno what, but I'd go along for a while and find out. I didn't come up the river on a bicycle, as people say. Not sure what it means, but it seemed right for this occasion.

'My sister, Marie. May I introduce Lovejoy, Marie?'

'Good morning.' She said it in hangman's tones, ten minutes before the eight o'clock walk. If she'd been a bloke I would have wondered what I'd done wrong, but females don't need reasons like the rest of us.

'Wotcher, miss,' I said politely. 'Nice, er, plants you've got here.' I looked at their soggy verdure with what I hoped was admiration. I can't understand people buying these things. I mean, I've never planted a single seed in my garden and you have to fight your way through the undergrowth. It's a jungle, which only goes to show plants know what to do if you just leave them alone.

'You're very kind, Lovejoy,' Metivier said. 'Isn't Lovejoy kind, Marie?'

'Isn't he kind,' she intoned funereally.

He winced. 'My sister doesn't like mainland weather, Lovejoy. I've been telling her that sometimes we have beautiful days, sometimes long hot summers.'

'Look, mister.' Mainland? This was getting beyond me. 'There's no point in talking about weather. The sky drops rain or snow, or shines hot, or it goes black and we go to bed. It carries on doing it whether we like it or not.' We waited. Nobody explained anything. I asked weakly, 'Why aren't you selling your, er, ferns?'

'Ferns,' Marie said, like I'd uttered an obscenity.

George looked about. Rain speckled his glasses. 'People don't seem to like my wares, Lovejoy. I had hoped—'

The field was now crowded. Twenty or so lines of motor cars and assorted vans, trestle tables set up beside each, stretched from hedge to hedge. Among them wandered upwards of five or six hundred people, more arriving.

'You've no antiques here, then?' I asked hopefully.

'Not here, no.' He shot his sister an apprehensive glance. Well, I'd shoot her a few worried looks if she were mine. 'Elsewhere.'

'What are they?' I surveyed his offerings. There were twiggy things in plastic pots. Some glass domes housed gnarly shrubs. It was a boring soggy mess. The quicker he got shut of this load and back to antiques the better.

He began, 'These are miniature variants of *Cydonia japonica*, very colourful. The trays are early . . .'

Gardeners are dull. I switched off. They're all desperate to preach their particular gospel – plums more succulent, flowers more dazzling, roses more floribunding, whatever. They're like anglers, yawnsome fibbers. I mean, even if their tall tales were all true, so what? My gardening philosophy is that everything that grows is fundamentally grass, and that's that. It varies a bit – here, it swells into a big woody thing we call a bush; there, it lurks and goes blue and folk call it a harebell, but basically it's all grass. Anybody who says different doesn't know Mother Nature like I do.

I wandered over to the flower stall opposite while Metivier prattled on about *Armeniaca vulgaris*. 'Here, Christine,' I said. 'Is that bloke's stuff any good?'

Christine's a rawboned lass from Hertfordshire. I like her. I'm not really sure what rawboned means, because anybody whose bones are raw is in pretty serious trouble. I suppose I mean hefty. She did me a favour once when I was escaping from three horrible people who said I'd forged a painting and sold it to a rival. I had, actually, but whose fault was that? She sells big spuds, big fruit, big vegetables, in boxes she hauls about as if they contained air. She owns two farms and brings two sulky cats. They miaowed and stalked towards me, but they only ever want to sit on my chest and nod off, lazy sods.

'You two can get lost,' I told them. They looked at each other, put out.

'Him? Good, but weird.'

She was wrapping fruit in a paper bag for an elderly couple. I watched admiringly. She spins the bag so it finishes up with two ears, the bag tight as a drum. I've tried to do it but it falls apart, then I look stupid.

'Weird how?'

She rested a fist on a hip. 'Lovejoy. Do me a favour? As a friend?'

'Yes, love. What?' I went all anxious.

'Don't ever go into market gardening. You'd starve.'

'I promise, love.' A promise I'd keep. 'Weird how?'

'It's . . .' Christine stared over, judging Metivier's layout. 'It's like from some time warp. Nothing real, y'know? For Christ's sake, look round.' She hauled me round and round on the spot.

'I'm looking, I'm looking,' I bleated. 'What at?'

'At folk, Lovejoy,' she said in exasperation. 'See these bedraggled droves? We have a special word for them – customers. Yes, love?'

A bonny woman with two children bought some tomatoes, lettuces, mushrooms. Christine did her spinning bag trick, chatting the whilst, gave the woman her change.

'See, Lovejoy? It's a new invention called a *sale*. I grow produce. I give it to *customers*. They give me money in *payment*. It's catching on everywhere. That lady's gone off happy. I'm happy. My vegetables are happy.' She embraced me, laughing, wet through. It was teeming. 'It's called commerce, you ignorant nerk.'

Like I say, we've been friends. I told her ta and sploshed

through to the fifth line of stalls, where Marker – GARDEN SIGNS TO THE NOBILITY – agreed to do me instant lettering on a giant piece of hardboard. I returned to Metivier and his merry sister. Latest bulletin on his stall: George had sold nothing.

'As I was saying about *Clematis viticella*, Lovejoy,' he resumed. 'It was introduced by Mr Hugh Morgan in 1569 from Spain—'

'Good old Hugh,' I cut in. 'Have you got a couple of poles?'

'Poles?' He inspected his area. 'I'm so sorry, Lovejoy.'

'Then we'll use your awning. Take it down. And your garden umbrella.' I hauled it from its concrete disc, giving Marie a bright smile. 'Shift, love.'

She stood there exposed to the rain, speechless. It's an ill wind does that, right?

Marker and his little lad brought the hardboard and rigged it up. It dwarfed the patch. I like Marker, a real artist. We stood admiring it.

'Genuine Gerard's Herbal Healing Herbal Power Plants!' I read. Capital letters, no two the same colour, the hues so brilliant they looked lit up. 'A masterpiece, Marker.'

'*Aphrodisiac alkaloid plants?*' Metivier read, aghast. 'Rheumatic balm?'

'Look around you, George.' I tried to spin him, like Christine had done me, but failed ignominiously. 'We've a word for all these folk. Customers.' I feigned exasperation. 'Do me a favour, George. Never go into business. You'd starve.' Christine's words sounded great.

Marker left. I promised him the money in an hour. He said he'd send his little lad for it, untrusting swine.

A woman approached, asked which of the plants was best for rheumatics. I frowned, all sagacity.

'What sort, love? There's ninety-two kinds of that illness. We have,' I added airily, 'all the right plants. The *Cydonia japonica* is probably the one you need—'

'Excuse me,' Metivier interrupted. 'Feverfew might assist—'

People really get on your wick. The woman decided to ignore me and listened to him. I went to where Marie was sitting in their motor.

'Are your antiques far, love?'

'Further than you'll ever know, Lovejoy.'

'Many, are there?'

Her grey-blue eyes raked me. 'More than you'll ever see, Lovejoy.'

She sounded like pantomime, what big teeth you have, Grandma.

An hour later, me watching Metivier's rotten weeds do a roaring trade, one of Christine's rivals came across and bought the remainder of his stock outright. I helped to negotiate the price, one-off for the lot.

We packed up. George was delighted by his success. Marie was not mollified.

'You want me to suss out your antiques now?' I asked, stowing the awning.

'Yes, please, Lovejoy.' He gave me a smile. 'Albansham Priory.'

'I know where, ta,' I said, thinking, Oh hellfire.

His sister, hateful still, gauged me to see the effect the name had. I tried to remain nonchalant. It was then that an odd thing happened. A mounted rider – I mean on a horse – came through the press. George Metivier brightened.

'Glorious, eh, Lovejoy?' he said, filled with emotion.

'What?' Glorious? There wasn't an antique in sight.

'That's in the Tey point-to-point.' He was in awe. 'It'll be favourite. Thirteen to eight.'

He meant the horse. 'Oh, aye? A nag's a nag.'

Just then Arty passed us. He said hello to George Metivier, then to me, an interesting exercise in priority.

'Nag, Lovejoy? Lovely beast, that,' he said, admiring.

'Lovejoy, you absolute bastard!'

Somebody pushed herself in front of me and took a swing at my face. I shoved her. She fell, spitting fire. Good old Irma, that I'd got Michaelis to rescue from clink. I was about to leg it among the stalls when something even odder happened. Marie Metivier stepped up beside me. Her face looked odd. I realized it was a smile. Not doing too well, but giving it a go.

'Stop that,' Marie blistered as Irma scrabbled to her feet. Marie blocked her path and raised a hand, nails in claw position. 'Control yourself, you silly bitch. Lovejoy behaved perfectly properly. I can testify to that.'

Irma simmered, glaring. I tried to look pious, almost as if I knew why Marie was suddenly crazy about me.

'That bastard,' Irma ground out while everybody all about cheered and laughed, 'put me in gaol. His stupid advice—'

'Which was . . . ?' Marie purred.

Irma said nothing. She could hardly blame me in public for having taught her to steal.

'Right, Lovejoy,' she said at last, ineffectually trying to brush mud off her clothes. 'You'll have to get it back for me yourself. I'll call round with the details.'

And she stalked off.

'Ta, missus,' I told Marie, clearing my throat. 'Loony Irma's from the lunatic asylum. Often escapes.'

Marie was amused. 'Please call at Albansham Priory,

Lovejoy. I'm truly pleased you are advising my brother.'
She offered a hand. No claws. We shook, all formal.

By then George had packed up and got the car mobile.
I waved them off and crossed to Christine.

'Here, love,' I said while she served customers. 'How
could you tell his stuff was from some monastery just by
looking at the greenery?'

'No, Lovejoy,' she said, weighing out apples. 'It was
written on the side of his estate car. Albansham Priory.' She
laughed at me, ruffled my thatch. I wish women wouldn't
do that. 'Do me a favour. Don't ever go into commerce.
You'd starve.'

I went to find Freddy. I needed more help than I'd got.

6

OUR TOWN HAS a parade of antique shops. The name's a hoot, invented for tourists. Last year three Dutch visitors brightly asked me where the parade was – when they were standing outside the five down-at-heel junk shops that our town council meant. The middle shop, the Eastern Hundreds Grand Antiques Emporium, if you please, is owned by Vesta. Her name has absolutely nothing to do with the vestal virgins of Ancient Rome.

'Like a drowned rat, Lovejoy,' she said.

'Good morning, Vesta.' I stood aside for a man to leave. He was trendily casual, but with a lean senatorial face. His glance spoke volumes. He got into a car that was illegally parked and sped away. 'Never seen a bobby this early in the morning. Have you been misbehaving?'

'Yes and no.'

That answer would normally have called for thought, so like a fool I forgot it. Vesta is what polite ladies call ample. She's big and vigorous, cheerily inventive.

'Rockingham,' I gave her. 'And how's Nightmarish?'

She brightened. Her brother Mike, a.k.a. Nightmarish to his fans (don't be alarmed, he's only the lead singer of a pop group of that name) has been planning a robbery for all eight years I've known Vesta. It's of Rotherham's brilliant and massive collection of Rockingham china, which is why I was visiting today, prompted by that exquisite Rockingham vision at Gimbert's. Nightmarish can tell you the museum's alarms, electronic tacky-mat locations, where the infra-red beams cut to and from, who's on the security team. Except he'll never do it. His robbery is like an Aborigine's dream-time, but less real.

Her face melted. She loves Nightmarish, and has scuppered three of his proposed weddings to prove it. A sister sometimes has a lot to answer for. She herself has lovers like a net collects tiddlers.

'Nightmarish is lovely.' She beamed fondly. 'I used to take him for walks in his pushchair . . .' et reminiscent cetera.

'Mmmh,' I went, wandering the shop while Vesta talked.

You see the problem? Nightmarish, like every bloke, needs a lass. Vesta's a welcoming Rottweiler whenever he takes a new bird home. You'd think she'd be glad. Women usually like people to get married, don't they?

There was only one piece of Rockingham in, a crude fake, of course, but priced like something from the hands of the immortal Brameld menfolk. It was a funny L-shaped jug, with a little goat on the brim. So far so good. Underneath was *Brameld* in purple. Some local fakers had done their homework. It didn't thump my chest with a gong-like shudder, so it was a dud.

The antiques trade says, 'When the Queen came, Rockingham went', meaning that after young Queen Victoria's coronation, the firm sank with all hands. The historical fact is that when King Billy IV died in 1837 the fancy-carriage families who'd adored Rockingham porcelains simply turned their faces away, being fickle old public. The famed Swinton–Brameld–Rockingham pottery closed in 1842 amid universal lamentation. There's no accounting for taste. I don't understand fashion. I mean, what suddenly makes one kind of blouse or skirt the overnight toast of London and last week's priceless frock a rotten old rag women wouldn't be seen dead in? Answers on a postcard, and we'll bottle the profit.

'. . . kick his little shoes right off, Lovejoy!' Fond tears were in Vesta's eyes.

'Mmmh,' I went. No antiques here either, just dross that ought to be down on Roman Marsh. 'About Rockingham.'

Her face changed. She concentrated on foes.

'Mike's got some tart sniffing around him, the conniving bitch.'

'What's she like?'

'I haven't seen her yet.' Vesta's hatred is impartial. 'I'll fix the slut. Huh! A name like Irma?'

'Irma!' I chuckled. 'Honest. A name like that!' I should talk.

My response pleased her. 'You want that Rockingham, Lovejoy? It's named underneath, has the right handle. See?' She held it up proudly. 'Horse-tail and hoof?'

I hadn't missed the characteristic shape, for the handle's top started as a horse's tail and finished as a hoof. But one swallow doesn't, does it?

'Beautiful,' I lied, mentally apologizing to genuine antique china the world over. 'I wish I'd the money.' If I had, I'd not spend it on a dud made last Saturday.

She wagged her eyebrows fetchingly. 'An arrangement, Lovejoy?'

'Who's been after Rockingham lately?'

'Everybody on earth.' She swore at a nail that split. To my consternation she simply ripped it off and searched for her handbag. False nails, I realized. Those and eyelash crimpers give me the willies. 'Mostly that Mrs Crucifex.'

'That who?' I said innocently.

'Crucifex. Has three homes, a husband in each.'

'She likes Rockingham?' I already knew.

'She eats it for breakfast.' She seated herself and busily started gluing a fingernail into place. She paused to eye me. 'Don't do it, Lovejoy. She eats men for breakfast as well.'

'Three homes, eh?' I grinned, to loosen up. 'There's money in antiques!'

'In charities, you mean.' She resumed painting the new nail red, her tongue out to concentrate. 'She's a milker.'

One who espouses charitable causes in order to nick the money.

'Then she can't be all bad,' I said mildly, to goad.

Vesta reacted with a snort. 'She's in with that Albansham crowd's new charity. Had the frigging nerve to come asking would I help.'

'To which you replied?' I laughed my way to the door.

Her remark stopped me. 'Lovejoy. Why Rockingham of a sudden?'

I hesitated, overacting. 'There was a piece going at the auction, Gimbert's. It got withdrawn.'

'Irma the wormer got herself arrested,' Vesta said with relish. 'Some crank got her sprung. She hates her auntie. Nightmarish told me.'

'Her auntie?' I raised both hands to fend off more explanations, and shot out.

My smile died in the street. Auntie, as in Mrs Crucifex?

I wanted a word with Nightmarish, but not until I'd sussed out Irma and this Mrs Crucifex. I rang directory enquiries from the Bay and Say tavern. Yes, the operator told me, Mrs Crucifex was a subscriber, Saumarez House, Albansham village. I said ta.

That worried me, the name. Wasn't Saumarez some historical character? I'd not time to visit our town's hopeless library.

It stopped raining! I got Hunter from the tavern darts team to drive me to Albansham Priory. He's a pest, talked about income tax all the way. A couple of miles from the coast I told him to hang on a sec.

'The priory must be near.' A signpost showed in the leafy hedgerow.

'It's OK, Lovejoy,' Hunter said. 'I know the way.'

And he did. We headed for the sea, nearly were into Aldeburgh itself when he turned into a narrow drive. It's all countryside there, and I don't recommend it. Suffolk is as depressing as fields, rivers and undulating woods can make it. Shown on canvas by Constable, it's safe and beautiful. In the raw, it's lonesome and scary. East Anglia runs out of towns faster than anywhere I know.

We trundled into a walled courtyard. I got out. Hunter said so long.

'Got the darts championship later, Lovejoy,' he said. 'Big money.'

Hunter the Punter, they call him. Thought intruded. 'Here, Hunter,' I asked, as he backed his van. 'How come you know this place?' For all I knew he might come to church here. A chapel adjoined the main building.

'Prior Metivier was in our punter syndicate.' He braked, gravel spouting. 'Good brain, but unlucky.'

I watched the vehicle recede.

Albansham Priory was of astonishing red brick, with angular tall chimneys, leaded windows, ramparts and leaded roofs, a flagpole on a turret, an archway for coaches, climbing plants doing their picturesque stuff. It was a post-cardy Queen Anne, lovely and venerable. I liked it. Would it like me?

'Hello again, Lovejoy.'

Marie Metivier waited at the foot of broad stone steps. She wore a stunning electric blue day dress. Her hair looked different. I couldn't remember if she'd worn a hat. More importantly, hate was back in style. Her eyes flashed with contempt, if eyes can do such a thing.

'Hello, er, missus.' I didn't buss her, in case she had me shot.

'Why did you come with that man?' She spoke with disgust.

'Eh? Hunter? He gave me a lift.' Did she expect me to jog the eighteen miles?

'Why didn't you come in your own car?'

Some women make you thoroughly fed up. 'Look, lady. My motor is the corroding sublimate of rust. I've been trying to sell it for years.' I was suddenly hopeful. 'You want it? One owner, good condition.'

She faced me, apoplectic with fury. 'Where's the famous antique dealer, then, who can detect antiques just by sense? Why *are* you broke, Lovejoy? You're the only dealer who can never ever be!'

'Women,' I said, adding nastily, 'women like you. Who have ideas of betterment. Who have worthy causes and know what's best.' I gave up. I could walk into Aldeburgh. Olivia the coastguard's wife might be free, run me away from these lunatics back to civilization where I was mistrusted but safe.

'You identified the Montagnana. Where's *that* money gone?'

'Eh?'

Italian names need spelling out before they come to their senses. Painstakingly I said the name to myself. Then I remembered.

I'd been in a shop near Telford and got talking to a tourist from Omaha. She was a pretty woman, who wanted help at an auction. I went with her, from lust. The globular porcelain she'd hoped was genuine Wedgwood 'Fairyland' lustre was an obvious fake. I told her that its lid rim was too uneven. But there was this violin.

It was in a shoddy frayed case, a throwout you can get for a few pence anywhere. But the violin was magic. I heard it playing to me in its case as I drifted round. I opened the case for a look, and instantly became a supplicant before majesty. The woman – was she called Barbara? – didn't notice, admiring crummy forgeries and discarded jetsam. I was broke, as it happened. I told her to buy the violin whatever it cost. We had a brief breakdown in communication. She said she wasn't at all musical. I said I'd kill her if she didn't buy it. She tried to pass my venomous remark off as a joke, so I had to do some forceful persuasion that I won't describe, if you don't mind.

The upshot was that Barbara from Omaha, wherever that is, bought it for a song. Some expert later identified it as a Domenicus Montagnana violin, 1727. It sold later for a sixth of a million, which was a percentage or two up on the nineteen quid Barbara bid for it. It made the headlines in Telford's mighty press. Barbara gave gushing interviews on TV. By then I'd slipped from the firing line. Once she'd got the gelt Barbara gave me the sailor's elbow.

'The violin?' I smiled, recalling the feeling. She had been so beautiful, almost a returning dream. It was purest sexuality, the music washing my soul in that musty dusty

hole of an auction. 'She was exquisite. I'd give almost anything to have her still.'

'The woman?' Marie Metivier asked.

'No, silly cow. The violin.'

'Why didn't you keep it, Lovejoy?'

'Lady,' I said bitterly. 'If I couldn't afford nineteen quid
to buy it in the first place, where the hell d'you think I
could get a fortune?'

She suddenly smiled, took my arm, and began to walk me
towards the archway. I gaped. Was the woman demented?

'Lovejoy,' she breathed, fondness itself, 'I really do think
you and I are going to get along. Would you like tea before
lunch? The novices grow their own tea. Personally, I think
the greenhouse is somewhat too arid.'

Caution in every step, I went with her because there's
not much else you can do when a bonny bird squeezes your
arm, but I was ready to run. This Marie Metivier ought to
try consistency for a change, give blokes like me a chance.
As we went into the interior courtyard, I tried to work out
what turned her switch on and off.

Her brother narked her, for one. As did Hunter. And
Arty, when praising a horse. The horse too she hated. So
what pleased her? Me, being broke. And me again, for not
having a viable motor. Me a third time . . . *for not being a
gambler?*

Her George had mentioned odds at the Tey point-to-
point races, what, thirteen to something? Hunter the
Punter. And Arty, who'd taken up antiques to become even
more broke when gambling. Aha, I thought. I'd invented
the wheel, and smiled with new confidence at the lovely
Marie Metivier. This gorgeous bird didn't care for menfolk
who blued their loot on tardy nags in the three-thirty at
Aintree. Simple as that! I felt relief, tried out my theory.

'Nice little place you've got here,' I quipped, standing before Albansham Priory. Time for a firing. 'Did you know that some ancient priories were actually wagered in ancient days?'

Her features clouded, abruptly Wicked Witch of the West.

'Don't talk to me—'

I was happy. 'Gambling is utterly wasteful.'

Her face unwrinkled and the dazzling sun shone. She squeezed my arm. I beamed. I was a hit! Eagerly I went on, 'Once, I knew a man who chucked everything he owned on a game of cards, bet his entire shop – a pokey little antiques place, but still his livelihood – at a poker championship. I tried to talk him out of it . . .'

Her face was rapturous. I kept up the patter. Once a crawler. But look how politicians get on. There's mileage in grovelling.

7

YOU CAN'T SMELL antiques, but you can sense them. It's not a guess, not a feel. It's like suddenly hearing an enormous shout. You know that feeling in passion, when she becomes the ultimate goddess and it's heavenly violins? Well, add a clamorous bonging and there you have it. Fakes don't do it. Forgeries don't do it. But antiques? Oh, yesyes.

It's because antiques *have been lived with*. People loved them, polished them, cried when they had to sell them, watched heartbroken when bailiffs took them away. Antiques *are* different. Is it any wonder? It's how they were made. Anybody can make a chair with modern glues and an electric drill. And if you're too idle even to do a hand's turn, simply buy the pieces ready carved and stick them together. Then, like most furniture manufacturers nowadays, claim that you're as good as the immortal Sheraton or Hepplewhite.

Except you're phoney. The reason was plain at Albansham Priory.

The interior courtyard was busy, busy. Workshops abounded. I'd been sniffing tantalizing scents ever since alighting from Hunter's van. The aromas of glues filled the air. A workshop – chairs, tables, even a small bureau – stood in plain view. Two smocked monkish figures beavered away. I almost puked at their frigging nerve. They had a bandsaw, two jigsaws, a stack of machined beechwood chair legs, more devices than the parson preached about. It was obscene.

Further along, three figures in nunnish apparel sat at embroidery frames in a large bay window. They too were going at it like the clappers, adjusting auto-holders, sliding their adjustable frames beneath arrays of focused spotlights. No mediaeval eye strain there.

And I heard the solid thunk of a kiln door, heard the switches go, the first muted belch of gas-firing sequence. At a ground-floor window, there was the erratic flicker of a welder at work.

'Marie?' I asked, appalled. 'What *is* this place?'

'Albansham Priory, Lovejoy.' She didn't know whether to be proud or depressed. 'George's idea is to make reproductions, for income.'

'No, love.' I stopped, wouldn't budge. 'Albansham Priory is holy. With monks and a convent. And a hot pool, where pilgrims are baptized.'

'And . . . ?' Marie prompted.

I strove to remember. 'The holy pool's mud cures you. It chucks up fossils.'

'Better than Wiltshire's hot pools. But priories have debts.'

She had a knack of making me feel daft.

Somebody inside one of the barns gave a shout. I saw the lights flicker as they decanted molten iron into sand moulds, and heard the rattle of gantry chains. I could even smell the wet-blood-and-coffee of the Bessemer process. Making things the old way, but assisted by every mod con. Obscenity ruled.

She smiled, a real winner. 'You thought it was all nuns preparing parchment and the Venerable Bede cutting quills for illuminated calligraphy?'

'Sort of.' I didn't like being laughed at. I ought to try hate again.

'You're a romantic, Lovejoy.'

'I didn't expect a factory, Marie.'

Which raised the question of why Mrs Crucifex – trigamist of the three mansions – was creating yet more charities to help this hive of antiques fakery.

I'm no saint, honest I'm not, though Marie Metivier's jibe about me being romantic did sting. I've forged everything from a Georgian hourglass to the *Mona Lisa* and back again. I've faked Gainsborough one week and Chippendale the next. I've forged Ancient Egyptian necklaces out of plastic, and William and Mary pearl coronets out of fish-scale paste (use the Canadian paste; it's far the best). OK, I know that folk buy them from me then sell them as genuine. I'm not thick. Well, not often. A Lovejoy model of a man-o'-war, allegedly French prisoner-work of the Napoleonic era, won't be made of bone slivers honed out by an electric drill-and-grinder. My forgery is worked by hand. The metal pins will be cut by hand. The holes for the pins (so's not to split the bone) will be drilled by hand. Even the hand drill is made by my own scarred lilywhites. In other words, I do what the old master geniuses do, did.

Marie sighed. 'It's dwindling, Lovejoy. There are no new novices coming in. Costs soar. Religion is out.' She walked me on. Her brother came forward to welcome me. He wore a monk's russet habit and looked really delighted, wrung my hand.

'How marvellous!' He waved at the activity. 'You approve, I trust?'

'He doesn't, actually, George.'

Marie said his name funny, slurring each g. Was it actually Georges, like the French say?

'I'm sure he's impressed deep down.' He did his twinkly look, came to my other side to take my free arm. I felt a prisoner between them. 'Do come inside.'

'One thing, er, George.' I couldn't say it like Marie. 'Why aren't you at compline or vespers, or hoeing the field ready for the Angelus bell?'

'Have you looked at the calendar, lately, Lovejoy?' he said with phoney sorrow. 'Time marches on.'

He ushered me in through the main door. A nun glided past, her habit sweeping the wooden parquet flooring. Flowers, light falling through stained glass windows, bannisters gleaming, it seemed about right. Metivier seemed authoritative, merely responding with a nod when the nun quietly greeted him.

'What does that mean?' I asked.

They still held me, making sure I wouldn't run away. We went through into a sumptuous book-lined study. It was all oak panels and leather armchairs. It would have done credit to a London club. Once in, they visibly relaxed.

'It means, Lovejoy, that all you see about you—'

'Is duff.' I let them assimilate that. 'Look, how am I to call you?'

'I am Prior George of Albansham Priory.' He grimaced. 'No religious titles, between friends.'

His roguish twinkle was starting to nark me. I saw an old print, badly mounted, across from the window. Stupid to hang it there, where sunlight would ruin it. An engraving of islets, an escutcheon, a massive compass, a border with lozenges. Phoney, of course. The outlined islets seemed familiar.

Saumarez. Nelson's second in command at the Battle of the Nile was a Saumarez. And Prior George's name, Metivier. I tried not to study the engraving. So I was a friend. For how long?

'Yes, Lovejoy. All the priory's antiques are gone.' He walked the study. His sister sat by the bay window, a pretty picture. 'Which raises the question of what I've persuaded you to come and see!'

'Not exactly.' I said. 'Why did you ask people about me in the first place?'

'Maybe because of this, Lovejoy?'

And he brought out a musical instrument I'd made. I recognize my own forgeries like old friends and started forward eagerly.

This was a small can-shaped structure. It was the great bass racket, a renaissance wind instrument that can play as low as a double bassoon. I'd made it of nine parallel-bore cylinders of wood – I'd used pear, but laburnum does as well if you can get it properly cured. It looks ridiculous, seen from a distance. Goons call it the pocket bassoon. Much they know. Close to, it looks even dafter, with a thing like a small smoking tube sticking out of the top. Its sides have holes. But play it right, it's a dream. One of the few musical instruments that sound good enough to eat.

'Here,' I said indignantly. 'What frigging idiot replaced the reed?'

'Me,' said Marie sweetly.

'Ah, well,' I said lamely. 'Don't do it again.'

'Why not?'

'Each reed has to be cut properly – cane, bamboo – as personal as the shoes on your feet.'

'Can it play?'

'Cheek,' I said, before remembering where I was. 'Er, begging your pardon, reverend.'

The reed was too thick. She'd carved it out of solid wood. Shaving it thin is the trick, that and soaking it in spit.

'Wrong reed.' I huffed and puffed for breath, then played a few notes of that Purcell gigue, then collapsed exhausted.

'Bravo, Lovejoy.' Metivier let me recover, then asked, 'Would you make us a few more?' He sounded quite wistful. 'We could sell them.'

Haven't you got any wood carvers on the Channel Islands? I didn't ask in case I'd got it wrong. Least said, quickest profit. I needed to find Mrs Crucifex, maybe get something out of her faster than I would this close pair.

Marie didn't like 'mainland' weather. It's what a Channel Islander would say, their having a sunnier clime. Saumarez, the last admiral to fly his flag on Nelson's *Victory*, came from Guernsey. That accented way of saying names. And even the name Metivier – hadn't a Metivier done some notable Norman dictionary? Possibly a Channel Island name. I looked at them both anew. I couldn't call to mind any famous Channel Island antiques. Had I missed something?

'I might.' I had no intention, though, what with having Prince's famous forgery to finish. And I didn't want Summer lurking around my workshop. Mind you, George had talked about filthy lucre, so I added, 'How soon would you want them?'

'We had a travelling antique dealer call less than a week ago, Lovejoy. He wants old violins, cellos, wind instruments.'

'Does he.' A likely tale. Anybody in the Eastern Hundreds wants anything, I'm the first to hear. Except I was barker blind, Tinker being in gaol, the unhelpful old swine. You can't depend on anybody.

'We happen to have a very cultured lady who knows a good reproduction when she sees one. She guessed your name. Hence my message at the boot fair.'

'Is this the "antique" you wanted me to suss?' I was disappointed. I'd forged the wretched thing.

'No, Lovejoy.' Marie stared at her brother. 'It's not that simple.'

'Now, Marie,' George soothed. He stood behind his desk, very Churchillian, and smilingly explained, 'My sister wishes that Albansham Priory were still mediaeval. I say we move with the millennium.'

'Your one remaining antique is pretty valuable, then?' I cleared my throat, feeling greed coming on. 'Is it the abbey's own property?'

'Yes,' said George.

'No,' said Marie.

'Er, are you sure?' The best I could do, confronted like that.

'Lovejoy,' Metivier said gravely. 'How well do you know the Eastern Bloc?'

'Eh? I thought that was over and done with.'

'It's still there, like a historic tribal war. We can't ignore it.'

Well, no. I wouldn't want history to forget, either. Yet here we were in a soporific old priory, with a few remaining monks and nuns trundling out antiques replicas for tourists. Politics has nothing to do with life. I told him as much.

'No, Lovejoy. It has everything to do with us.'

'Show him, for heavens sake,' Marie spat out. 'It's the only way.'

I wondered whether to ask. 'Find out what?' I said after a bit.

'Whether you are the one we need for them,' George said.

'Whether you *aren't* the one we need for it,' Marie said.

They both spoke together. For it? For them?

'Shall we go and see it, then?'

'Oh, it's here, Lovejoy. Behind you. It's a rare engraving, a valuable historic map.'

Carefully I didn't laugh. I didn't even bother to look.

'Thank you,' I said, polite as a kiddie leaving a party. 'Ta-ra.'

'Why are you going?' Metivier, baffled, started after me.

'You've not got an antique, George. I'd feel it.'

And left, out through the ornate hall with its gliding nuns, across the courtyard. I met Gesso there. He was with a tubby monk, who was furious.

'Wotcher, Gesso,' I said.

He brightened. 'Wotcher, Lovejoy. Going to help our Open Day?'

Each year, Albansham Priory has a gala. Village children dress up in Tudor costumes, and the whole place is given over to ancient times. Wheelwrights do their stuff with old implements, joiners, embroidresses, farriers, leather workers, parchment stretchers, wool spinners, everybody goes back several hundred years. Visitors pay an entrance fee, and a high old time is had by all. Imagine the gaiety.

'Er, ta, Gesso, but I'm visiting my sick auntie in hospital.'

'The oven failed to fire properly,' the stout monk moaned. He looked as if he wanted to be in a hell of a temper but was too holy.

'Hard luck, er, reverend.' I made to move on, then

paused. 'Here, Gesso. Was it you told old Metivier about me?'

'Course.' He brightened. 'Thought there'd be a quid in it. Any joy?'

'Not really. Is there a bus service hereabouts?'

Gesso and the monk smiled the smile of the rural trudger and let me go. I was almost out of the door when a lady arrived in a sleek reddish motor too posh for me to recognize the badge.

'Lovejoy!' Metivier came out, trotted after me. I kept going.

'Oh, it's you. You're that Lovejoy, aren't you?' The lady got out, flashing a mile of leg. Smart red suit, hem cut just so, necklace that could have bought me, cottage and all. 'Wait for the abbot.'

'No.'

'Stop him,' she said quietly, and I was grabbed in a flurry of habits. A monk held me. He looked old enough to be my grampa, but God he was wiry. There must be something in this religion business.

'Phone the police, Gesso,' I called out. Gesso shook his head like you do at a disobedient dog. 'I'm being kidnapped.' The woman was the one from the auction, Irma's Auntie Crucifex.

'You're being stupid,' said the woman. 'Take him to the vigil cell.'

And they did. And me innocent, if there is such a thing.

An hour later I'd cooled my heels. The cell had a small altar, two modern candlesticks of machined brass, a plain cross, a tabernacle. The window showed where the original stained glass had been excised, for a cheapo painted glass replacement concreted in. I'd seen holier sheds.

You can't do much in a vigil cell, except vig. So I pondered.

The Channel Islands were news to me. I'd never been there. What did I know about them, offhand? Jersey, Guernsey, Alderney, Sark, Herm. Were there more? Odd facts, like the Dame of Sark never lets motor cars ashore. There's no love lost between Guernsey and Jersey, word is, because the former feels disadvantaged and the latter's a snob. Herm is minute. Tourists abound. Did I know anything else?

Bits of the Channel Islands still have their own variants of the old Norman lingo, varying parish to parish. No antiques I could think of. No great tradition of joinery or jewellery, no dazzlingly brilliant silversmiths slogging away.

End of message. I'd been chucked into the priory's pokey, I was especially narked to remember, on the orders not of Prior George, but of a trendy bird.

Two hours later, I'd searched my cell top to bottom. From outside I could hear some plainchant, nuns' fragile warbling contrasting with the monks' uneven bass. I felt daft and embittered. What God lets visitors get imprisoned? I'd only come from interest, to see how a religious community actually works, hadn't I? Well, no. I'd come because Prior Metivier promised me filthy lucre, but I was still a person interested in God's rotten old priory. I sulked.

After a third hour I wanted to pee, but there was no loo. The doors were locked. I decided to wait until everything went quiet – even the Inquisition had a rest now and then – whereupon I'd break a window and do a moonlight into Aldeburgh.

Just when I was getting really desperate there came a

rattle of keys, locks, bolts. The door opened. A midget nun stood there.

'Please come, my son,' she piped. Son? That crinkly white biscuit-tin paper round their faces makes them all look like comely teenagers.

'Where to?' I didn't budge.

'To the prior's sanctum.'

'No. I've had enough.' I stalked past her. Three monks stood in the cloister. Noisy, they'd have been formidable. Silent, they looked scary. 'Which way?' I asked the nun.

She walked ahead. Following a nun is quite boring, whereas following any other woman's quite interesting. There's always something to see. I heard the monks' sandals going slap-slap-slap behind me. They let me have a pee in a spartan loo.

Then I felt it. We were going along a cloister when I stumbled. For a second I thought somebody had clouted me. I looked about. Nobody, except the nun, turning to see what the heck, and my trailing gaolers.

We were on one side of the inner courtyard. Work had ceased for the whilst. Against the cloister wall, no windows, was an array of artefacts on loose tiered shelving. Prior Metivier had evidently learnt display from his trip to the boot fair. Some had labels. CIBORIUM – TWELFTH CENTURY; and VELLUM HOURS OF THE VIRGIN – ENGLISH, FIFTEENTH CENTURY, and the like. They were covered by plastic.

'Are you well, my son?' asked this little titch in her saintly falsetto.

'Eh? Ta, er, nun,' I said. 'I feel a bit queer.'

'Please rest a moment.'

She pulled away the plastic, giving me room to perch.

The feeling worsened. I doubled with a groan, sweat coming down my face. I felt really giddy. Then I saw it. Up and to the left, almost burning my shoulder, was a metal animal mask. It looked home-made, as if some kiddie had worked it in Plasticine. Two recesses showed where eyes had been. Less than five inches wide, its mouth held a metal ring. Flecks of goldish colour gleamed, where inlay had once been. It was a simple handle. I looked, felt, listened. No, just the one. The other of the pair was missing.

'Is he unwell, Sister Cecilia?' one of the monks said, voice sepulchral.

'He seems overcome, Brother Gervaise. Please bring his friend.'

Friend? I hadn't any friends. Somebody brought me water. It tasted foul. I sipped, grimaced.

'From our own healing pool, Lovejoy,' the nun said with asperity. 'People come on pilgrimages to drink it.'

The more fool them, I thought. I moved away, vigilantly followed by the sandalled soldiery. Gesso appeared, with the prior, who dismissed my guardians.

'Hello, Lovejoy. Which is it?' Gesso looked pleased. 'Is it that pewter tankard?'

There was a tankard, a modern Spanish fake looking every day of its age – about four weeks. French forgers buy these pewters wholesale, and age them by either burying them in new-cut grass for a few weeks or giving them a black acid-stained patina. As genuine antique pewter pieces have soared in value, so has the number of fakes and their quality. No, it wasn't the fake tankard.

'What d'you mean?' I asked, but the game was up.

Gesso pulled the plastic, left it crumpled.

'Stand close, Lovejoy.' Gesso was grinning, like traitors always do.

'No.' I nodded at the bronze handle. 'That.'

'This old handle?' Prior Metivier lifted it down, truly amazed.

'They used to make them in pairs. Chinese. There should be semi-precious stones for eyes. The fact they're missing won't lower the auction price much.'

'How old, Lovejoy?' Metivier stood. 'We priced it at ten pounds.'

'It will buy a new house.'

The bonny lady approached. She held a cigarette, determined to look out of place, and succeeding.

'What is it?' she rasped.

You know when two people look at each other and you know there's something between them? Well, I felt exactly that. She and the prior were more than just good friends. Metivier determinedly kept his eyes averted. She had no such inhibitions. Her eyes were only for him.

'Lovejoy's identified an antique.' He looked at me. 'Chinese?'

'Older than all you saints, Prior. Remarkable that it's preserved.'

'Indeed.' He smiled at the lady. 'And to think, Mrs Crucifex, that we were about to invoke Lovejoy's assistance in a—'

'Where do we sell it, Lovejoy?' Mrs Crucifex cut in.

'London auction, or a private broker-buyer.' I shrugged. 'Don't let Gesso melt it down and make Christmas cracker brooches.'

That was nasty, because Gesso had once nicked some gold Roman staters from the castle museum. He'd melted the coins down to make pendants. That way, he changed rare ancient coins into cheap trinkets. He coloured in anger.

'Now, gentlemen,' Prior George placated. 'Lovejoy, I

would like to thank you for coming. Mrs Crucifex, would you care to offer Lovejoy a lift home?'

'Is that it?' I said. 'Can I go?'

Metivier smiled. 'For now. We'll need you later.'

8

I T WAS DARK, leaves brushing my face. I wasn't very old, maybe ten. I was scared, but I had a flashlight. Somebody was among the bushes, I didn't know who. I hadn't been following them but somehow I was there.

The ground was wet. In the air hung a strange cloying smell. I heard the person returning, so laid myself flat in the thick coarse grass. A beam cut the air but couldn't get through the low-hanging trees. I could hear the strange sucking plop noises of the hot muddy pool. It was that that I'd come to see.

The moon shone on its surface when I raised my head to look. Odd scrubby reeds grew there. Nothing grew in its middle. It was some ten feet across, and was having one of its gurgling and spitting fits. Not spectacular, like those New Zealand geysers or the American volcanic spouts, but it was the best East Anglia's undulating countryside could manage in the way of horror.

Every so often, it bubbled up enough to source a stream once the water cooled. The great thing was, fossils came up from deep under the earth. They had their original colours, too, unlike those that had been buried for millions of years. Rumours abounded of dinosaur bones, vertebrae and suchlike, still linked, being found in the stream bed, almost as if the pool had reached down and—

'Aaaagh!' I screeched, fighting the hand off.

'Goodness *sake*, Lovejoy!'

'Ergh, ergh!' I was frantic.

Moonlight, yes, but the voice was Florida's. I was not ten years old.

'Oh, hello, love.' Cool, calm Lovejoy.

Shakily I scrabbled for a match, lit a candle stub. Florida was about to climb in beside me.

'Honestly! I hurry to you, and I'm the monster from the deep!'

'No images, please.' I relaxed. 'Have you brought any grub?'

'You're sweating buckets, Lovejoy.' She got a towel, mopped me briskly. 'Turn over. Worse than any child. Having a bad dream?'

'Yes. The hot pool at Albansham Priory.'

'Hardly the most frightening puddle in the universe, Lovejoy. Yes, to food. And thank you, Florida darling, would be super.'

'Ta, dwoorlink,' I said obediently.

Waking up in the early evening, hardly dark yet, gives you a headache. My headaches go for gold, real temple-splitters. Waking up from a nightmare makes things worse, not better. I dangled my legs over the edge of the bed.

'Did you get it?'

'Get what? The prize money? Soon, darling. I bet far too much!' She trilled a laugh. Florida's gorgeous and rich. She gambles heavily on her horses. I could scent the grub. It was in those tin foil boxes that startle you because they're hotter than you think.

'Not your nags. I meant the glass vase.'

'Oh, that,' Florida said, airy. 'I forgot. But guess what, Lovejoy? My lovely boy Sharples got through to the semi-final of the Bycroft Cup!'

'You forgot?' I stared at her. Lovely, but a pest.

The previous Saturday, Florida had shown me some photographs. Like all pictures of horsey gentry, they were of stupefying dullness. Except one. It showed Florida laughing with her friend Tara. They were somewhere indoors, a massive boudoir – lady's room 'for sulking in', according to the original French.

On the dressing table was a piece of Gallé. It was indistinct, because Florida and her pal were the centre of focus, but it looked for all the world like an artichoke vase. 'Standard Gallé' glass, collectors call it, but you can't mistake the white opaque mutton-fat look of the body, with the marquetry-on-glass coloured covering on parts of the vase's lovely curved form. Its base looks solid agate. Genius. And Florida *forgot*?

Emile Gallé was a glass-maker's son in Lorraine, and studied in Weimar (yes, that one) before starting up with his dad in Nancy. Before he died, in 1904, Emile was world famous. I like his art. He experimented with glass night and day. A man after my own heart. He became the glassmaker hero of Art Nouveau, and I do mean everybody's champ. There's a rule of thumb among antiques dealers that if a piece is signed by Gallé it was made some time after 1889, but that's not always true.

When I'd first asked Florida about the vase, she'd said, 'Oh, Tara wants to get rid of all her old stuff, have a real throwout.'

Needless to say, I'd begged her to persuade Tara to chuck the vase my way. Now I get, 'I forgot.' Yet she remembers that her stupid nag jumped over some sticks. You're in a bad way when you call a horse a lovely boy.

'Can I go and see Tara?'

Florida was undoing the foils. 'Lovejoy. Tara wouldn't touch you with a barge pole. She's not into rough trade yobbos.'

'Like me?'

She darted me a mischievous smile, battling the luscious aroma.

'Lovejoy. Eat up like a good boy.'

'Ta, love.' I got the plate, and screamed as the scalding thing charred my naked thigh. I almost spilled the damned thing. Florida laughed so much that tears came. Her beautiful form shook and quivered. I eyed her, wolfed the grub. Sometimes your mind doesn't know what comes first.

We made hectic love. After a rest we imposed further demands, and then slumbered in a sweaty conglomerate. Instead of dozing, for once I found myself thinking. It's always a hazard.

There's this theory about civilization, isn't there, that it travels ever westwards. As one civilization fades another starts, but always west. Like, China, India, then Persia, Egypt, Greece, Italy, England and now America. I think it's rubbish myself, because what about all the civilizations we miss out? Anyway, what *is* civilization?

Many folk say it's crime.

Not long since, everybody in our village left cars unlocked, babies in gardens, doors unlatched, let children walk to school. Now, we think Carnage City. Everything has floodlights. Our very doors are wired to the Plod. Think of Victorian England, where every known vice abounded. If civilization does move west, and America does tote Lady Culture's lamp, then the flame singes the populace. Maybe crime and culture are inseparables. Now? Now it's Russia and China. Round and round it goes.

By the time I'd recovered and brewed up, Florida was awake. I got her talking about Irma – whom she knew – and Mrs Crucifex, whom she disliked with a woman's indelible passion. I asked why. Florida said, very disapproving, that Mrs Crucifex had too many husbands, in too many places. I did my ???, and got it on the nail.

Mrs Crucifex, from the Channel Isles. I said how I'd met her, and where.

'That place?' Florida almost spilt her tea in fury. She made a wondrous sight, sitting up in the candleglow, her breasts curved and her shoulders with that lovely sheen. 'Albansham Priory is on its last legs. That phoney man and his sow of a sister.'

'Oh,' I remarked innocently. 'I thought Prior Metivier was holy—'

'He's gutted it! My husband was educated there. We remember when it was a real priory, not just a few geriatrics putting on fêtes and catchpenny stalls.'

'Your husband?' I didn't like that.

'Didn't I tell you? He's home.' And this paragon of virtue added with sweet smiling innocence, 'I'm glad. Things are back to normal.'

'Er, look, love.' I started to get up. 'I'd better—'

She held me. Her tea spilt anyway. 'Not *that* normal, Lovejoy.'

Women have ways of delaying you when you ought to

be gone. Finally we dressed. She prattled about the Metiviers. In my wisdom I didn't listen much. Once a loon, always a duckegg.

Gesso was in the taproom of the Welcome Sailor. I'd tried eleven pubs. I needed Tinker. He'd have simply known where Gesso was, saved me hours.

'Drink?' I tried to get tick from Maisie, but she wouldn't and I had to fork out my last groat. 'Rum old place, that priory, eh, Gesso? What were you doing there, anyway? Bit religious for you, I'd have thought.'

I've known Gesso a long time, since he used to prepare gesso walls for me to paint murals on.

He's got a face like one of those mournful comics who can make you laugh just standing there. In fact he used to be a pub comedian. Once, he tried to set up restoring antiques, but he was useless. He helped me at the occasional house robbery, until I realized I wasn't really much good at it. His ex-wife Desdemona's a friendly lass, very gregarious.

'Mmmh.' He took the ale with a nod. 'I was at their open day, got talking to Prior George. He asked me about antiques. I told him about you. He's got some old painting he wanted you to shufti.'

So why didn't Prior George just call? And a painting? Not that priceless Chinese bronze handle?

'They're going on retreat soon, Lovejoy. Here.' He nudged me suggestively. 'His sister's a cracker, eh? And that Mrs Crucifex.'

'She ran me to the village. Not a word.'

'She's his fund-raiser. Hates Miss Marie. Women.'

'Aye.' I thought of Gesso's skills. 'What exactly are you doing?'

'Me? Bricking that mud bath they have. It's taken me three days. None of them monks can lift a bloody shovel. Worse than useless.'

'A bath?' I was mystified.

'Like for the Roman springs in Bath, but smaller. Visitors'll soak. He'll make Albansham a modern place of pilgrimage like in olden days.'

'Why not just put a rope round the hot pool, five quid a head?'

Gesso guffawed at my ignorance.

'You're off your trolley, wack. A farmer tried to fill it in years back, chucked in a hundred tons of rubble. Know what? It just vanished, glug, glug. No, Lovejoy. Sit a tourist down in that, it's goodnight Vienna.'

'Wise, then,' I said, uneasy, 'your little brick bath. I can see that.'

He came to the end of his pint. 'What you want me for, Lovejoy?'

'Eh? Oh, aye. Help me to burgle it, Gesso?'

He stared. 'To what?'

'You heard. Tomorrow night? You know the monks' routine.'

'Here, hang on—'

Maureen Jolly waved at me from the saloon bar. I went to her.

'Did you meet him?' Maureen breathed eagerly, bussing me and shoving her friend off a stool for me.

'Who do you mean, Maureen?' I pretended a roguish ignorance.

'Jonno Rant, you fiend!'

Phew. I'd forgotten the name I'd made up. 'Yes. He's resting at my cottage.' Good lies are reckless.

'He's a lovely man,' said Maureen's friend wistfully. 'I nearly auditioned for him once. Some younger bitch got the part.'

A *real* Jonno Rant? I eyed Maureen's friend. Until then I'd been admiring her on the sly – redhead, elfin and pretty in a green woollen dress. Now, I wasn't sure I liked her one bit. I needed gelt to finance a burglary, not truth. Also, I wanted my lies to stay lies, not suddenly turn into realities. Life's a mess.

'Are you sure it was Jonno Rant?' I said, sleet. Where the hell had I got the name from? Maybe some subconscious news bite lingered in my cortex.

Maureen laughed, slapping me playfully. I wish she wouldn't do that.

'Lovejoy's always joking, Patty. Take no notice. Jonno's famous! He's produced more shows than anybody on *earth*! When can I meet him, Lovejoy?'

'Tomorrow.' I heaved a sigh. 'I've been trying to borrow enough to take him out for a proper meal. You know these . . .' Christ, what were Jonnos called? 'These, er, show-business types. I don't want him to think badly of East Anglia.'

Maureen groaned. Patty groaned. We all groaned.

'I've got it, Lovejoy! Everything is looks. It's the *world*. Here!' Patty brightened, me thinking thank God the penny'd dropped. 'How about we lend you the money, Lovejoy? That way,' the lovely goddess explained while I fell in love with her, from the bottom of my heart, 'he'll be really impressed.'

'That's it!' I cried. 'We're noshing in the George, you stroll by—'

'Right! Right!' they both squealed, rummaging in hand-bags. Angel voices warbled fit to burst.

On my way out I gave Gesso the nod, then phoned Florida to say I was delayed at an auction.

She was outraged. 'At this hour, Lovejoy?'

'It's a ring auction, love. I'll see you about eleven o'clock. OK?'

'I don't know if I can be bothered to wait.'

Then don't, I thought but wheedled, 'Please, dwoorlink.'

Then I gave Thaddeus Harrod a few quid to lend me his motor and drove to Saumarez House, the home of Mrs Crucifex.

9

THE MOTOR WAS basically defunct. It had suffered. Twice it conked out on the bypass. On the outskirts of Alban-sham I flagged down a passing motorist. He was heading to the snooker match. His brother ran the team.

'You're lucky, mate,' he said, laughing. 'Don't stay out tonight.'

'Why? Is it All Hallows?' I can never keep track of these ancient folk festivals. Hereabouts it's all 'next Lady Day' and 'three nights before Michaelmas', and 'on Lammas Day' and suchlike nonsense. I can't see the point, when we've got calendars.

'No. The hare coursing's tomorrow.' For a second he looked stricken. 'Here. You're not the Plod?'

'Give over.'

'Thank God.' He really did seem relieved. 'The prior would kill me.'

'Prior George?' I chuckled, putting it on. 'He's a lad, eh?'

He said, guiltily, 'It's harmless fun, the dog racing.'

Now, hare coursing's illegal. It's been so since the law was passed through Parliament in 1841. It's pretty grim, if you've never seen it. The real hypocrisy is we've fine upstanding moralists who enjoy such sports. There's even an annual Waterloo Cup, real dogs and real hares. Sportsmen (sic) say the hares love it.

Hare coursing's done for a bet. Gamblers come from every corner of our creaking old kingdom to run their dogs in East Anglia's fields. You don't want to miss seeing some poor harmless creature being brutally exterminated, do you?

It's done like this: you catch a hare. Your dogs are the competitors. At a signal, you open your sack and release a hare. You also release dog A. It chases and kills the hare, while you enjoy the grand spectacle. Then you release a second hare, and dog B. Timekeepers clock the killing times, et evil bloodthirsty detestable cetera.

It's called rural sport. East Anglia's riddled with them, each as barbaric as the rest. Within ten miles of my cottage, you can see bare-fisted prize fights of a bright frosty morn. And cockfights, and pitbull terriors savaging one another, God knows what else. I'm not talking of some primitive backwoods (or am I?). I'm speaking of clean, quiet East Anglia. Civilized folk like me – and maybe you – might remember that there's legal greyhound racing at Romford and Swinton, if you crave seeing your dog running after an electric stuffed toy hare, where you can have a pint and place a bet as well, if you've a mind. OK?

No, not for the barbaric tribes among us, because there's no blood, no whimpers as the poor prey—

'Here, mate. You all right?' the driver was saying.

'Fine, ta. I get giddy in cars. Sorry.'

'Just as well we're here, then. Put your head down,' he said helpfully. He was a nice bloke. 'Have a pint. It's Magee's Ale, which is a bit grim, but—'

'No, ta. I feel grand. Saumarez House is three furlongs off, you say? Cheers, mate.' I grinned and strode off into the dusk. I was still trembling at the thought of the hedgerow creatures that would finish up in sacks later tonight, then have to run in terror for their little lives.

Saumarez House lay along the curved drive. I knocked. A policeman I knew opened the door, smiling.

'Do come in, Lovejoy.'

'Mr Summer.' I hesitated. 'Have I got the right place?'

He beckoned me into the light. 'You pretend you haven't, Lovejoy, but that's your way, isn't it? Always doing wrong, but accidentally, so it's never your fault?'

'Now then, Mr Summer.' My attempt at humour didn't work.

'Mr Crucifex is to join us in the living room. Go through.'

The Old Bill always like to follow you – their training, I suppose. I crossed the hall. The modern room was sumptuous. A huge painting occupied the wall beside the fireplace. A hero was dying, red-coated soldiery under fire, crowded streets.

'I thought that was in the Tate, Mr Summer. What've you been up to?'

'A copy.' He smiled. 'Or a fraud. Like so many things, Lovejoy.'

'If you say. Is this a posh do?'

'You mean tonight?' asked a man, entering and advancing with outstretched hand. 'No. Just a glass of something, while we iron out the details.'

'How do. I'm Lovejoy.'

'I'm Martin Crucifex. Welcome to our mainland abode. Yes. *The Death of Major Pierson*. Very graphic.' He said with heartfelt candour, 'I would give anything to possess the original.'

Summer smiled. I looked from one man to the other. I might not have been there.

'Now, Martin,' Summer said evenly. 'That's totally out of the question.'

'If you say so, Tony.'

Loudly I cleared my throat. If these two were squaring off for a scrap, I didn't want to get between.

'Iron out what details, exactly, Mr Crucifex?'

'Martin, please. We'll soon be on the very best of terms.'

How come? I said I'd dropped in on the off chance of seeing Mrs Crucifex about some antique she and Prior George wanted me to look at.

'Prior Metivier asked me to the priory, to look at something, then changed his mind.' Nobody answered me. 'If I've come at the wrong time—'

'Not at all. We expected you.' Martin poured me a drink. 'White wine?'

'Ta,' I said politely. 'You like the *Major Pierson* painting, then.'

He gave drinks round. Summer took his like a poisoned chalice. I thought, for Christ's sake, calm down, the pair of you. Or go outside and scrap it out. Frigging kids in a schoolyard.

'Like it, Lovejoy?' Crucifex turned to stare. 'You know the story? It was 1781. The all-conquering French invaded Jersey by night. Our lieutenant-governor surrendered in his bed. Can you imagine anything more contemptible?'

Aye, hare coursing. I said nothing. I know how surrendering feels.

'Surrender?' Martin laughed harshly. 'Not our brave Major Pierson. Barely twenty-four years old, he disobeyed the order to surrender. Gathering what men he could, he attacked with such courage that he won a signal victory, dying in triumph. He is buried in St Helier Parish Church.'

His lip curled. I watched it, fascinated. You don't often see that. I knew I'd try to do it – failing – in front of a mirror as soon as I got home.

'His foe – the Baron de Rullecourt – lies outside, in the churchyard.'

'God rest both,' I said. I only meant hard luck, but Crucifex angrily rounded on me. 'That's typical, Lovejoy! Our islands have a portentous history, just like the mainland!'

'Sure, right, OK,' I stammered, retreating before his venom. 'Jesus. I'd not meant anything bad. It's just a shame when people get dead.'

Summer rescued me. 'Evening, Jocina,' he said smoothly as Mrs Crucifex entered. 'Lovejoy, you've met our hostess?'

A maid followed, trundling a trolley of edibles. My belly rumbled audibly. I smiled a weak apology, trying to guess where the girl might leave the grub so I could get there first.

'Yes. Good evening, missus.'

'I didn't hear your car, Lovejoy.'

'It's laid up.' I avoided Summer's sardonic eye. He had booked me the last three times I'd driven it, hence its sessile atrophy.

'You might need it, once we get under way.'

'Once we've ironed out the details?' I can give as good as I get.

She was quick. 'One of Martin's phrases! Have you been filled in, Lovejoy? Our group's re-forming, to fund the priory. You figure in it.'

Swiftly I shuffled sideways. 'Sorry, love, but I'm meeting

an, er, impressario!' I almost shouted the word, delightedly remembering it at last.

'A percentage, Lovejoy,' she said. I stopped inching towards the door. 'Prior George leaves the money angle to us.' She dismissed the maid with imperial indifference. I wondered if she knew the lass's name.

'He does?'

'Our funds will have three destinies: the priory, the organizers and expenses. You, Lovejoy, come under me.'

A cat leapt on to her lap. We all sat. The cat sneered, clearly taunting: I'm sprawled on this exquisite woman, so get stuffed the lot of you. A cat is living proof that God was a rank beginner, all thumbs and no skill. He should have made cats without that inbuilt smirk.

We all ignored Mrs Crucifex's double meaning. Except me. Us cowards want definitions up front.

'Under you how, exactly?' I asked.

Summer coughed on his wine. Martin shot me an impaling glance. Mrs Crucifex crossed her legs carefully, but her long dress parted on a mile of delectable leg. I wondered if women do it deliberately. I suppose I'm wrong.

'For distribution of emoluments, Lovejoy.'

'Am I an expense?'

'Charity is a simple process, Lovejoy.' She stroked the cat. 'We organizers receive the appeal funds. Expenses come out. The residue goes directly to Prior Metivier.'

'I don't like charities, missus. They're frauds.'

'Not this, Lovejoy. Prior Metivier is chairman. I am secretary.' She indicated Summer. 'We have senior police. The charity will be registered.'

'We rattle tins in supermarkets, sell flags or what?'

'Nothing so exhausting,' she said, loving this. 'We advertise for antiques – however small – from parishioners, friends, churchgoers. We have already published in the religious press. You evaluate the antiques.'

'And who sells them?'

She sighed. I was being tiresome. The cat raised its head and stared with malice at unthinking peasants who had the nerve to intrude at food-and-lap time.

'You, Lovejoy. Or you arrange an auction.'

'I'm sick of arranging auctions.'

This is trouble. Because of BBC TV's *Antiques Road Show*, and a million *Road Show* lookalikes that tour every village and drill hall, there's a growing conviction that you've only to tack up a notice announcing one, and up bowl waggonloads of Rembrandts and Wedgwoods and Chippendales. It's greed. You want proof? Watch the TV show. You'll hear an expert waffle on about some porcelain piece. Nobody pays much attention, for who cares? Then he says, 'You want to know how much it's worth!' All conversation stops. You can hear a pin drop. See? Greed, more greed and nothing but greed, swelp me.

'Of *course* it must be you, Lovejoy. Ably assisted,' she said evenly, 'by Mr Summer. You are said – forgive me, Lovejoy – to need somebody beyond reproach to be close by.'

'Meaning I'm a crook, and Mr Summer's not?'

She smiled. 'I *did* entrust myself to your care.'

Well, if she put it like that. She meant driving me home.

'I found that thing at the priory,' I said, eyeing the grub. I was starving. 'That should keep Prior George in holy water for a week.'

'What thing?' Summer and Crucifix asked simultaneously, then quickly looked away to dissociate.

I told them about the Chinese handle. 'Pity there wasn't a pair. See, one is always less than half the value of a pair.'

There was silence. Martin looked at his wife. She started an immediate chatter about which friends might help, volunteer committees she'd written to.

'Er, any chance of . . . ?' I asked the trolley.

'Good heavens!' Mrs Crucifex trilled, relieved at the diversion.

She beckoned. I leapt an Olympic leap. It's very hard not to grab grub when you're hungry. Summer only picked, which is unusual, because the Old Bill are famous cadgers of grub and booze. We talked of this and that. I said a boot fair was hopeless and that asking antique dealers for gifts would provoke derision.

'It's the fancy,' I concluded. 'Meaning your level of society. You'll have enough money to advertise once you sell that Warring Period bronze.'

'Don't underestimate the problem, Lovejoy.' Crucifex spoke sombrely. 'Albansham Priory has fallen on hard times. We fear closure.'

'I heard about the holy pool.'

'Yes.' He heaved a sigh. I collared a plate of fishy circular things, only cavity fillers. I pretended to listen and got on with devouring. 'It's a long-term project, Lovejoy. Pilgrims mostly go to Walsingham, Lourdes.'

'Why not try something phoney, like Knock, in Eire?'

'Don't blaspheme, Lovejoy. Such places might be specially chosen.'

Well, OK, Martin sounded vaguely holy, but his wife? About Mr Summer I harboured not the slightest doubt, and me I knew all about. We were a mixed bunch all right. The priory had had it. I finished the chocolate things, so small your fingers met in the middle. They had crinkly paper round each morsel. If they hadn't been tasty they'd have been a nuisance.

'Oh, aye.' I wasn't convinced. 'How much debt are we trying to blot up?'

'The debt is confidential, Lovejoy,' Martin said, frosty.

'How soon do I scan the antiques, then?' The trolley had run out of grub. Time to go.

'We'll let you know. Two days or so, probably.'

'Lovejoy,' Mrs Crucifex said. Her foot was gently oscillating, up and down, up and down. I tried not to look, but women make politeness hard to come by, so to speak. 'You *are* committed to us, aren't you?'

'Er, yes, missus.' I did a gruff throat clearance. 'Just send word.'

No sign of her niece Irma. No feeling of genuine antique Rockingham pieces littering the house, no vibes of bliss-giving antiques clamouring away.

'I'll be off. It's quite a way back,' I hinted, helpfully giving them all the chance to hurtle forward with an offer of a lift home.

'Sorry we can't drive you back, Lovejoy.' Martin came to show me out. 'Our major fund-raising supper starts soon. You understand?'

All my life I've been told that I understand folk who're anxious to show me out, so I said sure, fine, ta, and went into the night.

No rain. I went down the drive, cut back and found a niche in the hedge. I stood waiting. 'Soon', he'd said. What time was it, half-eight?

Why hawthorns and blackthorn trees drip on you when they're not even wet is life's greatest mystery. It narks me. Twenty minutes passed before a large saloon arrived. Outside lights went on. I could see the house's façade, auto floods, I supposed. Prior Metivier alighted, with him his sister Marie. I watched them go in, wondering if they really were sister and brother. You can't always tell.

Then Irma, in a ratty little car so near the floor it seemed to snarl at the gravel. She flounced, her coat half off even before she vanished inside. Irma would be a ball tonight. I was glad I wouldn't be sitting next to her.

Two sedate couples came, dressed to kill, one pair parking their grand old Rolls, the next letting their car go. I tried to see who they were, but got spooked by another, a modern saloon. The bloke who strolled up the steps wore uniform, but not military. Airline pilot, perhaps? I was too far off to see the insignia.

No more came. Could there be a better time to do a burglary?

10

'WHERE THE HELL have you been?' I groused at Gesso when he arrived at the tavern. I was scared Prior Metivier would finish his nosh, zoom back to the priory and spoil everything. I don't know what priors do at night.

'Keep your hair on,' he grumbled back. 'Ready?'

'You look dishevelled.' I eyed him. They were making a real din in the taproom, darts reaching crescendo. 'You all right?'

'Fine. Let's go.'

He looked nervy, more on edge than I'd ever seen him, as we left the Fox and Hounds. Like I say, our paths had diverged when he took up burglary full time and I didn't. He'd get the job done, I was certain.

'We leave the motor at the crossroads, Lovejoy.'

'Won't people notice?'

'Not where I put it.'

Good enough. We drove through the night. He cut the lights once, scaring me. Then we'd emerge on some narrow side lane, with distant orange lights strung over trunk roads. I didn't know where I was when finally we coasted to a stop.

'Shhh,' he said when I made to speak. He listened for an age.

He got out, whispering to leave the car door ajar. He'd aborted the interior light. I heard a faint clink of metal as he hefted a bag.

'Follow me,' he whispered, and set off.

I couldn't see a thing. To the right the sky was less than pitch dark. I guessed it was the lights of a town, but which?

Characters like Gesso are really pretty naff people you don't think much of in cities among the milling millions. Yet put them out here in the dark, among strange night creatures, the ground turning suddenly into quagmires or flint, and they become the man. They're the ones you have to rely on, or go blundering, night blind, into some river. I bumped into Gesso.

'Shhhh, Lovejoy.'

I really wished he'd stop saying that. I was being as quiet as could be. We kept coming up against brambles. Twigs plucked at my face, leaves down my neck, and that daft non-rain kept dripping on me. I was fed up. I started off after Gesso, only to crash against him.

'What?' I whispered, scared we'd been rumbled.

'We're here. Shhhh.'

Where, exactly? All was darkness, no buildings anywhere.

'Where?' I whispered.

He made a susurrus reaching back. Slowly he took my hand, pulled it to my left. It touched stone. Brick? I felt further. Another, then another. A wall. I groped upwards. And down, to lovely solid paving. We'd reached civilization.

Then I heard it. Off to my right, a thick plopping sound, very irregular. Plop, suck, pitter pitter. Loud pause, then plop again. It was the hot pond, the pungent sickly fumes detectable as the breeze shifted. The priory wall.

Gesso tapped me twice, the burglar's universal signal that it's safe. We advanced, me having kittens. We were moving slowly, ten paces a minute. He stopped. I stopped

'I'm going in, Lovejoy,' he whispered, drinker's breath into my earhole.

'Here, Gesso. I need to come in too.'

'Shhhh, you burk.'

I heard a faint muffled clink, as metal wrapped in rag makes on stone. Two scrapes, then down over me gushed warmish air, not the hot pool's acridity but indoor air, faintly scented with incense. Gesso guided my hand down to his bag of tools, telling me silently not to fall over the damned thing.

Then he was gone. I felt him ascend somehow, with an almost imperceptible grunt of effort. His boot brushed against my shoulder. I felt all around, ahead, to the side, but I was on my tod. He'd climbed in.

For old time's sake, I started counting slowly, like you measure the distance of thunder after lightning. I reached a hundred, then wondered if I'd missed any out, which usually happens to me about sixty. My old Gran used to say my head was full of jolly robins. I tried a second time but gave up. What's the point?

A pencil torch blinded me for a second, from on high. I almost leapt out of my skin. The dark rushed back, pitch black.

'Shhh, Lovejoy.'

'I am, you pillock.' I leant against the wall until my heart stopped hammering.

A hand descended, felt my shoulder. I grabbed it, hauled myself up, found the edge of the sill and clambered in. He hissed at me to stay still. I crouched down, felt gingerly about. Parquet flooring, that scent of polish. No carpet. I'd once almost got caught by falling over a coal scuttle in a house in the Midlands.

Curtains did their muted screech along rails. Then, impossibly, Gesso's pencil torch light came on. There he was, falling about laughing.

'Your face, Lovejoy!'

'Nark it, Gesso.' He shone it round the hallway. I could see the upward curve of bannisters. 'Is it all right to talk like this?' But I was mee-mawing like I'd seen mill workers do when a child, lip reading across crowded streets.

'Yes.' He whispered that the nuns were in the far wing. 'Where do we look, Lovejoy? And for what?'

'How the hell do I know?' I wasn't scared, not in the least. And I reckoned I could scarper faster than the monks, if push came to shove. But being in somebody else's house puts the wind up me. Even when arriving somewhere I've been invited, I hum and ha before ringing the bell. 'Look, Gesso. You said a painting.'

'I didn't hear where they'd locked the bloody thing away, did I? I'm depending on you to feel the antiques, like you did when we was partners. You're the divvy, not me.' He capped his torch with a hand, letting only the thinnest glim from between red-glow fingers. 'Honestly, Lovejoy. You're all ideas and no frigging do. You make me effing sick.'

'Where's his study?' I was a bit disoriented. 'It'll be there, won't it?'

'How the hell would I know?'

Gesso's refrain. Tiptoeing to the prior's study, I began to remember how unreliable Gesso actually was, with his perennial urge to brag to the lads at the pub. He was always keen to show his thefts, explain to anybody how he'd actually popped the bottom lock on a mortised french window.

We creaked open the prior's study door. It would have to be here, right? I mean, if he'd discovered a da Vinci in some theological seminary, surely to God he'd keep it under his own eagle eye?

But he wasn't your average mundane prior. How many do you see selling plants at your weekend boot fair? And how many religious leaders send for a criminal like me to help out with antiques, legit or otherwise? None.

'Gesso?' I hissed, a brainwave. 'Is there a chapel?'

That's what a priory is for, after all.

'Yes. This way.'

He still shone his torch through his fingers. I saw that his tactics had changed. He used to have a thin plastic glove painted blue, because blue light is hardly visible in the dark. His confidence had grown. We went down a lengthy corridor past a refectory, and Gesso opened a door, miming for absolute silence.

'Sometimes one prays all night,' he whispered in my ear.

Great, I thought bitterly. An audience. Just what I needed.

The door, mercifully, was oiled. Not a squeak. A small chapel of a dozen pews, a central aisle. A pulpit, altar dressed in feria green, a red oil lamp giving an amazing amount of light, a central crucifix. That scent of polish, Stations of the Cross round the walls. A statue or two, heroic or mournful according. Too garish for me, but whatever turns God on.

No nuns, no monks at nocturnal penance. Too holy, no doubt.

Gesso silently closed the door. Above was a gallery,

presumably the organ loft. Flowers with that rather rankish perfume they get in the candle hours, gleaming brass vases.

'It's OK, Lovejoy.' Gesso spoke almost in an unwhisper, frightening me out of my skin. 'This is soundproof. I've knocked a nail in here a few times.'

'Wait.' I listened inside myself, rummaging about my senses. Not a blip. There was no antique here. But Prior Metivier was no normal prior, and this had to be the place. 'Can I look round?'

'Don't be too long.'

Why not, if it was as safe as Gesso said? I walked, silent, down the aisle, round to the sides. A plaque, IN MEMORIAM for some brother long gone. A list of nuns who'd died overseas in the missions. A brass rectangle commemorating four monks who'd died 'in service', dates twenty years since. It was all so transient. Were they in fact remembered, prayed for? I felt so down. This is what life amounts to, a pious memento read by a night-stealing stranger.

'What's that noise?' I whispered in a sudden panic.

'What?' Gesso whispered back, dowsing his torch.

'Thought I heard a motor car.'

He chuckled. 'You always were scared, Lovejoy. That's why you'll never be any good.' That from Jack the Pad, expert cat burglar.

'If you say so.' I walked along the south wall.

This painting was on the wall beside the plaque. I don't suppose I'd have paid it any attention whatsoever if I hadn't been struggling to pick out the lettering on the reflecting brass.

It was about three feet by two, badly framed in dark greenish bulbous wood. I thought, What on earth is that a painting *OF*? It seemed to be squirts of colour put on in strips and blobs, so thickly that the surface looked – and felt – corrupted. I reached up and tilted it to one side, trying to catch the reddish oil lamp's shine. Gesso's torchlight cut into my brain and almost made me yelp. No signature. Was it a child's daubed landscape, of houses among fields? Dull as ditchwater. Except it wasn't. The painting was eccentric, but you had to look at it. I knelt, my trick to get an oblique slant on any painting I see for the first time. Had I forged anything like this? Yes, definitely. It wasn't Van Gogh, but certainly one of his followers. Could it be O'Conor? I crouched lower, peering up, always the best way to see the brushwork on any—

And I heard '*Who's there?*' in a loud stern feminine voice. Marie?

I almost bleated in fright, but heard her advance, high heels striking the marble flooring, and hunched down. The chapel's electric light came on. I was blinded. Like a fool I almost stood up and said sorry, but cowardice came to my rescue.

'Sorry, Miss Metivier,' said Gesso's nervous voice. The echoes took time dying away. I felt a perverse glee, that he was caught, not me.

'What's going on?' Marie said sharply.

Her footsteps stopped. I was still below eye level. I kept silent, my heart banging away so hard I was sure she must hear.

'I forgot my torch, miss. And my feeler gauges. I need them for a car job.'

He was trusting to her ignorance.

'How come you left them here?' She didn't believe him. Who would? I seethed. Even I could have invented a better tale.

'The prior'd complained that one of the pulpit's risers was loose.'

'Very well.' She paused, probably doing that woman's circular look. She hadn't come far enough in to see me. 'Collect your things and leave.'

'Thank you, miss.'

'One thing,' she asked. 'How did you get in?'

'The side door was ajar, miss.'

Feeble, I screamed silently. I heard her say something as she left with him, but couldn't quite catch the words in that small echoey place.

Click went the light, leaving me dark-blind, and thunk went the door. I was alone. Or was I? The trick is to stay motionless. When you're burgling a place, and you think they'll come back for another quick gander, then you must clear out before they do. These are the golden rules the lads tell you in the auction rooms and junk shops – after they've got away scot-free. But what rules work when you're trapped? I'd be sure to choose the wrong one.

I heard a distant door go. Marie, letting Gesso out?

My vision slowly returned. I wondered about the vestry. Priests never come in from the front, do they? They emerge dolled up and ready to go from the vestry. I eeled, keeping to the wall. A door led off to the right. I tried it. It opened! I entered, felt ahead, found myself in a confessional, a kneeler and a hatch to pour forth my sins. No exit. Well, I'd no sins. I got claustrophobic and crept out, made the only other door by the red oil lamp's sheen.

Ahead, I could see a faint grey-stencilled arched area, face height. A window. I almost knocked off a brass candlestick in my eagerness, but caught it in time. It was a narrow window, hardly room for me to escape.

Door? I felt round the walls, came upon a door with an old Suffolk latch and a heavy lock, the key still in. We'd had one almost exactly the same at home. I put my weight on it, and almost floored myself when it turned with astonishing ease. There was the outer courtyard. Freedom!

Except there was that painting. I stood there like a prune.

Now, Prior Metivier had definitely asked me to come and look at an antique – all right, stretch a point, a near antique, though Customs & Excise define antiques as fifty years or older. I'd come, at vast expense and trouble, hadn't I? O'Conor lived a century ago, and that isn't quite old enough to set my antiques bell clonking. But O'Conor's in the Tate Gallery. Multo gelt hung uselessly on the chapel wall.

Here I was in the gloaming, within yards of riches. I had a choice. I could either scarper to safety or I could go back for the painting. But I might get caught, and they'd not believe that I was only doing my job.

Could I *take* the painting?

Who'd know it was me? Answer: nobody, except Gesso. He'd never tell. Let's face it, I'm not a thief. No, honest. And I'd not be stealing as such. Good heavens, I'd never do that. I'm more truthful and reliable than anyone I know. I mean, hadn't I given up my entire night just to take a look at a painting I'd been *invited* to examine?

After a quick listen, I left the door slightly ajar, glided back and hefted the painting down. I was careful, because they're tender things. Quietly, I left via the vestry door, keeping to the wall until I was close to the hedge, then walked slowly – that's the trick in the dark – until I blundered through the hawthorns, heading for where I imagined Gesso had left his motor.

It was gone. The selfish swine had done a flit, leaving me. That's friends for you, I thought bitterly. I checked the direction of maximum skyglow, and struggled through the undergrowth until I came on a feeder path of an apple orchard. It gave me the way to Aldeburgh, from where I knew the way home.

Five hours later I tottered into my cottage. No sign of Gesso. The night was a success, one way or another. I lit my candle and stared at the painting.

'Roderic O'Conor, as ever was.' I actually said the name aloud, marvelling at what I'd nicked – I mean borrowed, for research purposes.

Now, the 'squirt-and-flirt' school of painters, exemplified by Vincent Van Gogh, were laughed off from mid-Victorian days until the 1930s. Derided, ignored by all except close friends or perceptive shrewdies. This is where greed comes in, because there were scores, hundreds, of starving new-style artists.

As the twentieth century rolled in and on, collectors, museums, galleries all infarcted in horror at their ghastly oversight. They'd passed up valuable works of art that they could have got for a groat! The great scramble began. Gaugin, Van Gogh, Mondrian, all the now-famous names were hunted. Greed spread. Fortunes were made as folk bashed and cashed in. A glimmer of realization, maybe even understanding too, God help us, shone on lesser artists like Gilman and Roderic O'Conor. This latter bloke is typical. He was 1860 to 1940, give or take, and hung out with Gaugin's followers at Pont-Aven. Never super-famous, or ever likely to be, he's still notable. And very, very collectable.

Which raised the question of what should happen to works of art like this. I stared at the picture until the candle guttered and left me only the glow of its dying red wick. Some days you can't depend on anything. I carried the painting out to the workshop and set to.

11

NEXT MORNING I was wakened by a pounding on my door. Normally it's only bailiffs. I clad my waist in a towel. It was Prince, in high dudgeon.

'Lovejoy!' He used to have a waxed moustache, to twiddle in outrage, but now he's gone native and does without. 'You trick me!'

'How?' I had, but in which way specifically?

He stood quivering. Pistols for two, coffee for one.

'My furniture is unready!'

'Well, yes, Prince.' Florida can wrap herself in a towel and it'll stay put all day long. It's because women have waists. We men are cylindrical, so I had to clutch my towel. 'There's a good reason. The gloss on furniture—'

'You flannel me!' He marched off. 'Come this instant!'

Blinking, I followed into the drizzle, donning my hat, a tweed business with a feather. I nicked it from the Treble Tile hatstand one rainy eve. Three little children were in the lane. One shouted.

'Lovejoy!' He's a little brute called Roy, famous for stealing tortoises. He has six so far. 'Your mam'll tan you for not having anything on!'

Little Charlotte called, 'You'll catch cold, Lovejoy. Get dressed.' Females are born with the right to tell you off.

'Right, love. In a sec.'

She said to an overcoated man, 'His new auntie'll be here soon.'

'Will she?' Summer asked her politely. 'So early?'

'Yes,' said little Charlotte Blabbermouth. Five years old, she knows everything which she tells everybody so they'll know everything too. 'She sleeps on top of Lovejoy, but you've not to tell or she'll be cross.'

'Will she?' Summer didn't know whether to be intrigued or amused. He glanced my way. 'Why?'

'Because she's secret.' Charlotte was really motoring, a harbinger of doom and loving every syllable. 'She laughs in bed at night. I hear her.'

'Charlotte,' I called, not wanting Summer to hear of Florida's bedroom vocals. 'The bus'll come soon, love. Don't be late.'

Some hopes. Charlotte was determined to have the last word. 'Mummy says you have too many aunties, Lovejoy.'

'Right, love,' I said weakly. 'Tell your mummy OK.' Charlotte puts these strong views in her free-writing compositions at school.

'Here!' Prince shook the workshop door. 'Witness all!'

Summer followed us. I hate wet feet almost as much as I hate a wet head. I stepped on to the wood shavings. They hurt like hell.

'See!' Prince brandished his cane. 'Unreadiness!'

'I can explain,' I said wearily, but I couldn't think up a single excuse. I'm useless in the morning until I've had my stand-up bath and a shave and breakfast.

'How?' Prince howled. He marched to the painting on the easel, sending my heart into my throat. I'd killed myself working at it. I'd only been abed an hour before the wretch had arrived ranting. 'Doing superfluousness!'

Summer strolled in, shavings crunching. 'What is it, Lovejoy?'

Prince yelled, 'I tell what iss, commissar! Iss Lovejoy daubs!'

'It's a copy of a copy,' I said, stung. 'Better than the original.'

Summer tried to scratch it, the disbelieving swine. I stared truculently at him, but praying inwardly that he wouldn't have the wit to sniff the canvas. Phenol and formaldehyde will 'dry' new paint pretty quickly. I'd gone like a mad thing, covering the O'Conor with a new thin canvas (please protect the surface with gelatin if you try this) then over-painting its surface. My new painting was a Klee, white and a stringy stylized bird. Klee did hundreds of the damned things. So did everybody else.

Summer looked intently at the frame. I'd deliberately carried thick pigment over. It was rock hard, thank God.

'Damage that,' I complained, 'even police slush funds couldn't buy me off.'

He gave a sleet-filled smile at Prince. 'Lovejoy's joking, sir. One of our famous East Anglian wags. Imagine how amusing I find him.'

Prince boomed, stamping with rage. 'He demeans me!'

Prince finds words like 'is' and 'daub' difficult, so how come he's perfect with demean?

'Has he defrauded you, sir?' Summer was trying to rile me.

'Certainly not, Tony.' Florida arrived like a goddess, radiant and alluring. 'Lovejoy never defrauds. He simply . . . errs.'

'He defraud!' Prince swished his cane. I backed away.

With no clothes on, you feel vulnerable. 'That heap not finished!'

He indicated bits of the Nicholas Brown bookcase-desk that lay about in various states of undress. I knew how it felt.

'Lovejoy,' Florida said. 'Why are you practically naked, wet and wearing a stolen hat?'

'Hat and wetness, from rain. Nakedness, from intruders.'

'That's sufficient. Inside, Lovejoy. I shall deal with these two.'

'I didn't know you knew Mr Summer,' I said to her as I passed. She didn't bat an eyelid. I said to Summer, 'I didn't know you knew Florida.'

'Mr Champion and I were young constables together,' he said.

Florida eyed me to judge the effect. Summer smiled. I don't like it when the Plod smile. They've every reason to, being above the law, but I wish they wouldn't.

'Police?' I croaked. Florida's husband an ex-Ploddite?

'He's above all that now, Lovejoy.' Summer wandered about the workshop, studied the bowl of water by the easel. 'Isn't he, Florida? Owns his own security firm. Locks, alarms, vehicles, men.'

I said nothing. I didn't want Summer poking around too much, though the O'Conor canvas was concealed under my hasty Klee.

'Lovejoy. Why is your palette under water?'

'Oil paints are expensive. Oil and water don't mix. Immerse your palette, then take it out days later, blot dry, and you can start painting straight away, see?'

'Clever.' He weighed out another smile. 'Not like acrylic paints, then?'

'No. They'd dissolve like watercolours. You store acrylics on kitchen cooking paper in an airtight sandwich box.'

What the swine meant was, could I have done the whole painting in the night that fast with acrylic paints instead of oils. And what I meant was, whenever I'd painted the fake Klee, I'd used slow-drying oil paints. I hammered it home.

'If I'd had to fake a painting fast, I'd have used egg tempera. Except I've no money to buy fresh eggs,' I added pointedly for Florida's sake.

'But you can't remove that. Am I right?'

'Hire me for a lesson. I'm going in. Thank you all for coming.'

'Allow me to present myself, madame,' Prince was saying as I left them to it. 'I am His Royal Highness . . .' et regal cetera.

So Florida knew Summer. What with Barko and now Florida's bloke leaving police employment the Plod would be pretty shorthanded. I dried myself on an old shirt, and rolled into bed. I would have slept, but Summer walked in.

'Lovejoy? Were you marauding during the night?'

'No,' I said, muffled. 'Sod off.'

He flicked the bedclothes off me. I grabbed, hauled them up.

'Not Albansham Priory? Stealing paintings?'

'If you can find it, we'll split the proceeds, OK?' I glowered up from my pillow, one-eyed.

'It?' he asked smoothly. 'I said paintingzzz. Plural. You said paintinggg.'

Wearily I sat up. 'How the hell can I know what you're on about if you don't tell me? I worked until all hours. Ask the milkman. Ask Jill the postie.' I'd made sure of it, calling out to each at six-thirty.

'I believe that bit, Lovejoy.' And as I sank thankfully back into my pit, 'Gesso's your pal, right?'

'I used to know him. Why?'

'You've not the skill to burgle Albansham Priory alone, Lovejoy. I have reason to believe Gesso visited there last night. Someone stole a work of art.'

'Get after them, then. And good luck.'

'There you go again, Lovejoy,' he said. 'I implied *one* burglar. You said *them*. Why?'

'Because I'm half asleep,' I said nastily, and flopped down. Dozing, I heard him and Florida talking, mutter mutter. Prince had stopped creating. At least, I heard no more screams. After what seemed hours, I felt Florida slide in beside me. And that, said Alice, was that.

From the Antiques Arcade I phoned Albansham Priory.

'I am sorry,' some nun said. 'But the prior is supervising the closure.'

'Whose closure? What closure?' I bleated.

'Our Order goes into retreat in two days.'

Retreat is contemplation and silent prayer. I knew this, from a misspent childhood. To a priory, it's a time of holiness and uselessness all round.

'Does that mean he goes away?'

'Our Order disperses to different convents and monasteries. Prior Metivier has his own private devotions.' She paused. 'It is not a holiday, sir.'

'No, no. I can see that doing . . .' That doing sod all was praiseworthy? I ended weakly, 'Look, er, nun. The prior asked me to ring Miss Metivier.'

'I'm afraid she is busy with the constables. We suffered an intruder.'

Condolences. I rang off, and stepped two paces to my right to cadge some tea and toasted tea cakes from Jutta, who runs the Antiques Arcade café. The caff's only an electric kettle and a wonky toaster that chars your bread down one side. It's bring-your-own-mug and pay a penny a slice. There's nowhere to sit. Jutta knows what love is.

'Phoning Albansham Priory, Lovejoy?'

Thank heavens she'd heard. I'd bawled myself hoarse, making sure.

Jutta's a bonny lass who, like many, wastes her life lingering in unrequited love. She's fortyish, plumping up like they do at that age. She has fetching dimples you could bath in and merry eyes that always look young. Her hair is so long she has to sweep it out of the way to sit down. It flies about even when there's no wind and covers you in bed. When she rolls on you you're like inside a canopy. I like Jutta.

For twenty years Jutta has achieved two astounding failures. One is antiques: she loves jewellery, but can't tell jade from jam. The other is as tragic. She's in love with Reverend Dougal MacTavish, an unyielding vicar hooked on bringing the world to total misery and despond. He tried to get the street carnival banned. This year he's trying to ban Guy Fawkes Night bonfires, with their wassailing and joviality. He belongs to some stern north British sect that preaches gloom. He's on a loser, yet there are people who finance his campaign. Jutta, poor lass, has cried the night away in my cottage, begging me to show her how to seduce Reverend Dougal from righteousness into the path of merriment. God knows I've tried, but Jutta always fails, reporting that her Dougal is still hard at it damning everybody to hellfire for being happy. She keeps house for him. See the problem? But she was going to be useful.

'It's religion, Jutta.' I perched on her one stool.

In the Arcade, dealers pay rent for a cubbyhole to display their wares. Some have nothing more than a short plank on an orange box. Jutta has a small glass display case I made up for her after a particularly long night of seduction training. Today there were few dealers in. Mantra was tapping out hammered silver coins of Charles II period from home-made dies on his little anvil – he's always indignant that nobody buys his Rare Genuine English Hammered Antique Silver Coins, when everybody can see him making the wretched things. Fonks was there with his lone piece. He's like John the Baptist, sandals and beard, and does everybody's electric lights. He sells only one antique at a time, usually some cutlery or knife box, illuminating it on a stand. Nobody knows how he makes a living. He never seems to eat, just sits there, but he does like a chat.

'Religion?' Jutta passed me her tea. It tasted really neffie.

'Yes.' I heaved a spiritual sigh. 'Deep talk, with Prior George.'

'*You're* not getting holy, Lovejoy?' She was all trepidation.

'Not really.' I smiled, sort of sad. 'What about that priory, love?'

'Albansham?' Mechanically she passed me her toast. Thank heavens one woman hadn't forgotten her manners. 'Well, it's not the same as Reverend Dougal's, of course.'

Chalk and cheese. Mouth stuffed, I put some slices in the toaster.

'It has fallen on hard times.' She eyed me, working out if my soul was in spiritual moil. 'I'm making no religious judgement, Lovejoy.'

'Course.' I frowned. 'That would be morally wrong.'

'He's said to be a gambler.' She whispered it, leaning

forward confidentially. 'Racing. Cards. Those lottery things, you know? Everything the Good Book condemns. Rightly,' she added, standing by her man.

'Mmmh.' I didn't know whether to agree or not, so I did. 'Can't Prior Metivier see that gambling is sinful?'

'They say he spends priory funds.'

'No!' I was deeply – nay, religiously – shocked. The toaster growled. I went to butter the charred slices. No marmalade, frigging typical.

'Yes, Lovejoy.' She swished her lovely mane, to confirm the horror of her story. 'His sister – she's worldly – was sent for.'

'Oh, dear!' I managed to say, mouth full. 'Is she a nun, then?'

'No.' Jutta couldn't resist getting in a dig at another woman. 'She's very plain. Works for some business firm, at home.'

The Channel Islands, perhaps? 'How very sad it all is, Jutta, dear.'

You have to talk all Jane Austen when winkling news out of Jutta, otherwise she doesn't hear a word you say.

'Indeed, Lovejoy! Reverend Dougal heard that the prior expects a windfall.' Her mouth set in disapproval. 'Satan funds his own.'

Straight from the horse's mouth, I almost said, but caught myself in time.

'How marvellous!' I cried, spiritually. 'What sort?'

'The prior has had some antiques bequeathed to him.' She glanced about, even more secret. 'They will bring a fortune to the priory, but . . .'

She looked about, straightened up. 'Would you like some more toast, Lovejoy? We can talk about your spiritual plight at the manse this evening, with Reverend Dougal.' She went prim. 'Please do not mention anything, well, physical that might once have occurred between us.'

Me waiting for the silly cow's cliffhanger and she invites me to a wake?

'But what?' I almost shouted, stooped to whisper. 'They'll bring a fortune to the priory but what?'

'But,' she said quietly, 'Prior George might gamble the proceeds.'

'What antiques, love? Do we know?'

Jutta said sternly, morals to the fore, 'If we did know, it would not be proper to discuss them.'

'Course not!' I said, offended at the very thought. I had one serious question to ask. It was about Gesso, and was worrying me. I looked about hopefully. 'Dwoorlink, is there anything I can scan for you?'

Her eyes lit up. 'Yes, Lovejoy. That mahogany tea table. I've had the wood dated. It's genuine eighteenth century.'

The small round-top table did feel genuine. Mahogany, yes. Three-legged base, sure. Beautifully carved rim, with carefully carved knees to each leg, all matching, with feet cut as paws. Any dealer would leap at it. Not me.

'Love, no.' I said it low and sad. 'I'd not buy it at a giveaway price. You didn't look at the carving, did you?'

'It all matches, Lovejoy!' She was indignant, scared. Must have paid a fortune for it.

'Aye, love. But never trust appearances without kneeling down. Look at it sideways. *None of its lovely carving stands proud.* The carving should rise above the profile. It doesn't.'

Frantically she rummaged in her handbag. 'But I've the lab results. The mahogany's—'

'Genuine eighteenth century, love. But your tea table was made plain. Some loon did the carving hoping to up its value. They ruined it.'

She protested, wept, groaned. Then she pulled herself together, dried her eyes. She left the table's label uncorrected, though. She might be a minister's holy housekeeper, but she's not daft.

'Dwoorlink, can we keep in touch?' I asked piously. 'We ought not to consider buying any wrong antiques from, say, Albansham Priory. It might only prompt Prior George to be even more profligate than hitherto.'

Her eyes went misty. 'Lovejoy, sometimes you can be so sweet. Shunning profitable antiques to help a fellow human being!'

Hastily I looked sweet. What Jutta said was true, because I am really like that. After all, wasn't I trying to help her to collar Reverend Dougal by teaching her how to make love? I'd tried, I'd tried.

The bread had run out. I'd drunk her tea. Time to go. I bussed her a so-long, then paused. Here came my question.

'Oh, love. Seen Gesso?'

'Haven't you heard? Gesso's gone missing. The police are looking.'

'But it's not been long enough for Gesso to . . .' I halted, stricken, implicated by my words.

'What's not been long enough, Lovejoy?' Jutta asked. Her eyes widened as she realized. 'Lovejoy? *You* didn't see Gesso recently?'

'Me? No!' I gave a disarming chuckle, but it didn't work. 'I met him recently at the priory. He showed me round.'

'Oh. I see.' She called, 'Here, Lovejoy. Did you eat all that bread?'

Some remarks can be ignored. Hospitality's not stealing. It's a gift. And sharing is holy. Stingy cow and her measly rotten bread. So Gesso had cleared off, had he? I didn't blame him. At least I knew now what was going on, more or less. All I had to do to get back to normal was to find Irma, and teach her better this time.

Except there was a bad discovery waiting at the cottage. My Roderic O'Conor painting that I'd laboured all night to disguise was gone. I thought, Gesso. See what I meant about help? Help plunders your very dreams. This is the antiques game all over. My motto? Rub out and start again.

12

THE NEWS SPREAD, in taverns, betting shops, doctors' waiting rooms, nosh bars. I heard it from Tomtit, who ran after me by the war memorial.

'Lovejoy!' he howled. 'The scrap! It's on Horseheath! In an hour!'

Two passing blokes throttled him into silence, peering anxiously round to make sure no peeler was in earshot. East Anglians have the tact of a grenade. I ignored Tomtit, but it made me change my plans. I went to a phone box, dialled the lovely Mrs Crucifex at Saumarez, got Martin her husband.

'Ah, er, Lovejoy here. Can I speak with Mrs Crucifex, please?'

'No.' And get ye hence, varlet.

'I have three Rockingham pieces. Unless I get a better offer—'

'Rockingham? Wait.' He said it in the nick of time. I'd have only allowed him another hour to snap the bait. She came on the line, her voice taunting.

'What Rockinghams?'

'Unmarked and early.'

'That old myth?' she sneered. I'd love to learn how to sneer, but you have to be rich.

'Now, missus. I'm a divvy so I can tell. One thing, though. Your Irma has to be there when I show them to you, or no deal.'

'Irma?' She spat the name. Detestation, revulsion, all in there. I sighed. Women unsheathing claws at each other wear me out.

'Tell her to contact me. Cheers.' I cut her off.

Work done, so to Horseheath, to see a bare-fisted prize-fight straight out of the eighteenth century. It's not only porcelain and furniture that are antiques in the Eastern Hundreds. We have barbarity as well.

Tomtit gave me a lift in his cousin's estate wagon. We drove to the heath practically asphyxiated – it recycles fumes through the cabin. When the vehicle can't go above twenty, you need the doors open to funnel oxygen through. He grumbled all the way.

'You rotten useless bastard, Lovejoy,' he kept saying. He wears an old uniform, a begging tactic, and plays dirges on a mouth organ in the market. Another dedicated gambler.

'I keep telling you, Tom,' I repeated.

'You're a divvy, you burk! So you *know* what's frigging what.'

'Being a divvy only works for antiques, Tom, not for boxing.'

'Why not?' He eyed me with suspicion. I wish he wouldn't. I'm always scared he'll drive into a ditch. 'You're always on about how the antiques speak to you, the crafts-man's frigging soul still in there—'

'Antiques, Tom,' I kept saying wearily. 'Dead craftsmen.'

'Boxing's people, Lovejoy. We'd make a killing! Tell me who's going to win. Split fifty-fifty, OK? Look,' he pleaded, brushing the hedgerows as he went, 'close your eyes. Maybe the winner'll come to you. What happens when you look at an antique? I saw them mesmerize somebody on a stage once. We could borrow a watch—'

Round and round Tomtit wheedled. Folk just don't understand. For peace, I said I'd try, and nodded off with him saying, 'Find the winner! Find the winner! Find . . .' in what he imagined was a hypnotist's voice, silly prat.

He's a man famed for misjudgements. He's called Tomtit because he reported some rare bird on the coastal marshes. He told the newspapers he'd seen a white-polled bufflehead, whatever that is. The nation's twitchers caused traffic jams that paralysed three counties. During the kingdom's fren- zied hunt to photograph this exotic feathered friend, Tomtit made a fortune selling T-shirts, colour-printed with a buf- flehead's picture, to the long queues of motorists stuck in the lanes. The bird turned out to be a tomtit. His wife's as daft as he is.

With relief, I roused at the roar of the crowd, and leapt out on to the greensward calling a quick ta over my shoulder.

The fight was already well on. Two thousand spectators, at a guess, craned to see two bruisers brawling. I eeled in. A Cambridgeshire bloke told me it was the third round, but after that the news became garbled as a dozen others told me different. I already knew the match was between two contenders for East Anglia's bare-fisted championship.

Rules haven't changed since the Middle Ages. Seconds mark out a ring with ropes and four poles, but it's arbitrary. Prize money is provided by the pugilists' backers. They're often bookies themselves, their lads taking bets all round.

It's been illegal for donkey's years – like the cockfighting that goes on at Grand National Day and Derby Day, and like the hare coursing I've already said about.

As I watched, one fighter knocked his opponent down. A bell clonked and a hubbub arose. A round isn't timed like in legal boxing. It comes to an end when one bloke fells the other. Somebody counts a minute, after which both fighters must 'toe the line' – hence the saying – that marks the ring's middle. That's all there is to it. If you fail to 'come up to scratch' you lose. Bets are paid off and arguments begin about how the fight was unfair/fair/rigged/not rigged, et tiresome cetera.

Bare-knuckle scrappers are mostly from travelling families, gypsies. Each tribe has a champion. There's a very definite pecking order, so you've to be really polite. I mean to say, don't greet some lowly contender with a cheery hello until you've grovelled a greeting to the champ, or you're for it.

'What's the odds?' I asked, but the next round started and the answers were lost in uproar as the fighters came out. I wouldn't have known who to back even if I'd had any money.

Occasionally shouting encouragement in case anybody thought I was a bobby sneaking by, I wandered. I'd gone round three sides of the square before I saw him. There he was, in a long brownish raglan, deerstalker hat, green wellies. For all the world Prior Metivier looked a countryman.

That round took about eight minutes. During it, he made two bets. One was with a sour-faced bloke that I didn't recognize but guessed was a bookmaker, one of a string. The other was to somebody I couldn't see but standing facing, across the other side of the ring. Metivier did it with great slickness, a couple of gestures, eleven to eight on, from his tictackery. Three *thousand* zlotniks, though? I don't know all the signs, but regular punters can translate bookies' signals faster than they can read. This prizefight seemed home turf to the high-rolling Prior George Metivier.

A fish out of water, I went to the pie stalls and beer tents. There's always a following mob. I stayed there, thirsty and hungry from unco-operative servers, until the roars reached a crescendo about an hour later and pandemonium told me the fight was over. I flagged Tomtit, asking him to wait until the crowd had drifted and all bets were settled. I promised him a scheme for betting on antiques by the following Thursday. Surly, he agreed and went to drink himself stupid in the ale marquee while I mingled self-effacingly.

The bookie was easy to find. I hung about the outskirts of the throng surrounding his pitch. At these illegal matches bookies don't have stands, wooden shingles and gonfalons like their on-course pals. They're just there, handfuls of dockets in their fists with maybe a half-dozen touts. By the time the punters had evaporated I'd seen Prior George leave, head down, and I grabbed the bookie's head tout.

'Here, wack.' I did my northern accent. 'Yon clergy won, eh?'

The tout was enormous. I've never known one who doesn't swell when you speak. He eyed me with suspicion.

'What's it to you?'

'Only, he owes my gaffer, see? If he's well up, my boss'd be real pleased'.

'Don't hold your breath, booy,' the tout said. He spat, hitting a dandelion head at seven paces. I really envy skill. 'He's a born loser. Beats me what the fuck they do it for.

Loses every time. Hare coursing last week. Cock mains last month. Who's your gaffer, then?'

'Ted Hoawson from Harrogate,' I invented, pretending gloom. 'Ta, pal.'

The crowd had dispersed when I approached the fighters' caravans. They were set apart on the heath in a small encampment. One scrapper was sitting swilling ale at a campfire among a dozen cronies. It was all very raggletaggle gypsies oh, with little children playing and dogs on the roam. Two women standing by to serve his ale eyed me belligerently.

'Congrats, Charley,' I said, standing off a pace or two.

'Who might you be, then?' the champion said.

'Punter, that's all.' I knew better than to sit down uninvited. I heard one of Charley's men mutter something. His mates stared me down. 'Er, I met your brother two years ago, in Suffolk.'

He beckoned. A woman came for his glass and strolled off for a refill. Why didn't she just bring the ale bucket? It was by the caravan door.

Charley had bruises across his forehead, like they'd been laid in place. His knuckles were raw, bleeding away, his cheeks savagely cut.

'Our Dicker tellt me of some *jinney-mengro* he once sellt to.'

Jinney-mengro: their talk for a wise man. It can also mean know-all.

His brother Dicker had robbed a St Edmundsbury bloke I didn't like – still don't, come to that. Dicker had no idea. He'd nicked nine fairings, those cheap garish pottery figures they give you on fairgrounds. He'd also thieved a candlestick. God knows why, but there's not a travelling man born who can resist a candlestick. This had been a creamy

earthenware, shaped like it wished it was Georgian silver –
these clues scream early Wedgwood. I loved it, hadn't the
heart to do Dicker down because he'd once given me a
bicycle tyre for nothing. I'd bought the fairings for a few
quid (those were the days; I was loaded) but tipped him off
where to sell the Wedgwood candlestick for a mint.

I was pleased at Charley's compliment. Being called a
wise man was better than a clip round the ear, especially
when he'd kindly used his own speech.

'Nice bloke, him,' I said, 'that Dicker.'

'The *gorgio* gave him back a genuine old thing. He could
have kept it, but was honest.' He took the replenished mug
from the woman without saying ta. Well, if I was his size
and king rabbit, maybe I'd be offhand. 'I forget his name.'

'I'm Lovejoy.' Was more proof needed? 'Your brother
plays what he calls a *bashadi*. Looked like an ordinary fiddle
to me. He ever get the tune right?' We'd argued about
how to sing 'She Walks Through the Fair'. I'd been right,
of course, but gypsies are stubborn.

Charley grinned, jerked his battered head to the grass. I
sat, relieved.

'Are you really a *chohawno*, a wizard?'

'Me? Nar, Charley. I just listen. Antiques shout the
truth.'

He nodded. One of the men started to cut in, but
Charley gave him a stare and the bloke subsided. I recognized him. I'd been on remand, in clink, for ringing
auctions. He'd been in the same cell.

'We thought you were a *moskey*,' Charley said. I looked
askance. My gypsy lingo had run out. 'A spy, Lovejoy,
skulking around the churchman.'

They'd seen more than I'd wanted. Me and my clever
skullduggery.

'He's taking money from church charities to gamble with,' I said, shrugging to say it didn't matter to me either way.

'Not the first *rashengro* to steal.'

'Some priests do thieve,' I agreed. 'Have you seen him at other meets?'

'Grass races. Local matches. Football. Wherever there's a bookie or a bet.' He spat again. 'Brings a grand *gorgie*. Some churchman, eh?'

'A posh lady?' Now, I wonder who?

'*Grasni!*' his woman said under her breath. I knew that word: bitch.

Charley beckoned her closer and cuffed her. She went back, satisfied about something, God knows what.

'The woman's maybe the prior's *mort*, his shag on the side,' he said. He then described Mrs Crucifex to a T.

'He's a man without luck,' he concluded. Gypsies are big on luck. 'Gets a rich woman, is an important *rashengro*, yet still he loses.' He asked his people, doing no more than cock his head, 'What was his last plan?'

My ex-cellmate answered, still looking hard at me, 'Walnuts, Charley.'

'Eh?' I asked. Had he said walnuts?

Charley chuckled without moving his swollen lips, in case they haemorrhaged some more into his drink.

'Albansham Priory's got a bonny walnut orchard, Lovejoy. Not a selling orchard, like at Boxford, just been there from olden times. The *rashengro* decided to install a walnut press to make pure walnut oil. Walnut oil's expensive, see?'

He rolled in the aisles. His men made huff-huff noises like kiddies playing trains. After a brief ponder I recognized it. They were laughing. The women, more obvious, screamed with hilarity.

'What's wrong with walnuts, Charley?' I asked, blank. It seemed quite a good idea to me. This, note, is my native land. I hadn't a notion. They fell about at my stupidity.

'See, Lovejoy,' Charley resumed, wiping his eyes, 'my tribe've stolen from that orchard for four hundred years. Walnuts that grow here don't *make* oil. The weather, see? English walnuts peel like a dream. But no oil. He hocked the priory's silver for it. A fool. Everything he touches turns to dross.'

'People the same,' my old cellmate said. I remembered his name: Pral. 'Prior George's a bad-luck man.'

He was trying to warn me. Waiting for our respective cases to be called, Pral'd shown me card tricks using an unmarked deck. When I'd got sprung – I was going out with a woman solicitor that week – I'd begged her to take his case, and she'd somehow got him off after a bit of remand. Well, it's an ill wind.

'A bad-lucking man,' Pral said direct to me. I nodded, ta.

Saying this kind of thing is all very well, but who believes in luck? Luck's got an abysmal record, like God, like purity. Even the idea of luck worries me. I'd rather just trust people's faces, and do the best I can.

That was all the information I got. I had to drink four pints of his women's beer as the talk became general. The ale was unbelievably rough. No wonder Charley was moving up the bare-fisters' stakes if this was his staple.

When his women brought out a tin bath and started filling it with hot water to bath him, I rose, politely shook hands and left beerlogged, all his mob calling '*Rak tute*' after me, take care. The sky was nigh on dusk.

So Prior George nicked the priory's funds, gambling his

way into debt. But hadn't Jutta told me he'd just got an antiques windfall and would soon be in clover? Yet so desperate was the prior's plight that his fund-raising team of Summer and the Crucifex pair wanted to include me on their side, for a sale of antiques.

Where was Gesso?

13

'I PAID PRINCE OFF, Lovejoy.'

Florida insisted on meeting me at the grandest restaurant in town. She likes to show off. It's called Franco's, being Spanish you see. It doesn't look much, being opposite the sleaziest auction rooms our town – indeed, the world – has got. Inside it's unprepossessing, but the grub's the best. Every dish they bring is magic. Makes you wonder who'd go to all the bother, working everything out for each recipe and cooking just so. A triumph of mankind over misery.

The truly amazing thing is that the waiters love Florida. They are crazy about her. I can't see why, because in a restaurant she's nothing but trouble. For one thing, she insists on going backstage to inspect the raw food. Is anything more gruesome? For another, she argues the hind leg off a donkey. They offer single cream, she insists on double. They've got fresh tomatoes, she'll want sun-dried. Yet they love it, dash about obeying. Once, she sent some lettuce leaves back, played merry hell. So we both had to starve to death, everybody in the restaurant pretending we didn't hear the screams coming from the kitchen while they swapped frigging lettuces. I mean, who'd know? More to the point, who'd care? A lettuce isn't a space shuttle or neurosurgery. It's a frigging leaf.

Once, I asked Franco why he admired Florida so. He said, eyes dreamy, 'Ah, she beautiful! She *know* cuisine!', proving that he's as barmy as she is. Her beauty matters less to him than her expertise on aubergines.

You have to be careful, though. Florida can go berserk over even less. She asked me to marry her once. I smiled politely, thinking it some joke. She got really furious, stormed out. See what I mean? Even a simple misunderstanding can send her mental. Women are odd. Where was I?

'Ta, love.' About Prince.

'Hence, Lovejoy, you and I are now inextricably linked.'

'Hence, eh?' I was well into the grub. Franco's the only bloke in captivity who gives you enough mushrooms. Nobody else does. Ever notice that? 'What do you mean?' That's my commonest question with Florida, ever since That Time I Misunderstood Her Proposal.

She smiled, acknowledging that I was now properly trained. I wasn't happy. Subservience is nothing new to me, but what with Mr Summer, Irma, Mrs Crucifex, Prior Metivier, Prince, Gesso's disturbing absence and my own chronic penury, I'd had enough serfdom lately to be going on with.

'This forgery in which you engage, Lovejoy.'

She smokes between courses. This doesn't mean her ladyship actually had to slog it out alone, find her own handbag, rummage for a fag, struggle for a match, all the exhausting business that can wear a lady out, oh no. Florida calmly poses, forearm upright, fingers gently parted, and waits. Waiters instantly sprint up with fags of every hue and carcinogenicity. She deigns to select one. They hurtle for a match. Sometimes she wants her fag lit from a candle, a lighter, a taper. They dash to comply, and Creation is saved for the next millennium. It's a hard life.

'You make it sound grim, love. Can I have your soup?'

Carrot and something. She'd had half a spoonful. Makes me wonder why she orders it.

'I gathered from Prince, when I was purchasing the commission he gave you, that you are an expert forger?'

I eyed her warily. What was she up to? 'Forgery's legal, as long as you don't sell it as a genuine antique.'

'I visited Tony's office.' I stopped spooning her soup, in terror. Secret meetings with the Plod? 'Oh, dear! Is there too much coriander?'

I gaped. 'You stupid—' I lowered my voice to a loving whisper as heads turned across the restaurant. 'You stupid cow. I thought you meant I was in trouble with the police.'

'Prince says you can fake anything.'

'Anything can be faked,' I said. 'And I'm good.'

'Why?'

That stopped me in my tracks. I noshed on, trying to work it out. Yes why, exactly? I'm possibly the best there is. Is it because I'm the most careful? Or is it because I know how the original antiques feel, in this sordid world of money where beauty is judged only in gelt? Or because I feel how the old craftsmen felt at their wondrous labour?

'Maybe all of those, Lovejoy,' Florida said, which worried me even more. I hadn't known I was speaking aloud. Thoughts are private.

'I forge things to be the same as the original, love.'

'You just said that.' Had I? 'This Nicholas Brown bookcase-desk, Lovejoy. Millions upon millions?'

'The original went for a king's ransom in the USA, yes.'

She toyed with a spoon. Waiters sprang forth. She ignored them. They faded, in tears.

She said softly. 'Darling, I bought Prince out. You're now my partner. If?'

The main course came, some fish I'd never heard of. The spuds were really small, but there were tons, in butter. I like spinach, asparagus, and those eat-all peas – flat things; you eat them in their swads. I started, mutely apologizing. I can never quite work out what things need apologies. Burps, I can understand. But being hungry? Or wanting a woman? Or hoping she'll leave her salmon if your own meal isn't enough?

She hardly ate, but that's the way women tackle a meal, hoping it'll evaporate first. I slowed. Something was lacking. Ah, the rest of her sentence.

'If?' I prompted.

'Just "if", Lovejoy.' She smiled. 'Maybe it's an illegal if.'

'You mean . . .' She did. She meant what if I made the desk for her and she sold it as genuine.

'Could that be done, Lovejoy?'

My meal just made it. I stared at her plate, a whale going to waste over there.

'Don't you want your salmon?'

'Sewin, Lovejoy. Please help yourself.' She made some signal. Waiters zoomed her meal to me. I could have done it in half the time, but didn't want to spoil her fun, so sat with my hands politely folded. They brought more wine.

'Selling fakes is done all the time, Florida. There are obstacles.'

Her eyes closed in bliss. I'd only seen her do that in other circumstances. I watched, enthralled. Was it a hint?

'I haven't finished yet, love,' I said. 'I'll be quick.'

'Take your time, darling,' she said dreamily. 'Tell me those risks!'

'They're not pleasant,' I warned her. 'Scary, sometimes.'

'That's where you're wrong, Lovejoy,' she said.

Her hand reached under the table and stroked my thigh. I thought, What the hell am I to do now? I'd told the silly bitch I'd hurry up. Without pudding I'd not last the night. Starvation's no fun.

'Nark it, dwoorlink.'

'Eat, Lovejoy. And tell me the risks. I love *risks*.'

Whatever Florida said, people who really do take risks don't care for them. I mean, look at me. I used to be careless crossing the road. Now I gape, gander, dither before sprinting for the opposite pavement like a cartoon cat. No, risks are for TV tales. Risks, in short, are for those who never take them.

I told her lovely eyes, 'Each obstacle represents several risks.'

'Oooh,' she moaned softly. 'Do go on, darling.'

'In antiques, there are thieves. Criminals. Blaggers. Delffers. Every kind of killer you've never dreamt of. The thuggery and sheer lethality in the antiques trade make Hollywood smash-trash epics look like Keats poems.'

She whispered, 'I love it, darling. *Love* it!'

See? They're different.

'In the forgery game,' I went patiently on, 'are hundreds of thousands of rivals. They're a homicidal bunch who will stop at nothing.'

'Stop at nothing!' She crooned the words. 'Savages!'

'Then there's security folk, with their own private honchos. They're supposed to stay within the law.'

'Yet they don't?' Her eyes glittered adoration. I thought, The woman's off her frigging trolley.

'Course not. They just seem legal.'

'Anybody else, darling?' Her fingers dug into my thigh. 'Tell me there are more *brutes*!'

'Yes,' I said bitterly. 'There's a third rotten mob. The Plod.'

She came to, affronted. 'But Tony's in my husband's club. He goes to our church!'

'He's the Old Bill, love,' I said bluntly. 'So he's enemy of all he surveys. He surveys me. And, if you come in on the forgery game, you.'

She shivered deliciously. 'I like the first two groups.'

'That's the cast,' I said rudely. 'Now listen close, and I'll tell you the scene.'

In antiques, there are three options, and no more. It's a three-by-three problem.

There's selling, honest or otherwise. There's robbery, H or O. And there's forgery, H or O. That's it. The powers ranged across the board are the mobs, the guardians and the Plod.

Nothing to it. Living in the antiques trade depends on how you permutate the options and the mobs. See? Basically a three-by-three problem – but so is the maddening child's game of noughts and crosses. Which is why the antiques game has got the globe's police forces, every known artist living or dead, and every villain, government or businessman on Planet Earth in a flat spin. Now read on.

If you rob a bank, you get shot, arrested, hunted, and maybe end up penniless. But knock on any door, con some widow out of a wardrobe or a piece of jewellery, and maybe you're an instant millionaire.

Silly legends abound. Like the Raffles tale, which assumes that any art thief is learned, professorial, an expert in Titian, knows the paintings of Leonardo da Vinci, has brilliant insight into the art market. It's all balderdash. Your art thief is like Gesso: quick, slick, and doesn't know one 'smudge', as they call paintings, from another. He's just told where to go, which wall it's on, what alarms are installed, and which roadside caff to drop the 'dodge', i.e. the stolen antiques. It could be a roll of wallpaper for all he cares. Like the Longleat robbery in Wiltshire, when they nicked the Titian – what was it, eighty-eight seconds for the entire crash-smash-dash?

There's another daft assumption, that famous paintings can't be sold because 'everybody will know it's the famous stolen Goya, Turner, Constable'. Wrong. It's barmy to think that crooks won't know what to do with a famous painting/vase/Queen Anne desk/necklace just because it once was legitimately owned by somebody else. They'll sell it. Or barter it. Or hock it to some fence. Or use it as security for a loan. Or swap it for a house, yacht, even a lifelong pension paid monthly on the nail. In other words, use it just as you would if you'd been (legitimately!) left it in your great-uncle's will.

'Then there's the ALR,' I continued to Florida.

The Art Loss Register belongs to the insurance companies. Instead of working in modest sheds in poor disadvantaged Salford, the ALR has built itself expensive glamorous offices, centrally heated and air-conditioned, near Buckingham Palace – all at clients' expense. There, some 100,000 stolen antiques are on computer file, with 20,000 more cascading on every year. The insurance companies say, eyes raised heavenwards in gratitude, that they finance the ALR themselves. They don't, of course. They charge you for each antique you tell them has been stolen. Then they have the nerve to charge you a percentage if the antique is recovered with their help (so what the heck did you pay the ALR for in the first place?). They have offices in New York and Australia, for staff holidays.

Antiques trade newspapers have 'Stolen' sections, more for general gloom than anything, and some run data bases, just to make antique dealers suicidal. They give gossipers something to gossip about, nothing more.

That's about it. Oh, almost forgot. The police.

Scotland Yard's mighty Art and Antiques Squad (all four police officers), now merged with the Flying Squads, has lately become part of the new Organized Crime Group, OCG. They've not yet spotted the embarrassing ambiguity in this title. The Specialist Operations – like art and antiques – are called Focus Units and are all in one pool. Good, eh? Not really, no. For when you have so many names for so many units/groups/echelons/whatevers the soap clogs the funnel, if you follow, and nothing flows the way it should. Nowt more to say about them, except that there are fifty-five whole police forces in this creaking old kingdom of ours, and only eight have as much as even one single art/antiques bobby on their staff.

The final laugh at all this ineptitude? It's the Scotland Yard Art and Antiques Squad's very special, very secret and wondrously superb ACIS. It's a brilliant data base, been designed by deep-thinking computer criminological taxonomists for national use! Really super-great. ACIS stands for Article Classification and Identification System, would you believe?

It gives everything about stolen antiques – any fingerprints, shreds of wool from burglars' jackets, records of suspects, photographs from security cameras, all that jazz. Essential, vital, eh?

Well, not so's you'd notice. Because ACIS isn't on-line for the whole country. Police forces all over the kingdom may – if they've a mind – send information to it. Most, though, can't be bothered, being far too busy, you see. So there's this great computer weapon, built, installed, created, to be ignored by the majority of those who could, if moved to consult and use this engine, actually do something effective. Thank goodness, says I, because the Scotland Yard A & A Squad – as people still call it – isn't mainly there to investigate particular thefts.

'That's about it,' I concluded. I'd had a date pudding by then, keeping the wolf from the door. 'Except for attitude.'

'Whose?' She was in a drifty languid mood, almost as if we'd made something more passionate than talk. 'Yours?'

'No. The police's. The one thing they hate, all of them, is being made agents for the insurance companies. Documenting road accidents, making detailed records of stolen antiques, they see as being unpaid insurance clerks.' I smiled. 'They skimp it every chance they get.'

'Lovejoy,' Florida said huskily, 'you're a vicious beast of prey.'

'Eh?' I said. Some new tack?

She ground out her cigarette and rose. 'Come, darling. Home time.'

'Oh.' Not a new tack at all. A very old one.

She left without signing anything, without paying. I thought only queens did that. In her Rolls, she told me that she'd joined Lovejoy Antiques, Inc.

'What for?' Maybe we should have gone to Woody's nosh bar? She likes to go sordid.

She laughed, carolling, before she sobered. 'Lovejoy. You really understand nothing. To *rob*, of course. What else?'

In the night, Florida kipping beside me with that fragile snore all women develop about two hours after midnight, I suddenly remembered the word I'd heard one of Charley's men say as I'd said my so-long. It was Pral, my fellow ex-prisoner. They'd all said their '*Rak tute*', take care, after me. But Pral shook his head and said, '*Dinnelo.*' It means somebody touched in the head, even sinister. It's also their word for a fool.

He meant me.

14

FLORIDA LEFT ABOUT four o'clock. As I put the robin's cheese and the hedgehog's saucer out I tried to remember exactly what I'd agreed. She'd insisted it was really important. Connie, from down the lane, drops in and leaves some unspeakable meat for Crispin. I don't look at it, just leave out a clean saucer every day. Where was I? Florida, leaving.

She'd pressed her face down on mine, me hoping she'd get gone so I could kip. I felt worn out.

'It's agreed, then, darling? I'll be late tonight. Be ready.'

I hate women telling me what I've agreed. It's a kind of polarized untruth.

Alone, I bathed. Florida wrinkles her nose up at everything in the cottage. She won't eat here, won't have a bath, only goes to the loo on sufferance, then complains about draughts, how I should mend the broken window – I'd once had to climb in because of bailiffs. She has no idea. At the start of our 'relationship' – God, how I hate that word; we use it only when we've really got none – Florida upbraided me because I didn't have a single antique in the place.

She'd stunned me by saying, 'I'd have thought you'd have a Sheraton bureau, Lovejoy.' See what I mean? Florida, like all the rich, thinks profanity.

What had I agreed?

There were windfalls in the garden. I washed and sliced some apples, and fried them with bread. I'd washed my only other shirt. It was still damp and I'd no way to iron it, but put it on, shivering. If ever I get rich, I'll have dry clean clothes every morning and somebody to rub my nape when I'm tired. Is there that sort of heaven out there? I combed my hair with a fragment of green plastic comb, then set out into a bright new day. I shouldn't have. The robin ballocks me for not digging. I've got nothing against worms and told the cheeky little sod that, but he only chirped, angrier still. Omens were everywhere.

Normally I wouldn't have bothered much with Leach's Auction Emporium at Little Henny, but it was the only normal one until weekend. I felt I'd been among troglodytes and asteroids for days. You can feel out of sorts for no reason. And I'd no barker, except the useless Freddy Foxheath. And where was he?

The auction was due to begin when I stepped off the Mount Bures bus. It's three miles. Everywhere's uphill when you're in a hurry, so I was puffed out when I tottered in, Florida still making her nocturnal presence felt.

The lads were in. Big Frank from Suffolk – his home territory, this – was being modestly congratulated on his new wife. I waved, grinned, gave him the thumbs up. He changes wives every tide. I'm exaggerating, but it seems so, the rate he goes on. Big Frank has strong views on alimony. He's currently suing his seventh ex-wife for maintenance. The week before, he'd tried to get me to sign a petition saying he was destitute – he was giving me a lift in his new Lagonda at the time. Margaret Dainty was also in, with Liz

Sandwell. The former – and the latter too – is my favourite. She limps, has a husband vaguely around, but you don't ask. She is an older, wiser woman, and my friend. I'm not sure if I'm hers. I try.

And the blonde Paula, she of the glitzy earrings and miniskirts, high heels and skimpy bolero. Paula's enormously fat, so somehow her clothes – what there is – look wrong. Women give each other meaningful looks about Paula, but I like her. She really packs on the cosmetics, rouge, mascara, lipstick, so you're knee deep if you get within striking distance, and wears scent enough to make you gag. She's an expert dealer in eighteenth-century English porcelain, so she tells customers.

'Lovejoy?' Desdemona was suddenly there.

'That you, love? Where's your bloke?' I was narked at Gesso, but didn't want to tell her off. She was Gesso's ex-wife, water under the bridge now.

'Not here.'

She looked pale, led me out to the car park. It was coming bright, gusty. I like Desdemona, though her name embarrasses me. Just saying it makes me feel I've started a speech, then I feel daft because I've nothing else to say, and silence isn't much where women are concerned. She stood there, pretty, quiet. It was only then – honest truth – that I felt the first twinge of anxiety.

'Have you seen Gesso?' I said nothing, looking at her eyes. 'Only, he's not been about since you took him to rob the priory.'

So much for secrecy. 'I've not seen him either. No,' I went on as she drew breath, 'I've not put word out. The Plod are asking.'

Dangerous ground, this. I told her what happened that night. They divorced some two years since when

Desdemona gave up over Gesso's bad spell of remands and gaol sentences.

She said bravely, 'I'm frightened something went wrong.'

'It did. I told you. Gesso got—'

'Normally he phones. He crows about robberies he's just done. This is the only time he's not called.'

'The only time?' I asked, even more uneasy.

'Lovejoy.' She held my hands tight. I tried to pull away. 'You know how things are. In his way Gesso was all right. Weak, but what man isn't?'

This falsehood made me try to look strong, utterly reliable.

'I never gave him away. His calls were like a bond, the only bit left between us. You're not hiding him, are you?'

'Me?' I heard them call for the start of the auction. 'I'll find him, love. Honest.'

'You will, Lovejoy?' She scanned my face, found enough near-truth in my lies to be going on with. 'Just so he's all right. Nothing more.'

'Right, love.' I watched her go. She has a little Continental motor. What on earth was Gesso thinking of, chucking her for an inept life of robbery? Mind you, I should talk.

Back inside, Paula collared me. The crowd had swelled enormously, to at least a dozen, drifting among the trestle tables and home-made cabinets.

'Lovejoy,' she breathed. 'Come and look!'

'There's not much here, love.' No chimes in my chest. Everything was modern – for modern, read dross.

'That dancing girl, Lovejoy!' She pretended to be chatting, but deceived nobody. Her excited breathing alone gave the world clues enough.

'Fake, Paula.'

'It can't be!' she wailed. Dealers everywhere sprang out of the floorboards to hear. I was tired, wanted out. 'I've put a dog in!'

Dog is the dealer's word for a written bid delivered just before an auction. You scribble the amount you want to bid, give it to the whiffler and lurk about pretending you've not bid at all. Some dealers do it to increase the price of an antique – having themselves put the antique in for auction – but risk buying their own antique. This means that they lose serious money, commission, tax, premiums on the transaction.

There are more fakers about now than ever, but they haven't the skill, patience or the understanding. And they certainly don't have the feel for the original antique. So they use wrong glazes, clay, paints, enamels, or fire things at the wrong temperature. Modern forgers get me down. They won't experiment. Worst of all, fakers nowadays don't bother to learn. Like trying to write yet another sequel to *Pride and Prejudice* without having bothered to read the original – though that's done often enough, God knows.

'Duff it, love. Be sharp. They've called starters.'

'Yes! Yes!'

She hurtled, a formidable velocity. Margaret Dainty smiled, came near. I bussed her a hello.

'We were all wondering about that piece, Lovejoy. Thank you.'

'It's a shame.' I eyed the little figure. 'She could have been lovely.'

In London, about the 1750s, a small factory blossomed. It's known by one of its principal figures. The Girl-In-The-Swing factory only became recognized as something really special in the world of genuinely old antiques about the mid-1930s, when collectors realized their quality. One of these rare figures was of a little dancing girl, with a yellow flower in her hair. So far so good, until the Torquay Couple started faking. The man-and-wife pair lived in Devon, and swiftly upset the porcelain collectors' market by turning out fakes. Tips: the Torquay Fakers *never* got a girl's shoulders and waist right. They seem thickish, clumsy. And the poses are strangely inelegant. The really best tip, though, is this: stare for a full minute at the colours on, say, the porcelain girl's dress. They look as if they've been put on with a gluey paintbrush. If that's the impression, don't – repeat, *do not* – buy. It's fake. Let somebody else snap the little figurine up. Never mind that your friends'll boast afterwards, jeering that you've missed the bargain of the year. Let them. They'll change their tune when they try to sell it.

'How much, Lovejoy?' Margaret asked.

Sadly I looked at the pathetic little fake. 'Nowt, love. Not a groat.'

'Are you all right, Lovejoy?'

The auction was starting up. I wandered with Margaret among the tables, listless. It was all gunge and semi-gunge, old bikes, record players, old throwout plastic toys, tatty furniture. I felt really down.

'Heard anything of Gesso, Margaret?'

'No. Only that you and he . . .' She grimaced. 'They're saying you did over the priory at Albansham, the night it closed.'

'Closed?' I thought a moment. 'Went into retreat?'

'No. Closed. It's going to be amalgamated.'

'For good?'

Gesso hadn't said. But the priory had been very, very quiet that night. And Marie hadn't exactly been silent when she'd barged into the chapel. Nobody else had come running. No alarms had sounded. Because the abbey was empty, or because me and Gesso had been especially cunning?

'Yes, Lovejoy. It was in the paper.' She put a hand on my arm. 'Are you sure you're all right?'

'Best of order, please, ladies and gentlemen!' the auctioneer chanted, gavelling away. 'Item one, a beautiful ormolu clock, probably made by Vincento Ostrakis and Sons of Norwich in 1720 . . .'

This morning the whole world seemed dross. Dross attitudes, dross fakes, dross bargains, dross people. There never was any Vincento Ostrakis, 1720, clockmaker of Norwich. So even the blinking auctions begin with a non-existent non-craftsman. The fake clock was a feeble replica of a Harrison work of genius. It's our civilization. Right there and then, I could have stopped the world and got off. In that single moment everything seemed betrayed and dirty.

'Come home, Lovejoy?' Margaret suggested. 'Positively no obligation?'

It's what antique dealers say on the knocker. It was her attempt to make me smile. I tried, didn't make it.

'Not now, love, ta. Can I come later on?'

She weighed me up, sighed. 'You'd better, Lovejoy. I can't leave you to the tender mercies of others, the state you're in.'

Two quips from Margaret in one morning? Paula had captured a hangdog whiffler who was feebly trying to escape. Much chance.

'Anyway, enjoy the meet, Lovejoy.'

'Meet?' I paused. 'What's a meet? I thought that was horses.'

'It is.' Margaret gazed at me. 'Noon start. Isn't it Florida's big show?'

'Oh, aye. I was just on my way.' That must be what I'd agreed.

Margaret's motor was outside. I got in, scraped the wires with my thumb, splitting two fingernails, cursed a few curses, and drove like a fiend.

Sometimes a whole area can feel really strange even when you know it well. There's a place near Wivenhoe village on the Colne estuary where the road narrows. It's the least spooky place on earth. You can see the whole countryside, farms, distant houses, trees, cows doing their somnolent best to look thrilling for some passing watercolour artist.

But I hate – *hate* – that bit of road. Won't drive there at any price. I've looked it up. No savage Ancient Britons waylaid Romans there. No Viking marauders hacked peaceable wagons on the way to market. No Great Civil War skirmish, no highwayman got hanged there on the gallows tree. It's the one furlong of the kingdom that is seriously boring.

The moral? Don't trust history – there's no future in it. I simply don't believe the facts. Once, it was an Ancient British trackway to the coast, then a rollicking road to the ancient Christian missionaries' seashore chapels. Later, a horse road for mediaeval merchants, then simply a road to the seaside.

It's eerie. There's something wrong with it. That road, I don't go on.

Even in Margaret's nicked car, I belted along the coast to avoid it, came on Albansham before I could think. I stopped the car and stared towards the priory's tower. I was worried, because I'd brought that Wivenhoe road's weird feeling along with me.

No mysteries, though, in antiques. You have to get on, get gone or get none. I drove in, whistling. Into a spooky silence.

'Hello?' I called out.

No noise. Not a sausage. No merry monks pouring molten metal into sand moulds. No nuns bent over embroidery. Nobody carrying hoes to merry work in the fields. The place was quiet. I almost thought it a deathly quiet, but that would have been stupid. I mean broad daylight, a holy priory, deathly?

Now, I'm big on quiet. I like it. I'm pleased if the town's emptier than usual, as when a tourist ferry fails to come in because of storms at Harwich. But there's quiet and quiet. By the latter, I mean an ominous protracted silence that itches.

'Hello?' I shouted, listening. My own voice, nobody else's.

Worrying, I walked along the walls to where I'd eeled out of the chapel. I tried the vestry. Locked. I tried jumping up to look inside, but the curtains were drawn. No red votive light that I could see.

The forge? You simply can't close a forge in a few minutes, not like laying aside your embroidery. I tried the big door. It was firmly padlocked.

'Hello?' I shouted, rattling the handle. 'Gesso? It's me, Lovejoy.'

Quiet.

My fingers could reach the sill. I hauled myself up to chin the window, toes scrabbling, and saw inside.

A glow from the furnace still, but dying. Bellows, sand moulds on the stone-flagged floor ready for the molten metal. Gantries above, haul-and-tip chains. I got out of breath, dropped down, did it again, had three or four looks until I was shaking from effort. I stood and thought.

The wind was rising slightly, leaves blowing across the courtyard. Funny-sad how desolate a place becomes the instant folk leave, isn't it? A house can have all the family warmth imaginable, but within minutes of the last child's departure, mum getting on her coat and dad locking up, a house grows as sad as sorrow. Is it that it's no longer lived in? Or that the house feels left behind? That's exactly the difference between an antique and something modern. An antique's been created, been lived with. People are in it, their feelings, hopes, dreams, their very selves.

The priory felt dead.

Drainpipes aren't difficult to climb. To any burglar, even a hopeless one like me, they're simply hollow ladders. I've heard real burglars say that. I shinned up, peered into the nuns' embroidery room. It took a minute for my eyes to adjust, but it was sedate, vacant. No hurried cast-off stitchery here. I slid down, walked about some more.

Margaret Dainty was right. This place was closed for the duration, not merely resting between shifts. I was worried sick. You don't start the Bessemer process – that difficult, chest-corroding manufacture of molten metal – unless you intend to go through with it. Only days ago, the monks were hard at it. I mean, you need melted cast iron, through which you force air. Since its heyday – it was promulgated in 1856 – furnaces have come and gone. It killed most of its workers from silicosis and injury. What I'm saying is, the Bessemer process isn't a whim. Valuable metal when you've finished, but there's a price to pay for every solid pig. Yet the furnaces, still not cooled, had been shut down in mid-cycle. It'd be hell to start the foundry up again. So they were dud for good.

'Gesso?' my voice quavered.

This priory had been hurriedly abandoned, a landlubber *Marie Celeste*. It hadn't just been closed for the hols.

For a sickly hour I trudged the priory, knocking on doors, peering in windows, trying handles. I scaled more drainpipes than the parson preached about. I called out my hellos and anybody-theres like a fool. I even went round to where there'd been some sheep. Gone, the pen open. Tyre tracks indented the soil, showing where they'd been loaded. Market? Transferred to another farm?

The nuns, I knew, spun the wool that the monks sheared off the sheep, and made it into cardigans. I knew this because I'd made some hand carders for their history gala. I'd sent them over with some schoolchildren who'd asked for help on a history project. I'd also made them a Lancashire spinning wheel, but had run out of heartwood. I'd got them woad seeds, and showed the children how to make the most beauteous dyes on earth – blues, yellows, greens. They hadn't paid me, but you can't really take umbrage about mere gelt when people are reworking ancient beauty, can you?

The dye vats were cold, a residue of soggy wool, the cauldrons gone.

It was starting to drizzle. I sat on a wall. Empty is as empty does. The place was vacated. Nobody was coming home, not to Albansham Priory.

'Well, Lovejoy,' I said aloud. 'Time to clear off.'

And didn't, just sat there getting soaked, trying hard to move. My feet wouldn't do as they were told.

Behind, on the rising hillside behind me, there was a faint sound. Plop, bubble, plop. I hated, still hate, that sound. I found myself trying out different tunes in time with its gurgling. 'Marching To Pretoria' almost slotted in, but missed out after a few bars. I tried 'Goodbye', no luck, then 'White Cliffs Of Dover', but had most success with 'Abide With Me'. I rose humming, nervous, and walked towards the hot pool.

Once, I'd been up there and thought it a waste of time. Like most pools, springs, wells, they are venerated by locals, especially in East Anglia's remoter spots. Folk leave garlands and wreaths of flowers at most wells in south Britain anyway. But the few hot ones that we have – in Bath, in Wiltshire – are especially holy, heaven knows why. The Romans got organized. Bath, for instance, became a major tourist town two thousand years ago. Me, I leave wells alone. Stop and drink if you've a need to, then scarper. I help our village schoolchilden to 'dress' the oldest well, but it makes me feel uneasy. I'm always glad when it's over.

The hot pool was plopping away. I stood looking down. It's actually like a boil on the greensward, a hot splurging pustule. No more than ten feet wide, it has a freshet that starts there and dribbles away down the slope. Children sometimes find things in the water – coins, bits of bone, the odd tooth, a single claw with scales still attached. Like I said, such ancient relics still show their original colour, as if they'd been dropped in the hot slime only minutes before. One was the vertebrae of some small extinct dinosaur creature. It isn't stain from the hot mud, because the hues fade within days of exposure to modern air. It's as if deep down there's a subterranean chasm filled with silent creatures, gazing somnolently at each other in a kind of archeological purgatory, waiting to be raised to life. It's eerie.

Attempts to fill in these hot pools always fail. The hot pool continues plopping away, unaffected. It simply engulfs whatever's offered.

The view was feeble. Distantly, the church, Aldeburgh

way. Undulating farmland with a copse or two, trees where the woods began. Flatter fields a mile north where, gulp, Florida's many mounts were presumably champing. Nearer, the priory, windows shuttered or blanked out. Not a chimney smoking.

Time I reported to Florida. Still I didn't budge.

A yard away, I saw what I didn't want to see. I'd actually stepped over it, ignored the silvery shiny thing. I made my feet take a step.

Gesso's pencil torch was bent in the middle. I don't know if you've ever used one of these, out at night on one of your burlary jaunts or maybe creeping home late after some love tryst. If so, you'll know how tough they are. Not mere plastic for Gesso, no. Solid metal, with one of those tiny pointed bulbs. It had a clip, to latch it to your pocket. The bulb was shattered, soil clagged inside its cavity.

Without doubt, Gesso's. He'd painted two black rings round it, Halford's matt black anti-rust paint, so it didn't slip in his gloved palm. I made myself pick it up. I saw a groove gouged in the earth where it must have scraped savagely along. The line led directly to the hot pool. A large rounded flintstone – the only stone we've got in the Eastern Hundreds – stopped the groove. A mark showed where the torch had scraped the surface of the flint cobble before almost snapping from the force of whatever was being dragged—

'What's your fucking game, mate?'

I jumped a mile. 'Eh?'

A security man was standing a few yards off. He was ready for trouble, with his London accent. He could have made three of me. I grinned, instant yokel.

'Sorry, booy,' I said. 'Juss seein' if the sheep be gone.'

'You see any, you stupid get? Sod off. No sheep here.'

'Roighyt, booy.' I walked down the slope. He came with me, disappointed. 'When be the old prior be comin' back?'

'Mind your own fucking business and clear off.'

Which was how I left Gesso's last glimpse of light and life, coward that I am. The security guard ballocked me all the way to the motor. I said a cheery so-long and drove off to meet Florida. I felt Gesso's reproachful flashlight in my pocket, and even stopped the car.

'Look,' I told the windscreen angrily. I could hardly see for my stupid eyes watering. 'What can I do? If I go to the police, what evidence is there? Gesso's just scarpered, that's all. He often does. And Marie wouldn't harm a fly.'

I blotted my eyes, yelled out, 'Everybody leave me alone, for God's sake!'

Margaret's wheels I left by the war memorial just in time to get abused by Florida for being late again, and by Margaret coming up in Paula's massive truck, furious with me for stealing her motor. Honestly, women get my goat. Some days, you wonder if it's all women do, tell blokes off for nothing. OK, so I'd nicked Margaret's car. What was it, for heaven's sake, a crime?

15

'Y OU ALWAYS GRUMBLE, Lovejoy,' Florida fumed, driving fast. 'A point-to-point meeting is *exciting*. You're like a child!'

'I've already seen your horse,' I said, but you can't be reasonable.

'Once! Horses are for life, you stupid...' Et county cetera.

Forlornly I looked out of the car window. Horses mean countryside, and I'd had quite enough of it, ta for nowt. Fields appeared. Woods, farms, a river. Civilization receded. Out here was religion, every shade of pale and dark, and we all know what horrors that breeds. I could cope better with Florida if only she'd keep her cars for more than a week at a time. Whenever we meet, it's new. I can't keep track.

'Where do all your old motors go, love?'

'This horse is a darling!' she cried. 'Hand off my knee, please.'

My hand had moved, quite innocently. I folded my arms. Why the aggro? Florida epitomized the sixteenth-century saying 'Woman is in church a saint, in the street an angel, in kitchens a devil, in bed an ape'. Now, no knees.

'And you can stop sulking,' she scolded. 'You're only happy over some stupid old pot or piece of wood. Get real, Lovejoy. Get a life.' Her phrases mean I'm wrong and Florida is right.

We drove to her wretched point-to-point. It was two miles from Albansham, close by where Florida lives in a fourteenth-century house. She's restored her mansion to resemble a condensed housing estate. I've only been there once, when her husband the ex-policeman was out of the country. I wasn't allowed in. Me and Florida made use of a summer house (hers) down by a pleasant river (also hers). Even her nine-acre grounds have been flattened. I said nothing as we drove into the fields. They seemed rimmed by tents, pavilions, horseboxes in rows. Horse-inclined ladies congregated round the car. Horses were everywhere. A pretty girl leant in, screaming.

'Bobbinella's entered the second race!' she shrieked. 'Simply super!'

'And Leaper!' others howled.

I got out saying how happy I was at this fantastic news. A lass – I could only see one man, and he looked about as much a part of this scene as me – collared me. She was holding the reins of a horse so huge it didn't matter any more.

'Are you Jocasta?' she demanded.

'No. Lovejoy. How do, love.'

'No,' she said impatiently. 'Are you Jocasta's *owner*? I've Mulish and Peterloo to see to, and it's a two o'clock start.'

The horse sidled towards me, friendly. I sidled away. Horses are all right, but being pals with two tons of brisk muscle is unwise. I have enough trouble with bluetits.

Florida struggled against a tide of women all wanting decisions. The field was laid out with fences and hedges, even a watersplash. The place was knee deep in nags. I was the only living thing here without a fetlock. I'd been in the clubhouse once before, so I signalled Florida that I'd call in the pavilion for some tea. She nodded suspiciously, tapped her watch, spread a hand. I mimed eager agreement, back in five minutes to share in her ecstatic equestrian frolicking, and headed for the last vestige of sanity among these barbarians.

A girl trotted beside me. She wore jodhpurs, riding boots, a velvet crash helmet, carried a whip. Riding horses is warfare, and looks it.

'Lovejoy? He wants you!' She almost fainted with pleasure. The lone man was standing by the judges' table surrounded by admiring ladies in elegant dresses. If I'd been that lucky I wouldn't have bothered watching me.

'Right, love. I'll talk to him in a sec. Er, good luck with Jocasta.'

'Mine's Robber King,' she said.

'Well, never mind. Horses are all the same.'

Inside the pavilion I scrounged some tea and toast and cream scones from the waitresses. They, of course, gave me verbals. 'The minute we get straight you disrupt everything, and leave those Chorley cakes alone . . .' Beats me how I survive, forever getting my hands slapped. If it isn't Florida's knees it's their measly Chorley cakes. Though some people don't survive, of course, like a certain friend whose damaged pencil torch was burning my pocket. The waitresses shooed me out, laughing and scolding. I drifted, hands filled with purloined grub.

There was a club room. Photographs of horses – honest, somebody had wasted their time actually taking snaps of the beasts – and cases of trophies round the walls. Nobody in, fire burning in the hearth. I stood, peered, gazed, I began to think at last, and to remember. As we'd driven into the point-to-point fields, I'd smelled woodsmoke out there. It had a definite tang that ordinary fires haven't. For a long time I stared at a glass case. It contained a wooden object labelled EARLY HUNTING HORN, PROB. FRUITWOOD. Beside it were two old biscuit tins, one shaped like a toy aeroplane, the second like a Rolls-Royce. PRESENTS FOR OUR FIRST CLUB GYMKHANA somebody had written, exclamation marks all across the card, very humorous.

It's hard to believe, but the fastest-soaring prices are for collectables, not real antiques as such. Maniacs, like birds, flock so. It's a sort of modern sickness, because who cares when these items aren't proper antiques? Answer: collectors care, by the million. I looked closer.

Biscuits used to come in small tin boxes pressed to resemble anything from buses to planes, tanks to golf-club cases. The two in the display were a Dutch mandarin-red monoplane, complete with propeller. Everybody in the antiques trade (including me) brags to have seen one of these, but I hadn't until now. The English one was Crawford's Rolls-Royce. Miraculously, both had their original box. GIVEN IN THEIR WRAPPED BOX!!! a handwritten card announced jovially, TO MISS WENSTONE AND MRS HAWKSWORTH!!! Some details of nags, with yellowed newspaper cuttings, were on a faded card. If Florida knew the value of these two biscuit tins, she could rush out and buy another couple of motor cars instantly.

The absurdity of collecting would make you laugh, if it didn't drive you close to tears. Everybody wants these biscuit boxes, the rarer the better. A French bloke called Nicholas Appert's the man who's given credit for starting to store food long term. He did it for Napoleon's soldiery. Industries swiftly shelled off Appert's bottle-and-cork methods and turned to metal boxes. After 1810, food was never the same again. This doesn't mean that the oldest are the costliest, not by a mile. The better the Victorian industrial processes, the pricier the antique tin today. So Benjamin George's posh transfer-printed tins, then the French offset lithography designs (neatly stolen by our Mr Barclay's patent in the 1870s) brought in every shape you can imagine. They compete at expensive international auction houses: Huntley & Palmer's, Peek Frean & Co, Macfarlane, Lang & Co, all the biscuit people. There are hundreds of designs.

Anybody could nick these from this shaky display cabinet and make a mint. I should have done Gesso a good turn, brought him here instead of getting him killed.

'Can I come in?' I turned to look. It was that staring bloke.

God, he was a scruff. And I'd thought I was shopsoiled. At least I wash all over every morning. Even if it's in cold water from my garden well I do a dawn bum-balls-armpit soap and rinse, teeth, gargle, plus hair every three days. This geezer looked like some tatty vagrant, hair a-straggle, shabby jeans, shoes well on the way to being slippers, faded soiled coat. Yet he was the one being adored out there by clusters of gorgeous women. Is this justice?

'You a barker?' I said through a mouthful. 'Freddy Foxheath send you?'

'Barker?' He considered the word. 'You mean, like on a fairground?'

Thick, as well as gungey. 'Not that sort. A sniffer of antiques.'

'No, I'm not a barker. I'm Jonno Rant.'

'How do.' I nodded, affable. 'Lovejoy.'

'I know.' He moved in, sat on the arm of a couch. I

realized waitresses were peering in through the door, giggling and whispering, clearly worshipping the leather he lolled on. I smarted. They'd slung me out of their posh tearoom but were desperate to grovel to this apparition. 'And you're under arrest.'

'Who says?' I didn't panic, because lots of people try arresting me.

'Me. Two lawyers. Three policemen. And my bodyguard. They're waiting outside, in unmarked cars.'

Which stopped me. He didn't look a diplomat. His name caused me sudden anxiety. I didn't know why.

'At all the exits.' He smiled. 'When you're ready, Lovejoy.'

'Why?' Quickly I finished my grub. Speed was called for.

A waitress came and asked if he wanted tea. He said coffee, didn't even say please. She fled with a whimper of ecstasy. Things like this make you bitter. Some women wouldn't recognize tact if it slapped them in the face. She'd completely ignored me.

'Why, Lovejoy? Because you're not Jonno Rant.' He was amused. 'And I am.'

Seemed reasonable enough, I was just about to say, when the name registered. Rant? Jonno Rant? Hadn't I spoken his name lately? But why on earth would I want to do that? I'd never heard of him.

'Couldn't we agree that you're you and I'm me, and leave it at that?'

'Not when you've made illegal contracts for me.'

Had I? Then I remembered. Whoops, Maureen Jolly in the tavern, her mate Patty, when I was on the cadge. I'd promised her an interview. This yokel, then, was the great impressario? Vague primordial memories trickled in. He'd been a pop star once, turned to promoting West End musicals. And him a grown man.

'You took money, Lovejoy, and made verbal contracts in my name. Naughty.'

'Ah.' I beamed, advanced smiling with my hand outstretched. He didn't shake. 'I think I can explain, er, Jonno. It's a simple misunderstanding. That lady's very sick, mentally disturbed. To please her . . .'

I gave him the full monty. He listened, took his coffee with a smile the lass almost fainted at.

'You simply don't realize, Lovejoy, do you?' He sipped, causing the growing mob of waitresses peering in to swoon and scream. 'You've upset me, and seven great production houses in a multi-million business. Your fraud must be fully exposed.'

Multi-million business? I thought in wonder. What, for a few songs? He was deranged, certifiable. Time for exit, pursued by bear.

'Look, mate,' I begged, summoning lies. 'Will you give me half an hour? I won't run away.'

'You can't bargain,' he said reasonably. God, I hate reasonable people. They make you sound thick as a plank. 'You can't leave, Lovejoy. You're going to a police cell. A con man's promises aren't worth the paper. Also, I have two journalists and a photographer here. They want the scoop.' He nodded, as if I doubted him. 'Publicity's the name of the game, Lovejoy. Showbiz needs it. I'll be in every national tomorrow morning, free of charge. Bliss.'

This was a problem for Florida. I find that women are the ones you need when in this sort of scrape. They're born with luck and cunning, and we're not.

'Can I shout Mrs . . .' I'd forgotten Florida's surname '. . . Florida? She's boss of the cavalry. I came with her.'

He shook his head, stood with an air of finality. He was enjoying himself. I put my hand in my pocket for a scrap of paper, thinking to leave Florida a note, and touched Gesso's torch. I turned quickly to face the trophy case.

'Can I ask, Lovejoy,' he said, 'why the tears? I can't believe this kind of incident is unfamiliar to you.'

'Shut your stupid teeth, pillock.' I stayed put. 'I'm just reading about these interesting things, so shut it.'

He came to peer. 'Two old tins and a bugle upset you so much? What's the connection? Were they your dad's?'

'It's one of the commonest mistakes,' I said, to get speech going again. 'René Laennec invented the modern stethoscope. That's one. It doesn't look much like a hunting horn.' I blew my nose. He waited in silence. 'I often wonder if Laennec thought it up from the musical instrument – he played half a dozen different instruments, including the hunting horn. Died,' I added, free of charge, 'in 1826. His stethoscopes are all sorts of shapes, some in two or three pieces.'

'What's the matter?' He was staring again. 'Are you OK?'

'Can I go to the loo, please? Send word to Florida. Won't be a sec.'

'Very well.'

He went into the corridor with me. I turned left, he right. The waitresses crowded for his autograph. A cook said to me, agape as I went through her kitchen, 'It's Jonno Rant! He had three number ones in the charts!'

I said, 'Isn't it wild?'

Outside, two rows of horse vehicles were lined up about a hundred yards away. I walked alongside a girl leading a horse. If I'd known how, I'd have stooped to inspect its hoof, but didn't risk it. Horses can spot a duckegg a mile off, though they're basically dimwits. At the horseboxes I ducked low, and made the boundary unmanacled. In a trice I was among the trees heading for the scent of woodsmoke.

They call him Logger Yelk, for reasons that aren't clear, because his name is Bernard Marlborough. He's our cleverest charcoal burner. It mightn't sound much, but to me Logger Yelk's a series of plusses. I approve, and that's a fact.

'Logger,' I called when I'd gone a mile through the undergrowth. The scent was stronger, so I was heading in the right direction. He hates being surprised.

No answer. Shouting for people who didn't respond was becoming a way of life. I seemed to have done a lot of it lately.

'Logger!' I yelled. 'It's me, Lovejoy.' I plodded on.

Woods are grim places. Farmers shoot squirrels, crows, magpies, and hang them up on trees to warn Mother Nature to get it together or else. Much notice she takes, being in league with God. They're a right pair, more carnage than the rest of us put together.

Woods baffle. I can never work out where east is. Even stars don't work, because they go round instead of pointing stoically north. You'd think they'd make themselves useful for a frigging change.

At last I came on the clearing. It was a scene from the past. Breathlessly I sat, panned out.

Logger was hard at it. He'd just returned from a cutting session, I noticed. His logs are no more than six inches across, two inches diameter the thinnest.

'Hello, Lovejoy. Come to hide out again?'

'No, ta, Logger.'

Logger lives in a makeshift hut at the corner of the

clearing, year in, year out. I'd had occasion to befriend him
when I was on the run a couple of times. He's a good bloke,
says nothing. I got him the charcoal-making concession that
started his career, by persuading Her Ladyship of Ashwood-
Pentney, a famous manor, to let him manage this woodland
free of charge. I used unorthodox but successful methods,
until she said I was getting too friendly with her cousin's
wife from Basingstoke. I think jealousy's really naff, but
women are full of it.

He poked his fire. It's in a great iron pot some ten feet
across and a yard deep. He has two, burns three tons of
wood a week. Each fire pot has a huge metal lid. You start
your fire with alderwood, hazel, oak, ash, about teatime, let
it burn until the roaring dies down. Stick the lid on for a
sixteen-hour smoulder. There are four chimney-like vents
in the metal. It's an ancient career.

'Wipe that expression off your face, Lovejoy,' Logger
said, cheerful as ever. 'I'm not killing the trees. It's care that
brings butterflies and insects, starts flowers growing again.
I only clear the underbrush, make way for new. I've rescued
whole species. Did you know that ninety per cent of the
world's species aren't yet identified?'

'No.' Because I didn't.

'East Anglia's got sixty thousand acres of derelict woods
rotting away. They could be bettering the world.' He
stopped, angrily shook a stick at me. 'Manage our woods
properly, we'd not need to import charcoal from the tropical
rain forests, save the planet . . .'

He continued like this. I listened, agreeing every now
and again. Eventually he worked the lid on to his fire
tin and went for a pint of ale.

'Sycamore this time, Lovejoy.' He gave me a pint glass.

'Cheers, Logger. Ta.' It was his famous tree beer.

Logger produces ale from great trees like the sycamore. He makes slits in their trunks, with a sort of half cup clamped to the bark. I looked. It had no flies in it. His sap cups are always filled with the damned things. He laughed. He thinks me amusing because I'm out of my depth when civilization vanishes.

'That ale is crystal clear, Lovejoy. You're no countryman.'

'Course I am.' I was indignant. 'I like everything.' I looked round the clearing, with its stacks of branches cut ready for burning. 'It's really, er, good.'

'Because I give you wood, Lovejoy, ready labelled.'

He checks wood for me, especially unusual ones. Only rarely does Logger come to civilization, always calls on me. He borrows a McArthur microscope from somewhere. Lately he's been going over a batch of the unusual arbutus wood – it's the sort I call the strawberry tree – that Killarneyware trinket boxes are made from. They take ages to fashion, being intricately inlaid, but ideal for long winter evenings after your woman's walked out in a temper. Other fakers make these Victorian Killarneyware items from infilled teak and Japanese oak instead of strawberry tree wood, which only goes to show how low some forgers sink.

'The prior himself praised my learning,' I grumbled back.

'Did he now,' Logger said laconically. He sat on a stack of cuttings.

'Aye. Nice priory he's got there, eh? Lovely old place.'

'Balls, Lovejoy.' He cocked an ear. 'It's no more ancient than that blaze yonder. It was, before Prior George gutted it and sold everything off.'

'Did he?' I asked, innocent.

'My dad remembered it well. Prior George brought in his monks, nuns. Good riddance, I says.'

'Oh,' I said, even more innocent. 'He's gone, has he?'

'Scattered. Monks to Preston, nuns to near Lindisfarne.'

'I didn't know you could. Thought religious foundations were sacrosanct.' Though Henry VIII didn't do a bad job. 'Led them off himself, did he?'

Logger didn't answer for a minute. He went to listen to his cauldron, kicked it, returned to sit, looking directly at me.

'You mean where has he gone, Lovejoy?' he said. 'Does he owe you money? He'd gamble on a weather vane, that one. You're in goodly company.'

'I'll come clean, Logger. Where's he gone?'

'Like that, is it?' he said, scuffing the earth with his boot. 'He's a Guernsey man. Him and his sister. Do anything for a farthing, especially if he could pop it on some nag. That meet,' he said, pointing at some nearby trees. He meant the point-to-point. 'It's the first time there's been gambling without him for years. Beats me how he does it. Gets women to collect objects, money, endowments for his priory, then milks it and loses it on everything, dogs to donkeys. A menace.'

A suspicion was growing within, and I hated it.

'He's gone to Guernsey?'

'Eh? Oh, sure. His sister's going about the county settling up.'

'What with? Is she rich in her own right?'

'Not her. She's had a slice of luck lately, dunno what from.'

'Ta, Logger. Look. Is there any way—?'

'Hold it, Lovejoy.' He stood, went to put a hand on a tree trunk at the edge of the clearing. He listened. 'There's people coming, six or seven. And a motorbike on the Alban-sham road. Somebody after you?'

'Me?' I said innocently. 'No. But I'd best be off. Ta, Logger. Oh, pretty soon I'll need some pear wood, maybe laburnum if you can get it.'

'You don't ask much, do you, Lovejoy?' He sounded peeved. 'Do you know how much pear heartwood costs? A mint.'

'Get some,' I said, narked, starting off. 'You're the frigging woodsman, Logger. Oh.' I stopped, sheepish. He was grinning. 'Er, please could you tell me which way? Only, I fancy a quiet walk. I don't want to be bumping into others.'

He pointed, rolling in the aisles at my embarrassment.

'Go that way for six furlongs. You'll come to a coppice of ash with a medlar. Turn half right for three perches, and you'll meet a footpath. Turn left, and the Albansham road's a mile. You can get a bus.'

He might as well have spoken Tagalog. A coppice of ash with a medlar?

'Thanks, Logger,' I said politely, and simply walked in the direction he pointed.

'Lovejoy,' he called after me. 'Give my regards to Guernsey.'

Who'd said anything about going to the Channel Isles? I thought this, but did not say, striding away from that Jonno Rant and his mob.

I wondered what the fare was.

16

MOST TOWNS HAVE a drill hall. His-
torians say they're relics from days
when bowmanship was compulsory
and every lad worth a grain had to trudge out with his
bow and arrows to the fields to learn the art. Hence the
abundance of Butt Roads and Archers Lanes. Nowadays,
territorial platoons do their stuff, and whist drives raise
funds there for hopeless causes. They're also where the
ultimate embarrassments are enacted. I use that last term
loosely. Performers were assembled, a real motley. Many
were in leotards, tights. Some carried sheet music. To one
side a juggler frantically juggled. Is anything sadder than a
juggler hoping for a job?

'Next,' a woman called. She looked in off the road, a
dragster, smoking her head off, scratching lazily.

Next to her was the Power In The Land, the pop music/
impressario boss. He drank volatile liquid with fevered
intensity. The pair were seated at a trestle table in front of
the stage. He looked a cheapo version of Jonno Rant. The
itchy lady had a clipboard. They looked an unsavoury pair.
I'd come miles to find this grotty scene, paid my all in
phone calls. For this? But I needed money. If a derelict
scruff like Jonno Rant could get instant adoration from one

and all simply by being in show business, then the whole thing was a con. It was a career made for somebody like me, who needed to travel fast on no resources and catch up with Prior Metivier.

The producer cleared his throat. Everybody froze in terror before realizing there was no message from Olympus yet awhile. A pianist, already well drunk, was at a tinny piano. The hall held some thirty hopefuls in various stages of confidence.

A man started singing 'Heart Of My Heart'. I thought he was quite good.

'Next,' the itchy woman said, bored.

'Can't I finish?' The singer was youngish, tousled, anxious.

'You already finished,' the woman said, huffling at her quip. The singer left, red-faced and despondent. 'Next.'

A girl stepped forward, looked about for adequate lighting, realized this was it, and announced shrilly that she would do an Ayckbourn speech.

'That fucking *voice*,' the assistant woman said, grinding out her perfumed fag and instantly lighting another. She called, 'Do your Shakespeare piece, lovie.'

'Very well,' the girl said, '*So oft it chances in particular men—*'

'No, dear,' the woman bawled. 'It was a fucking *joke* for fuck's *sake*. Like I mean exit left and leave your CV in the wastebasket and go. Next.'

The girl went, in tears. I found myself heartbroken at the sheer waves of desperation among the actors waiting to go on. Auditions are hell. I advanced at an indolent stroll. I wished I'd not given up smoking. You can be so much more confident in a con trick when you're smoking.

'Hold it,' I called, casual. 'You're . . . ?'

'Barnie Woodfall.' The woman glared, spoken to by a mere mortal. 'I'm Sam Costell.'

'Hi, Barn,' I said to the man. He looked ill, could hardly sit upright. Her, I ignored. 'Jonno said to drop by. Got the list?'

Barnie Woodfall's eyes descended from orbit, fixed on the woman. 'Jonno? We talkin' Jonno Rant here, Sam?'

'No.' I gave him bitter sarcasm. 'I mean like Jonno Two-Shoes. Have you got the fucking list? She rang for your audition schedule, for Christ's sake.'

'She who?' Sam Costell demanded, suddenly gone edgy. My demand had done Barnie some good. I wondered if pupils should be quite that size, and leant away from their aromatic smoke in case. I'd rather have Logger's clean charcoal any day.

'Her who, exactly?' I thumbed a thumb insolently. If she wanted to be called a man's name that was her lookout, but she'd already proved that bravado ruled. 'You know what Jonno's like, Barn. He'll have her balls.'

'We talkin' failure here?' Barnie erupted in an insane screech. He fell over backwards, the chair going with a crash, couldn't get up. A dying fly.

'Oke. Take the poke. See yous aroun',' I intoned, drifting. I sounded ridiculous.

'We talkin' cock-ups here, Sam fucking Costell?' Barnie shrieked from his moribund position at his scratchy bird.

She raced after me, caught me up at the door. Barnie's shrill tantrum echoed in the rafters.

'Look, er . . . ?'

'I'm Miles,' I said. 'Jonno's oppo, but don't frig about, willco?' It was as near as I could get. I'd heard them say willco on telly police procedurals.

'Here's the list, Miles.' She'd have been really attractive

if she stopped smoking, got proper clothes, had a bath, did her hair, cleaned her teeth. Or not. 'I'm sorry about the cock-up, truly. Look.' She whispered it, looking scared. 'Is Jonno back? Please tell him it was all a terrible mistake, OK?'

'Ten frigging more minutes, that's all.' I stuffed her list in my pocket.

'Take my card, Miles. Please. Anything I can do for you or Jonno—'

'Sure, sure,' I said, like in American films.

At least I had a list of performers. The drill hall's notice outside read, AUDITIONS/CABARET/MUSIC HALL/EQUITY. I left it untouched. I can be really forgiving.

Then I went to see a man about a painting, and got Irma.

Paula's antique shop's just round the corner from the Hippodrome. They have a bar there, though it's no longer a great old-fashioned music hall. Symie Doakes drinks there, three hours in the day, six at night. He never moves, but sometimes is exactly the one you want. I perched on the next stool.

'Wotcher, Symie.'

'Hello, Lovejoy.' He stares at himself in their ornate mirrors. I'd look at the barmaid if I were him. He wears a pork pie hat, a tweed overcoat and wellingtons, summer and winter. 'What?'

'How much, Symie? I'm broke, mind.'

'What's new?' he said, sarcasm. He puts on this Jewish act, hands up, plaintive at penury and all that, but I don't know. 'Aren't we all?'

'What paintings have been sold lately? Modern, lookalike Expressionists or Neo-Thingies?'

'Ov vey,' he said, but it came out somehow wrong. 'From round here? Only one. It went for a king's ransom, through a London broker.'

'From where?'

'Gelt first, Lovejoy. My old saida used to say, God bless her, always get the dinars first, ma booy.'

See what I mean? Saida's their word for a relative, I think, and they don't use dinars. Like a bad act. The purpose escapes me.

'I've got money, Symie.' I feinted at my pocket. 'Who sold what?'

'A modern, they say, Lovejoy. Horrible. Squirts of colour. O'Conor, they're saying, though I didn't see it myself. Thank God it wasn't Russian. I should praise a Cossack painter yet?' He chuckled, inspected his empty glass. Gladys the barmaid shook her head, smiling, then looked harder, then nodded, pulled Symie a refill. I thanked her kindness. Maybe she'd seen something in my eyes I didn't want to have there.

'Woman or man, Symie?'

'Holy man's sister, bad cess to him. Frigging Jesuits. Cheers.'

'Cheers.' I went for gold. 'Symie. I need names. Prior Metivier owes me a mint. Was it him?'

'His sister Marie sold it to Benbrooks and Dellors.' Maybe he'd seen something in my gaze too because his jokes ended, and his act with it. 'He's escaped Gellbridge the bookie's honchos. She paid in full. They let him go.'

'Go where?' As if I couldn't guess.

'Guernsey, folk say, but who knows? His sort's a bad

penny, leave a trail of punters' papers across the kingdom. A brother like him, I'd let him sink.'

'Look,' I said, in a hurry now I'd got it. 'I'll ring you the next couple or three days. Suss out any more antiques from the priory for me. I'll see you gain, Symie.'

'Right. You'll phone here?'

'Sure. Have my drink, Symie, and ta.'

'Here, Lovejoy,' he exclaimed. 'You owe me for that. Twenty.'

'Haven't got it, Symie. Ta and oy, er, whatever you said.'

Gladys called so-long. I waved, and left him grumbling.

Paula wasn't in, so I told her shop minder – it's her unpaid mother – to clear off, brewed up and found a vegan pie in her fridge. You have to make do.

Using Paula's phone, I rang Desdemona. No news of Gesso. I said he'd turn up. Then I called Benbrooks and Dellors of London. Some plum-voiced article condescendingly answered. I asked what time I could call tomorrow for the painting, expressionist or something, that I'd paid a deposit on. I made myself sound a twit, not difficult. They became flustered. I became angry.

'Now look here,' I yelled. 'This is Colonel Haffton Morley, Grenadiers. I have the receipt signed by Miss Marie Metivier, and I want my picture!'

'Colonel, Miss Metivier's painting has already been sold on.'

'Sold on?' I thundered. I began to enjoy myself. Being apoplectic's quite invigorating. 'Describe the painting! If you've sold mine, my lawyers . . .' et cetera.

The man described. It really did sound like my O'Conor. He had the nerve to say that it had been badly overpainted with a badly faked Paul Klee, which really got my goat. I rang off spluttering, turned to see Paula standing there, massively miniskirted.

'What on earth, Lovejoy?'

'Paula. Didn't you used to go out with a stonemason?'

'From birth, Lovejoy.' She checked that I'd not nicked anything. Such trust. 'He's my elder brother, Horace.'

'Ah. I knew.' I put my wheedle on. 'Would he do me a job?'

'Look about, Lovejoy, while you're here. Earn your keep.'

Sighing, I started towards the only piece of furniture in the place that looked anything like. I was actually glad to help, because I badly needed to nick some small antique to sell. I urgently needed the fare to the bonny isle of Guernsey.

We made our way among her antiques in the cramped shop, me helpfully moving chairs, display cabinets and trinkets out of her way.

A genuine sideboard, the piece had been heavily punished in its time. There's more daftness told about inspecting drawers than anything, but I showed Paula the motions. We took out a drawer. Drawers were – should still be – made short of the full run, otherwise they bang on the inside back panel. That last bit of the supporting bar – the 'runner' – and the dividing panel have to be darkened (by grime, air) for the thickness of your thumb nail, while the adjacent area stays pale. Also, the last bit of the runner's length should stand proud, because it never becomes worn, the drawer not sliding that far in.

'Always look at the dovetails, love. Machine dovetailing was really motoring by 1890. It tends to be even – the "female" and "male" wedges are all of a size. Look at the drawer from the side. See? These are narrower against the drawer's facing. So it's before that date.'

'Is that it?' Paula looked amazed.

'Not all, but it'll do. This piece is old.' I felt the old piece's heart warm.

'But it's got turned legs, Lovejoy.'

'So? Treasure it, love. It saw Trafalgar out. And it's not been ...' I hesitated, sickened by the word '. . . improved.'

'Cheek, Lovejoy.' Her eyes were shining. 'I'll sell it to a Continental buyer!'

My spirits sank. That meant she'd have it glammed up by some faker like Glosser Ackroyd, whose sole job in life is to 'restore' antique furniture so it looks glamorously new. It's all the fashion in Germany, France, Switzerland and elsewhere. Glosser laughs about my distress. He calls Europe 'Pure rope', thinks it's a hilarious pun.

'Don't, love. It's been made by a craftsman.'

'Who?' she breathed, wanting me to say Hepplewhite.

'Dunno, love. Keep it, to lend lustre to your junk.'

Money, as profit, excites. She asked, 'Lovejoy, is my mother still in?'

'No, I sent her packing.'

'While you did that pongo on the phone?' Pongo is a fraudulent chat intended to deceive and elicit information, antiques or both. 'Silly cow, that Marie, paying off her brother's debts.'

'Did you see the painting?'

'O'Conor, I heard. Ten ton of paint daubed on canvas!' Paula hooted with laughter. 'Cheaper to buy the farm, don't you think?' This was proof beyond doubt. No way I could evade the responsibility now.

'O'Conor, who was influenced by Van Gogh?'

'Want to stay, Lovejoy?' She fluttered her eyes roguishly. 'I owe you.'

'Get your brother to carve me a headstone.' I came to earth. I hadn't got long. 'Carve it "Gesso, RIP". Put the date of a couple of days back. Tell him to stand it above the hot pool at Albansham Priory.'

She drew back to inspect me, sober. 'Are you serious?'

'Never more, love.' I bussed her and left – no mean feat, those two together.

She stood in the doorway looking after me as I crossed the road.

The small silvers I'd nicked as we'd talked were a George V enamelled silver mounted cut-glass scent bottle with its matching box. Five inches. I couldn't check, but I was sure the river landscape engraving was by the brilliant Daniels of Birmingham. No older than 1934 or so, but collectable and easily sold. Harry Bateman for once had some ready gelt, and I kindly lowered the price for a quick sale. I'm a fool to myself sometimes. I could have got twice the price if I'd hung on.

Then I went to the travel agents in Red Lion Walk. By seven I was on the train to the airport. Hand on my heart, I'd no intention of killing Prior George Metivier for killing Gesso, honest. Vengeance just isn't my thing, and I mean that most sincerely.

17

IN AIRPORTS YOU either spot your destination everywhere on those consoles, so it seems unlikely that anyone is going anywhere else, or you can't find it. I imagined a Biggles goggles-and-helmet job, with some Tiger Moth to cough and blip her way over the English Channel. Not a bit of it. The world and his wife were heading to Jersey, Guernsey, Alderney, wherever, and all on my plane. Hopefully I tried to see if anyone wanted Paris, Madrid, Moscow perhaps, but no. Stanstead Airport was thronged by wicked hordes aiming for my seat.

A lady sat near me in the airport lounge, talking about routes. I listened desperately, because I'm scared of flying. I said I was Jonno Rant, impressario. She, Enid, said not to worry, air was the safest.

'Of course, I could have flown from London City Airport – do you think they're as good? – though BA Newcastle's excellent, don't you find, Mr Rant?'

I drew breath to answer. Some hopes. She rattled on.

'Do you usually come this way? A lady I bumped into last week – the De Garis family? She has such a clever girl, but troublesome – said flying from Birmingham is simply a must, though I positively *swear* by those Condor multi-hulls from Weymouth—'

You get the idea. Planet Earth's population was emptying into Guernsey. One airline advertised ten flights a day. Nervously I watched the clock, thinking of us crowds shoaling from the skies to perch on a gaunt rock that surely couldn't have enough flat bits to land a kite, let alone a zillion squadrons. The flight was called.

On board, everybody except me seemed to know everybody else, except me. The air lady greeted passengers by name. ('Did Jess get his music examination? Marvellous! Tell Olive that Harry'll be delighted . . .' all that.) She assured me that the aircraft was wonderfully safe, that it wasn't all that small, that, yes, there was a life jacket under my seat. The possibility of our crashing into the cold waters of the Channel was remote. She said.

The man next to me was going to do some Roman and pre-Roman archeology on Guernsey. He had cameras, and wanted to talk zoom lenses and f-stops. Enid waved, announced loudly that I was the famous impressario Jonno Rant, bringing in a big Guernsey summer show. I smiled weakly. Two aircrew checked that I'd not fainted when the engines started up. This was a bloody nerve, because the one thing I never am is scared. Six passengers passed me tablets, drinks, pillows, an inhalant, meanwhile loudly recollecting their worst-ever flights, a particularly bad form of psychotherapy. A lady advised me on how to breathe, another said thinking of rhododendrons in sunshine cured flight fright. One thing was sure, Radio Guernsey must be superfluous. Already my fame had soared through the stratosphere.

My first inkling of real problems, however, came after we'd taken off. I was trying to waft air at my damp forehead. The lady on my left, hitherto broodingly silent, suddenly exploded to me, 'Mr Rant? *Don't* take your show to Jersey, whatever *they* say. You *mustn't* believe *their* travel brochures. Our mean summer highs are less than two degrees below theirs, so there!'

'Eh? Oh, good,' I said weakly.

Which prompted the photographer and a cluster of others to lecture me about how much better Guernsey was than Jersey.

'Jersey's *slightly* increased warmth is caused by their north-to-south incline. Guernsey slopes up southwards.' He drew me a helpful map of the island's geography. I said ta, pretended to fall asleep, didn't make it.

By the time we landed I was worn out. Friendship's all right, but it's not the sort of thing you should get too fond of. We disembarked into fresh air. Guernsey's done what every place in the kingdom's done, planted its airport a million leagues from its capital.

'Excuse me,' a lady said. By then I could hardly focus. 'The capital isn't St Peter's Port. It drops the possessive. St *Peter* Port, please. I hope you don't mind my drawing your attention . . .'

By skilled feints I narrowly avoided a lift, and got a taxi. The driver knew of a decent place to stay. I'd thought I'd escaped Guernsey's instant palliness until he said a merry 'Have a good stay, Mr Rant' as he dropped me off. I sighed, hefted up my shoulder bag and knocked. Well, I would have, only the door opened before my knuckles made it.

'Mr Rant!' the lady exclaimed. 'Wasn't it a nice flight!'

'Er, aye,' I said, wondering vaguely what was wrong with that sentence, but she'd got some grub on the go so I surrendered while she told me what I wanted to see during my stay and how eager I'd be to see this and that. Drawing breath, she added, 'You won't want to go to Jersey, thank goodness!' I began to wonder if the two islands were at war. She said she was especially sorry I'd been so airsick, especially 'as Bill himself was at the controls!'

The grub filled me. I was invited to watch the telly, stay up at least until X, Y and Z 'get here because it's not often we have an impressario come to cast his new summer show . . .' I began to hate Jonno Rant, wished I'd never thought to nick his identity. If I'd guessed right and Prior George had arrived back here, I'd never dare make surreptitious inquiries about him. With Guernsey's gossip velocity it'd be like giving him a ring. I tottered upstairs to bed.

They had hold of me and dragged me along the grass. It was dark as pitch. I tried screaming but it was like one of those dreams where you're trying to shout, Help please, Grandad, and you can't utter a sound.

Somebody had filled a great net with flintstone cobbles. It trailed along roped to my ankles. They were bleeding. The nylon cut my skin. I struggled, tore at the gag round my face, couldn't free it.

Then I got hold of some small cylindrical object, slender and thin like . . . like a torch, a pencil flashlight. I yanked it from my pocket even as I heard the muted splutter of the hot pool, and I dug the slim metal into the soil and for a second felt them halt as it bit.

They cursed. Someone's familiar voice said, 'What the fuck', usually so friendly but now utterly venomous, and I was dragged and gripped by three of them and the metal thing scraped on some flint cobble and then bent and was gone—

'Chuck the bastard in,' the voice said, breathless. 'Not

that way, stupid. Feet first. Why the fuck d'you think the stones are there?'

'Bet it takes longer than twenty seconds,' somebody said.

'You're on,' said the educated, venomous voice.

Somebody chuckled. I screamed without managing to, now so near the hot pool's quiet but totally evil sounds, and then I was hurtling through the air a short distance and I screamed and was dragged down into the heat.

'Mr Rant?' some woman was saying cheerily.

'Help!' I bleated, battling to get the gag out of my mouth, flailing.

'My goodness!' the lady said, coming into the room. 'It's that flight that did it. Will I give Bill a piece of my mind! I had a visitor last year came to visit the North Beach Marina who was positively terrified of flying, well luckily my sister's husband – he taxied you from the airport – has a connection with the Condor boats from Weymouth, isn't that a lovely place . . .'

I was drenched with sweat, the bedclothes tangled. I emerged, eyes screwed against the light, and found safety.

Guernsey. A boarding house, locally a 'guesthouse'.

This lady with the tray of tea and whatnot was the one I'd come to stay with. I remembered the taxi driver. I was not sinking weighted down with flint cobbles. Life was great.

'Good morning,' I said. 'You're beautiful.'

'I hope you mean that!' she trilled, laughing. 'Shall I open the curtains?'

She did, and it was truly beautiful. I could almost see down into the harbour. She put the tray on my knees and poured the tea, started to butter the toast. I watched weakly.

'Mrs, er . . . ?'

'Mrs Vidamour, Mr Rant.' She judged me, decided, 'Rosa

to you. I'm a Guernésiaise born and bred, widow, and very proper. I have four guests presently. They're tourist workers, so are almost *never* in!' She served me the toast and tea. 'You're the sort who wants sugar I can tell so drink up because breakfast will be in thirty minutes and I expect you to eat it and not leave it like folk tend to nowadays but you'll want to know about Guernsey before you start out—'

'Ta, Rosa,' I said, recoiling, still overcome with relief at not being Gesso sinking into some place I didn't want to think of. 'Er, two things. Where's Bailiwick?'

She drew back, the better to inspect me. 'Bailiwick? The Bailiwick *is* Guernsey, and four small islands. Jersey is its own Bailiwick. The second?'

'Have you any museums, art galleries?'

She smiled. 'Oh, dear, Mr Rant. It truly *was* a ghastly flight, wasn't it? I can see we've quite a way to go. Guernsey has everything the mainland has. Let me tell you about them.'

'Please, Rosa,' I said, loving Guernsey. 'Call me Jonno.'

Rosa Vidamour's house was about a mile from the harbour. Nice, but I wasn't here to stare at water, with or without distant ships. Prior Metivier and his clique had used the O'Conor masterpiece to clear his gambling debts, sure. But he'd got another windfall, courtesy of me. That Chinese Warring States handle that I'd divvied was about as valuable as the O'Conor, so Metivier probably had a bit of money spare. And word was, he'd scarpered home to Guernsey. Fine by me. I wasn't here to suss his reasons. I was here to express my sense of reproach. And I honestly wasn't thinking of vengeance, retribution, reparation, all those ugly tit-for-tats that keep politics and wars going.

So I walked down the slope into the bonny town of St Peter Port.

The port itself had two marinas. One wasn't enough to cope with the number of yachts. The main harbour had ferries. Esplanades ran along the sea front. From there the town rose quite steeply to a skyline where the port's taller buildings showed – churches, a castellated turrety sort of tower. The cafés and shops were busy, people all about. Mrs Vidamour'd told me cars were forbidden on Sark, but you could hire one on Guernsey. 'Cheaper,' she interrupted herself sharply, 'than on Jersey.' Swift into local camouflage, I agreed that wicked old Jersey was extortionate about motor cars, the rotten lot.

Antique shops weren't plenteous, but there were some. In two hours I'd drifted past the main ones, and started hunting out others. By confessing myself the famous impressario, I received attention and advice from everybody. St Peter Port is lovely, the people a delight.

At the gallery, visitors were being taught about paintings. I listened to the gent who was giving the talk. Very knowledgeable. I heard him out and went to him after the group moved on.

'Morning,' I said. 'Liked your talk.'

'Dealer?' He was a rubicose man in a blazer, brass buttons with nautical emblems, club tie, moustache, innocent beery face except for the eyes.

'Me? No. I'm in showbiz. Just came in out of the rain.'

'Not across the harbour on a bicycle, presumably what?' he twinkled. I still hadn't got the hang of that saying. 'How can I help you?'

'Who's the expert on paintings?' I asked politely. 'Is it yourself?'

'Hardly. I'm a guide. Jimmy Ozanne. Old Guernsey name.'

'Good, er, good.' I tried to look pleased. 'Only, has anywhere here got a massive collection of modernist paintings? Expressionist, that sort of period? I'm due to meet a pal, and I've forgotten the name of the place he told me.'

He said, endearing himself, 'Your pal's possibly going to tackle Victor Hugo's house. Hugo wanted to be near Normandy, and lived here.'

Mrs Vidamour had already shown me how to look for the Normandy coast, 'should you wish to, Jonno'. I hadn't yet felt the need.

'Thought Victor Hugo was French?'

'Rum cove, him,' Jimmy Ozanne said. 'Settled here after being exiled, in 1855. Lived here fifteen years. Bought Hauteville House the following year and packed the place with bits of everything. He sliced up old furniture, diced and re-stitched carpets. Wandered half the night. Amusing old codger, what what?'

'Are his furnishings still there?' I asked, ill at the notion of an antiques slicer.

'Yes. You OK, Mr Rant?'

So much for secrecy. 'Bad crossing yesterday.' The thought of some silly old goon wantonly murdering antiques made me feel worse.

'There are tablets for airsickness. Ask Rosa Vidamour.'

'Ta,' I said. 'How do I find Hauteville House?'

'It's way out facing South Beach, Jonno. Quite a walk.'

He meant just over a mile. I made it at speed.

Three hours later I was sitting in a nosh bar – they're posh in Guernsey – almost sobbing into my coffee. Victor Hugo must have been a psychotic nut. The guide books seem so proud, of how he took pieces of craftsmen's genius and dissected them, then assembled the chucks as he thought fit. He painted and wrote, but at what cost? I went all over Hauteville House and felt ravished, my brain clattering about untethered in my skull from the daft old buffoon's massacres. OK, he did design tapestries and 'created'. And he collected, so it was well worth a robbery or two. Or three. But honour for Victor Hugo? He gets none from me, the destructive swine.

He built a glass-walled studio at the very top of the house. Sometimes he'd go and stare at France. Myself, I wish he'd done more gazing and less decorating. Everywhere, they give his quip, '*J'ai manqué ma vocation . . .*' Whatever it means, I hope it was a profound apology.

No Expressionist-like paintings there, though.

A shabby portly bloke with a garden gnome's beard and bedraggled attire came and sat opposite. He wore a grubby knitted wool hat, but it couldn't keep his locks in. I'd never seen so much hair on anybody. He watched me eat.

'Bit underdone, this,' I said, stopping. It was one of those long thinnish sandwiches, cheese and tomato, lettuce. I'd just started.

'Going to waste, hey? Pity.' He said it pit-ee. A local.

'Unless you could finish it for me?'

'If it'd help.'

'Ta.' I pushed it across. He fell on it. I gave him my tea. He slurped it. I was hungry, but hadn't much money left and dared not risk my last groat while he was around.

'You hate Victor Hugo, eh?' he said, scooping up the crumbs.

'I didn't. But any genius who uses a Sèvres dinner service as wallpaper is a prat.'

He guffawed, clapped. A waitress wagged a finger and called over, 'No trouble from you, Walt. Y'hear?'

'That Sèvres set was a gift from Charles X of France. Hugo did the same with Delft, porcelain from Rouen.' Walt eyed me. 'Upsetting, hey? Like the tapestries.' He stuck out a hand. 'Walt Jethou. You're Jonno Rant, *n'éche puis*?'

We shook. 'I'm looking for a decent painting, say 1890s or so, as a present for my cousin Ada. Looks like I'm on a loser.'

'Painting, hey? You need Gussy, hey?' He came to a decision with a slap on my arm. 'I'll take you! I know everything about every thing on Guernsey.'

A harbour tout. Well, I could do worse. 'Ta,' I said. 'One thing, Walt. Can you stop saying "hey"? It's driving me crazy.'

'Oh. Right, Jonno.' He stood. 'I'll get the wheels. Ten minutes, hey?'

Getting some quick replacement grub, I was in the middle of it when I decided to ring Symie at the Hippodrome back home, got him with Gladys's help.

'Any joy that end, Symie?' I asked straight out. I hated the thought of a wasted journey, and this trip was starting to look dicey.

'No, son,' Symie said. 'The bird's flown after her bruv. Where are yer?'

'Here and there, Symie. Sure she's gone from East Anglia?'

'Sure. Oh, Paula's brother Horace come in. Asks if you want a cross or a slab.'

'Cross, tell him.' I didn't like the thought of a great single rectangle of stone standing up above the hillside like half a jaw with the other in the earth beneath. 'Symie? Ask

Freddy Foxheath to suss out any of them painting look-alikes, eh?'

'Right. And Desdemona's asking what the hell you erecting stones to her old feller for. She's narked, Lovejoy.'

'Ah,' I said. 'Hang on.' I bipped, made a burring noise and clicked my tongue, replaced the receiver. People do nothing but quibble.

'Who're you trying to get, love?' a waitress asked. 'Ask Directory Inquiries.'

For a second I looked at her. She looked back. I thanked her, did as she said. After which I also looked in the phone book. Prior Georges Xavier Metivier was listed, at Metivier Mansion, in the parish of St Sampson.

'Will you marry me?' I asked the lass. She said, 'Get on with you', and scolded that my tea'd get cold.

They must have a lifetime of handling duckeggs like me, so many cocky visitors. I ate until my money ran out, but things now weren't all that bad. From the café I could just see the place where Guernsey had burnt its witches at the stake in 1580. Maybe Jersey had behaved even worse? I went out to meet my new ally.

18

WAITING ON THE pavement for Walt Jethou's car, I thought how to get money. Antiques? In a place you don't really know, fast gelt can be difficult – I mean quick enough to pay for your next meal, your lodgings. And Walt Jethou would need a few bawbees for chauffeuring me about. Plus, I'd need to pay Rosa Vidamour for the pad. I stood watching happy holiday-makers arriving. When you're broke, happiness makes you think of con tricks, doesn't it? Being here wasn't my idea. I'd been driven to it.

A toddler came along the pavement, chuffing at its reins. It clasped my trouser leg.

'Dadda!' it bawled. I said hello. Its dad tried hauling it off.

'Sorry, mate,' he said, red-faced. 'He sees a leg and goes for it.' Passing women laughed, making me redden.

'Like that for life,' I said. The little family barrelled on down the pavement.

But a glim of truth shone there. See one, see all. See one painting in the feeble gloaming of a dim chapel, and you think of lots of others. After I'd proved their O'Conor worthwhile by nicking it – Gesso obviously babbled before he'd, well, whatever. Then somebody had stolen it back from my workshop – plenty of suspects for that, including Prince, even including Hawkeyes Summer of the Plod. Then Marie Metivier confidently sold it off. A new big question was looming in my mind. Was their canvas from a hidden cache of many?

A scarecrow flapped up on a wheezing moped which coughed to a standstill in front of me as I waited. The figure wore a bulbous crash helmet, black visor, and beckoned. I was about to tell it to sod off, then peered closer.

'That you, Walt?'

'Hop aboard, Jonno.'

Chauffeur, indeed. I hopped and clung. A policeman waved us down.

'Helmet, sir,' he said. 'It's the law.'

Walt grunted, gave me his. I put it on. Inside it stank of brandy. Walt unfolded some home-made leatherette thing, inserting mysterious slabs into slots. The policeman watched, sighing.

'I'm not sure that's legal, Walt,' he said.

'It's my own patent design, Pete,' Jethou told the bobby, muffled.

We puttered off in style. Within a furlong I saw a likely antique shop, but the blighter wouldn't stop.

Augusta Quenard's gallery – Walt kept shouting its praises over his shoulder – was basically a wooden lean-to shed with half a window and a drunken door. The board cladding was rotting. Eight feet square, no more.

We drove up, the little two-stroke croaked to silence, and we alighted. Walt took off his helmet and shouted, 'Gussy! Customer!'

'Hardly that,' I said, uneasy. 'Where are we?'

'Where it matters, Jonno,' Walt said. 'She'll be out in a minute.'

The shed looked slammed against a brick barn wall. I noticed an improvised chimney stuck on the gable. Talk about ramshackle.

'When tomatoes were the thing, Jonno,' a lady said, emerging, 'this barn was filled with workers, packing produce for the London markets.'

You try not to gape, but some women deserve astonishment. This lady looked elegant, but in a demented way. Wide golden hat, flowers adorning its brim, white lace gloves, a full skirt with high heels, a neckline frothy to her chin, so much make-up that she looked camera-ready. Thick red lipstick, rouge, eyelashes caked with black mascara, earrings dangling to her shoulders. Beautiful, needed only a little more make-up. My old Gran would have called her 'mutton dressed as lamb'; but what's wrong with mutton?

'How do you do, missus.' Regally she extended her hand. I almost bent to kiss it, but squeezed instead. 'Er, everything changed, has it?'

'You can't imagine, Jonno. Things have gone sadly down.'

That surprised me, though you always get knockers who can't see good in anything. To me, Guernsey looked on the crest of a wave, friendly and lovely, as long as you came for the right reasons, unlike me.

'Really?' I did a crest-of-a-wave plug. She wasn't from – gasp! – Jersey?

'Certainly not! Enter.'

She said it like admitting me to the Sistine Chapel. Into the shed Walt leapt, switching on a light. He too felt this urge to serve in the presence of a lady. One naked bulb, half an erg, showed a wall crammed with paintings, mostly copies of Victor Hugo's useless daubs in Hauteville House.

'Superb reproductions, Jonno,' she breathed. 'Don't you think?'

'Mmmmh,' I said, walking round. Two paces, two across, then back. They were rubbish, the sort that fills boot fairs to no purpose. A kiddie could have done better with a paint-by-numbers birthday box. 'Really, er, ta for showing me.'

'Tell me, Jonno,' she trilled, spinning quite like a ballerina on an off day. 'Which one *really* gets your fancy?'

'Well, Gussy, they're all, er . . .'

She sagged. I really do mean drooped. Her shoulders slumped. It's a terrible thing to see hope drain away so nothing's left. Men do it differently. When it happens to us we more or less look the same outwardly, but it's our spark that fades as our irises hollow out. But women somehow reveal it as a whole, as if their life is condemned.

'I know,' she said in a broken voice. 'They're no good, are they?'

'No, love.' You have to be honest.

'Here, you,' Walt said. I gave him the bent eye. I didn't want a brawl.

'Did you paint them, Gussy?'

'Yes.' She tried a smile, which was even worse. 'When Walt phoned that he was bringing a rich customer I put out my very best.' She blotted her eyes. The mascara ran. 'I've others, but they're more or less of a kind.'

'No harm looking.' God, they were dreadful. She'd have done better chucking the paint at the canvas and calling herself a neo-modernist.

'Gussy's a great artist, hey,' Walt growled.

She led me into the barn. The end was partitioned off,

wood erected on a dicey run of breeze blocks. Derelict, except for old fruit boxes.

'Come in.' She did her heart-rending smile, pulled aside a screen.

It was a dosser's quarter. A truckle bed, one chair, a lopsided chest of drawers. In the corner stood an easel, with paints, brushes, jam jars. Paintings sloped against the wall. Above, girders and rafters. So she lived here. Well, she was behaving like a real artist, if nowt else.

'Don't you get cold?' Women are always on about cold.

'Terribly. I have an electric fire.' She spoke dully. She turned her canvases like leaves of a book while I stood.

'She's marvellous, hey?' Walt Jethou almost choked on admiration.

'Mmmh.' Love comes in many a guise, they say. It wasn't for me to pop his balloon, but I couldn't honestly encourage Gussy. It'd only end in tears. 'Hang on, Gussy,' I said, noticing. 'That's the fifth.'

She had exposed several paintings more or less identical – 'of a kind,' she'd said. Greys, muted patches of greys variously tinted, with black intersecting curves across its face. All five were bigger than her pathetic copies of Victor Hugo's daubs. An artist is crucified by expense – canvas, frames, paints, brushes. I really do believe that artists should be heavily subsidized, if not by tons of actual money, at least by making pigments and materials untaxed and cheap as possible. The point was that Gussy, broke, had copied a single painting time after time, on large canvases she couldn't even afford. This phenomenon shrieks of the artistic impulse, whatever the result.

She laughed self-consciously, but bitter. 'Guernsey people call it my mad picture.'

'Gussy does it often, that's all.' Walt would take a swing if I sneered.

'Excuse me, please.' I stepped round him to see.

Nine? She'd done nine. I sat on her chair unasked and had her arrange them in a line in front of me. They were the same, as near as anybody could tell. Now, one artist painting the same vision over and over varies things, however slightly. Like Paul Klee's simple bird paintings, never the same twice, and he turned them out like Fords. These were copies, but not of a vision. They were copies of a painting.

I cleared my throat, looked from Gussy to her row of canvases.

'What's the matter with him?' Gussy asked Walt nervously.

'Gussy, love,' I said. 'Brew up. You and me need a chat.'

She'd clearly been obsessed, over and over. I'd done right, coming to Guernsey. An idea germinated.

Her tea was execrable, but under Walt's glare I drank it good as gold.

'Nice tea, Gussy,' I said.

'I paint a painting I once saw as a child,' she said. She felt awkward, confessing to a secret neurosis. 'Does that sound silly?'

I told her, 'I paint paintings I sometimes haven't seen at all. When and where was the original?'

'I was a little girl,' she said, going dreamy with reminiscence. 'I used to walk by the shore. It's quite safe here in the Channel Isles. I was trying to paint.' She smiled shyly. 'I was always like that, artistic, without talent.' She dabbed her eyes, had a go with a hand mirror, gave up. 'I was drawing a huge offshore rock called La Grosse. It was a fine day, so I walked down to the beach, climbed over some rocks, leaving my drawing box up above.'

'The scene evoked the image?' I said doubtfully.

'No, silly. I saw the painting.'

'Somebody else was down by the sea, painting it?' There was that famous short story, wasn't there, of a man meeting Picasso, who was sketching in the sand with a walking stick, and the tide came and washed the sand drawing away.

'No. The painting.' She spoke as if to an imbecile. 'There was a pram standing out to sea, a man rowing round the headland. The light was glary, too bright for me.' She laughed, shamefaced. 'I was always poorly sighted, though Dr Oldham has done wonders and I see quite well since—'

'The picture, love.'

'There was a rock tunnel, for ammunition supplies, an old gun mounting. Water was on the ground, a trickle down one wall. It caused the eeriest reflections. I can see it now.'

She was so tranquil it worried me, her voice sounding far off, staring into space.

'I saw a stack of canvases propped against the sea cave's wall.' She came to, to explain, 'You do that in case the surface—'

'I know, I know.'

'I felt really excited, like in some brilliant adventure, you know, Enid Blyton, those children's writers?' I nodded. 'They were all beautifully framed, some gilded and heavy looking. I was naughty, but a look could do no harm, could it? It was quite bright in the tunnel, only a few yards in, that horrid sea glare reflecting everywhere. I pulled the end one away, and stared at it.'

'And it was the painting?'

Her expression was so utterly serene that I couldn't help wishing I could have painted her there and then.

'Yes. Grey, seeming at first nothing more, with thin arcs of black intersecting each other. Simple touches of greens, fawns, blues, rose madders, all so faint that you'd think there was nothing but grey.' She smiled, wistful. 'It seemed the purest thing I'd ever seen in my life. I do mean purest. I still see it in the night, in my mind's eye. It was an artistic miracle.'

'Purest?' That was an odd word.

'Watch it, you,' Walt growled, thinking I was criticizing.

'Shush up, Walt,' Gussy said sadly. 'He knows what I mean.'

'It was exactly like these that you've done?'

She spoke with the longing of sorrow. 'Exactly? No, hardly that. But I try.'

'What did you do?' She looked back at me blankly. I went on, guilty. 'Well, there you were alone in the sea cave. Plenty would have nicked it, and scarpered off up the cliff.' I added quickly, in case she got the wrong idea, 'I don't mean that I would, of course.'

'Steal it?' said this emotion-filled saint, in horror. 'I'm speaking of a work of art, Jonno!'

'Course you are,' I said weakly, avoiding Walt's accusing eyes.

'I climbed back over the rocks, making sure the pram was now out of sight. I went up to the greensward, got my sketch box, and went back down. I had the silly idea of copying it while nobody could see. Going down to the sea took me quite a time.'

'And the man in the rowing boat?'

'Gone. So was the lovely picture. And so were all of them,' she said in sorrow. 'I hurried to see if he was rowing

the paintings out to some boat anchored offshore. I hoped
to recognize it, you see, if it came into the Marina.
Nothing.'

'That was it?' I couldn't take my eyes off her copies.

'Vanished. Quite like a dream. I tried drawing it that
same night. I even sent my copy painting in to the children's
art competition.' She sniffed, blew her nose. 'They laughed
at me, and said I was deranged.'

Not while Walt was around, I'll bet.

'People think me silly in the head.' She rummaged in a
handbag for another tissue. 'I painted it every chance I got.
Still do. I became a figure of fun. I started dresing up to
match their perceptions.' She looked defiance at me.
'Flinging a pot of paint in the public's face, you see.'

John Ruskin's famous condemnation of Whistler that led
to the notorious lawsuit in Victorian London.

'Were there any paintings left in the cave, love?' I asked
gently. 'You did check?'

'Of course. I went again and again. I was always there,
until Father stopped me going. He tried to get me into an
art school on the mainland. I wasn't good enough.' She
smiled, gathered herself. 'But I won't be beaten. You see,
those who deride me never saw the original, did they? But
I did. I shall carry on. One day Walt will bring somebody
who likes my work. Then maybe people will stop laughing
at Daft Gussy.'

'Walt?' I asked. 'You bring customers here. Is that it,
how you manage?'

'Yes.' He did his glare, until I told him to knock it off
for Christ's sake. I'd had enough trouble without nerks like
him.

'Let me get it straight,' I said. 'Gussy does her paintings.
You haunt St Peter Port where the ferries dock. You try to

wheedle tourists here, and sell them Gussy's copies of the Hugo pictures?'

'Yes. It's how we make ends meet.'

A shore tout and a repro shed. Hardly a scam to keep Scotland Yard sleepless.

'Have you any antiques at all?' I asked this loony, not so loony, pair.

They both said no. Gussy was looking. I don't like women to look at me closely like she was doing, quizzical but with a half-knowing obliquity.

'Do you know anybody who has?' I asked.

'Well,' Walt began. 'There's three shops in St Peter Port.'

Gussy laid a hand on his arm. He went quiet.

'One thing first, Jonno,' she said quietly. 'Who are you?'

'Me?' I said. 'I told you. I'm an impressario from . . .' I petered out. She was a laser gazer, and a man can't resist much of that. I shrugged. What harm could it possibly do? Jonno Rant, impressario, or Lovejoy the wandering antique dealer, I was still broke.

'First, you can call me Lovejoy. It's my name. Forget the Jonno Rant bit. Next thing, maybe it's time you exhibited your pictures properly.' I thought of Florida, Mrs Jocina Crucifex and her husband Martin, Irma Dominick and a gambling-addicted prior. Oh, and Gesso.

'Exhibit?' Hope fired in her eyes, and died. 'Nobody would come to see them,' she said forlornly. 'And they'd only laugh.'

'We could show them in a way that nobody would laugh, love,' I said bluntly. 'Let me explain a couple of things.'

So I did, but only a couple. My plan wasn't much good, but what plan ever is?

19

'**H**ELLO? CAN I please speak with Florida?'

'Who wants her?' the bloke groused.

'Bert Postlethwaite, her horse trainer,' I snapped, really narked. Try to help people, all you get is aggro. 'Hurry, please. Her horse Benjamin has got distemper.'

Silence. 'I thought only dogs got distemper.'

See? 'It's terminal, tell her.'

He clonked the receiver down, grumbling. 'Some lunatic, Florida. If it's that barmy antique dealer—'

'Hello? Mr Postlethwaite, is it?'

'Yes.' I heard her stifle a laugh. I'm usually Lieutenant Carruthers of the Dragoons when I ring her, but her husband long since sussed that. 'Look, love. I need gelt—'

'Wait a moment, please, Mr Postlethwaite. I'll get a pencil.' A door clicked, and she returned, breathy. 'Lovejoy. What the hell are you playing at? The police took off after you through the woods . . .'

The phone ate my borrowed zlotniks.

'Listen, dwoorlink, I rang you because I'm daft about you, and want to know how to organize a gambling game.'

'Darling,' she said, all misty. 'You're a swine.' Then, sharply, 'Gambling? You, Lovejoy?'

'Sort of,' I said. 'It was you gave me the idea. That conversation in Franco's restaurant, remember? And we *are* partners, after all. There's lots of real sordid risk, dwoorlink,' I ended in a burst of genius.

She said thickly, 'Real *sordid* risk, Lovejoy? Can I bring a friend?'

'Be my guest,' I invited grandly. 'Only, I can't quite work the odds out. It's not horses. I need a few quid to set it up. Could you advance me—?'

Click. Purr. I cut the phone in the nick of time. I winked at Gussy, waiting with me. Walt Jethou was at the kerb on his machine.

'Ready, steady, go!' I cracked, smiling. 'Can we all get on that thing?'

'No, Lovejoy,' Gussy said. She'd added more make-up, looked nineteenth century in her vast flowered hat and lace gloves. 'I'll phone for a car.'

Which arrived ten minutes later, and off we drove to the abode of a middle-aged couple.

The bungalow was what I'd call average. The antique dealers Meg and Joe Carriere, had converted their parlour into a small showroom. They were nervous, treating Gussy warily as some madwoman. Meg definitely saw Walt Jethou as somebody to avoid, all but asking him to wait outside. I began to wonder if I should have thought twice before teaming up with this rum couple, but by then we were indoors and I had to brazen it out.

'I ran into Mr Jethou at the harbour.' I was calm and proper. 'He overheard me asking the way to the nearest antique dealer, and offered to put me in touch with you. Good of you to let me call.'

Meg said eagerly, 'What are you interested in, Mr, er . . . ?'

'Lovejoy,' I told her. In for a penny. 'Any antique. I'm doing a sweep of the Channel Isles. After this, Winchester, then Cornwall and Dorset. Only limited funds, mind you—'

'Of course!' Meg cried quickly. 'You've a spending limit!'

'As long as the antiques are right,' I finished for her. Antique dealers always chant this litany. Politeness, before a joust to the death.

She ushered me in. 'Take your time, Lovejoy.'

'Ta.' I gave Gussy and Walt the bent eye, and they faded into the garden. We'd agreed that I'd do better on my own.

And I was left alone with homely Meg and her antiques. Her artisan husband went to make some coffee. The room was fitted out with long shelves, a dais and display stands. Every inch was covered in some antique, near antique, fake, ranging from dross to desirable. Not too bad. I felt quite lifted.

Meg's accent was Midlands, almost Birmingham. She was fortyish, quite dumpy but neat. I often wonder how women see us, because they've not as much to go on from men's clothes, whereas their own gear always gives more clues. I often wonder why women's dress varies so much. I mean, two birds in different frocks look gorgeous, but two in similar frocks is total war – barmy, when they're both still just as gorgeous anyway.

'Lovely piece of brass, that,' I said, nodding, smiling. 'Have you got a ruler?'

I'd left my essential antique-hunter's kit behind. They're what every antiques fan needs when scavenging for bargains. (Don't pay more than a few pence for this kit, incidentally.) Simply buy a tape measure, marked in metric and imperial, a folded colour chart of artist's pigments – they're never perfect, but colourmen suppliers give them away free. Then buy a loupe of ×10 magnification for close work – and *don't* believe the fallacy that the more powerful the lenses the better. Add a tiny pencil torch (sorry, Gesso; sleep sound, pal) with a concentrated beam. If you can afford it, get a McArthur microscope. This is a work of outstanding genius, being a powerful microscope no bigger than a box of matches. You plonk it down on any surface and inspect everything from wood graining and sawing marks to lathe cuts and artists' brush strokes. They make children's versions now – not as good as the real thing. If technology scares you, forget the little microscope and make do with the tape measure, the colour chart, the hand lens and the torch. They'll save you a fortune, and maybe earn you one.

Meg returned. 'It's our daughter's school ruler, I'm afraid, Lovejoy.'

'No matter.' It took a minute to measure the armillary sphere. Every dimension was accurate, but in modern metric. I pursed my lips, judged Meg for a second. Like I said a second ago, in for a penny.

'Love, did you buy this as genuine eighteenth century?'

'Yes.' Worry washed age into her pleasant face. 'Isn't it?'

'Some reppers – blokes who copy old instruments like navigating quadrants, astrolabes and such – use old machinery. Lathes, hand engravers, old chisels, heaven knows what.'

'But how can I tell that?' she cried. The age-old whimper of the dealer who's overspent.

'Measuring helps, love.' Sadly I returned her ruler. 'Reppers are often weak on learning. The great old encyclopedias – Abraham Rees's *Cyclopaedia* that he finished in 1820, or the huge French *L'Encyclopédie* of Diderot and D'Alembert; there are others – cost a mint, but contain all the guidance you need to rebuild antiques of the period. The giveaway is that most reppers can't afford those books, see?'

She looked at the ruler in her hand.

'So reppers use modern metric for ease, love. They don't have an original to copy from, either. They just hope a buyer will be impressed by appearance.'

'It's a fake?' Meg was dejected. She must have paid a lot.

'Always do two close-ups on early brass instruments, love.' I pretended to go Sherlock Holmes, imaginary magnifying glass at the ready. 'Sheet-rolled brass came in the seventeenth century. You can see the striae, scored lines in the surface, very fine. Reppers use modern brass, and 'dab' its surface with a small round hammer, to deceive you into thinking all its bits were hammered. You see a pock-marked surface on forgeries.' I nodded at her armillary. 'They'll be there.'

'Even though you didn't look?'

'I've no loupe lenses, Meg.' Then I remembered I was supposed to be a rich dealer on a sweep. 'Er, I always forget my tackle.' My chuckle sounded unconvincing. 'Which of your antiques is the best?'

'That chair.' She sounded so proud. It stood in a corner, labelled PLEASE DO NOT SIT. 'Chippendale. Isn't it beautiful?'

No fake is really ever beautiful, though a dealer trying to sell it would believe it exquisite. It emitted not a single chime. I walked past it to look at a small brass snake, raised as if to strike, its tongue hooked downwards.

'Ugh,' Meg said with a shiver. 'Horrid thing. I tried to talk Joe out of buying that, but he's so stubborn.'

Good old Joe. Time for honesty. 'Listen, Meg. This snake's a watch stand, maybe a century and a half old. That diamond-seated corner chair's a terrible fake – the

decorative back splats are too wide. Besides, the dowel pins
– those little wooden rods in the legs holding the chair
together – should stand proud.'

'They do, Lovejoy,' she cried, horrified. 'Feel!'

'Yes, love,' I explained patiently. 'But not because the
wooden leg's shrunk. The faker's made them to stand out,
and then had to stain them darker so they'd look old.'

'You haven't looked yet, Lovejoy. So how—?'

'Because he does.' Joe was standing there, holding a tray
with five cups and some biscuits. 'Know, I mean, Meg.'

'Know?' She looked, him to me and back. 'Of course he
knows. He's a rich antique dealer, Joe!'

'Don't be daft.' I did my laugh, worse than ever.

'He's a divvy,' Joe said evenly. I decided I didn't like Joe.
The swine must have been listening. 'He can feel the real.'

'Oh.' Instantly Meg was all panicky glances. I chucked
in the sponge.

'I have to read up the prices just like you. But Joe's right.'

'Oh, dear.' She almost broke down. 'You'll know the
Rockingham, then.'

'Yes.' Lot of Rockingham about. Well, there would be,
in the land of Jocina Crucifex, famed collector. There was
a little dish. Somebody had painted it skilfully with countri-
fied scenery. 'To forge Rockingham, love, make sure the
rococo decoration's asymmetrical. It's very tempting to
balance it up, because that's neater and easier. Forgers do
one half like you've done here, then make a simple reverse
cast mould of it for the opposite. The old workers didn't.
They weren't scared of art.'

'No wonder . . .' Meg drooped. Lot of drooping today,
too.

'Shhhh, Meg,' Joe warned. He distributed the coffee.

'No wonder what?' I asked, tense.

'There's a lady here in Guernsey who collects Rockingham. We wrote to her and offered the dish. We thought we'd get away with it. She took one look and left in a temper. No wonder.' Meg sniffed. 'We thought our dish was so beautiful, Lovejoy. Dove worked *so* hard.'

At least Jocina wasn't a fool. So this couple had a private faker. 'Dove?'

'She's our daughter. She's not very active. She does our painting.' Meg dismissed Joe's cautions. 'It's no good, Joe, if he's one of those witch people, a sorchier.'

'Steady on, love,' I said, uneasy. 'I'm the same as everybody else.'

'We do reproductions. Joe makes the furniture. I do embroideries and pottery, but the glazes are a terrible trial. Sometimes they're completely wrong.' She smiled diffidently. 'I'm not very good.'

'Do you label them all as repros, fakes?'

She avoided my eye. 'Of course.'

Oh, aye, I thought cynically, don't we all.

'Your daughter around, is she?' After all, the Rockingham dish wasn't so bad.

'I'll see.' Joe left. Me and Meg politely toured her wares. Joe returned and ushered me down the corridor to a bedroom.

'This is Lovejoy, Dove. He's a divvy.'

For a second I could hardly see anything, the room was so cluttered. Then my eyes accustomed themselves, and there was this girl in some sort of frame on a bed, with rods, cords, pulleys over her chest. She had a brush in her teeth. Her dad took it out, placed it on a rack that floated above her on strings. I advanced cautiously. I never know what to say to sick people. I penetrated the tangle, bussed her.

'Hello, love. You the artist? Gussy and Walt never said.'

She smiled, rueful. 'I get in rather a mess. I'm so sorry.'

'Well, you would, in all that gear.' She did it with her teeth. I realized my hand was stuck out for a handshake, snatched it back and hid it, going red.

She forgave. People up against it always do. 'I can do so much more now Dad stays at home. We're famous forgers, you see.'

Her smile lit the room. I thought, how the hell does she keep going, for heaven's sake?

'You're not bad at Rockingham, Dove. I was just telling your mother.' I searched for something to praise. 'I liked your artistic stuff in the showroom.'

'Oil painting's the worst, though you'd think water-colours'd be hopeless, having to paint at this angle.'

'Try tempera. You can work with a much drier brush, unless you're doing dry-brush mid-Victorian watercolours.' Tip: dry-brush antiques look wondrous, but usually go cheaper in antique shops nowadays, so watch out.

She was interested. 'Maybe I shall. But tempera paints are very expensive, aren't they?'

'Make them up yourself. All you need is the powdered pigment and a raw egg yolk.' She had a whole bookcase filled with art books. 'Could you do some forgeries on parchment for me, on commission, once I get straight?'

She smiled mischievously. Meg adjusted her pillows carefully, offered her a drink from a complicated curled straw. 'You already have a local artist, Lovejoy!'

'I bumped into Walt at Hauteville House.'

Dove was lovely but goading. 'With your divvy sense you managed to avoid buying one of her Mondrians?'

My face must have changed because she looked suddenly apprehensive. 'Oh, dear. You *didn't*!'

'Er, no.' I stood beside her bed, seeing in my mind those endless paintings, those black arcs on teeming feculent greys. 'Mondrian, you said.'

'Have I got him wrong?' Dove asked seriously. 'She's brought some here once or twice. I don't think Gussy knows very much about painting, actually. But it's nice that she keeps trying, don't you think?'

'Oh, definitely, love.' I edged to the door. Action called.

'Lovejoy,' Dove said. 'Will you come again?' She could see I was suddenly nervy.

'Definitely, love,' I said. 'Definitely.' I said definitely too often, but I meant it. I wasn't here by accident. Once Metivier decided to enlist my help, it was inevitable. 'Definitely.'

20

OUTSIDE THE CARRIERES' house I interrogated Walt Jethou and Gussy without mercy, going over and over the same ground. Was Joe Carriere safe? How long had he and Meg been married? Was Dove really ill, all those pulleys? Where did they get their antiques, what could they afford, who came from the mainland to visit? I wanted reliable answers, ignoring Gussy when she finally screamed that she'd had enough. She rounded on Walt, for bringing her an obvious madman and crying who needed an idiot anyway, all that.

'I've already *got* morons!' she cried, wagging her lace-covered hand for Walt to drive her home.

He said, 'Go on, Lovejoy. Where do we come in?'

'I want to sell my paintings!' Gussy screeched. 'All Lovejoy keeps on about is who Meg Carriere brings home for tea.'

'No, Gussy.' Walt was calmer, peering at me. 'Lovejoy's wondering whether to bring the Carrieres into his scam.'

'Scam?' Christ, I thought, they'll hear in Jersey. 'What scam?'

'To make Gussy's paintings famous?' Walt asked me, by

way of reply. 'To pull a big money hook with antiques? Which, Lovejoy?'

'My paintings, famous?' Gussy gaped, clutched my hand. We were friends.

'Shut your teeth, love. Who're the Carrieres' friends?'

'The Gascons,' they both answered together. Gussy, suddenly more intense, took it up. 'She's not real Guernésiaise, of course, but at least she's not from Jersey.'

'Do they go to church?' I sighed, tired, as their expressions changed. 'Answer the frigging question.'

'No.' They glanced at each other. 'They had a row with Prior Metivier and changed parishes.' Gussy added frostily, 'You don't *do* that sort of thing.' She spoke like it was spreading leprosy.

My sort of people, the Carrieres. Maybe I could trust them, along with Walt Jethou and Augusta Quenard? Trust only fifty per cent, of course. Well, maybe thirty.

'What's the matter?' Joe was there beside the driver's door, Meg peering anxiously out from her steps. 'Can't you get her started, Walt?'

'Er, got a sec, Joe?' I said, wearing my sincere smile. 'I've an idea.'

'Antiques,' I told them, sitting on this stool in Dove's french window space, them around me like Sunday school children, 'are among the biggest illegitimate sources of gelt in the world. Some say that we – I mean,' I added hastily, '*they*, the forgers and thieves in the trade – come second, after arms dealers, drugs and banking frauds.'

'Lovejoy.' Joe was worried 'Why're you telling us this?'

'Background, Joe.' I smiled my sincere smile at Meg. Dove watched intently from her pillow. 'I want us all to understand where we're at.' It sounded wrong, because I can't talk that modern slangy stuff. 'Where we're coming from,' I tried doubtfully, and gave up. 'Understand,' I said firmly, my own lingo. 'You can't know what's fair unless I tell you what's unfair, right?'

'But—'

'Daddy!' Dove scolded impatiently. Like a good father Joe shut it.

'There are three levels of antiques, and of dealers who find them. Sometimes,' I added, unsmiling, 'dealers include real people, but not often. Think of an ocean. The bottom level of antiques is plankton. That means cheapest. Second come the plankton feeders – the dealers who find antiques in junk sales, fairgrounds, vicarages, house clearances, any-where Out There. These plankton feeders can even be giant whales – TV scouts on a countryside sweep happening across some valuable painting in their telly *Antique Road Shows*. Or the plankton feeder can be stickleback size, meaning a casual collector or low-grade dealer who just blunders onto some valuable ornament. Fakes and forgeries are rife at plankton level,' I added, looking at Meg. 'And plankton feeders aren't all honest. They'll sell you a fake Sheraton chair as genuine, if they can.' Meg had the grace to blush. 'Or,' I added, 'an armillary sphere.'

'Is that us?' Dove asked with delight.

I eyed her. Some folk can be too quick for their own good. 'You're no giants, Dove, but yes, I mean you.'

'Which is our ornament?' she asked, smiling.

'You'll have us here all frigging day,' I complained, but went and brought the stone carving. It was some nine inches high, a small mountain-shaped reddish sculpture of nine intertwined dragons. The top one had a small ball in its mouth. They were coiled about a large Chinese coin carved in the centre. The stone had been hollowed out, but must have weighed nearly three pounds. 'This.'

'You're wrong, Lovejoy,' Joe said. I looked at him, seeing where his bolshie daughter got it from. 'I did its density. It's not jade.'

'I know. It's Shou-Shan rock. It's not as tough as jadeite jade, but carves easier. It's more opaque. But it's an important carving none the less. Hong Kong includes Kowloon. It means "nine dragons". Count them on your carving.'

Shou-Shan is a small town in Fukien, less than forty miles from Foochow. It's famous for this stuff.

'The yellowish stone's most sought after, for carving Chinese seals – those "name chops" everybody buys on holiday. Your name in Chinese characters, y'know?'

'Is it valuable?' Meg breathed, keen to get back brownie points.

'Not very, but not cheap, love.' And, as she brightened, 'It'll look pretty, washed clean, mounted on mahogany against scarlet velvet. Nowadays it's a historic document. It might buy you a good used car.'

'See?' Meg squealed and clapped her hands. Gussy looked on, waiting. She wanted news of my scam that would sell her paintings. I smiled to encourage the little bit of jubilation, because artists can be a right frigging pest.

'I'll write it out. There's another place, Chin-tien in Chekiang, which markets stone used to imitate jadeite jade. It's quite easy to fake this stuff, using Suffolk flint ground small in Polyfilla powder, but I can't stand those acrylic paints you have to use . . .' I realized what I was saying, and went red. 'Er, I've *heard* that's what forgers do.'

'I think I've seen another carving like that, but smaller,' Joe said.

'Keep it up, Joe. They're all over. People sell them cheap *because* they're not jade. Ever heard anything so daft? So many people were out East in the days of the Raj. And keep an eye out for medals, anything from brasswork to ivory buttons. Never a boot sale but what there's four or five suchlike on the stalls.'

'Oh, weren't we lucky!' Meg marvelled, while Gussy looked askance. She was impatient for the world to focus on her.

'It happens, love.' I wanted to get it across that finds are not as rare as all that. 'Finds can be apocalyptic. Every week there are stunning windfalls. Somebody lately found the city of Urkesh, 4,500 years old, underneath a town in Syria, where the ancient Hurrian civilization flowered. The very next day, Alfred Gilbert's statue of Perseus popped up in some tiny flat belonging to a defunct headmaster in Bristol.' I described the exquisite cast in high bronze, almost weeping in jealous rage. The lucky swine had discovered the original commissioned version, inscribed *Fonderia Nelli, Roma*, the Italian centre of Victorian lost-wax bronze casting. That mark on a bronze sculpture is the giveaway, the gateway to the highest prices, so keep an eye out.

'It's not fair,' I went on miserably. 'See, we deserve some massive find like that. Think of what we could ... er.' I collected myself, noticing that they were all staring at me. 'Sorry,' I ended lamely. 'I get carried away.'

'What're the last, Lovejoy?' Dove asked. 'You said three levels of antiques and dealers. Plankton, then plankton feeders, then ... ?'

'Sharks, love.'

There was a momentary silence.

'Which will we be?' she asked, really enjoying herself.

'Plankton.' I smiled, innocent. 'Though we might feed a little.'

'Antiques sharks, Lovejoy?' Dove pressed. 'Here in Guernsey?'

'Good heavens!' I cried, laughing. 'Who'd even think such a thing? Sharks are voracious, use any savagery to snaffle antiques!'

That's antiques for you in a nutshell. Plankton, the plankton feeder and the shark. I hid the ultimate question: which of the three is the next antique hunter you'll meet? You never know the answer to that.

On which high note we ended. I listed the best of Meg's stock – hardly worth more than she'd paid – and borrowed a few quid. We all shook hands on the deal, which I'd carefully omitted to define. I promised to come next day with the whole plan.

Walt and Gussy drove me back. They put me down on a small cliff near the harbour, from where I could watch the boats.

My only remaining obstacle was to legitimize my presence on Guernsey. I watched two small yachts – cutters, were they? – luffing, or whatever it's called, rounding the headland. I looked at every promontory anew, now I'd heard Gussy's childhood tale. I had to think of a legit way to *be* here. I was already disguised as the showbiz bloke called Jonno, the one who'd sicked the Plod on to me. I wanted to be here as me, Lovejoy the innocent, Lovejoy who could be forgiven for masquerading as somebody else.

Forgiven by whom? By those in power, who might arrest me for impersonation. It was small beer, really. Antique dealers are always at it, pretending this daub is by Leonardo da Vinci, that manky hatchet work is by Michelangelo, this pathetic scribble's in Shakespeare's hand, and so on. I didn't care if I was here as Jonno Rant or King Kong, as long as I got nearer whatever treasures Prior Metivier was hoarding. I swear it was only that. For all I knew, Gesso was fine and I was jumping to conclusions.

How had I come in the first place? A distant ferry hove into view, steaming cross the horizon.

It had all started with Irma Dominick's desire to steal a worthless necklace from Gimbert's Auction. She gets herself arrested for stealing, not her necklace, but some Rockingham jug. I get Michaelis Singleton, wino lawyer, to spring her. The porcelain anyway belonged to Mrs Jocina Crucifex, her aunt, famed Rockingham collector. I'm meanwhile faking, with brilliance, a rare bookcase for Prince, blue-blooded spendthrift with hardly a neurone between his ears but who has money plus a shrewd sense of deception. Then – I'd lost track – I finish up pretending to be Jonno Rant, after encountering Metivier and his lovely but hate-filled sister Marie at the boot sale, who admit to having antiques they want me to divvy. 'Farther than you'll ever know, Lovejoy,' Marie'd said at our first meeting, and 'More than you'll ever see.' So Prior George had a cache of antiques. And where else but here in Guernsey?

Estranged from gorgeous Florida because I wasn't a gambler, I gain approval from Marie Metivier for the same reason. (Don't ask me to explain *that* paradox.) Gesso, part-time worker at Metivier's financially strapped Albansham Priory, proves me a divvy by that trick in the cloister. Good old Jocina Crucifex has me join her fundraising team to support the priory. The Plod's in there too – Summer, no less. I suspect that he's barmy over Jocina – well, weren't we all, including none other than Prior George himself?

Martin Crucifex is fiercely loyal to Guernsey, loveliest island in the world.

The dark secret is that Prior Metivier is a notorious gambler. Like all gamblers, he loses. At horse racing, at field sports, at whippet racing, even at the illegal bare-fist fights, as Charley the champion told me. Me and Gesso burgle the priory. Gesso gets caught, and vanishes.

Here I had to blot my eyes, clear my throat from the terrible frog growing in there as I remembered that gruesome scrape on that flint cobble near the priory's hot pool. I'd found it the day I discovered that the prior's holy order had finally taken to the hills – some religious retreat, spurious or otherwise. Out on the sea the yachts were turning round a buoy marker. A longer thicker boat was coming round the headland, pale cream sails, Red Ensign.

Summoned to Florida's point-to-point, I get chased by Jonno Rant's bodyguards and the police. Into the woods. I find out from Logger Yelk that the priory's closed for ever, submerged in gambling debts, all its money-making schemes done for. Marie's 'slice of luck' – the O'Conor painting I'd nicked, that they'd stolen back, and sold to that posh London firm – pays off Prior Metivier's gambling debts, the naughty man.

Symie Doakes at the Hippodrome tells me it's no mere chance. It's a painting that had come to the priory's rescue. I nick Barnie Woodfall's list of auditioning performers and hoof it. I also nick a small antique from Paula to sell to Harry Bateman, and set sail for the Channel Isles.

And here I am at Mrs Rosa Vidamour's in beautiful Guernsey. Prior Metivier is in the phone book at Metivier Mansion. I find Gussy, an eccentric painter ceaselessly copying some stupendous painting she once glimpsed as a child in a local cave. Walt Jethou, the Carrieres – low-grade antique dealers – with Dove the paralysed artist daughter, become my allies, sort of. I phone Florida, hint that I'm into some gambling scheme. She's as daft over betting as Prior George, but doesn't lose quite as catastrophically. With luck, she'll be on her way.

So now I needed to legitimize my presence here on this marvellous isle. If they'd topped Gesso they could easily do for me here on their home ground, especially as I didn't know who 'they' were.

Who'd complete my foolproof plan? Women.

After all, it's a woman's world.

Once, as a teenager, I tried to work women out. What does a woman invariably forgive in a man? Looking out at the ships, my bafflement returned. Lust, say? Does a woman *always* forgive a man who lusts for her? No. Films, newspapers, are full of evidence against.

Well, desire, then? It's perilously close to lust. No also, same evidence, same reasons.

Love? Could love be that special thing that women always find forgiveness for? Women's magazines are crammed with what passes for love. Literature preaches that love wins out, when we all know deep down that it doesn't. Love conquers all, they say, but it can't so it doesn't. My frank opinion? Never in a million years do women forgive love just because it's aimed their way. I had a great-great aunt whose headstone reads, with terrible ambiguity, ON THE TENTH OF THE FIRST MONTH OF THE YEAR OF GRACE, ALMIGHTY GOD DID PLEASE US ALL BY TAKING UNTO HIMSELF MY BELOVED WIFE . . . The family's party line is that her husband loved her even though she treated him like dirt all their married days – this back when you didn't divorce.

See? Love abounded somewhere, but to what end? God's probably still puzzling her out up there on some cloud.

Aye, love is a dangerous word. Years ago there was a famous musical in which some geezer sang the question 'Do you love me?' His wife sings in answer that she washed the dishes, cooks his grub, does his clothes, raises his kids. He rejoices – she loves him! OK, she might have, but he was taking an unimaginable risk. Love isn't a long-service medal. I once was in hospital because a woman had stabbed me. In the next bed was this old chap. Convalescing, I used to sit and chat, though he was quite off his trolley. He plucked my sleeve one evening in fright. 'Son,' he babbled in delirium. 'Promise me you'll not let your ma take care of me if ever I'm ill.' I promised, hand on my heart. He'd been married, the nurses said, over forty years, but nobody ever visited him. He was sent to some nursing home. No, love definitely is not mere longevity.

Two years ago I made love to this older woman who had a genuine Tudor apostle spoon, London stamped. Don't laugh – it would buy your house. It was honestly Henry VIII vintage, with the maker's fringed S mark. It even had its own little history, bless its beautiful little soul. Fakes of these are legion, but beware missing an honest antique as costly as this one was. (Sorry, digressing.) She'd dressed afterwards as I watched. She prattled, 'No dozing today, darling. Mark's taking me to a dinner dance tonight. I haven't got long. My Mark's a wonderful dancer.' I said, penny dropping, 'You've no intention of selling me that apostle spoon?' She trilled a merry laugh, gay as a sprite. 'Of *course* I haven't, Lovejoy!' I demanded, 'Then why this?', meaning why make love. She'd sobered, sat on the bed. 'For two reasons, darling,' she cooed. 'One, because I like crude!' I'd asked what two was. 'How dim you are, Lovejoy!'

she said, rolling on her stockings. 'The reason is, I hate him.' She was fifty-three. They'd been married twenty-one years, two children at university. No, longevity isn't love. It's not vice versa either.

I then wondered about longing. Does a woman unfailingly forgive a bloke who longs for her? Doubt it. There are times a bird wants action, when soulful isn't enough. No action, she'll hate you with anything she can throw into the ring.

Respect? I felt myself getting close, a hint of 'maybe' in there. After all, you can seduce, use, betray even, but you've got a lifeline if you respect the lady for her style/class/wit/looks. (Delete any, as long as you leave any two). Yes, respect edged close to what I was searching for.

Synonyms for respect? Adoration got a bit closer to the right answer. But a pedestal's so damned hard for a woman. And sooner or later even goddesses want to descend, to sojourn a while among us sordid mortals and experience our passionate imperfections.

Worship, then? *Yes!*

Excitedly I rose, paced a yard or two, resumed my perch. It was *worship*! With worship she's in the driving seat, can put her own ascription on a man's grovelling. Worship gives a woman an emotional blank cheque, to cash in any time. And a handy slave. And worshippers don't ask questions.

Worship was the key. I thought to myself, 'Dear Mrs Crucifex . . .'

An hour later I'd found the post office and had composed my letter filled with hidden – not so hidden – passion:

Dear Mrs Crucifex,
Don't be mad, this coming out of the blue. I'm in Guernsey. You'd better let me help. I won't have them

taking advantage of you the way they are. I wouldn't have written, but can't get you out of my mind. You deserve the very best. I'll do anything. If you tell me to get lost, I'll do as you say and just wish you luck. I truly am sorry about intruding like this. I'm not usually so stupid, not even about pretty women, but I'm hopeless where you are concerned.

    With worship,

Lovejoy

Naturally, every word needed changing a score of times, like everything else I write, until it was almost what I'd started with. Women like words.

I posted it, and got Walt Jethou to drive me past Metivier Mansion for a look. It was beautiful, set back from a narrow road in its own grounds. No expense spared there.

Then Walt took me back by way of the Crucifex's residence. I was surprised to see that it stood next to a posh hotel. For a second that set me thinking, but I was tired. Far too much thinking for one day. I went home to Rosa Vidamour's. She whipped up salmon and chips for supper.

That night, I went to bed full of optimism. Once a nerk, always.

21

SLEEPING UNAIDED IN a strange bed makes me restless, dreaming, into nightmares. Sometimes mine are fairly innocuous, but often they're sweat-and-yelp.

People find antiques. It's an eternal law. (Really the law is that everybody *else* finds antiques, but you know what I mean.) God having this wicked sense of humour, it's mostly the undeserving rich who visit auctions from sheer boredom and bid groats for a trinket on a whim – hang it all, there's the afternoon to kill – and whoops, the trinket turns out to be a genuine antique and jewellery dealers are clamouring at your front door. I once saw a lady do exactly that. I'd just got to Gimbert's Auction rooms, out of the rain and late as usual. This lady – in furs, if you please, smoking with an ivory fagholder to amuse stray environmentalists – was there. She saw something flash when the auctioneer's dodgy helper made his traditional call, 'Showing here, sir!', and held up this little necklet. She bid on the auctioneer's, 'Who'll start me at twenty . . . ?' which no dealer ever does, and got it, to chuckles of disbelief. I was the only one who groaned, because even across the distance it radiated beams that set me juddering. It was a small diamond, sure, which is mistake enough to make, but there's one type of setting you must promise never, *never ever*, to miss. And this was it. Easy to spot, easy to miss.

Back in the dim dark days of the 1860s there lived in Paris a Belgian jeweller. He made a living setting small semi-precious stones. Working away, he suddenly thought, 'Hey! What if I invented a setting that made a small stone look big!'

So he did. Oscar Massin created the famed Illusion Setting.

It's a peculiarly pleasant thing to fake. I've done it often, when I could get somebody to buy me the gemstone and the precious metal. You need both.

You take a gemstone – he used midget diamonds – and make an ordinary ring. Nothing special so far. Bare rings already fashioned up, you can buy in dozens, no problem. The marvellous trick is in the setting.

You build your collet, in which the gemstone will nestle, and burnish it as brilliantly as possible. I use Massin's technique, make the precious metal dazzlingly reflective to start with. Go for reflectance at all costs. When its brightness is practically charring your retina, set your stone and shape it. But make sure you cut away so much of the setting that *the margins of the remaining collet look like part of the gem.* See the trick? The lady slips it on her finger, extends her hand to see – women always do that – and suddenly that tiny little diamond of maybe a twentieth of a carat will look maybe twice, three times the size! Clever, eh? Now, why isn't such a piece of superb craftsmanship always spotted? Because antique dealers looking at a 'reserve tray' on a viewing day, see a gem, bend closer and quickly move on – spotting of course that most of the gleam comes from the setting, not the stone. These 'deception' or 'mirage' settings were all the rage in Victorian and Edwardian days, but betokened smaller stones. After all, a posh lady doesn't want proof that *her* jewellery is made up of minuscule gemstones, thank you. The French still call them *montre illusion* rings. Find an original Oscar Massin ring, you're in clover.

Antiques get discovered by others equally undeserving. Lady Erica Pearce was wandering in her Sussex garden one day, pleased at how her garden did grow. How nice, she thought, to write about the garden ornaments that she and her husband – distinguished judge, Lord of Appeal, et wealthy cetera – had bought over the years. Good idea! So she and his lordship filled their long winter evenings doing just that. Drawings, photos of their statuary showing each sculpture against the plants, a lovely little volume well worth, people said fondly, a few shillings. Among the statues was a bronze no more than thirty-one inches tall, of a dancing faun, very like the work of De Vries. *Hold it.* Could it – *gasp!* – be the missing Dancing Faun of Adrien De Vries, that obsessional Dutchman who back in Renaissance times made and cast *single* statues, so that each of his bronzes is unique and pricelessly special? Of course it was! So the Dancing Faun, which was originally sold in a job lot (meaning chucked in with several tatty others, not being worth a special listing) forty years earlier for less than eight pounds, became a cool ten million US dollars and got shipped out to the Getty under armed guard. I know antiques thieves who still weep at the missed opportunity, because it was only the village bobby who advised his lord-ship to sell. The Plod don't want priceless statues among shrubberies in the lantern hours. See? People who find priceless antiques should be me.

Of course, I come across more than most, being a divvy.

Unfortunately I'm thick, and too soft for my own good. That's why I'm always broke. I thought on, staring at the ceiling.

Suppose Gussy Quenard really *had* seen some genuine painting in that sea cave when she was a little girl? And suppose there was a cache of similar vintage art works somewhere here in Guernsey, and that Marie and Prior George Metivier had it hidden somewhere. Further suppose that I got close. Could I trust my divvy sense to bong me as senseless as if, say, I was put next to a much older Chippendale bureau, or an invaluable Doctor Johnson-vintage gouty stool? It's all very well for the Customs and Excise nerks to redefine 'antique' just to rake in tax revenue; my sixth sense doesn't work in quite the same way. But I'd definitely felt odd when I'd overpainted that picture I'd nicked from the chapel at Albansham Priory that night.

Thinking always sets me grumbling in a half-doze. Luck always goes to the undeserving. Take Lee Bon. He was a Chinese official back in the Wanli days – contemporary of our good Queen Bess, give or take. Lee Bon was retiring to Imperial China from Burma, having done sterling service for the Ming Dynasty. He brought with him some seeds of the Burmese Egg Plant. They grow in a simple pod like a broad bean. Take one out, though, and it's rather like a miniature egg in an eggcup, a bulbous little dome on a squat stalk. You can polish the seed to a black-blue burnished gleam. Harden the seed's stem in the sun, and it carves like ivory. Well, this grand Imperial Chinese official had several of these seeds set in jewels and gold, a gift for his Emperor, gained multo points on the Ming Dynasty creep chart. Then, miracle of miracles! After Lee Bon died, the exotic plant was found growing freely in his courtyard, where some dud old seeds were accidentally chucked. Thus was born the wholesale production of carving the hardened stems for use as personal seals. These little cheapos date from our Tudor times, and those old originals cost the earth. They're also replicated in every junk barrow on the China coast, so beware. The lesson is that rich emissaries profit while you and me worry about bus fares. To them that hath and all that.

I was still awake when Rosa Vidamour knocked with a cup of tea. She looked lovely in the dawn light. She put the tea on the bedside table and said, 'You can stop looking like that.'

Sighing, I had my tea. I'd only been thinking that today Mrs Jocina Crucifex would get my letter. I hadn't even been thinking of how Mrs Vidamour's breasts would be naked under her blouse. Is life fair or what?

'Somebody's downstairs, Jonno,' Rosa called before I was even dressed.

'Tell her to wait, please.' I was just out of the bath. Jocina!

'It's a him.' She sounded full of humour.

Last Candlemas, I washed my cottage floor. Dunno what came over me, but I did. Got a bucket, filled it with water from my well, got some of that detergent powder that makes you choke, and actually knelt down and washed – that's *washed* – the flagged floor. I even shifted my chair, shoved the divan up (it lets down from the wall), did it exactly like Gran used to. I ended up knackered. I'd never done it before. Afterwards, though, instead of feeling really proud, sitting there like Noel Coward hoping for somebody to happen by and say, 'Gosh, look at glitzy Lovejoy's floor,' I just stood there. It looked no different. And I thought, why the heck did I do it? It's like making your bed. What's the point? It only gets tumbled again. It's women who decide these cycles in life. Wash, polish, dust, watch for a sunny day to hang out the washing. Like Rosa Vidamour was doing now, singing in the kitchen.

'Hello, Lovejoy.' Martin Crucifex was sitting at the kitchen table, a cup of coffee before him like a trial judge's mallet. 'You came to Guernsey, then.'

'I didn't know I was expected.'

'You've met Mr Martin Crucifex, Jonno?'

'His name isn't Jonno Rant, Mrs Vidamour. It's Lovejoy. He's an antique dealer of ill repute and worse behaviour.' Martin glared at me. 'I have checked. Jonno Rant is still in Suffolk. Lovejoy is an impostor.'

'Got breakfast for a cheat, Rosa, please?'

She sparkled, really rising to the occasion. Maybe I provided more excitement than she usually got from holiday visitors? I'd have settled for a peaceful start to the day. I'd done nothing criminally wrong yet, though I had hopes.

'Yes, Lovejoy. What an unusual name!' She bustled about. Eggs, fried spud, fried bread, tomatoes, loads of bread, strong tea. 'Mr Crucifex?'

'Thank you, Mrs Vidamour, but no.'

He exuded malice. Rosa constantly deferred to him, smiling and coming near to curtseying. To her, Martin was nobility. I wondered if he had one of those ancient titles.

'You haven't time to fill your face, Lovejoy,' Martin said, cold. 'Mrs Crucifex wants to see you instantly, to explain your presence here.'

'I'm busy, Martin.' I smiled at Rosa, who gasped at my effrontery. 'Mrs Vidamour and I have to find a concert hall. To put on a show.'

'How dare you come here and—'

Ignoring his splutters, I started my nosh. 'Haven't you heard?' I said through a mouthful. 'Me and Jonno Rant go way back.'

Martin stormed out, Rosa peering through the curtains. 'You're in trouble now, Lovejoy,' she said, eyes like saucers. 'They won't forget that. Please pay your room and board by teatime today.'

Notice how women go straight to the heart? It's not their fault that money gets there ahead of them.

'We've a lot to do before anybody gets slung out into the gutter.'

'What was that about a hall, Lovejoy?'

'More bread please, Rosa,' I said. 'We've not much time.'

'Me too?' She sat, nervous. 'I don't know anything about music halls.'

I said, narked, 'What did I just say? Get a move on, love.'

Some days just have rotten beginnings. She did as she was told. Several times she started to speak, but wisely saved her breath. Nine o'clock, we were out into St Peter Port, the light of eagles in our eyes.

'This is a waste of bloody time, Lovejoy,' Walt grumbled.

'We've seen some marvellous places, haven't we?' I sounded unconvincing, but grinned at Rosa.

'For what?' She was lost, though I'd explained several times.

'For cheating.' Walt was fed up. I recognized the exasperation of the drinker wanting his noontime pint.

'For a show,' I countered, narked. 'Look, troops. This scam'll founder unless we keep cheerful. Keep smiling, look optimistic.'

Rosa said, 'We've found twenty halls. You've rejected them all. Why?'

'Not big enough, love.'

We stopped at a hotel rather larger than the others we'd seen so far, the Roi de Normandie.

'Here, Lovejoy?' Rosa exclaimed. 'It's a five crowner.'

Hotels in Guernsey have their own signs of excellence, one to five crowns. Fewer than half a dozen hotels boast five, the max. Across the way was the OGH, as everybody calls the Old Government House Hotel. This other one opposite was a jaunty newcomer, and more my style. It had neon lights, coloured fountains. Music blared. The restrained OGH sneered, full of disdain.

'Why not?' I asked, eyeing it.

Walt spoke. 'Because it has discos. And it's brand new.'

That might have settled it, until Rosa said something that swung me all the way. She said, nervous, 'Martin Crucifex bought it two weeks ago.'

'Did he now,' I said in a whisper, remembering that sooner or later I had to visit the delectable Jocina Crucifex. 'Drive in, Walt. Have your midday pints on me, but somewhere else. Rosa? Come with me.'

There's an old – I mean 1648 vintage – milliner's shop in my town. If you go in, the manager calls quietly, 'Forward, Miss Faversham!' or whoever, and an assistant lady, attired straight Charles Dickens, steps forward respectfully to serve. I felt like saying that as we alighted, our own foray into the unknown. Rosa was pale, Walt nervously looking round in case his mate Pete the harbour constable was on his tail. These were all excellent signs. Con tricks in antiques are my home ground. Things were finally looking up.

In the quiet foyer they said Mr Underwood, the manager,

would be out in ten minutes. I looked about, and sure enough there was Mrs Crucifex's hallmark, a display case containing glass and porcelain. A nice lass was on reception, busy with new arrivals. I bought some cigarettes, but not to smoke, and told Rosa to look at the display cabinet. I went downstairs, ostensibly looking for the toilets, and found the maintenance man's hidey hole. They're never locked. I filched a tube of super glue – vicious stuff, this, so mind your eyes.

The display cabinet had several small cup-and-saucer items, a bonny jug, a decanter. Some loon had put a glass of water in the cabinet, presumably for humidity. I groaned aloud until Rosa nudged me.

'That's ridiculous,' I told her quietly. 'We'll have to rescue the decanter.'

'Rescue?'

'Steal, love, to save the poor decanter's life.'

I had to explain, or she'd have gone moral on me.

'Glass is the most abused of all antiques.' I hated whoever had put the lovely thing at risk. 'Worse even than silver. See, glass is susceptible to moisture. It makes the glass's surface opaque. You can never cure it.'

'Tell them!' Rosa said, womanlike, trying to shirk responsibility.

'Our duty is to thieve it to safety. Keep being fascinated.' I stood her at the cabinet. 'Give me a nail file.'

She said, ever helpful, 'Is one split? I'll do it.'

Unaided, I took her manicure set from her handbag. A couple of women were talking over coffee, and some bloke was phoning. Nobody noticed. I worked the nail file into three by bending and straightening it quickly. The metal gets hot, but you finish up with three small usable screwdrivers.

The cabinet had a lock the Tower of London would have envied. But its end panels were held by six-sided recessed nuts. Extolling the beautiful porcelain on display in quiet tones, I made a mash of four cigarettes, and rammed it into the nuts' recesses, squirting the glue in and tamping it down, then jamming a piece of the nail file in. This glue's dynamite – it sets within seconds and holds fast. I did it all one-handed, quicker than it takes to tell, while apparently admiring the antiques. I was actually shown this tobacco-and-glue trick by Luna, a pretty housewife from Croydon who did it every chance she got. I took Rosa to sit down.

On the couch – lovely huge ferns in that lounge, but who likes ferns? – I borrowed Rosa's comb and drove her manicure set's nail scissors into its shaft until I'd created a tiny though reasonable slot.

Just then the manager emerged, friendly, so I postponed the theft.

'Please wait, Rosa, dwoorlink,' I said. 'Won't be a second. Admire the antique porcelain. That decanter's beautiful, eh?'

'We pride ourselves on our lounge displays,' Underwood said affably. 'The Crucifex family bought the hotel, so we persuaded Mrs Crucifex to display some items from her famous collection.'

'You did us all a real favour,' I said, truthful.

He took me into his office. I started my patter.

'Mrs Vidamour is used to waiting,' I said, smiling fondly. 'Isn't that what family is for?' Chuckle, chuckle.

Mr Underwood was a pleasant, decisive bloke, determined to hide his bald pate by flattening his remaining strands of hair crossways. Portly, a waistcoast brimming fountain pens, he sensed business. So did I, for I was an impressario, big show to put on, right?

'Frankly,' I got in straightaway, 'other venues have not impressed, Mr Underwood. Too staid. Too small. Too . . .'

'I know.' He instantly condemned his rivals' reputations, beaming. 'We have everything you'll need here. Our show-space is . . .'

You can fill in the dots, like I did. His office wall was crammed with diplomas, pictures of stars in holiday mode, Christmas celebrations with streamers. It all happened in Mr Underwood's domain, the Roi de Normandie.

'Entertainment,' he was pontificating at a drop chart of his empire, 'is the game, Jonno. Our ballroom hosts the Channel Island championships.' He boomed a stentorian laugh. 'You'll know the fame of *those*!'

'Certainly,' I said. It's hopeless trying to be as hearty as the world's Underwoods. They out-hearty the rest of us without even trying.

'Right, Jonno. Which of our magnificent facilities will you leap at?'

'Floor show, Mark. TV's signed. My band's on the way. Full advertising.'

'Mainland advertising too?' he asked, eyes wider.

'Is there any other kind, Mark?' I leant forward. 'Not in my book.'

'Right, right.' He had to swallow to say it. 'Isn't it short notice?'

'Notice, schmotiss,' I shot back. I didn't know what it meant, but felt sure I'd heard something similar said in those American TV musical extravaganzas you can't escape. 'I'm talking numbers here, Mark.'

'Right, right,' he said, eyes glazing. 'I'll need to OK it with—'

'Jocina already OK'd it,' I said, strolling out. 'Nice doing business with you. Ciao.'

'Er, ciao, Jonno.'

He stayed in the office. I went into the lounge. Rosa was admiring the cabinet, more worried than ever. I'd kept her comb. I told Rosa to stand talking with me. A tourist was booking out, and the receptionist fully occupied. I fitted the slit I'd made in Rosa's comb over the projecting pieces of nail file, gave each one quick turn. The glass-sided panel swung out. I reached in, took the decanter, sleighted it to Rosa – gasp, gasp – and replaced the panel. Rosa hadn't had the sense to fold her coat over her arm. I sighed.

'Remove your coat, Rosa,' I said.

'But it's quite chilly—'

Shedding my jacket, I did the hiding job. We left, casual, the decanter under my jacket. Walt wasn't there, but the motor was in the hotel car park. I broke in and blipped the wires.

'What are you doing?' Rosa bleated. I dragged her on to the passenger seat and gunned the engine.

'We're going to see Mrs Crucifex, love.'

'We? But I'm not dressed properly for—'

Women can get you down. 'Direct me, love. We've a fraud to perpetrate.' The plan's final details had come to me in Mr Underwood's office, a triumph of mind over environment. 'Notice those bloody horrible ferns? Get rid of them.'

'Me?' I could tell that her head was swimming. 'Me? Get rid—'

'And that table arrangement in the restaurant's useless. Scrap it. And those curtains'll make me puke in strobe lighting. Ditch them.'

'How can I, Lovejoy?' she said faintly. 'It's not my—'

Suddenly I'd had enough. I yelled, 'Won't anybody do

as they're told? Do I have to do every single thing? You'll have me carrying the bloody pots and pans.'

Driving us out into the main road, I ranted and raved a bit longer, just to help her focus. I was getting really nervy, trying to help people. I mean, here was I upping her dull landlady's life to mega showbiz, giving her a life in the fast lane with the famous Jonno Rant – well, me – and all I get is earache. If I wasn't a saint I'd give up.

We arrived at the manor house. I drove in, parked before the steps.

'Can you drive?' I asked as we got out.

'No. I'm sorry. I did try once, but—'

'Just agree with everything I say, OK? Bring the decanter.'

'I'm frightened, Lovejoy,' she said in a small voice. She stood close.

I stared at her, astonished. 'So am I. It changes nothing.' I rang the bell.

The door opened on Jocina. Showtime.

22

S HE WAS EXQUISITE, and knew it. Her contempt for Rosa was instantaneous.

'I sent for you, Lovejoy, not her.' She walked inside, furious.

Was that the full welcome? I beckoned Rosa. 'Come on, love.' We walked down to the motor and were just getting in when Martin tore out. A man with a mission.

'Lovejoy! You're to come inside.'

I ignored him, firing the engine by slipping the wires together, hurting my quick so I swore. He stood resolutely in front of the car's bonnet, Horatio on the Bridge. I eased the motor at him. He backed, protesting, commanding.

'He says you've to go in, Lovejoy,' Rosa whispered, frantic. She was for the social proprieties, this one, and no mistake.

'He can sod off.' We approached the road, him backing away, desperately looking towards the house for orders.

Then the wind changed. He raised both hands in surrender, wearily waved me down. I reversed to the mansion. We were at the front door before he came puffing up. Rosa was in mortal anguish at such carryings-on, especially when I entered without knocking. She kept trying to pull me to a standstill.

'Lovejoy,' she hissed. 'For goodness' *sake*. I haven't got my best—'

'Rosa,' I said wearily. 'Will you shut it? I'm in enough trouble.'

'Trouble?' she squeaked. 'You're in . . . ?' She was almost in tears, 'I don't know what's happening, Lovejoy.'

'It's the antiques game. Nobody ever does.'

'I've got no hat.'

We stood waiting in a hall the size of Crystal Palace. Martin followed, slammed the door. I asked Rosa conversationally, 'Did you count the locks on that display cabinet at the hotel, like I asked?'

'No.' She looked stricken. 'I thought you were joking.'

'There's no jokes in the antiques game either.' It wasn't her fault she was honest. A misspent childhood. I looked at Martin. 'Which way, b'wana?'

'The withdrawing room.' He ushered us in. The room wore Edwardian wallpaper, guinea an inch, had great bay windows and a wealth of antique furniture so beautiful I groaned aloud.

Jocina Crucifex turned her glare on us. Unhappiness reigned.

'In future, Lovejoy,' she said, voice a blizzard, 'you will comply—'

'Oh, aye. Much good compliance has done you.'

'Silence!' she screeched, so loud that Rosa jumped a mile. 'I will not have you coming here with some cleaning woman and—'

'Lover,' I said calmly. Rosa gasped. 'Not cleaning woman, please. Mrs Vidamour and I are lovers.'

'Lovejoy!' Rosa bleated. 'This will be all over the island!' She couldn't quite make outrage, and settled for annoyance.

'It's no good, love. Mrs Crucifex knows everything here

and on the mainland as well. Please respect her superior position.'

'But it's not—'

'True?' I said gently, looking at Jocina. 'If you say so, Rosa. Mrs Crucifex will respect our confidence. She's a lady.' I could have throttled Rosa. Had I or had I not told her to agree with everything I said? Talk to the wall. Women and infants never take a blind bit of notice of me. 'I brought Rosa to prove I'm concealing nothing, Jocina. Mrs Vidamour will help unconditionally. I need her.'

Mrs Crucifex took her time lighting a cigarette from an onyx skull on the Sheraton table, her very movements silent music. The way I felt, looking at her, my letter wasn't far wrong. I stood like a kid caught scrumping.

She finally spoke. 'Why?'

'She's essential for the con trick.' Rosa started yet another denial. I quelled her with a raised finger. 'I've had enough from you.' My voice was tight. 'Give my plan away, I'll do you. Not another word.'

Martin's voice cut in. 'Lovejoy's prevaricating, Jocina. He has no plan.'

'Then why am I here, nerk?' I shot back. 'You're desperate to raise money for the prior's religious order. So here's what we do. We pull our con trick, and make a king's ransom. You keep ninety per cent, to help . . .' I heard their intake of breath, and relented. 'To help anyone you care to.'

'Impossible!' Martin for once ignored his wife. 'You're as secret as a parade, Lovejoy. A confidence trick needs subterfuge.'

I smiled at his error. 'The best con tricks are the ones with the biggest publicity. Remember the brilliantly successful Beraha? He forged gold sovereigns, each containing

124.64 grains of measured gold, 1.37 grains *more* than England's official coin. He got away with it, by simply thinking big and bigger!'

'It's gold, then?' Jocina demanded, quick on her toes.

'No. It's an antique. It's the commonest trick in the book. Everybody who ever buys something for herself, some trinket to wear, falls for it every single time.' I turned to Martin. 'We advertise it. Nonstop, every TV channel, every newspaper.'

He gaped. Jocina stared, judging and guessing, angry at knowing that she was missing some obvious thing by a mile.

'Will you bear the cost, Lovejoy?' she said after a few throbs.

'No.' I tried to look like Big John Sheehan does, restful but lethal. I couldn't. 'But I'll arrange it – free. Will that do?'

'Here's the catch, Jocina,' Martin said, all satisfaction.

'I have proof I can do it.' I felt cool for once. Simple theft always creates an impression. 'Your lounge display of porcelain at the Roi de Normandie Hotel. Those locks were picked today. One of your pieces was stolen.'

'That's impossible!' Martin almost shouted. 'It's thief-proof. And it's electronically tagged.'

Jocina was close to a smile. She wasn't as bad at guessing as I'd thought. She held out her hand. I nodded to Rosa, who passed her the shopping bag.

'You felt lovely while you lasted,' I said sadly to the decanter in farewell. Carefully Jocina placed it on the table. She signed her husband to keep quiet.

'Where does Mrs Vidamour come in, exactly?'

'Rosa will run the floor show,' I lied. 'She has already booked seven of the music hall acts we'll need. I'm banking on twelve. The first arrives tomorrow.'

Rosa quavered, 'But I haven't!'

'Rosa thinks we'll only need ten,' I thundered to shut the gabby cow up. 'She's wrong. You can't stint a con trick in antiques. Not with the amount of money I'm going to bring you.'

'Jocina—' Martin began, but got nowhere. His wife sank on to the couch and motioned us to be seated.

'Martin, be a dear. Ring for tea. Lovejoy marches to a different drum. Let us listen. Maybe we shan't make the same errors *this* time.'

He winced and obeyed. I began speaking. I too was eager to hear me, to find out exactly what I planned. I'm at my best out-guessing my own lies, if nowt else.

As I talked and talked, I couldn't help looking about, feeling the loveliness of the antiques around me. Women really have the knack of positioning furniture. Men can't do it. People call it style, but they're wrong. It's character. I once knew a woman in Bloomsbury. She kept a young bloke – her methods I won't go into – in a flat overlooking Queens Square. I brought her a small Victorian twiggie, a wicker basket chair folk still call a twiggen in Lancashire. It was free of that hideous varnish that dealers forever spoil such treasures with. I was really worried, carrying it up the lady's stairs, because twiggies are notorious for ruining a room's look.

She belonged to the University of London, very august. She always looked lost, scatterbrained, and smoked like a Battersea chimney. No 'style' as women's magazines define it, no. But she seized that twiggie with a yelp of glee, got me to shift a genuine Earl of Pembroke table – made by George Kemp of Cornhill about 1760, nowadays worth a street – then moved a small Richard Wright oil painting. It blended like a dream! I looked at the room in the early hours the following day and marvelled. Move this a few inches, balance that, and harmony reigns. See what I mean? No style as such, but character by the busload. I still can't figure it out. Chromosomes, I shouldn't wonder.

Jocina had it too, but with style in abundance. Talking and inventing – note the absence of explanation in there – I wondered if you could make a general rule for women. Style plus character equals class, like that?

'How do we—?' Martin interrupted.

He'd poured the tea, brought by some minion. I wondered if I'd glimpsed the serf before somewhere. Albansham Priory, perhaps? She went out before I could place her.

'Let me finish, Martin.' I'd only just got going. 'My display is on show. The public will be everywhere, grockles by the thousand.' Grockles are tourists. 'The climax is a raffle.'

'Displays of what, Lovejoy?' Martin practically bawled.

Jocina raised her eyebrows, amused that resolve was such a rarity among her men.

'A fair question, really, Lovejoy,' she ruled. 'You've already proved you can steal an antique on public display from a hotel foyer. But can you *provide* one, if that's your game?'

'No.' I saw her assurance flicker for just one anxious moment, Tinkerbell's wilting light before the audience applauds it back to life. 'I'll provide the dross. Someone else provides the genuine priceless one.' I smiled. 'Deal?'

'Priceless? How much is priceless?' Remember what I said, hearts and money?

'Enough,' I said, swigging my tea to the dregs and rising to go, 'to buy a priory and five mansions, with a farm or two. At the very least. Look missus,' I said as Rosa almost keeled over and the room went still in awe. 'Please don't think I'm a scavenger, but it wouldn't have bankrupted you to dish out a slice of fruit cake, would it?'

She looked at me, at Rosa. Martin she ignored. 'I do apologize, Lovejoy. Could you find time to come to supper? On my boat in the marina.'

'Not tomorrow,' Martin began. 'You have two appointments—'

'Pleased to accept,' I said, making for the door. 'Incidentally, that hotel cabinet's rubbish.'

'*Lovejoy!*' Rosa ground out in anguish.

'Don't worry, Mrs Vidamour.' Jocina, smiling, came as far as the main door. 'I'm beginning to get the hang of this.'

We drove away under Martin's glare. I was worried. If Jocina really was following my plot, I was in deeper trouble now than when I'd arrived. I complained to Rosa about always feeling hungry in Guernsey. We stopped at a nosh bar in St Peter Port for fish and chips. Rosa asked me what was going on. I was a bit narked, because something was irking me. Naturally I blamed Rosa. I borrowed money from her to pay for the grub. Then, staring at the harbour, I remembered.

Jocina's serf. She'd looked into the motor at that point-to-point, before I'd scarpered to the woods away from the Plod, when I was being taken to watch Florida's horses. It raised all sorts of questions. I couldn't answer a single one, having a load of music hall acts to hire, with no gelt.

Theft can be almost everything a woman is. Beautiful, bright, entertaining, really captivating. It can also be unbelievably vicious. My question for now, though, was how thieves get caught. My rule is this: thieves are *close by*. It works, with very few exceptions.

Not long since, Christ Church library, Oxford, missed two books. Then over eighty precious volumes – manuscripts, texts – went absent, from Oxford University and London sources. What intrepid thieves, you might think, to raid such ivory towers! Who on earth could those thieves be? Cockney East End scoundrels? Bounders newly sprung from Dartmoor Prison and up to their old tricks? The books were dazzlingly valuable: Isaac Newton's *Principia*, John Locke's philosophies, Copernicus, Edmund Haley of comet fame. It was especially clever burglary, because the only people properly admitted were academics belonging to ancient colleges, who of course were above suspicion. When I heard the news, I smiled. Sure enough, an eminent academic – composer, lecturer, Oxford University don of Oriel and Queen's, a BBC presenter no less – was arrested and slammed in clink, a further 113 counts of nicking and deception being included at Oxford's grim Crown Court. The blighter even had boxes of them under his bed. See? Thieves are never far away. Murderers are different; they sometimes nip to Guernsey.

I explained it to Rosa in her sitting room. 'It's a problem.'

'Why?' She baked her own bread, a godsend because it toasts better than that sliced latex our shops sell nowadays. Her marmalade was too thin. I wondered if I ought to tell her, or if she'd go mental. 'You told Mrs Crucifex it'd be public.'

Some people. I begged mutely for more crumpets. 'Rosa, love. Please remember that I lie.'

'Then why tell me about that Oxford don?'

'Because *somebody* will steal the antique I'm going to put on display. That's what my scam will be; an exhibition of several identical paintings, with only one genuine. Then I'll know it'll be him.'

She seated herself slowly. 'I'm frightened when you speak like that.' Then asked, 'It'll be who?'

'The thief.' I cleared my throat, quelling her question. 'Actually there might be two robbers.'

'You as well?' She put her hand to her throat, her eyes roving everywhere over my face. 'Stealing?'

'No, Rosa. You.' I looked at the plates. 'And not stealing. Putting something in. Is that the only grub? I'm famished.'

She hurried to serve, but looking at me. I hoped her phone bill was paid up, because I had a couple of dozen calls to make as soon as she'd gone to bed.

'Look, love.' I tried hard to appear thoughtful, though what good have thoughts ever done for mankind? 'Everybody cheats. Look at T. S. Eliot.'

My mind went 'Eh?' even as Rosa said, 'Who?'

'Well, everybody nowadays pretends that T. S. Eliot wrote *The Waste Land*, that he didn't nick it from whatsisname – Madison Cawein, the assistant cashier in that Cincinnati snooker hall. But he did.'

'What has that got to do with us?' Rosa asked.

'It proves it, see?' Actually, I didn't know. But somewhere in there was a vague truth. I felt it. 'Defraud once – antiques, politics, even love – and it's risky. The trick is to keep on tricking.'

'How can we do that?'

'We reveal only four-fifths.'

'Of what?'

Women's questions wear me out when I've no answers left.

'Of our fraud, love.'

'Must we tell the police, Lovejoy?' she asked, out of the blue.

We talked of shopping. I told her about a youngish bloke I'd once seen pushing a supermarket trolley. He asked a woman customer what he ought to buy to make a simple meal. His missus was in hospital, he was to cook for his two kiddies. The bird he asked was really pleased to help, told him about suet and cheeses. Another woman eagerly joined in. Then a third. Considerate, no? No, because acrimony broke out – cooking recipes, brands of butter, how you baste the carrots and God knows what. The blazing row finally engulfed the supermarket. The poor bloke silently ditched his wheelie and crept away unnoticed, probably took his children to their granny's instead.

'Too many cooks spoil the broth, Rosa,' I concluded. 'So no police.'

'But we will tell them eventually, won't we?' said this gentle soul.

I looked her squarely in the eye. 'Hand on my heart, dwoorlink. Sincerely.' I even squeezed her hand to show affection, in case she felt particularly kind towards a hungry guest. She coloured, shyly withdrew her hand. I felt cheated. I'd scrubbed my teeth like a maniac. Waste of time.

Soon as she was abed I rang the police. Wrong.

23

'POLICE?' I FAKED confidence. 'Can you tell me how to get in touch with a police officer? Name of Summer, in East Anglia.'

They passed me about a few times, then I got some thick-voiced bloke who told me nothing, said to visit the cop shop in the morning. I said I couldn't, I was busy putting on a show. He said to drop in anyway. I started phoning East Anglia, got mad when people were in bed, the unfeeling swine.

Rosa's phone bill took it on the chin. Three hours later I was done for. It was late, all Guernsey abed. With my last erg I phoned Gesso's Desdemona. No, Gesso wasn't back. Desdemona was now seriously worried, the police doing nothing, did I think something *really* could have happened. I said oh, Gesso'll turn up. I was halfway up the stairs in my stockinged feet when there was a knock at the door. A *pleasant* sort of knock. Restrained.

Her front door had a small vestibule. You could see into it through stained glass. I dithered. At this hour? Some guest off the late ferry, blundering around St Peter Port? I opened the door.

The chap standing there was portly, but neatly dressed, collar, tie, overcoat, specs.

'Your car's double parked, sir,' he said, all affable.

'Sorry, mate. I've got no motor.' Was he police?

He consulted a paper. His mufti, his geniality, a million other clues should have warned me, but I'm basically stupid. Did Mrs Vidamour have a motor she didn't want me to know about? Or one of the other four guests, workaholics all, I hadn't yet seen?

'Could you come and look, sir?'

I put my shoes on and followed him into the gloaming. He suddenly stopped. Hands grabbed, swung me round. I got clobbered. I'd been beaten by sticks before, truncheons even, and tried to make a run for it as two – two, I was sure – slammed blows across my shoulders, back, bum, thighs. I didn't get a yard. They held me down, kept up the steady and silent battering. The polite bloke was silhouetted against a street light, watching. I tried to shout, but I'd got my arms up to shield my head and my yells were muffled. My mistake. They were too cool to bother with bits that might show, and ignored my face.

Trying to run, I fell, scraping my knee hideously. Something ripped. I made another dash. The urbane bloke kneed me. Somebody chuckled, bastard, walking round me as I cowered, choosing spots to whack. I rolled about the pavement, conscious of the rising pain. It's odd. In case it's never happened to you, please observe that suffering doesn't come in spurts, one with each thump. There is that, of course, but the hurt quickly becomes an independent entity. It engulfs you in a rapidly swelling tide quite as if you were drowning in a pain flood. You start retching and vomiting after, say, fifteen seconds. Done expertly, punishment doesn't take long to reach this point.

'Leave, Lovejoy. Understood?'

'Mmmh.' My repartee.

'Tomorrow, no later. And I do mean go.'

They left me lying against Rosa's decorative hedge – boxwood? – of little bushes, no thorns, small leaves, actually not much use as plants go. I was sick for a while, drowning in my ocean of ache. It's only then that the real stabs start, doubling you over and making you retch every time you move. Somewhere nearby a car started up. Rain was falling. Guernsey wetness that seemed to start a couple of feet above my head. It's gentle stuff, not those forcible raps that clout your pate in East Anglia.

There wasn't much light. A little was coming from Mrs Vidamour's, feeble indirect stuff through the front door's fanlight. The skyglow, and that one street lamp . . . Should there be more? Organized punishers could have easily dowsed the street lighting. I gave up. Reason's no use at the best of times.

God knows how long I sprawled by the box hedge before I managed to creak on to my hands and knees. That was how I made it inside. I locked the front door after me – clever, eh? – and crept upstairs. I didn't manage to undress. The little clock said twenty to five. Thoughts started up about five past, stealing into my head and forming patterns. I wondered how long it would be before Jocina's husband called to gloat that he'd warned me.

Women are great. Give them their due.

Rosa came bustling in at seven, tea on that round tray. She put it down, stared. She left without a word, fetched bowls, flannels, and started. It made me worse. Being unpeeled and washed is embarrassing, not because you finish up naked as a grape while she whales at you, but because a woman crossly assumes you're deliberately impeding. For example, she'll want you to roll over when it's the last thing on earth you want to do, for pain surges and submerges you in nausea while she tuts and complains and holds the bowl for you to spew in. It's not dignified.

Also, women secretly know you're an infant. I reckon it's their genes. Suddenly they ignore speech, and completely forget communication except for curt gestures: on to your side, lift your arm, bend your leg. You get more talk when they're passionate. It's like they're blazing mad, as if you'd deliberately done yourself over, oh, it's Tuesday, I'll go and get clobbered senseless.

It's at least as bad for the injured party, namely me. Mrs Vidamour's breasts moved to and fro above me. When I miserably let her flip me onto my belly it was no easier. Her thighs kept brushing my legs, and her breasts squashed my shoulders. It's not fair. If I'd tried to reach for anything, I knew I'd be for it.

It took a good while. She did a fifth change of hot water, had the nerve to powder me, then hauled me vertical. I winced along the landing, my arm on her shoulders. She kept gasping because of my weight. I was slotted into a clean bed. She vanished, brought some tea, sat.

'My husband was a drunk,' she told me after a bit.

Oh, good. I felt encased in hot iron. My chest was criss-crossed with red marks, as if somebody had left the grill on overnight.

'I'm not sloshed. And,' I added pointedly, 'you haven't offered me a glug.'

'You'll get no alcohol in this house, Lovejoy.'

'Keep your hair on.' That's all I needed, a ballocking

because her spouse was a wino. 'Doctors say we must swig for our health.'

'He was always being brought home inebriated.' Tears shone in her eyes. I could tell that this annoyed her. Or maybe it was me? 'It was my job to clean him up, pretend he'd fallen. Any excuse. He died of it.'

'I'm sorry, love.'

She tried to smile. 'It's all right. Like old times.' Hesitation crept in. 'Should I call the doctor?'

That she hadn't spoke volumes. I shook my head, winced it motionless.

'I got beaten up. They told me to leave Guernsey or else.'

Rosa coloured. 'Why?'

'Why's always a rotten question, love.' I moved, groaned.

'Will you go?' Her voice had gone quiet.

'Look, dwoorlink. Any chance of you coming in to keep me warm?'

'You mean . . . ?' Her colour deepened, spread. 'Certainly not. I've only just got up.'

'Come to bed, and tell me about the antiques in Guernsey.'

Too much to hope for. Women can only co-operate in one thing at a time. I got some guide books with bits of ill-remembered local wonders.

'They've had some luck in Jersey,' she started, prim with disapproval of Guernsey's arch rival. 'A man found one or two tin things there. They put them on display, showing off as usual. We've far more interesting places.'

As she spoke I took her hand. She didn't snatch it back. Considering that she'd blanket-bathed me only minutes since, this was giddy progress. I listened to her miscellany. She was interrupted a couple of heart-stopping times by the doorbell. Once was the postman, the other some neighbour. When she returned the second time she surrendered her hand quite matter of factly.

Thinking of Rosa's vague accounts as she reminisced, I guessed that she meant the famed Cadoret Find. Never, I thought bitterly, the renowned Lovejoy Find, always somebody luckier. Except, the more you go out hunting with expensive equipment, the luckier you probably get.

He lived in Jersey, this detectorist, as they now call themselves. Out he plodded with his C-Scope CS2MX metal detector. He got a farmer's permission to detect on an oddly angular-shaped field. Instantly, he finds the island's hugest-ever Bronze Age hoard, over 170 genuine axe heads, sword fragments, bracelets and a small jeweller's hammer with side grooving for making drawn silver wire. Brilliant. The world's archeologists went into raptures. I remember hearing about the new dazzling find from Natty in the Antiques Arcade – the La Houge Bie Museum display was mentioned on telly. Dealers everywhere sobbed in their ale and blamed God for lack of fairness, et whining cetera. (No good telling them to get out there and hunt. Antique dealers find grumbling easier.)

Closer by inches, me and Rosa pored over her guide books. They were sadly dated. From about half a million years ago, when England was connected to the Continent and rhinos, lions, bears and giant deer roamed wherever they wanted. The seas rose over five fathoms. Land submerged. The British Isles hived off from the Continent. The peninsula of Jersey joined the Channel Isles; Guernsey and Herm parted company, all that boring geography stuff. Rosa prattled on through the tourist literature. I was thinking caves, and where paintings could be hidden. And where somebody trustworthy – me, say – could accidentally find them.

And thinking maybe that if there were no genuine Old Masters left, I could provide a *new* Old Master.

'The ancient people were called neolithic,' Rosa was going on, her hair falling over her face, showing me photographs in some crummy book. 'They made slab graves. They covered them with earth. Here, see?'

She showed me a picture. 'Mmmh,' I went, looking at her.

'The Guernsey family Lukis started listing them, to protect them from collectors.' She glanced at me to see I was paying attention, and edged away when she saw that I was.

Years ago I visited a place in Berkshire, not far from Henley. Some old Jersey governor retired there in 1788, taking with him the massive Mont de la Ville neolithic tomb from Jersey. He stuck it in his grounds. You can still visit it. It's a lesson. God knows what other priceless antiques wander from collectors' cabinets to auction rooms. Age-old innocence becomes depredation with historical hindsight. Every antique dealer on earth envies the La Hougue Bie, Jersey's massive 5,000-year-old mound that stands almost thirty-five feet tall and measures almost sixty yards round. Just think of the invaluable relics a burial chamber that size might contain. And what if you stumble across another in, say, Guernsey?

'The most famous remains are at Les Fouaillages, Guernsey's northern tip,' she said. Take that, Jersey, you upstart.

'Show me the museum and art gallery?' I asked. I had to get some perspective if I was going to pull any stunt at all.

'Will you be warm enough?' she asked, not looking.

It was a merry quip, I realized, about my asking her to come to bed. I smiled, forgiving.

'By noon,' I said gravely. 'Earlier, if you'd help.'

'Get on with you,' she reprimanded. 'I'll bring you a new breakfast.' Then she paused. 'Who did it, Lovejoy? I heard noises through my sleep.'

'Dunno. Your jealous lovers?'

Into silence she said, 'This doesn't happen in Guernsey.'

Oh, aye, I thought. 'Everywhere's holy until I arrive, is that it?'

One thing worried me. 'Three husbands,' I'd heard of Mrs Crucifex. Her legit one was Martin. No prize for guessing that Prior George was the second stud in her stable. I now knew the third, my home county's police boss Summer, benevolent helper on Jocina's fund-raising team. He must have formidable allies in Guernsey. From their supercool behaviour I could assume my assailants were Plod. My enquiries had stirred him up. Had they also listened in on my phone calls?

'Why are you arranging this show, Lovejoy?' Rosa asked eventually. She now wore make-up, I noticed, but not enough. Women can't wear too much, though they don't know this. 'If people don't want you to, why not give in?'

'Look, dworlink.' I mopped the grease with my last slice of bread. 'I have a cousin. She's elderly, really poorly. She runs this home for orphaned children in Manchester.' I watched my lies take effect. 'If I can earn a percentage – anything's welcome – it might help, see?'

'That's beautiful,' she said, eyes glistening. I too filled up, because it truly was. I mean it would have been if it was.

She came on to the bed, after I waxed lyrical on my imaginary cousin's struggle for imaginary orphans, but kept her clothes on and unfairly lay outside the bedclothes, selfish cow. Eloquence doesn't do much.

Eleven o'clock, I groaned my way into the world. After my marathon phone session, four performers were due in by one o'clock, followed by six more on the late afternoon flight. I was nowhere near ready.

'You kept me late!' I cried, floundering about for clothes. She rushed to get them from my bedroom, complaining that I hadn't warned her, where were they going to stay, dross questions women always ask when they're trying to escape blame for idleness.

'Get old Jethou and Gussy,' I shouted, limping to the bathroom. 'And tell them to find me a crook.'

'A *what*?' floated back along the landing. I turned the taps on.

'You heard. Where's a towel?' No towel, no love, no nothing. Was that a song? I looked in the fogging mirror. It's not something I do often, thank God. I saw a desperate face. I decided to avoid mirrors in future. If Rosa hadn't come to help me into the water, I'd be standing gaping there yet.

'Lovejoy,' she said at last, offering me a mothball-scented dressing gown – first outing of her husband's remaindered gear? 'I'm not sure of this behaviour. I think we ought to perhaps leave the island for a week or two. It's rather outside my experience.'

'We?' I sat on the edge of the bath to ponder. Did it mean what I hoped it meant? She wasn't looking at me, so maybe I was on a promise. But it would be daft to leave now because everybody that mattered was here in Guernsey. The fag ends were going to arrive in shoals, starting today.

'You expect too much of me.'

That was a bit steep. What the hell had I asked her for, for heaven's sake? Nothing had happened yet.

Just as I thought that, the doorbell went. And Rosa, in a kind and caring way, gave me an hour's notice to leave her lodgings for good.

24

'MORNING, MARTIN,' I said to the figure in the vestibule.

'Marteen?' said Prince. He gestured imperiously to the taxi. 'Iss I, Lovejoy!'

'Er, wotcher, Prince.' I'd not counted on this. Hadn't he sold his forgery commission, the Nicholas Brown bookcase-desk, to Florida? 'Why're you here?'

He thrust his way past and ceremoniously kissed Rosa's hand. ' 'Eez Roy' 'Ighness Prince Yussopopoff, madam . . .' etc. She went flustered. I don't know why he does this pantomime. Maybe it has some effect on the ladies? The duckegg certainly has an effect on me. He wore scarlet Cossack pants, Russian boots, a blue fur hat, and a vermilion cape with epaulettes. I needed secret help, and got a game show.

'I 'ear,' he boomed, twirling his earring, 'my fren' Lovejoy pulls a grett scam, no?' He reclined, beaming joyously on Rosa. 'Theess yor concubine?'

'Not yet – er, no,' I said. 'Look, Nev—'

He sprang up in fury. 'I no Neville, Loveyoy! I duelling, no?'

'We're just off out, mate.' I'd no need to be servile any longer. 'Find yourself some other place.'

'Oh, Lovejoy!' Rosa cut in, all eager. 'I'm sure His High-ness—'

'Clear off,' I said wearily. 'See you at the harbour nosh bar, sixish.'

I managed to shove him out, protesting. The taxi driver was just unloading the last of his sixteen suitcases. I slammed the door.

'Rosa, love. That duckegg lacks scruples. He's a bigger con than . . .'

'Than you?' She went to peer through the window. I'd already agreed before I realized what she'd said.

'Less lip from you. Did you catch Jethou?'

She bleated, 'When have I had time to phone? I've been busy.'

That's women. Excuses. Comes from having nothing to do.

'Lovejoy.' She seemed distressed, wrung her hands. 'I meant it. I have to give you notice.'

'Don't muck about, love,' I said, impatient. 'We've things to do.' I petered out. She was in tears. Was this serious? My heart fell. Suddenly I remembered the early morning rings on the doorbell, postman, then some neighbour. After that, she'd been solicitous, kindly and rather sad. She'd been given orders to ditch me. Also, how at ease Martin had seemed, drinking his coffee in Rosa's kitchen. The penny dropped. Silly me.

'Don't worry, love. I'll go.'

'I'm so sorry, Lovejoy.' She blotted her eyes. 'It's the stealing, your telling lies, those men beating you up. And associating with . . .' Drunken old Jethou and crazy Gussy?

'It's all right,' I said. 'Don't cry. I understand.'

She gave me a bill for the rent, with every phone call priced, every bit of grub costed, added to the amount she'd lent me. It came to a hell of a lot. I promised to get the money in an hour, soon as I could get to the bank. We parted with mutual expressions of regard. She said I could return any time 'in normal circumstances'. I walked, trying not to limp in case she was watching. Pride.

Hospitality's like eloquence. It doesn't do much. I longed for East Anglia, where I knew the hoods, bloods, duds. On this lovely holiday island I was out of my depth. Just my luck to have landed at Mrs Vidamour's. I felt sorry for myself. I had no illusions. Seaside places have systems to protect landladies from default. I'd be on everybody's list. Had I better hop it?

In a coldish wind I sat at the Quay, looking out to Castle Pier. Nights wear me out, and daytime only exists to be worn out in.

Even when you feel down, sea's somehow soothing. I'm not one of those romantics who're forever on about us being in harmony with the mighty ocean. I'm only in harmony with antiques. I tried to think. What had I promised Jocina, exactly? I'd promised a competition. I'd left it vague.

Some bloke stood nearby, pointedly I thought. I gave him a glance, then a couple more. He seemed familiar. One of my attackers? His stare intimidated me, so I moved to the North Esplanade. The Sea Link Ferry docks across from there. Walt hadn't turned up. Maybe they'd done him over as well?

It's knowing that you've no money to buy food that undoes you. By noon I was starving. Deceiving nobody except myself, I went to the ferry office on the pier and made enquiries.

Maybe I could pick up a groat or two at the marina doing odd jobs. But the rich only hire mariners who know what they're doing with valuable sailing craft. They don't hire inept scroungers.

In despond, I actually started wondering if I should stow aboard the next ferry from the island. If I stayed to face the mob of showbiz folk, I'd have a hell of a time. Nobody more murderous than an actor who fails the audition. For one wistful moment I imagined that maybe Maureen Jolly might be kind and understand the mess I was in, but it was a pipe dream. She would kill me dead, and go to the scaffold delighted she'd finally made star billing. She'd do her hair for the occasion.

If I hadn't been so kind to Irma Dominick, I'd not be in this mess. Demanding to be taught to steal so she could balls my life up, stupid cow. I'd murder her if I could get my hands on her. Which made me think. What on earth *had* happened to Irma? She'd got nicked, I'd asked wino lawyer Michaelis to spring her, but then what? I felt a glim of hope. Wasn't Irma the Rockingham porcelain thief *who hated her Aunt Jocina*? Had I a secret ally here in Guernsey after all? I used a public phone box, got the operator to reverse the charges by an inventive lie.

'Yes, Vino Wine Importery of Guernsey here. To place an order.'

They put me through like a shot. 'Hello?'

'Michaelis? It's me, Lovejoy.' He was partly sober. 'Sorry about the phone charges trick, but I've no money. What happened to Irma?'

'I bailed her, and she scarpered. You owe me her bail.' He mentioned a sum verging on the National Debt. I felt ill. 'Clients don't welsh on me, Lovejoy.'

Despite the threat my spirits rose, first time since I'd got marmalized. Irma had done a bunk. Where to? Here, of course! I could use Irma to betray Jocina.

'I'll not let you down, Michaelis. I'll see you're paid. I mean that with sincerity.'

'I warn you, Lovejoy. My people get nasty.'

Irma *must* be here. I wish I'd had the sense to think of this a couple of days before instead of wasting my time. It came on to drizzle. I was past caring and sat there watching the marina, ships to and fro. I scanned things in my mind. Antiques had got me into this, thanks to Irma. Antiques must get me out. Then I'd settle up with Metivier for Gesso's . . . I couldn't think the word . . . vanishment.

Then I recalled when Walt Jethou had given me that lift on his crummy motorbike. We'd driven down a street. I'd yelled in his earhole that an antique shop we were passing looked a likely place. He'd shouted back, 'Don't be ridiculous. They're not local!' laughed like a drain, didn't stop.

Two o'clock, in drizzle, I found the shop near the Parish Church. If the dealer was 'not local', I stood a chance. A chance is all I've ever needed in antiques to get in a worse mess. I went inside, the bell clonking overhead.

A woman, pleasantly tubby and harassed, was packing handies – small antiques you can palm. I waited for my gong to go. Hardly a chime. I heard a creak behind a curtain. Grannie in a rocking chair?

'Hello,' I said. 'Can I look, please?'

'Please do.' She brushed a wisp of hair with her wrist. I like them doing that. It's somehow touching. 'I'm sorry, but we're closing soon. The charity auction, you see. I'm due there.'

'Got much?' No more creaks. I smiled. Grannie was listening.

The place was no bigger than a living room, a curtain

dividing off the rear. Around the walls, furniture, paintings, poor-quality harbour scenes looking good from a distance but aged by tobacco smoke, one circular table that would have been worth restoring, except some loon forty years back had replaced the legs with modern dross and re-veneered the surface. Dealers do that, and finish up with one 'good' antique they can sell to some unsuspecting buyer who thinks she's getting a perfect eighteenth-century dining table. In the process, they've murdered maybe three honest old tables while doing their 'antique creation'. It's the in phrase. Plates hung from those modern hook-and-spring wires that have chipped (and therefore ruined) more valu-able Georgian plates than any carelessness. I once wrote to our MP, tried to get them banned. He wrote back that I was insane. That, note, from a politician.

'Not a great deal, I'm afraid.' She had a nice smile. A door closed quietly. The curtain wafted up then settled. Grannie leaving, not interested after all? I tried to avoid sniffing the aroma. Oil of cloves? 'We're practically brand new.'

'But you're Guernsey, Rita?' Her name was stuck on her lapel.

'Yes.' She was flustered, checking, forgetting where she'd put her list. 'I have no experience. I mean, antiques are special, aren't they?'

'I like that brooch.' Cardboard box, fewer than a dozen objects.

She glanced at the time. 'I see you know your antiques! That has to go for quite a lot!' Her voice hushed, big secrets. 'It's Berlin jewellery.'

Berlin work was made in, well, Berlin, at its Royal Berlin Factory, though it had started earlier somewhere in Silesia. I picked up the bracelet. Heavy, not very attractive. Its inside had the stamp GGIFE, meaning *Gold gab ich für Eisen*, proving that some lady had patriotically handed in a precious golden bangle to fund Prussia's efforts against Tyrant Napoleon. Such ladies received iron jewellery in exchange, a custom they repeated in every major war, though Napoleon nicked the moulds and started a French manufactory. There are even Wedgwood variants, valuable things if you can find them.

This bracelet was decorated with a single garnet jewel. I love garnet, a much maligned stone beloved of the ancients, almost as much as I hate the term 'semi-precious'. I mean, would we like to be called that, semi-human maybe? It's an insult to a gemstone that has lived millions of years and will be here long after we're gone. Sometimes Berlin iron jewellery was designed in parures, which are suites or sets, such as earrings, necklace, bracelet, brooch, plus an aigrette to adorn the lady's hair or headdress. You only come across them split up nowadays, unless you're rich enough to fund a search. It set me thinking. I looked closer.

Somebody had had a go at enamelling the bracelet's rim. It had blistered quite badly. I sighed. The antiques game is ruined by its players, who despoil in ignorance.

'Well, don't blame me!'

'Eh? Oh, sorry.' I must have spoken aloud. 'I wouldn't care, except this piece is genuine.' I explained about parures, and incomplete sets dealers call 'demis', meaning demi-parures. I laid the iron bracelet down, mentally told it thanks for not minding. 'You didn't do this enamelling yourself, then?'

'No. It was done somewhere on the mainland.'

'Well, tell him not to use a drying oil for painting in the enamel colour. It always froths up. Temperature faults, probably. It's a giveaway that somebody's tried to make jewellery more valuable.'

Enamelling is beset with these problems. The worst thing is to try some short cut. I've even known blokes who'll try to exclude cobalt oxide when doing a first enamel on sheet iron. Barmy. It can be done, but at prodigious risk.

She went to the curtain. 'Oh. Sorry. He's just gone. I'll tell him. Can you write it down? I know he'll be very pleased.'

So I did, like a burk. Sometimes I can't believe my stupidity. 'Got any Golden Syrup? Tell him to use gum mastic, syrup, glycerin, in equal amounts, with a little distilled water. Add a drop or two of wetting agent. Never mind those expensive mediums. They only carry the vitrified colours to the heat.'

She watched me scribble. 'Do you really mean household—?'

'Certainly. Golden Syrup's very underrated stuff. A spoonful in butter cleans grime, makes your hands like a baby's bum.' We forget these old remedies. Like, Cleopatra's ladies used natron – sodium carbonate – in honey as a contraceptive douche. They *said* it worked. Mind you, they said the same about crocodile dung.

'He's ordering a small kiln.'

'Tell your faker not to be so blinking impatient when he's forging antiques. Impatience is worst on precious metals. You have to do layer after layer, brief firings one after another. Save him a fortune, tell him it's hopeless firing enamels straight on to gold. Do it on silver first, then layer it in.'

'Thank you. Mister . . . ?'

Robbing this innocent lady would be like strangling a butterfly.

'Hang about, Rita. I'll have a look round your antiques.'
It took about half a minute. What was bad was horrid.
What had been good was ruined.

'He restored this painting himself, did he?' I stopped
before a Victorian seascape. With enormous restraint, I
managed not to sob.

'I think his partner.'

'He's ruined a perfectly good painting.'

'Oh, no. You're wrong. He's very proud of having
restored it himself. It was mouldy. He even scraped the
surface! Restoring is an art.'

Indeed. If you really want to learn the Great Antiques
Trade, learn by heart my nine truest calamity stories.
They're all terrible, and carry bitter lessons bitterly learnt.
I'll not give all nine. Here's just one – if you haven't a
nervous disposition.

Two Canadian blokes one day wandered through a local
auction. 'Hey,' says one. 'Look at that moth-eaten mouldy
oil painting! Vaguely like Turner, eh?' They had a laugh,
bought the begrimed canvas for a groat, took it home. The
more they looked, the more they thought of the immortal
Turner, greatest painter the world has ever known. And the
more they looked, the more it *felt* Turner. Finally they
thought, Fingerprints!

Cut to the police in West Yorkshire, Merrie England.
Whose fingerprint department checked, rechecked and
issued a few mild words. 'Yes, those fingerprints are
Turner's.' They'd got his originals off the *Chichester Canal*
painting in the Tate. Ecstasy! Paradise indeed! Oh, and
money. Mustn't forget money, because if you, me or Joe
Soap paints a daub as best we can we'd be lucky to get sixty
zlotniks. But if a crumbling decaying canvas is by Turner,

you're in zillionnaire land and no mistake. It was jubilation time in the old homestead that evening, to be sure.

(I know what you're thinking. A moment ago I said it was a calamity. So how come it's suddenly angel choirs and violins? Read sadly on.)

At Phillips, posh London auction rooms, in the gloomy rain of dark December, there was one shining beacon of light. It was gelt. For the newly found *Landscape With Rainbow*, proven handiwork of the immortal artist, was up for auction. Then (here comes our calamity) the light guttered and died. Buyers and Old Master experts came, saw and wept. For the painting had been 'restored' almost to extinction. Dirty, it had been worth millions. Now, it had been scrubbed free of all its artistic brilliance. The auctioneer knocked it down for peanuts, amid a stony silence broken only by the sounds of the sobbing newshounds in that Oxford Street pub and the loud ping of perforating duodenal ulcers. The owners had scrubbed off a king's ransom. Tip: if you don't know what to do to an antique, *don't do it*.

'That's terrible!' Rita was saying.

'Eh? Oh, well, old artists sometimes tried new media, different effects on colours, see? Turner was always at it.' I smile when I think of him. I can't help it. 'He'd used megilp, a stuff made of mastic varnish and linseed oil crammed full of poisonous white lead. It's brilliant to do forgeries – er, I've heard. But it starts wrinkling almost as soon as you walk away from the canvas.' Forgers use it, though, with ochres as a yellowing agent, to deceive people into thinking they're buying something truly old.

'Isn't that fantastic!' Rita looked from me to the box of dross. 'Why did you say thanks to the bracelet?'

Thinking aloud was getting out of hand. 'Sorry. I used to do it, er, as a lad.'

She was smiling. 'Would you help me out to the car, please? My dealer has gone ahead.'

'Certainly.'

So I carried her crummy box out through the back room. Where a peal of thunder stopped me.

'Can you manage, Mister . . . ?'

'Aye, ta. Just noticed that lamp.'

'Yes.' She spoke with distaste. 'I told Mr Crucifex it ought to be removed. We should have this room renovated.'

Above the back door hung a cresset. Scotch folk call it a crusie, Shetlanders a collie. In Lancashire it's a Betty. Basically a Roman design, it's just an iron stand with a hook to hang a glim. You fill it with oil, stick a wick in it, and there's your lamp. The Channel Islanders had this variant. Their word cresset is Norman, not English. This was an old, old version. One form is the basket and spike you see in Hollywood sword-and-sandal epics, burning torches on castle walls. This looked like it had been corroding there a couple of centuries.

'Rusty old thing. It's dangerous.' I was thinking, Did she say Crucifex? But Walt Jethou had said the proprietor wasn't local. 'Shall I get rid of it?'

'Have we time?'

'Only take a second, love,' I said, piously hurrying out and stowing her box in the boot. 'What if it fell on some little child, or a customer?'

'Exactly!'

She went back to get her handbag. I followed and lifted the cresset down. It had a metal loop that had discoloured the wall plaster over the years. It felt exquisite, that crooked old piece of bent iron and its flattish metal bowl. There was even a charred wick in the bottom under thick dust. Only a couple of hundred, but that's more than nowt. A year for each zlotnik? Cheap at the price.

'There!' I showed revulsion, acting away. 'Have you a dustbin?'

'In the yard. Collection's Mondays.'

'Right.' I placed it with reverence behind the bin, dusted off my hands. She got into her car. 'Did you remember to lock up, Rita. Front door and back?'

She smiled. 'Yes. And I put the "closed" notice in the window.' She gunned the engine. 'You're nice, Mister . . . ?'

'I think you're beautiful,' I said. 'But I don't go on about it, do I? Was that Mr Crucifex who'd left as I arrived?'

'No. Mr Slevin's not a Guernésiais. He's new, rents the shop from Mr Crucifex.'

'I'd like to met him.' Maybe black his eye, for damaging antiques by mucking about like that bad enamel.

'Thank you for your assistance. Are you a collector?'

'No. My cousin runs this orphanage in Manchester. I try and help her out . . .' I smiled nobly. Stick to a good lie.

'An orphanage? Look, please let me . . .' She fumbled in her handbag.

To my horror I heard myself say, 'Certainly not! I wouldn't dream of it. How could you be sure I'd send it to her?'

She pressed a note into my hand. 'I know people,' she said, all misty.

'Get to St Peter's,' I choked back my welling piety.

'It's not there. The charity auction's at Splendid Sejour.' She started the engine, a manoeuvre taking the best part of the day, and said shyly, 'Will you call in again?'

'Perhaps I'll follow you to the auction.'

She smiled, lovely teeth, dimples, and drove out of the yard. Follow her to where? I couldn't even say it.

On my own, I peered about. The back yard wasn't overlooked. I hefted up the cresset, and wrapped it carefully in old newspapers I rescued from the dustbin.

Fifteen minutes later, I'd sold it to the Guernsey Antiquery Emporium. I told the dealer I'd fetched it over on the ferry from Wiltshire. I invented a provenance. My mythical great-uncle, erstwhile soldier in the Guernsey garrison, had brought it back, etc., etc. The chap tried telling me it wasn't worth anything, sneering that I should take it back, and who nowadays wanted old iron lamps? I just shrugged, said OK, turned sadly away – whereupon he dragged me back and offered me what I'd asked. See? Confront antique dealers honestly, you get away with murder. I mean that with sincerity.

Half an hour later I found Splendid Sejour.

25

SPLENDID SEJOUR TURNED out to be a leisure centre packed with visitors. Unbelievably, it had a cinema. There was a fashion exhibition, swimming, bars, restaurants, other goings-on, it was all happening at Splendid Sejour. No antique shops, though. Planners wrong again.

The Gala Charity Auction was scheduled for three hours' time. I milled, looked, searched, saw nobody I knew. Presumably it was too small an event for Mrs Crucifex and her harem of tame males. No sign of Irma Dominick. This disappointed me, after my notion that she'd be a potential ally. No sign of Marie Metivier, either, which made me sadder still. No sign of Martin, of Prior Metivier – though I saw that his Holy Priory Charity was listed as a beneficiary.

Boxing clever, I surged only where there were crowds to surge among. Roller skating, the bars, a nosh place after a couple of hours. No sign of Rosa, ex-landlady who'd let me down by buckling under hard pressure from local bigwigs. Surprisingly, no sign of Rita either, though I could see her stuff laid out among the dross on trestle tables when I glanced in. Ladies were diligently numbering the items. No bongs that rendered me senseless, so any genuine antiques must be ruined or restored – same thing – out of all recognition. The furniture was especially pathetic. I noticed on the wall one of Gussy's grey-and-black line paintings. I was peering in at it, thinking, when a voice intruded.

'Hello. Jonno Rant?'

'Er . . . ?' The rubicund face of Jimmy Ozanne beamed recognition. 'Remember me? We met at the Victor Hugo Museum.'

'Of course.' We shook hands. I can't do it convincingly, like Americans. In East Anglia we only ever shake hands once, and it does for life. 'Are you running this auction, then?' Maybe he was the quiet manager of Crucifex's antique shop? I must clear that little side issue up, ask Martin Crucifex. As if he'd tell me.

'Heavens, no. I came on the off chance of bumping into you, actually. Mrs Vidamour said you'd gone home.' His voice became concerned. 'Not giving up your show, are you, old sport? Only, I've already drafted the newspaper notices. Small service I offer, y'know. Off the cuff, what?'

'You have?' I felt delighted. Here was an ally after all, even if he did speak like a crusty old harrumphing major. 'That's terrific, Jimmy. Time for a drink?'

'If you insist, old bean.'

Was Jimmy Ozanne real? I ordered grandly with money from the cresset. I'd not been called old bean since acting out some jingoistic nonsense in school.

'Good of you to take the trouble, Jimmy,' I said once we'd got going. I kept an eye on the time. 'Unexpected help, that.'

'Locals, old boy. Terribly proper, what? Sticklers for propriety. Worse than the mainland.'

Aye, I thought bitterly, remembering Rosa lying demurely above the quilt while I lay beneath, I'd already learnt how proper.

'Maybe I'll do the show here. My performers,' I added recklessly, 'arrive soon. Some are already here now, I shouldn't wonder.'

'Splendid, old fruit!' Old *fruit*? 'How soon's your show, Jonno?'

'Third night from now. I sussed out the Roi de Normandie Hotel for it actually, but I'm having doubts.'

'This is the place, Jonno. Splendid Sejour can cope.' He lowered his voice. 'I might wangle a special rate. 'Nuff said, what?'

'Er, great, Jimmy. Ta.'

'What's the campaign plan? Mum's the word.' He tapped his nose.

I was full of admiration. I'd not seen that gesture since *Oliver*.

'The artists gather. My show director's a lass called Maureen. She's dynamite.' God, I thought, lying away, can Maureen direct? And her pal, Patty. Hell fire. They *all* might be duds. I swallowed. Somebody announced the auction on the intercom.

'I need a factotum, Jimmy, to organize details. Any ideas?'

He cleared his throat, rocked on his heels. A shoal of children passing on roller blades made a swift diversion between us.

'Can I offer myself, Jonno? Local. Recce superfluous, what?' He tapped his temple. 'All systems, jump-off time.'

'You'll be the manager? Great!' And I meant it. 'Terms are eight per cent. Equity contract.' Eight per cent of what? I was making it up. I'd known a girl once, aspiring actress. She was always on about getting an Equity card. Or was that immigrants to America? 'Of the gross,' I ended on a flourish.

'Excellent!' He beamed, ordered a gin sling. 'Assembly what ack emma?'

What the hell was ack emma? Some sort of gun? 'You decide, Jimmy.' I raised my glass. 'You're in charge! Sign chits,' I said grandly, 'in the name of Jonno Rant Productions. Now, we do two things. One's the show. They're all splendid performers, so no worries there.'

'*Kwaiss jiddan!*' He rubbed his hands. Approval, in Arabic? My scam was going to be harder than I thought.

'At the peak of the music-hall floor show, Jimmy, the whole audience will be invited to gamble mightily on items I'll display. It's for charity. One person wins a genuine mega possession. Advertise it as an antique.'

'Antique, hey?' He brushed his moustache, doubt creeping in. 'Is it worth interrupting a show to dish out some old pot? Not losing morale, but—'

'It will make the winner a multi-millionaire, Jimmy.'

He stared, gaped, harrumphed. 'By jingo, Jonno! You take the biscuit, old chap! Thinking big, hey? Tickety boo. What *is* the antique?'

'Secret, Jimmy,' I said, going furtive, because I didn't know myself yet, though I had the glimmerings. 'Insurance, Sotheby's, Lloyd's. Security, you understand.'

'Say no more, old bean!' Solemnly he raised his glass. 'Chin chin.'

'Chin, er, chin,' I said. 'Six-thirty, press conference.'

'*Waaaw kyeh!*'

'*Waaaw,* er . . .' I left him a happy man. His back was straighter, stalking danger on safari.

The little auction had started to fourscore people in a mild carnival atmosphere. I lurked. Nobody I recognized, and nobody bidding with a recognizable 'signature', the auction pattern that's a dead giveaway. The way a regular bidder goes about his bids is as characteristic as handwriting.

There's never an auction but what something's worth buying, even in a small charity do. I bid a few coppers for five old posters in a cardboard roll. I tried to look indifferent, but was delighted to see that I'd bought the greatest of Victorian posters, practically mint. Advertising boomed recklessly in the nineteenth century – adverts even popped up on the Pyramids, on sacred national flags. People even had artillery literally firing wads of handbills for tooth powder all over the suburbs. Ignore 'advertabilia' if you like, but you're throwing money away if you do.

Collectables make purists mad, but if they make you money, do they have to be a Rembrandt? Any auction has sporting memorabilia, forgettables, watercolours, porcelain, toys, jewellery. Scavenging's not a nice side to human nature, but if looking round old junk shops was the worst we got up to, the world would be a pretty pleasant place. So I paid up and put the roll under my arm. Plenty of people make a living from new advertising, so what's wrong with old? For once I'd scooped the pool.

Andrew Pears, soap maker, founded his company in 1789. For his time he was a dynamite salesman. His granddaughter's husband, Tom Barratt, got the marketing bug. He'd do anything to sell Pears soap. It's a famous Victorian story, how in 1887 Tom bought from the *Illustrated London News* the painting called 'Bubbles', by that marvel Sir John Millais. A little lad, actually the painter's grandson, is admiring a soap bubble he's just blown using a clay pipe. Barratt had a bar of his soap painted in – and there was his tasteful advert. He even got Lily Langtry – the Jersey Lily – to sign that she used Pears Soap exclusively. There was a row, as only Victorians could row, but eventually even

Millais didn't mind. The modern advertising lesson was learnt: publicity ruled. A perfect 'Bubbles' poster nowadays costs as much as the original painting did. And I'd just bought one for a quid.

Barratt's the same bloke who imported tons of French ten-centime copper coins – then usable in the UK as legit 'pennies' – and stamped them with his advertising slogan, at fourteen to the shilling instead of twelve. The government went nuclear, melted them all down, and angrily amended the law. They showed Barratt the door when the cad offered to print the nation's 1891 census forms free of charge – if the forms carried yet another soap advert. I like Barratt, a true manic Victorian. The government's refusal made him indignant: wasn't the national flag being flown inscribed with beer adverts? And hadn't government allowed Barratt to print his adverts on the gummy side of the official 1881 lilac penny postage stamp? (In New Zealand, a rival's legend in 1893 came off on your tongue when you licked the stamps: 'Sunlight Soap for Washing Dogs . . .'). I was content. I knew four collectors of advertabilia. Is it my fault they're off their trolley? I once sold a Victorian advert for magnetic foot warmers. The most expensive are those shaped metal painted adverts advertising posh American shops of the 1870s; one will buy you a new house. Keep looking. Meanwhile . . . Eh?

'Hello, Lovejoy.'

'Hello, Walt.' He looked uneasy. 'Augusta's painting's the next lot?'

'People only laugh, Lovejoy. She won't come to these auctions.' He coughed. 'Sorry not to have been around.'

'Don't worry, Walt.' I can be quite kind when I'm lying. 'I leave Guernsey today, so I'm glad I caught you.'

He was relieved. 'Rosa told me. Glad there'll be no more

trouble. Gussy's disappointed, after your promise, but she'll get over it.'

So much for loyalty to principle. 'Remember me to her.' If I'd had a watch I'd have glanced at it. 'Better get down to the ferry. Cheers, Walt.'

Off I walked. I posted the cardboard roll of posters to my cottage, and got a taxi to drop me off a few hundred yards short of Gussy's antiques place, clever old Tracker Dan that I am. I walked in. She was at her easel, yet another masterpiece. I guessed what it would be. I stood there a few minutes, saw her do the preliminary underpainting. Christ, but she poured on the turpentine. It was awash, stank the place out.

'Same, love?'

She painted wildly on, hair any old how. 'Thought you'd gone back to the mainland, Lovejoy,' she said bitterly. 'Come to buy one of Mad Gussy's crazies?'

'No.' I went closer. 'I want fourteen.'

She rounded so fiercely I recoiled. Then she saw my face.

'Lovejoy. You're one person, then you're not. You're leaving, then still here. You say my paintings are balderdash. Now you want fourteen?'

'Yes. I can pay a deposit now, the rest later. How much are they?'

She started to laugh, tears streaming down. I grew uncomfortable. I don't like that noise between laughter and tears. Women laughing crying like that make me think something's wrong. Joy and pain ought to keep separate.

'What the hell for, Lovejoy?' she got out finally. 'You buy fourteen, *then* ask the price?' She sobered. 'I knew you were trouble, first time I saw you.'

'Not interfering, love, but is so much turpentine wise?'

Artists kill critics (and vice versa; fair's fair), so I was dicing with death. 'Play your cards right, a spoonful will do for a whole canvas. Think of the original. He never splashed it about like that.'

'You see?' Tears fell, plop, plop, on to her skirt. 'It's the same feeling.'

'Eh?'

'I knew a man once. We were close. He'd been in prison for manslaughter. I was young.' I don't know what a sardonic laugh is, but it sounded close. 'We were the scandal of Guernsey. He left because of the police.'

'Here,' I said, narked. 'I'm not a criminal. As for manslaughter—'

'It's the same feeling, Lovejoy. Doing wrong, the speed, not knowing why.' She looked at me. 'And not caring any longer if I'm doing wrong. Tell me, Lovejoy. What are my paintings to do with you?'

'When it's all over, I'll keep one. For my cottage. For now, I need a place to hide, and your gungey old motor. And paintings.'

We spoke for an hour, me and Gussy, mostly about her childhood. I listened while she talked. And the oddest thing happened. She became animated. The years fell from her. Her lunacy dwindled and vanished. We were suddenly the friendliest of friends. Augusta Quenard was the best thing that had happened to me since I'd arrived.

Later, laughing, she sought out the last of her grey paintings and we got them covered up in her car boot. Solemnly I paid her a note for deposit.

'Sale or return, Lovejoy?' she asked mischievously. 'And can I come?'

'No, love.' I got her keys and coaxed the engine. '*Waaaw kyeh!*'

'What does that mean?'

'Dunno. I think it's optimism. Cheers, love.'

I badly wanted to see Prior Metivier and his delectable sister, but things were more pressing. The crook, Gesso's killer, would have to wait. I drove to the airport to meet Florida.

26

WOMEN MAKE ME hungry. Sometimes, just a glimpse makes my mouth water. Don't misunderstand. Florida was no bimbo. She came into Guernsey's miniature air terminal like a goddess. Bright, alert, demanding. Powder-blue suit, pillbox hat, skirt trim and everything matching. In comparison the arriving crowd looked utter tat.

'Dwoorlink!' I cried, advancing, old times.

She swept past. 'Don't be ridiculous, Lovejoy. Where is it?'

That's what I mean. Florida was class. I know my place is humility, but why the reminder? She stopped, looking about. Three porters, three suitcases each. Probably staying all of two days.

'The scam? I'll show you, love.' I stutter when I'm edgy, worse when I'm flummoxed.

'Florida means the limo, idiot.'

A massive bloke was standing by her. Slim of waist, muscly, an inverted pear of aggro. Tarzan in trendy King's Road leather, long blond hair, tanned from alligator wrestling in some tropic. He looked a giant sixteen. Florida and him? I'd thought it was Florida and me.

'It's there.' I pointed to Gussy's wheels.

Tarzan stared at Florida. 'You were right. This worm's pathetic.' He turned to me, amid clusters of tourists. 'Get decent wheels, idiot. Pronto.'

He buffeted me so my head spun. I reeled. I don't mind these tough duffs, but feel narked when they decide they're Godzilla and us amoebas. I grinned, stored it up. I'm good at hate, but tend to forget why I'm seething.

'I'm sorry,' I said, humbly. 'Will they do for the whilst?'

We drove, him clipping my ear when I hesitated at intersections. I kept silent. Every one was a chit I'd cash in later, to his profound regret. They named a hotel I'd never heard of. To Dook, as she called him, my ignorance of its whereabouts proved I was an imbecile. Florida didn't deign to speak. I drove them to the Roi de Normandie, unloaded their luggage.

'This is the sister hotel,' I lied. 'Yours, sir, is in, er, superclass, through main reception.'

I promised to call later, take her and her primate to dinner. Florida ignored me, swept inside holding her gilded youth's hand. They left their suitcases in a heap. So did I. I'd assumed Florida, my mark one gambler, would be a superb ally. Wrong again. I drove off.

Thirty minutes later I knocked on the Carrieres' door, and asked to see Dove. They took me through.

'Lucky you caught me in,' Dove said cheerily.

Like a fool I found myself agreeing before I got the quip. I laughed shamefacedly. Joe was sculpting in the garden. Dove was painting in watercolours, using her pulleys, a brush in her teeth.

Meg seated me, brewed up. We talked of this and that. I asked could I crate some things up in their shed. They said why not. I got Dove laughing fit to burst, describing Florida's arrival and her bronzed stalwart.

'Dook,' I said when Dove asked. 'Honest. He's called Dook.'

'Don't be upset, Lovejoy,' Dove narked me by saying. 'She'll see sense.'

'Upset?' I laughed so merrily that I hurt my ribs. 'You seriously think . . . ? Good grief!' I went on about Florida's ugliness for some time, saying if I was *that* hard up I'd be really down, but I wasn't so I wasn't.

'So she's very pretty?'

'She's married, heaven's sake!' I told them. They were all listening by now, nodding. 'She has a terrible temper. She likes horses. Can you imagine?'

'No, no,' they went.

It makes you narked, when people misunderstand. Me and Florida? Give me a break. I'd have said it outright, but Americanisms sound daft when I try them. Conversation faltered.

Joe took me to his shed. It stood behind his workshop, where he was trying to model a Lalique piece in that new porous fast-drying clay – a boon to forgers, incidentally. Made in Swindon, but costs the earth. He had plenty of spare wood. I backed the motor in, said I could manage on my own, ta very much. They went about their business, so didn't see what I was bringing in, and I didn't say. Fourteen canvases don't take much space, even in frames. Two small flat crates, wood and fibreboard, that anybody could lift, three by four by two. Done.

'They're only garments and pottery,' I told them, Dove looking really excited, when they called me in for tea after I'd sat alone a while in the shed thinking things out. 'No peeping. No nipping out to the woodshed,' I threatened Dove grimly, 'in the candle hours, you. Understand?'

'It's very thrilling, Lovejoy. Are we in a dangerous adventure?'

'Yes. You're accomplices. And,' I said when she exclaimed in delight, 'I've never had such duckeggs helping in a crime before.'

The word sent them quiet. 'Crime?' Joe looked at Meg.

These glances between spouses get on my wick sometimes. Warning, alarmed, encouraging, they exclude the rest of us. Maybe that's why they do them? I think they should keep their private glances to themselves.

'You've gone all serious, Lovejoy,' Dove said. Her brush was a No. 4 hog bristle, floating suspended above her. I removed it, wiped the tip on a rag dipped in turpentine. 'I'm glad it's us, Dad. Honestly. I like Lovejoy.'

'Shut it, you,' I told Dove gruffly. 'Where's your twin dish? Separate dirty and clean, you trollop.'

'Can't manage.'

'Should be able to make you one.' I inspected her pulleys. Her mirrors seemed important.

'What crime, exactly?' from Joe. Meg didn't mind half as much. I could tell. Women usually don't.

'Somebody died.' I could have explained how Gesso'd gone missing, the evidence. I could even have said how I was starting to blame myself, but I'd have sounded as if I was to blame, and I wasn't having that. I eventually found the fudge formula. 'I want to bring a crime to light, that's all.'

'The Scarlet Pimpernel!' Dove squealed. 'Robin Hood!'

Joe was already throwing up logistical earthworks, a frigging pest. 'Why not simply tell the police? And why come to Guernsey to do it?'

'Because the murderers are here!' Dove shrieked. 'We must stake their place out!'

'Ta, love.' There's a point where help becomes hindrance. 'Not a word. I haven't been here, OK? And if you're asked, I brought nothing.'

'We should swear an oath!' Dove was saying when I left. Meg was full of merriment, Dove had never been so animated, Joe doubtful. Women are easier to con. They have such faith.

Twenty minutes later, returning Gussy's motor, I was arrested. Two tourists looked on, aghast. I tried to look casual about being apprehended, but fooled nobody.

Jonno Rant was at the police station. I was interrogated to within an inch of the truth. I admitted everything, most sincerely.

'I am Lovejoy, not Jonno Rant. I live in East Anglia.'

Grouville was as succinct a bobby as ever I'd met, if I've got the right word. He registered facts by writing one-liners, each no more than three syllables. I'd have hated to meet him on that TV word game. Stout, but he moved smooth. Like, he went for a file, and didn't seem to have to go through the motions of having to stand up. Tennis player? I tried, from curiosity, to read his scrawl upside down, see how he managed to encapsulate my tale so fast.

'That is correct,' Jonno Rant said, still amused. 'I'm me. He isn't.'

Even I could have jotted that down in three.

'Your purpose in this deception, Lovejoy?'

'Support for charity, Mr Grouville.' Trying it for size.

'Purpose,' Grouville reminded me. 'I said *pur*pose.'

'Oh. Sorry.' Hadn't I just told him? 'I want to support

Prior Metivier's holy establishment in Suffolk. I have no means of my own. I had the idea of running a show in some holiday centre. I know nothing about music hall promotions, so I nicked – borrowed – a list of performers—'

'From Barnie Woodfall,' Jonno said with scorn. I perked up. Scorn's useful when it's other peoples'.

'And rang some of them to come here,' I said hopefully. 'That's it.'

'Why Guernsey?'

'The best holiday centre on earth.' Get stuffed, Jersey. 'There'd be more support, seeing Prior Metivier is from here.'

'Why Mr Rant?' Grouville announced each question like a proposition from Euclid: construct equilateral triangles using a set square and compass.

'He's famous. He's popular. Everybody knows his name. His musicals are done everywhere.'

'Mr Rant doesn't write musicals.' Grouville wrote only two words this time on his rotten old paper. For my marvellous explanation? Stingy swine.

'Promotions and that,' I said lamely. Got three.

'Mr Rant?' Grouville prompted, wanting Jonno to demand the death penalty.

The impressario looked unkempt. Maybe from the flight? These pop stars are real scruffs. I've not seen one that couldn't do with a good tidying up. I felt like lending him a comb, if I'd got one. He was in green leather, a long fringed coat. He wore sun specs with vertical-strip lenses. His head looked a bisected arthropod, a real extra-terrest.

'Why Barnie Woodfall, Lovejoy?'

I explained how I'd come across the audition, and how the odd couple had reacted. I had to keep searching for his face beyond those glasses. 'The auditions frightened me.'

'Samantha Costell.' Jonno nodded. Anger plus scorn now? Bad news can be quite good, and anger even better. I perked up some more. 'Why did you choose these artists, Lovejoy?'

'Random, from the list I conned from that Samantha bird. Except for Maureen. I knew her once.' Jonno thumbed a list Grouville passed him. 'I phoned the other night from Mrs Vidamour's, told her to make the arrangements.' I cleared my throat. Honesty time. 'I've also taken on a local gentleman called James Ozanne, to—'

'Ozanne's activities are what claimed our attention.' Grouvillespeak, do an isosceles triangle without a set square. 'He is next door.'

'Please tell him sorry. Jimmy's a nice bloke.'

'You impersonated for financial gain,' Grouville said. 'You deceived airlines, ferry services, hoteliers, landladies and other residents here.'

'Excuse me, please.' Rant didn't speak for a bit, stood staring at me. 'Might I have a word?'

They made me stand outside. The disconsolate figure of Jimmy Ozanne was sitting in the corridor. I waved, called, 'Sorry, Jimmy.'

'Chin up, old chap,' he said. 'Ah, not Jonno Rant any longer, what?'

'No. It's Lovejoy.' I kept looking among passing Plod-dites for the blokes who'd done me over, didn't see them.

Jonno was signing something when they called me back in. I stood before Grouville's desk. The paper with its terse scribbles was gone. Grouville looked at me five full minutes in silence, I swear.

'Lovejoy. Visitors assume that this Bailiwick is the responsibility of our Duke Sovereign – that is, our monarch. Or Parliament, the Lieutenant-Governor, the Bailiwick, the

States of Deliberation, Uncle Tom Cobley and all.' He went on in this vein. I switched off. I wish I'd a quid for every time I've heard the speech.

Silence descended. It fired question marks about my head.

My usual answer was called for. 'And everybody's wrong?'

'Indeed. Because Guernsey is down to . . .' Again the ???? salvo.

'You?'

'Correct. As far as you are concerned, Lovejoy, I am the ultimate deterrent. Mr Rant has, out of a spirit of generosity, elected to employ you in the capacity in which you deceived and defrauded. Do not ask me why. I disapprove. Not, I hasten to add, of Mr Rant's welcome presence here, or of his musical talents. But of you. You are warned. Pay your debts. Stay within the strictures of Mr Rant's employment, and you will not incur my displeasure. Move outside them one iota, I shall lose my temper. You will be very, very sorry. Clear?'

'Yes, sir.' How the hell did this windbag précis everybody else's words to half a blot, and take hours saying watch it?

'Good day to you.'

Murmuring thanks to Grouville and any deity who might be tuned in up there, I left. In the corridor, Jonno Rant was making notes in a pocket book while Jimmy Ozanne was saying, 'Willco. Roger. Pip pip' and the like.

Jonno, my good pal Jonno, rattled through details of bookings, hitches, standbys. Jimmy was delighted. Here was a decision man, not a bumbler like me.

'Right. Any questions, Jimmy?' Jonno asked.

'Authorized changes to pattern?' Jimmy said, terse. Caught it from Grouville, likely enough.

'Individual switches, you deal with. Pattern changes, refer to me.'

'Roger!' Jimmy darted me a smile and strode off to some waiting battalion.

Jonno Rant turned to me. He'd started off a few inches taller. Now he seemed up in the stratosphere.

'Which leaves you, Lovejoy.' He wondered how much to tell me, then said, 'You know what? I remember you welling up, when we first met at the point-to-point. You wept, staring at a couple of old biscuit tins.' I said nothing. I don't like people who remember things. He gestured the silence out of the way, forget it. 'Frankly, you did me a good turn.'

'Eh? Oh, any time I can . . .' My weak blather petered out.

'Cut it. You brought to light a showbiz rip-off. Barnie seduced Samantha away.' I tried to look intelligent. 'She stole my lists of artists, the lot. I wasn't aware of it until you happened by. I'd have lost a mint.'

He seemed to expect some comment. I said, 'How can a producer lose money? Don't you just sit back while they send you cheques?'

He heaved a sigh. 'No wonder you get in messes, Lovejoy. You're an imbecile. Here's what will happen. I'm taking over your – *my* – production. In exchange for my not prosecuting, tell me everything. And tell it now.'

'Jonno,' I said earnestly. 'Honest. Sincerely, I'm hiding nothing. I swear on . . .' He took his specs off and put them away. We stood there. 'Right,' I said weakly. 'Place to sit, is there?'

We went to the harbour nosh bar where I'd lusted after the waitress, and I told him about my notion. He laughed at it. I was pleased. He looked so much more pleasant when he laughed, and I felt a lot safer.

By mid-afternoon, I was on the good ship *Jocina*. Jonno had gone to Splendid Sejour. Maybe he'd meet Dook and Florida. I wondered if he already knew Dook. If he did, I hoped he'd heed my warning and keep his mouth shut. I didn't want things to go wrong. And what on earth was an iota?

27

'IT'S NOT A "boat" as such,' the bloke said who kindly ferried me out to the *Jocina* in a cockleshell. 'A "boat", in strictly nautical terms, is a submarine.'

He, in strictly nautical terms, was a Jolly Jack tar, tanned to leather. In East Anglia, where estuaries and seas intrude, I've learnt to avoid sailors like the plague. They're like midwives, can talk of nothing but. I could have said, 'Er, doesn't some Old English Chronicle of 891 AD mention "boats" . . . ?'

Coward first and last, I said brightly, 'Oh, good,' clinging to the dinghy's rim for dear life. I can swim like a fish, but didn't want to. I'd once seen two nauticals have a terrible scrap over what a spar was, daft sods. (It's a piece of wood, end of message. Tell all your sailing friends.)

He rowed casually, one oar over the stern, brilliant. We glided among a million – well, a hundred – much bigger craft. People called down greetings, offered drinks. I grinned. My friendly nautical yelled back half-insults, as they do.

'You know Jocina?' he asked me. We approached the biggest vessel. 'Isn't she marvellous? If we didn't have the Duke, we'd have Jocina instead! Do you know, she maintains a whole priory? With her own funds! Of course, Prior Metivier is one of our own. Do you know anyone in Wolverhampton?'

'No, sorry,' I said. I know three antique dealers there, and a forger called Tulip, from skilled Dutch Old Masters he does. Better not say. 'Ta, pal.'

'Anything for Jocina Crucifex, Lovejoy,' he said. I'd not mentioned my name. His kindly ferrying was neither kindly nor spontaneous. I got the feeling that Guernsey was up to something.

A set of steps led up the ship's side. I grabbed, clung, climbed, waved. Jocina was sitting at a table, being waited on by that same lass. Prior George was there, graciously advancing to welcome me aboard. Boats, whatever, always turn out bigger once you're on, don't they. It had awnings, tables and chairs, doors, steps, three storeys, brass fittings. I know nautical expense when I see it.

Jocina looked beautiful. I admire that 1920s look, flared silks, drooping figure, hair looking carved, enough make-up to sink all but the strong.

'Wotcher,' I said in greeting. I didn't want aggro, just kept cool.

'Your tipple, Lovejoy?' Metivier was comfortably at home. I heard Martin shout something from below decks. A woman answered vaguely.

'Posh water, please.' I sat at Jocina's nod. The yacht started to move. Something splashed, engines throbbed. 'We going somewhere?'

'Just moving moorings, Lovejoy.' Jocina's smile lit up the harbour. 'You aren't a sailor, I take it?'

Lights and ships and the world turned, inchwise.

'No. I like land.'

She wore a diamond and peridot necklace, matching

earrings and two bracelets – presumably in case you didn't spot that it was all one glorious Fabergé set. The Russian master was barmy over peridot. So am I. The gemstone's lovely colour is as far as my nerve goes with green. Any greener, I literally go queasy, especially when red's nearby. I wondered if women guess these likes and dislikes, something instinctive.

'Glad you could come, Lovejoy,' she said. 'Sorry about Mrs Vidamour.'

'Easy come, easy go.' I shrugged. 'I still owe her for lodging. As long as the show goes with a bang.' I stayed serious, not wanting puns to show.

Prior George was vastly amused, detecting my lust for the exquisite Jocina.

'Don't take umbrage, Lovejoy. Plenty of people come under Jocina's spell.' He patted Jocina's hand. 'It's simply my good fortune that she wishes to show kindness to one such as I!'

Not so infirm that you can't drag my pal Gesso to his death, you rotten murdering swine. I thought this, but kept up a docile tranquillity.

'What will you do with the proceeds?' I asked, innocent. 'I've got Jonno Rant doing the show now. The performers'll start rehearsals tonight, I suppose.'

'It will be a success?' Prior George leant forward, intent, as my water appeared. Ice, French crystal glass. The lass didn't give me a glance.

'Course. It'll be big. Jonno's famed in show business.'

Jocina interrupted impatiently, 'The scam, dolt. Concentrate, Lovejoy, for Christ's sake.'

'That too, Jocina. I think we only need publicity. TV, radio, papers.'

Jocina spoke in some shushing Frenchified dialect to the prelate. He leapt to do her bidding.

'Don't "think", Lovejoy.' She watched him disappear inside. 'I want the details. Scam, start to finish. What is it? You've told umpteen tales. Versions to Jimmy Ozanne, Jonno Rant, dear Florida and her stud. To me, Martin, Mrs Vidamour. Uncle Tom Cobley and all.' Her smile made it impossible for me to remember who'd last used that phrase. Was it me?

'I'm not sure yet how much to tell.'

Her low voice was all but silence on legs. 'You do as I say here, or you do nothing. Do you understand?'

'Yes.' I'd struck some nerve. Did all her beaux get the verbals from this glorious supernova? 'Was it you had me done over?'

'Of course . . .' she trailed the meaning. I waited for that important negative. It didn't come. '. . . it was, Lovejoy. Who did you think?'

'I got hauled in by Grouville.'

'*Is*n't he nice?' she cooed, sipping. I tried to look away from her lips, failed. 'I was pleased you said nothing of significance. Good.'

'I don't know who's on your side, do I?'

'Of course you do, silly man! *You* are.' She laughed. It had been worth waiting for. I went weak. I can't understand why women don't simply have everything on earth. Women like Jocina Crucifex would only have to ask and we'd hand everything over, simple as that. 'That's all that matters, darling. When this is over, Lovejoy, I want you to join my establishment.'

Her lashes lowered. The ship's lights had come on in the dusk. We were still moving, but so slowly you'd hardly notice.

'Will you, Lovejoy?'

'What about Mr Crucifex? And . . .' I didn't want to get kicked into the briny. It was now frankly gloaming, St Peter Port a-glitter. Out at sea low ships' lights strung the horizon.

'My friends?' she teased, laughing. 'I simply use Summer for business, Lovejoy. And Prince is a joke, a lagniappe.' Did she mean *Prince* Prince, or was I missing something? 'Could he be anything else, Lovejoy? I ask you!'

She was so delighted by the idea of Prince being a threat that she had to have a cigarette fetched and fired by kulaks. She dosed herself with pink gin.

'Seriously, darling,' she resumed, pressing my arm confidingly. 'A lady of my rank deserves – needs! – a lapdog. Who is better qualified?'

'No.' I meant yes – me. That mental correction dealt misery to my plan. Three husbands, I'd heard of this elegant courtesan. I'd assumed Martin, Prior George and Summer. Now there were four, Prince in there. Walt Jethou'd be number five any minute. It was getting like the 'One Green Bottle' nursery song. Grouville to make up the half-dozen, then? She was getting out of hand.

'No more jealousy, Lovejoy!' She heard Metivier returning, said quickly, 'After it's done, come to me. We'll go away.' She greeted the cleric with a dazzling smile. 'Done, George?'

'The TV cameras will be here after supper. Newspapers, photographers and radio first.'

Marie Metivier emerged in a lavender cocktail dress. I tried speaking to her as Underwood the hotelier, with his bird in a frothy pastel pink frock, arrived. Marie's was like a spray of ground glass, pretty.

'You're to run a gambling competition, Lovejoy,' Marie accused. 'You lied to me about hating gambling.'

'Not exactly—'

'Don't ever approach me, speak to or contact me again. I hate you.'

'Where did you get it from, love?' I asked, trying my whisper out.

'What?' For a millisec she was almost thrown, but recovered. Steel in this lass's spine.

'You had a windfall, settled your brother's gambling debts. And such formidable debts. The bare-fisters, the racing—'

She drew away, looking. 'Who are you?' she said. The others were busy having a laugh with Underwood.

I felt so sad. Women never get over hatreds, so I'd had it now with Marie Metivier for good. 'I'm only me, love. Not sure about that lot over there, though.'

She moved towards her brother, glaciation back in place as she greeted Martin. You can always tell when people are special to each other, but I was really surprised to see her lightly touch Martin's arm. Was this why Jocina disliked Marie? Meanwhile I learnt with relief that my theft of the decanter didn't rankle with Underwood. He told me they'd increased his hotel's security.

'Some visitors, Lovejoy!' His eyes twinkled. I grinned.

'Bet your security's still not good enough, Mr Underwood. Like me to prove it?'

'Mark and Phyllis, please, Lovejoy.'

The whole of Guernsey clearly being in on my pathetic subterfuges, we settled down to talk about his experiences. I told him I was sorry to have misled two of his recent guests.

He frowned. 'I don't think we've had two singles in,

Phyllis, have we?' His frothy pink girl was the receptionist. She said no, only that couple who'd made a mistake. They'd gone to somewhere down by the harbour. We were all so happy and at ease. Floodlights came on. A television crew arrived, started laying cables and pinching booze. Radio interrogators – very much the Cinderellas – poked microphones at us, tried to make me reveal the Great Gismo (their term). I laughed, said aha! I estimated the raffle prize's value at over three million, fast rising.

To my surprise, Jonno Rant came aboard during the evening. We had supper on deck, where TV people could film us noshing and being glamorously tipsy. Jonno was good value. He had a million anecdotes about show business, theatre mistakes, flops and successes, performers' egomanias. He had everybody in stitches. Turn him to a camera, though, and he was an instant pro. He mentioned two names that made even the cameramen blink, so famous were the stars he was flying in. The women all went Ooooh! I was really proud.

'Glad you're on my team, Jonno,' I said as they moved to do another interview against the backdrop of Castle Cornet for some mainland TV unit.

He was amused. 'Wrong, Lovejoy. You're on mine.'

That gave me a laugh. It shouldn't have, but I've always been dim. I went up to the control deck. Marie and Martin were there talking quietly. I interrupted, asking brightly if these were the boat's controls. Martin rather sulkily said yes. He reluctantly showed me the starter and controls. I said how interesting. He gritted his teeth. I ogled Marie.

'Must be nice sleeping on a lovely, er, cruiser,' I hinted. 'Do you ever let visitors stay aboard? I'd like to try it one day.' Ponderous hint.

It failed. 'There's a security guard, Lovejoy. And crew.'

'Oh, good,' I said. 'This is a terrific evening, one way and another.'

Truly, I was sorry it ended. I left about eleven. Gussy had read the note I'd left on her dashboard and was waiting by the Station Marina. Not quite as posh as Jocina's boat pool, but pride mustn't interrupt when laying a false trail. We drove north.

'Does Guernsey need to be so blinking dark?' We'd stopped close by a small seaside village.

'It's not dark at all,' she said. 'There's the sky. Lights. My headlamps.'

It was pitch black. I peered, guessing directions.

'Where's the ship?'

'Don't worry. It's there.'

We alighted. Several houses stood there, lights mercifully still on in a couple of windows. I could hear a television. Wind was cold on my face.

'Will it be big enough?' I asked, nervous. Risking Gussy on the ocean wide was a small price to pay, but to risk me was absurd.

'He's an experienced sailor, Lovejoy.' She always seemed angry when I was sensible.

A voice said in the darkness, 'You came, then.' I jumped, clutched Gussy.

She laughed. The selfish cow thought it a joke. 'Hello, Boris. This is Lovejoy.'

We said hello. He sounded dour. 'She's ready. This way.'

He led us down a small path, shining a torch for us. The harbour was small, hardly room to swing a cat. His yacht was shorter, squatter than the *Jocina*.

'Is he going to drive it himself?' I asked Gussy nervously as we boarded.

'Yes, I sail her alone,' said Boris. 'Always.'

Gussy said, 'Get on with you, Lovejoy. Safe as houses.'

'I know, I know!'

We set out, Gussy proudly pointing out landmarks. I could hardly see a damned thing. The church of St Sampson's lay to the south. We pulled out into a vast black ocean, to the left Vale Castle – unseen, darkness all about – and to the north Bordeaux Harbour coming into view – a lie; darkness all about—

'Bordeaux?' I yelped in terror.

'Not the French Bordeaux, silly. *Our* Bordeaux. We'll pass the Channel Islands Yacht Club. It has its own marina!' And minutes later, triumphantly pointing, 'Over there! See?' Answer, no, darkness.

Gussy sat admiring the black world. I huddled in the cabin. Boris was steering. Why do these yachtsmen peer out when there's nothing to see? A screen swirled a green line. Another thing blipped and belched. The boat sounded on life support, in need of intensive therapy. Boris smoked incessantly, pungent cigarettes that, oddly, gave little explosive flashes now and then. They reminded me of something, couldn't for the life of me remember what.

I grew nervous. 'Aren't we a bit far from Guernsey?'

'Yes.' Boris looked surprised, shouted Gussy. 'You said La Grosse?'

'La Grosse,' she confirmed. She'd come alive, thrilled to be out.

'Where's La Grosse?' I should have asked earlier.

'Alderney, of course,' she said pleasantly. 'It's on the map.'

'So is L'Anse aux Meadows.' Newfoundland, where

Norsemen landed in the eleventh century. I didn't want to go there either, dark-blind on this night sea.

'Don't be childish. Boris is really kind, taking us.'

'Isn't this dangerous?' I bleated.

That set Boris off, talking of dangerous seas hereabouts in his curiously deformed accent. The Swinge, a wide channel down which we'd be travelling, was especially chancy. It passed to the northwest of Alderney. The swirling maelstroms of The Race, infinitely worse, boiled blackly to the east.

'I like those waters,' Boris growled, the nerk.

In fright I clung to some brass rail, and until we landed never let go. It was quite a time. I ignored the landmarks until Gussy, rolling in the aisles at the state I was in, finally told me we'd arrived.

'There, Lovejoy.' She handed me binoculars. 'Night glasses. To your right's the coast. Can you hear the shingle? That's Saline Bay. Don't stare, you'll see nothing. Relax. You'll see a great mound of black. See it? That's La Grosse. We can't go any closer because of rocks.'

'No more, ta.' I felt ill. 'Can we land, please?'

There was a small harbour, with a long pier thing projecting. We moored. I said a million thanks to Boris, stepped thankfully on to terra firma, and set off after Gussy's torchlight.

The road led upwards in a steady climb. It took us an hour. We blundered along overgrown paths, coming haphazardly on metalled roads only to feel them give out. Gussy was so sure of herself. I hadn't realized she'd meant Alderney, assuming she was Guernsey born and bred.

'That light?' She pointed. I couldn't see a bloody light. 'It's Fort Clonque, on an islet. It's got holiday rooms. You live out at sea! *Lovely* for painting.'

'Oh, aye.'

'Clonque's from Old French, means rocky cove,' she blabbed, walking on. 'There was a famous shipwreck, the *Emily Eveson* – the rocks are ghastly – but a dog barking led the crew safe to land. Isn't that romantic?'

'No. Where's the cave?'

'We're right over the path, Lovejoy.' How did she know? A dark windswept coast means nothing. 'Look northwest.' She rotated me irritably. 'Offshore is La Grosse, the rock I used to paint. It's opposite a megalith here on land. The burial chamber's only two uprights and a capstone, looted long since.' She laughed. It started raining, the wind colder, a really good time to speak of burials. 'I used to pretend it was Stonehenge.'

'Is this where?' I asked about the man rowing the boat and the cave.

'Down on the shore.' She prattled about Braye Harbour being used for pirate ships three centuries before. 'We're above it. The path is rather overgrown.'

'It can be reached from the sea?'

'Rowing, yes. Big craft, no. They'd get broken up.'

I swallowed. 'Whose cave was it?'

'Alderney was impossibly fortified during the Second World War, Lovejoy. It was an ordinary sea cave before the Germans enlarged it. They used slave labour. All old Aurniais – Alderney folk – still tell tales of the poor starving creatures who were forced to build the bunkers. The Nazis' famous Atlantic Wall started here.' Her flashlight raked the foliage. She pointed it down, didn't make it because of the angle. 'Our parents forbade us children to play in the gun emplacements, the caves, the tunnels. That's why I never told anybody.'

I was fixing it in my mind. 'Ta, love. Is there much doing in Braye? Supposing somebody wanted to hire a dinghy.'

'You're going to the cave, Lovejoy? There are other caves. The Channel Islands are riddled with bunkers. Alderney was heaviest fortified—'

'Forget it, love. Just wondered.'

All the time I'd been peering through her night binoculars. We started back, me asking this and that. Her answers I hardly listened to. It didn't really matter, because I'd decided anyway.

An hour, and we were aboard heading for Guernsey. Boris was glad to be at sea, yet another of his pungent fags polluting the Channel. Two things happened on the return journey, not much in themselves, but odd.

The first was his accent. He spoke of his first boat, chartering for tourists.

'Surprised you can't afford proper cigarettes instead of them rotten old socks you smoke, Boris.' Those fags and that accent were needling me.

'Oh.' He laughed, self-conscious. 'They're Moscow's home-made. We get Russian tourists now. I smoke them for old times' sake.'

'Your dad worked here?' I'd read they used Russian prisoners.

'No, Lovejoy.' I can see his expression yet, illuminated in the fluorescent green of the instruments. 'Slaved. Died. I came here to lay flowers and stayed.'

Mentally I placed ticks against his accent, his cigarettes, his name, Boris. 'God rest him.' I could still see hardly a thing, unlike these islanders, but guessed we were getting near that great rock. 'Here, Gussy. La Grosse. What was that white cow doing on its tod out there? Who looks after it?'

'What?' I swear her face drained of all colour in the cabin glow. Boris's boat swerved a fraction off course. 'What white cow, Lovejoy?'

'On the rock. You'd think the farmer'd have more sense.'

'You're imagining things, Lovejoy,' she said, and held my hand. 'There's supposed to be a ghost, a giant white bull. You're having me on.'

'Oh, sorry.' I didn't say another word about it. Let her and Boris guess.

By the time we got back to her place I was knackered. She let me stay, and we made smiles. It wouldn't have been fair to make me sleep in the draughty gallery, after all I'd done for her. Well, hoped to do. Tomorrow was the problem.

I made sure I was up and away long before she woke, and reached Splendid Sejour even before Splendid Sejour, so to speak.

28

ORNING IS MORE honest than night-
fall. You see joggers, and know that
humanity's still doing its teeth or on
the loo, or trying for a few more winks while the children
bounce on the bed. At the leisure centre, staff arrived,
extraverts slamming car doors shouting to friends. The rare
introvert went quietly in to start work. The tired wanted
breakfast before the coming slog. I went in, feeling a bit
scared now it was imminent. Jimmy was already there. He
was delighted. At this hour.

'What ho, Lovejoy!' He did that moustache-brushing
gesture with a knuckle. 'Preparations, hey?'

He detailed – his word – the show's layout. We toured
the stage. He said Jonno was in contract phase. I kept up
my monologue, 'Great. Excellent.' We saw dressing rooms
where the artists would change. He showed me how curtains
worked on complicated switches, how lights dimmed.

'Now, Lovejoy!' His eyes twinkled. 'Your competition
room!'

A partition rolled back. Eighty or so feet square, it had
windows with curtains, dance-hall flooring, podium and
dais. We acquired a girl.

'I'm Victoria,' she breathed, trying to shake hands but dropping everything. 'Jonno sent me.'

Clever old Jonno. We paused to assemble her. 'Welcome to the team, love. Look, Jimmy. Security problem, what?' I was talking like him. 'Er, those windows.'

He got the point, barked at Victoria, 'Occlude windows. Shutters. Blinds. Auto bleeps. Fire exits, secure by permanent sentries.'

'It's square,' I said of the room. 'Display stands in a circle, please, arrows to direct people clockwise. Ropes, to stop folk touching the exhibits.'

We went on. Jimmy was in his element, snapping out brisk instructions for Victoria to scribble, breathlessly mouthing his words. I couldn't help wondering where Jonno got staff from. I had a hell of a time keeping out of hospital and the nick. He merely turns up, and legions flock to his banner. Was it money, charisma?

We'd almost finished when there was a scream, and in rushed Maureen Jolly leading a charge of delighted people, who fell on me, wringing my hand, slurping kisses on my face. I'd never seen so many shapes and sizes.

'Lovejoy!' Maureen screeched. She was so thrilled I almost felt glad to see her. 'Did you see our telly interview? *It's been broadcast!* You darling!'

'I was in it too!' they all cried in triumph.

'You darling!' cried the elfin Patty, tinier even than I remembered, green dress and glorious red hair. 'We had doubts, didn't we, Maureen?'

'Oh.' I went all offended, was instantly fawned over. This was the way into their affections, that and giving them a part at the auditions.

Maureen introduced them while they shouted their achievements, this theatre, that show, who they'd acted with.

I was bewildered. One geezer did a sleight-of-hand thing, turned his walking stick into a hankie. I thought it was brilliant.

'We've met Jonno!' Maureen said proudly. She was their leader, knowing me, and me being Jonno's old schooldays chum. 'He's a *dreamboat!*'

Their adulation got out of hand as more performers joined us. I grew anxious. Had I ordered this many? Victoria showed her mettle.

'Everyone!' She tapped her clipboard imperiously. 'Nine-thirty call!'

Withdrawal began in an instant hubbub. Maureen kissed me, whispering, 'I'll never forget this, Lovejoy!' Patty did, said, the same. They retreated, chattering. I gazed at Victoria in admiration.

'How'd you do that, love? They wouldn't leave when I said.'

'Command structure!' Jimmy said. 'Leadership, what!'

She blushed. 'I'm his deputy assistant. He fired Samantha Costell.'

He being Jonno? So Victoria was indebted to me because of Samantha Costell? She was going to be useful.

'Look,' I said. 'Can we get some coffee? I need to find a lady called Florida. Her, erm, friend is Dook.'

'Hotel Roi de Normandie.' Jimmy harrumphed, as Victoria scuttled. 'Look here, Lovejoy. Man of the world, knees brown, what? Against the old grain, married woman, partners with an idle-back. Moral decay, hmmm?'

'Couldn't have put it better, Jimmy,' I said gravely, wondering what the hell he was on about. 'It's too sad. She'll be among the gamblers.'

'About that, Lovejoy.' We sat in the lounge area. It was already starting to fill with visitors. Victoria rejoined us.

'Gambling in the Bailiwick. Defined activity, say no more, hey?'

I'd lost track of whether his barks were questions or not. 'Let me go over what'll happen, Jimmy.'

'Ready!' Victoria squeaked, pencil flying, head down, drooping hair making a cocoon of her notepad. I drew breath.

'Fourteen exhibits, numbered consecutively, are on the stands. At a signal, people can enter. They put sealed – *sealed* – bids into an envelope.'

'Written bids? Like a tender?'

'Yes, Jimmy. Of all the exhibits, only one is genuine and highly valuable. The rest are duff, forgeries, false.'

'One is costly, the others not? Roger!'

'Right. Like, if you're a gambler and think number seven is the true item, you write seven, sign your card, write your bid.'

'What if—?'

'Let me finish.' This was the hard bit. 'We keep the money.'

They looked up. Victoria's face emerged from her nest of drooping hair.

Jimmy was uneasy for the first time. 'Punters very particular, old bean.'

I pressed on, firm. 'Take certified cheques, cash, authorized plastics. Victoria, you know about money. Do it. All bids, we keep the lot. Anybody who backs wrong loses their bid. That's how it goes.'

Jimmy nodded. 'No stake, no draw, what?'

'Here's the difference from a horse race: if there's only one bet on number seven, say, even if it's only a farthing, and it's the right guess, then whoever placed that bid wins.

If two people guess the genuine article, the *highest* bidder wins.'

'Can we announce its value?' Jimmy asked. I noticed that Jonno was standing near, still as a pool-watching heron. How long had he been listening?

'Yes.' I went on improvising. 'We must be honest, start to finish. The genuine item's value lies between seven and eight figures. There's one further stipulation. Whoever wins gives half its value to charity. And we name the charity.'

Jimmy glanced at Victoria, ahemed. She calculated, 'A million is seven figures, Lovejoy. Eight figures is ten times that.'

'A lot of money.' I said it sadly. The coffee came. 'Here, love,' I told the waitress. 'Is there nowt to eat? Morning, Jonno. Didn't see you. Join us?'

Florida was lounging by the swimming pool when I got there. Guernsey had donned a superb translucent day. Dook spectacularly oiled himself, posing.

'Wotcher, Flo.' I sat uninvited. 'How's hubby?'

'Tara's coming.' She peered through her sunglasses. 'Remember Tara?'

'Tara who sells antiques to other folk after promising me? Aye.'

Florida laughed, turned her exquisite body over. She knew the effect she was having. Dook indolently continued showing off his muscles.

'The rules for the gamble are in,' I told her shoulders. She looked away, satisfied that I was transfixed.

'Tell me.'

I explained. She listened in silence. A hairdresser started

on Dook's hair. Whatever Dook did for a living, I hoped he was good at it.

Florida considered my news and pouted. 'So it's fair, is it? We inspect the fourteen exhibits, and bet on which we think genuine. If we guess right and our bid's correct *and* highest, we win it?'

'That's it. It'll be international TV news by noon today.'

'Darling, what if you wanted a friend to win?'

'They might lose. A bet's a bet.'

'And what if somebody – me, say – guessed right, but only bid, say, five thousand, when some other bidder tendered ten?'

'You'd lose, love.'

She sighed. 'So many chances of losing, Lovejoy. And you keep the bids?'

'It's what gambling is, Florida.'

She turned her head. Her lovely hair tumbled over her face just like Victoria's, but for a brief moment Florida looked like somebody drowning in deep water. A breeze lifted it, thank God.

'I don't *want* to lose, Lovejoy. Bringing me all this way, then letting me down on a silly old bet. Is that fair, darling?'

'Not really, no.' Darling, now.

She smiled because my voice had gone thick. I tried to think how me and Gussy had made smiles, but the memory wouldn't stay. Florida's tongue touched her lips, slowly withdrew.

'It would be a smashing help to me, Lovejoy, if a friend told me beforehand which was the genuine exhibit.' She flexed a knee so she became even more curved. 'And what other bids were put in.' I'd always loved her smiles. 'You do see what I mean, Lovejoy?' She stroked her thigh.

'Yes.' I managed not to groan.

'Am I being frank?' She looked as somebody splashed into the pool, laughing. 'Whoever improved the odds for me would deserve a certain gratitude.'

'Yes,' I said, but no sound came out.

'Is that yes, or a groan, Lovejoy?' she demanded, smiling.

Both, but I'd no words left to say so.

'Time you left, squire,' Dook called via his hairdresser's mirror.

'I'm going, Dook.' I hate people who call me squire. 'Florida? One thing. Who're Mrs Crucifex's blokes?'

'Why, Lovejoy?' she asked mischievously. 'Are you interested? There are only crumbs left in her little web, I'm afraid. She gives her main course to others. To one especially.'

'Who?' The answer would be whoever murdered Gesso in that hot pool. It had to be Prior Metivier, right?

'Guide my bet, Lovejoy,' she said. 'And I'll tell you.'

Her smile dimmed even the pool's reflections. I left, cadged a cylindrical cardboard tube from the hotel's handyman. I bought a tiny pencil flashlight from a lass in the hotel shops. Then I made one call from a public phone box. The Eastern Hundreds Grand Antiques Emporium was already hard at it, Vesta in charge. It was an unsatisfactory conversation. I reminded her of when I'd called and we'd talked of Mrs Crucifex.

'You'd said she had three different homes, a husband in each.'

'Are you with her? I hear you're in Guernsey.'

'Who are they, Vesta?'

'Ask Mike. He's there with his group, Nightmarish. He'll tell you.'

'Did your Mike's band bring that Irma Dominick over with them, Vesta?'

'That bitch,' she spat. 'If he did, I'll strangle her.'

She rang off then, a customer coming in. I remembered the suited man, upper crust and smart, his posh car, and wondered if that had been him again, just arriving.

I managed to book on a day trip, a Condor Eight, whatever that was, a catamaran. I sat among naturalists and excited walkers sharing maps. I watched the sea, startled at the speed of the thing. I wanted to think about gamblers.

It's a definite but mysterious fact that our old kingdom has more motor accidents on any Friday the 13th than any Friday the 6th. Why? Dunno. And crime plummets in towns whose football team reaches the Cup Final. Dunno why that, either. And that gambling is normal, until it ruins your life. Gambling is the most mysterious stuff of all.

Did I know any gamblers? Plenty. Hunter, who'd given me a lift. Arty, who I'd nicked from. Gesso, RIP, used to, but his wife Desdemona was against it. Prior Metivier definitely, whose lovely sister Marie was contra. Florida, though she was mainly horses. Anybody else? Michaelis Singleton used to, before he learnt that wine was more pleasurably destructive if you worked at it. Irma Dominick was a gambler in her own way, of course, if she'd only get a move on and come out of her Guernsey hiding place. Barko, of course, ex-cop turned villain, who frequented boot fairs. Prince, too, though he was not easily talked into risk – hence his commission for that Nicholas Brown bookcase. Might Prince have eastern connections by way of Guernsey's wartime past history, that I'd only recently begun to think of? Another heavy gambler I know is Fireball – called from setting fires in museums so his woman can nick valuable antiques in the panic – but I'd not seen him since Fritter Thursday, when he'd left his old infirm dad in my garden while he torched that place in Norwich. It was in all the papers (the fire, not his dad).

Doc Lancaster in our village once gave a talk on gambling. You can get treatment, from psychiatrists to drugs. He said six out of ten respond. Obsessive compulsions are to do with part of your brain being smaller. So?

I dozed off, as I'd dozed back then in the village hall, this time from the catamaran's humming and the sea rocking. I hoped the captain knew about the dangerous channel called The Swinge.

Even half awake I get narked. People get things wrong. We create legends, and confuse ourselves. Not long since, a bloke investigated piracy. He turned up odd statistics. Like, how many pirates' captives in all those centuries were made to walk the plank? Answer: one. Only one prisoner went in with a splash from a piece of four-by-two. The pirate's average life expectancy? Not even two years. And so on. We create myths, when we ought to know better. I had a responsibility to Mondrian if Dove had got it right. No myths allowed.

Sometimes, we do know better. Editorials trumpet our scandals, despite libel laws. How, for instance, Peter Wilson, founder of the modern Sotheby's, was the notorious 'Fifth Man' of our famous spy shock-horror-gasper, and that his secret nook for meeting the spy Sir Anthony Blunt (yes, *that* antiques expert) was that oh-so-secret house in Chelsea. The trade also whispers about Christie's links with Rome's famous Red Brigade and all that jazz. Gamblers, in antiques and elsewhere, strut a very shifting sand.

Yet you can be lucky. This is the dangling carrot. The

richly beautiful Levens Hall at Kendal in Cumbria recently snatched the 'Garden of the Year' title from weedier rivals, yet three centuries ago Colonel Grahame won that lovely mansion on the turn of a card (the Ace of Hearts, incidentally). If it's different risks you want, go diving in the Kyle of Tongue in Sutherland, and bring up the 50,000 Louis d'or and English gold coins submerged there. Local people will even sell you a treasure map showing you exactly where the French war sloop *Hazard*, hunted down by the English frigate *Sheerness* in 1746, was wrecked when frantically trying to escape. They'll even prove where the invaders sank the gold – it's only two miles from the shipwreck – when attacked by 'Brave Captain Hugh MacKay'. You can bring up enough gold to rock the world's bullion markets. Just don't call me. If you're taking that particular risk deep in those dark waters, you're on your own.

You can be lucky too in theft, like in love. Dig anywhere in the Holy Land, you're bound to tumble into a Byzantine tomb sooner or later. Even one clay artefact can net you a cool two million, for a night's scratching. Myself, I'd chosen paintings. Or rather paintings had chosen me.

Tell you a story. Big John Sheehan back in Suffolk once ran a book, on a single bet. We all took part, being too scared to decline. His bet was this: name the six most wanted Old Masters – 'wanted' officially by Scotland Yard's Art and Antiques Squad and unofficially by the rest of us. None of us won. Know what they were? Titian's *Flight to Egypt*, stolen from Longleat; Rembrandt's mother, nicked from Wilton House, Salisbury; Turner's *Light and Colour* . . . , owffed in Frankfurt; a group of seven Picassos, whipped from Switzerland; Friedrich's *Wafting Mist*, also good old Frankfurt; and *The White Duck*, Oudry's masterpiece, lifted from the Marquess of Cholmondeley's Norfolk pile. It was the last that threw us. We'd been thinking of major thefts on the Continent, see? Two of the lads had just come back from a steal and grew very narked. While everybody argued, I rang the Art Squad's deathly secret special London number – 230 4974, but don't tell anybody. We shut up then. Also, Big John can get very nasty. But it was *The White Duck* threw us. See? We imagined we knew everything.

It's the age-old problem of who wants what. There's danger in buying an antique when it's been nicked. I don't mean because of the police. You might be buying a pig in a poke. Jelly Gosham – his real surname, incidentally – paid every penny his rich wife possessed for the stolen Goya portrait of the Duke of Wellington. It turned out that he'd bought a fake. He dared not go to the police, because they'd ask why he'd bought a stolen masterpiece. He went bankrupt. His wife left him for a window cleaner, taking the forgery. I saw it in a Brighton junk shop two years later, bought it for eighty quid, and exchanged it for a Roman amphora. The lesson: you can also lose.

Proof is vital, whatever proof means in antiques. Some methods aren't bad, like Turner's fingerprints I mentioned. Now, a US firm will do an artist's DNA profile for a groat – well, $3,000. Fine, if the artist is still alive, donating a hair, spitting his DNA into their saliva pot. They sell you ink containing the artist's DNA, with which he signs canvas, watercolour, contract, whatever. The trouble is, what if the canvas is by Constable, Da Vinci? Or Monet? Or, nearer my heart for the moment, Mondrian?

Which was my problem. And Jonno Rant's. And Florida's. And the evil murderer Prior Metivier's, and those other gamblers who'd be attracted like flies.

Which brought me to what I'd been avoiding all this time, the terrible, truly terrible, story of the incalculable zillions in antiques waiting for somebody lucky enough. The story is loot. It happens in wartime, on a massive scale. It was especially huge in the Thirties and Forties, when nations got swallowed up and their antiques with them.

Every country's done it. But we only now realize the scale of looted antiques. Never mind Catherine the Great's throne and Napoleon's sledge being lifted from Lvov, or the 1,700 priceless paintings 'moved for protection' from Minsk. The Eastern part of Germany wants 6,500 masterworks back. Budapest wants its 10,000 antiques of astronomical value, please, and kindly send along the entire Hungarian Jewish Library that, in truly impenetrable secrecy, is hidden in Nizhniy Novgorod. I could go on. Antique dealers' eyes are all on Russia. It's because of the famed – and aptly named – Grabar Plan. Igor Grabar in 1943 planned to acquire – for that word read loot – antiques from enemy countries. The idea was that loot would be assembled willy nilly and housed in a huge complex next to the Pushkin in Moscow. Grand, eh?

'Trophy Bridges' were set up, with transport, art experts, antiquarians, to collar precious objects. A looter's dream. I mean, whole units, armed, to snatch antiques, and you got medals for it? It's as close to paradise as antique dealers can dream. The Ukraine alone says please can it have its 25,000 missing paintings, no hard feelings – one is definitely a Frans Hals, another Correggio's *Madonna with Saint Sebastian*. So what are the other 24,998? The scale defies belief. Of course, some confiscated antiques *have* gone back home.

Dresden got some in 1957. Italy's Ministry for Cultural Heritage calls for 2,000 masterpieces – by mere beginners like Michelangelo, Tintoretto, Canaletto and suchlike – to be returned from Berlin, Hanover, Belgrade, God knows where. Some modern heroes plough a lone furrow, like the brave Rodolfo Siviero, who painstakingly slogged through the undergrowth and identified hundreds. But politics is ticklish. A nation doesn't want to annoy another more powerful than itself. And the victor one minute, who loots Michelangelo's *Mask of a Faun*, might easily become the vanquished, whereupon its loot gets looted in turn. So the priceless *Mask*, which started its journey from Florence's Bargello museum, travels on and on like Babushka.

The Pushkin Museum disarmingly put on a show called 'Twice Saved', of art brought from Germany. It did another soon after, 'Hidden Treasures Revealed'. It was then that realization hit the fan, for on show were Gaugin, Van Gogh, Renoir, Degas, Matisse . . .

It isn't always entire nations. Individuals are in it. Lone squaddies lift an ikon from a shelled church. A soldier dosses until daybreak and, waking in the rubble, nicks some trifle that takes his fancy. Or some gent offers money to some tomb robbers in the Middle East, maybe thinks nothing more about the old rolls of papyrus until they shazam into the Dead Sea Scrolls.

And don't say, 'How awful'. We'd all be at it if we could get away with it.

'Sir?' Somebody was shaking me. 'Braye Harbour, in Alderney.' I was asked if I wanted to join the island walk with a team of ramblers. I said ta, no.

Distances shrink in daylight. I went confidently up the

slope from the harbour towards St Anne's. Hikers accompanied me, telling me there were some good restaurants. The population is only 2,100 or so. It has thirteen good hotels. I said excellent. And was glad when they went on and I turned right towards the sound of waves on the shingle.

My cardboard tube was a nuisance. I carried it under my arm, cursing when it caught on foliage. I scrabbled down to the sea, directly below where I'd been with Gussy in the night, where she, a little girl, had painted La Grosse. Bloody great rock it was too, looming away like that. Not a white bull to be seen. I clambered along the shore – definitely not rambling territory, this – and came on the cave. At least, I supposed it was hers. Its mouth was wet, as if it had just been fed. I closed my mind to that vision, and went in. Pencil torch, poor light but enough.

Its floor rose a little. I came on a drier area, just made out the occasional initials carved on the wall. Nothing. A discarded oilskin, some driftwood – this far in? – and old tins from beer, fishing tackle. No colours staining the wall. I looked especially for horizontal lines – oil paintings leant against any support leave a straight mark of colour. None.

No zinc nails, for tacking canvas. No discarded tubes, no broken brushes flung in a temper. No linseed oil bottle. Nothing in fact to suggest that a painter had ever painted here.

That didn't mean that older, famous, works hadn't been stashed here, brought in years later by somebody who'd once slaved over building fortifications. Who, when nations crumbled, had returned to hide loot. I searched for an hour. It was empty, clean as a whistle. I emerged into the sea light empty-handed, looked up at the sky, and said, 'Ta, God.'

I really was glad that I hadn't found a cache of Old Masters. If they'd been there, they'd have been guarded, and Gesso already knew what happened to nosey intruders who got caught. It could go ahead.

29

THE LEISURE CENTRE was bedlam, with at least three competing TV crews. I narrowly escaped being interviewed. There's no such thing as reporters, journalists, critics – they are all merely newsagents, impure and simple, and that's a fact.

I burnt my empty cardboard cylinder in the incinerator, after making sure that no Old Master had nigged inside while I was in the sea cave. I got nabbed by Victoria, looking bonnier and more harassed than ever. She had a message: Jimmy reported two betting syndicates were due in today. Another group from Atlantic City had cabled a bid to pre-empt the competition, buy the genuine antique sight unseen. Jimmy was on the ramparts defying untold hordes, loving every minute.

'Seventeen faxes? Now?' I wanted out.

'Jonno,' she breathed his name like a saint's, 'said you must handle them.'

'Right, love. Where are they?'

'Our production office.'

Production office? I didn't know we had one. 'There in twenty minutes, Victoria, you're doing brilliantly.' Praise helps lies.

She coloured. 'Thank you, Lovejoy.' I cut through a crowd of holidayers heading for the swimming and walked into St Peter Port.

Luck brings luck. I saw a novelty teapot in the same shop I'd sold the cresset, right there in the window. Its purple bonnet caught my eye. I ambled in, a gormless grockle.

'What've you got for three quid?' I asked

'Nothing.' A sour, craggy bloke was in charge today. Obviously a minder, no idea. 'It's all prime stuff.'

'Give me any old pot.' I hawked out my money. I drifted, pointed to a piece of Doulton. He exploded with laughter, shaking his head.

'That saucer?' An exquisite Japanese kakeimon, precise colours hatched over the surface. I got derision. That Lowestoft jug, then? I was asked to leave.

'Anything,' I suggested. 'My missus is fuming. I broke a pot last night. She said I've got to get something for the landlady. That thing?'

He hefted it, saw it had no price ticket. 'She's not costed it yet. Four quid?'

'Leave off, mate.' But he wouldn't budge, so I put the money down. 'You'll have me begging in the gutter. Is there a lid?'

We studied it for a while, saw nothing but the name BUDGE underneath. Budge made cheapo fairings, pot novelties you won at fairground coconut shies. The teapot depicted a pansy-looking man wearing a purplish bonnet. One hand was the spout, very limp of wrist. The other was akimbo, very camp, for the handle. Turn it round, and the figure was now a lady wearing the same purple bonnet, but with a lily on her breast. The bonnet was the lid. I left rejoicing, with the teapot. God help him when his boss returned.

It would buy a decent second-hand car. Lily Langtry, the famed Jersey Lily, friend – more than friend – of kings and princes, was connected with Oscar Wilde. It's among the costliest of novelty teapots. Because it looks so daft, you can get it for a kopek, unless the dealer's done his reading, which isn't often. The minder, sadly, had just lost his job, and I'd made a mint.

Hurtling out in joy, I almost knocked this bloke down on the pavement.

'Sorry, wack,' I said.

'Not at all, Lovejoy,' said Michaelis Singleton. He looked bleary. 'Got you, you rotten sod. Can we get a drink?'

Just when things were looking up. I turned gladness on. 'Michaelis! What're you doing here? Thought you'd be getting sloshed in your cellar.'

'Delivering a writ, Lovejoy. You're for it. So am I.' He croaked the words. 'I've been driving about antique shops for three hours. I knew I'd catch you.'

We entered a respectable hotel near the waterfront, to watch the boats. I was getting sick of sea. The teapot warmed my pocket. Michaelis named a bottle of rare wine. The waiters loved him, hated me for wanting lime juice.

'Nothing wrong, Michaelis, is there?' The hotel was brimful. I liked Guernsey, but had to watch out for my night visitors. I didn't want chucking on to the ferry, alive or dead, now that I was so near Gesso's killer, my scam looming.

'Wrong, Lovejoy? Not unless you count me going bankrupt. I'm dunned for everything I own.' He sent back the glasses, chose new ones. The wine waiter was ecstatic. Michaelis sniffed the cork, dirty devil. Can you believe it?

I was really embarrassed. Pouring the wine took a year. He sipped, sat with eyes closed, finally nodded. Ecstasy spread, and the universe – Samuel Butler's crack – was saved.

'Where is Irma, Michaelis?'

'Here. I traced her.'

This didn't make sense. 'You sure? Then where's she hiding? I'd have heard. Mrs Crucifex and I are . . .' Careful. I couldn't say we were in this together. Guernsey had ears.

'You think I wouldn't check, Lovejoy?' He raised a hand. Competing waiters sprinted to decant. I thought, For God's sake. Wine's only fluid, not a religion. 'Miss I. Dominick travelled via Weymouth. She's here, all right.'

We paused. My thoughts were that maybe a little betrayal had crept in here. But by whom? Michaelis thought I'd betrayed him.

'Lovejoy,' he said bitterly. 'You and I go back a bit. I trusted you. You get me to represent your trainee shoplifter. Then you scarper with her. I'm her bail guarantor. I'm close to getting disbarred.'

History's fine, even when it intrudes into real life, as now with Gussy's Mondrian mock-ups and my scam that depended on everybody's knowledge of war loot. But Michaelis meant friendship. I sighed. History costs.

'I told you everything, Michaelis. And I didn't know she was here.'

A long beat, another bottle ordered with a flick of an eyelash, then, 'Very well, Lovejoy. I need a fee, though.'

'Agreed!' I cried with relief. Delaying payment's my thing. I sent for another lime juice. Hang the expense.

'My fee is winning tomorrow's bet.' In soft tones he gave the rapturous wine waiter commands about some mystique. They did the sacramental decanting. My lime was flung at me.

'Winning?' Not good. 'Syndicates are already here to bet fortunes.'

'My syndicate will also bid high, Lovejoy. They're on their way now from the North.' I remembered his family of Geordie hardliners, a real mafia. 'You'll have to take the cost of the bet out of the winnings, me being bankrupt.'

'Great idea,' I croaked. 'Any chance of a drink?'

Michaelis shook his head. 'Not this, Lovejoy. Your palate's like tarmac.' He sent the sneering waiter for a glass of house white. It did me no good.

For the next hour I chased Victoria demented, telling her to locate Irma Dominick. I got wild when she drew blanks. I went to watch the rehearsals, astonishingly good. It was a real mixture. Nightmarish, the pop group with Vesta's brother Mike, was tolerable, in a back-to-the-sixties way. I caught myself laughing at the comedian, then remembered I was in serious trouble. I'd promised to make sure Florida won the Gamble of the Century, Jimmy's name for my exhibition. I'd also promised Mrs Crucifex – and she controlled the night visitors who'd kaylied me at Rosa Vidamour's. Now I'd finally promised Michaelis and his Northern mob the same thing. Was there a way to kid all three syndicates that they'd won one and same bet? With a serious headache I watched the dancers at their glittering drill, Jonno exhorting, threatening, cajoling. He was a genius, right enough. The more I saw of him the more I saw, if you follow. I went backstage to find Mike. He's a long-haired earringed six-footer who pretends he's from Liverpool and wears a black eye patch and no shoes, very piratical. I reminded him who I was.

'We last met when you were on your way to burgle

Rotherham's great porcelain museum, Mike. How're plans going?'

'Pretty good, Lovejoy. You want in?'

'Give me a call,' I said grandly. 'Oh, your sister Vesta sends her regards.'

Alarm leapt. 'She's not here, the cow, is she?' He was with a lovely girl dressed like a navvy in clogs. She was practising her fingering on a solid gold flute, but it was modern rubbish. Vesta would go berserk. The bonny girl wasn't Irma.

'Keep your hair on, Mike. No. You're safe.' Somebody called for stage action. 'Oh, Mike. Seen anything of that Irma lately?'

'No, Lovejoy. She stood me up. Is that my stage call?' I wished him luck and left, with a growing conviction that Irma was now lurking at Prior Metivier's house for some reason. It was all wrong.

Victoria came tiptoeing to whisper that Irma Dominick was still nowhere to be found. I nodded, sick at heart. Irma was the only one who had any explanation. All I needed, I thought bitterly, was for Big John Sheehan to hove in.

'And there's a message from your friend.'

'Who?' I said, heart leaping.

'A Mr John Sheehan. He arrives in an hour.' Thank you for listening, God.

'Thanks, love,' I said, broken. So many friends. Time to leave?

'I knew you'd be pleased. Friends are so important, aren't they?'

Personal history, a.k.a. friendship, costs, or have I said that?

'Victoria?' Drowning man, begging a straw. 'Can I ask? You and Jonno . . . ?'

'No!' Her face flamed. 'He doesn't bother, not even with the dance girls.' A possible consolation? My heart rose. 'His, ah, friend is Mrs Crucifex.' Jonno also a contender? A headache began.

I said, shattered, 'Could you get me a drink, please?'

She looked pleased. 'I've brought you one, Lovejoy. Is house white all right?'

'Ta, love. That's me.'

30

'WE'VE DONE IT.' Jimmy's security man Stan showed me the display stands, and guessed my angst. 'No, Lovejoy. They're screwed down.'

'And—'

'Electronic central system.' He kept going. 'Fail-safe generators, if that's your worry. No fuse, no ruse.'

Jimmy Ozanne beamed as we went round the exhibition area. He was especially gratified when I accidentally stepped over the guide ropes and a siren gave an angry squawk, stifled by a pocket zapper.

Splendid Sejour truly was the place. They'd thought of everything.

'Unless you tell me otherwise?'

'No, Stan. Fine, fine.'

He suddenly shouted at some assistant who'd lit a fag. The man jumped a mile. So did I. 'Now, Lovejoy. This is your exhibition area. What crooks must I expect?'

'Somebody will steal one exhibit, Stan. Not all, not several. One. It won't be an outside job. The thief will be one of you, a true Guernésiais. Somebody among the bidders.' To their shocked faces I went on, 'Not riff-raff, either.'

Stan took this in silence. He was a tall assured man. He dangled three electronic bleepers, red diodes showing they were on the ball, everybody watch out. Guards material. He and Jimmy exchanged glances.

'That true, old boy?' Jimmy asked. He signed Victoria to step inside and close the door to exclude infidels. 'Guernsey has no crime.'

'I heard that.'

'Can't you say who it'll be, Lovejoy?'

'No. The thief might have a friend as decoy.'

They saw the sense of that. I told Jimmy to announce that a legal guarantee of umpteen million zlotniks was signed, sealed and banked. It wasn't, but the truth had failed poor Gesso, and it must be made to pay. They had four more TV appearances scheduled for Jonno in the afternoon. Already air waves were carrying chat shows about the combined variety show and The Greatest Gamble On Earth. Its capital letters were growing apace. Some billing. I was pleased that church dignitaries were hand-wringing about falling moral standards. Nothing promotes crime so much as moral outrage.

'Lovejoy's right, Stan,' Jimmy said. 'Live and learn, what?'

Live and learn's an old motto, except that folk abbreviate it. 'Live and learn – *die and forget*,' I completed for Jimmy. None of us smiled.

'Lovejoy, please?' Victoria shook her hair away to peer out. 'There are now two dozen urgent messages.'

'Any from a Miss Irma Dominick?'

'None of the faxes, telephone calls, care-ofs. The rest aren't open.'

Jimmy made me sign an inspection sheet, time, place, date, before I could leave for Victoria's production office.

God, it stank of fag smoke. Jonno was on the blower yelling insults. He still wore his long slicker, as if his faithful pinto was outside champing at the bit. I was glad to see him, but in the nick of time remembered that he might be one of Jocina's famous three. I was unprepared when he slammed the receiver down.

'Lovejoy, I sacked your pal,' he said. 'Stage call ten minutes, Victoria.'

'Maureen?' I asked in shock, as Victoria shot off.

'No. Nightmarish. I'm flying in a group from Aberdeen.'

'Oh, right.' I thought I saw one of Big John Sheehan's blokes walk past the window. 'Er, look, Jonno. I've to attend to these messages. OK if me and Victoria do it somewhere else? Only—'

We made it, among rehearsing dancers, a fairground area and marauding toddlers in sandpits. We examined the messages in the safety of Cambridge Park. They were all dull, apart from Big John's. It said he was teaming up with Michaelis Singleton. I handed them back to her. She was aghast.

'We must answer them all immediately, Lovejoy!' she cried. 'Bidders from Berlin, Marseilles—'

'No interest to me, love.' I looked at Guernsey's trees. Trees fascinate me. They're in one place for good, yet they wave about, always busy. Autumnal shedding, burgeoning buds. I like them. Same as birds, really. I reckon you could get a lot of consolation and even love from trees and birds if you stood still.

'Yes, I think that,' she said gently. Whoops, talking thoughts aloud. 'Lovejoy? You took desperate risks to bring Jonno's show and set up the exhibition to help Prior Metivier's priory. Why don't you bother about urgent calls?'

I said nothing, watching the trees.

'It would be like Jonno setting up a West End show, then not caring.'

A little lad was trying to fly a kite. It reminded me. I'd watched a kiddie fly one somewhere long ago. Me?

'I had a mate once, Victoria. He had this ambition. A massive roadside caff. Actually got one. You know what? He ordered all traditional things, beef, burgers, made it grand – and nobody came. You know why? The weather temperature went up, from 19°C to 20°C. He went bankrupt.' I looked at her across my shoulder, leaning forward, elbows on my knees.

'Well, I do sympathize, Lovejoy—'

'You don't see, love. Everybody else knew that that one degree up to 20°C stops East Anglian folk eating meat, beef, pork, burgers. They change their foods. It's common knowledge.' She was still doubtful. 'Like, every woman knows that Good Queen Bess had a thirteen-inch waist – what's that, thirty-two centimetres is it? Achieving it is the problem.'

'Thir*teen* . . . ?' she gasped, then concentrated. 'Are you actually speaking of the exhibition, Lovejoy?'

'Aye, love.' I tried to smile. 'Cope with the messages. Tell Jimmy and Stan I'll need a security van at four o'clock tomorrow morning, OK? Give me your mobile phones numbers.'

She watched me stand and stretch. I bussed her so-long. She looked so forlorn, clutching her sheaf of vital messages.

'Lovejoy? Where will you be?' She coloured, went for it. 'If you have nowhere to stay tonight, you can, ah, stay . . .'

I started towards St Peter Port. 'Ta-ra, love. Another times. Thanks for all you've done.'

'Not at all, Lovejoy,' floated after me down the slope.

She was forlorn? She should have been in my shoes. From the stern rail of the Weymouth ferry, I watched Guernsey recede. I spent the whole journey thinking of the antiques I'd found restored so badly in the Guernsey antique shops, especially Rita's. Couldn't get them out of my mind, as a matter of fact.

Back in East Anglia by late afternoon, I went to see Desdemona.

She'd moved to her auntie's, only three doors along. She was glad to see me. I asked what Gesso'd been up to when she'd seen him last.

'I don't know, Lovejoy. Remember, we're separated some time.'

'What work did he do for Albansham Priory?' I asked, not knowing what the hell I was up to. My plan was in Guernsey, bubbling to the boil, while I was home gnawing at a non-existent bone. Daft.

'He did a lot, Lovejoy.' I took her hand. She pulled away. 'No, Lovejoy. Not now. The children will be home soon. Another time?' I said yes, but I'd said the same to Victoria.

'Can I see his toolshed?'

She took me into the back garden. The shed looked untouched, just a few trinkets lying about, a tube of paint, brushes, a dusty canvas. Nobody had worked here for ages. Powder in jars, a midget electric kiln with a temperature slab drooping like a Dali watch. I gave myself a splinter feeling along the window ledge.

'Was he well paid?' I wanted to ask if Gesso had happened on some scam of Prior Metivier's, like a fool hunting for motives, when motive is always dud.

'I never knew,' she said, aggrieved, 'after he took up with Irma.'

'Irma who?'

'Irma Dominick. Him and her. That's why I went to Little Henny – I met you there, remember? They had a holiday chalet.'

We returned to the house, leaving the shed door ajar. 'Did Gesso ever go to the Channel Isles, find anything there he shouldn't?'

'Him? Stick-in-the-mud?' She started laying for tea. I heard the school bus arrive, whoops and shouts. 'That plain-clothes bobby came asking the same.'

'Oh, I know,' I said, casual. 'I was just checking he'd, er, asked the right questions.' I made for the door. She plucked at my sleeve.

'I meant it, darling, about another time.' She smiled, coming close. 'I'll promise you, if you promise me. Yes?'

Her two children burst in, flinging satchels. I zoomed to town, only a few hours left. Why do women and promises go together? Maybe because promises aren't for keeping anyway. What policeman exactly? I hadn't dared ask who, in case it gave me scarier thoughts than usual. Gesso was Irma's mate, and Gesso got killed. Had Irma in fact stood to gain most from his death? What Gesso'd found out about the Priory's cache of war loot, Irma must also know. And I knew from Michaelis that she was among the merry holiday-makers on Guernsey. Had she led Gesso unsuspecting to his doom at the priory?

I was beginning to sound like the Black Hand Gang myself.

*

Jutta was in the Antiques Arcade, hair still unbridled. I was relieved the dealers had left. Racing at Doncaster, the results in at Penny Dev's, bookmaker of this parish. I said hello.

'How's Guernsey, Lovejoy? Did you hear Gesso's gone walkabout?'

'Nice, and yes. How's Damnation Dougal?'

She was dusting her rotten antiques so they'd look buyable. Some hopes.

'He's wonderful, Lovejoy. Maybe one day.' She sighed. 'Oh, Paula's on the warpath after you. You stole a George the Fifth silver and sold it to Harry Bateman. She's livid.'

'I'll call in and see her,' I said pleasantly. 'Look. Did you ever see Irma Dominick? She was that girl who—'

'Fortune on wheels, that one.' Her vigorous dusting almost sent her items flying. 'I hate a rich buyer who won't buy when she should, stupid bitch.'

Which flabbergasted me. Into Jutta's voice had come That Tone, a whine dealers use to blame punters for not throwing money at their tat. What set me on my heels was rich. Irma? R-i-c-h rich? Or merely got a bob or two?

'Can't be the same lass, love. This Irma was virtually broke.'

'That's her, smarmy cow.' Jutta threatened me with a duster. 'You stupid sod, teaching her how to shoplift when she could buy every auction house in the Eastern Hundreds.'

'Eh? But she jumped bail.' I almost whimpered it, lost.

'Typical rich, that is. The mare.' She came close, fingered my lapel. 'Lovejoy. Could you show me that technique we tried once at your cottage? Only, this Friday I'm in with a chance. Reverend Dougal has asked me—'

Typical. Starving for lack of a woman, I start getting offers wholesale when I've no time. I promised, hand on my heart, etc., etc., and fled to Florida's home, a little cot in the Suffolk meadows.

Her home occupies vast tracts of prime farming land, which explains the shortage of grain products, but the splendid mansion, the gardeners slogging at the verdure, make you trust Florida's profane contention that wealth is justifiable – as long as it isn't wasted on worthless social causes like the poor.

'Remember he's an ex-cop,' I told myself, knocking. A maid let me in, made me wait in the marbled hall. I'd been in smaller cathedrals. The staircase soared up in spirals to a majestic domed belvedere.

'Lovejoy? Eddie Champion. Come in. Drink?'

Gentry aren't often pally straight off, so I trod warily. He poured me orange juice, had whisky in a beaker that made me groan. Eddie Champion chuckled. He was the man I'd seen leaving Vesta's Emporium. Now, he looked kindlier.

'So it's true, eh? Genuine antiques do make you gag?'

'Only an idiot could mistake that yellow.'

An expert decorator of porcelain in old Vienna was Anton Kothgasser, who lived to well over eighty. He loved colour. His pal Gottlob Mohn showed him his new palette of transparent hues – Gottlob's dad had developed them long before 1815, when he popped his clogs. The shock of all time was this brilliant clear yellow. They'd used it for painting window glass, and Anton fell in love with it. Glass which the Mohns did for the Austrian Emperor is more pricey, but for me Anton's is second to none. I winced as the beaker clanked gently on Champion's teeth. Signed, with his address, a Kothgasser beaker names its own price.

'Irma Dominick gave me this,' he said wrily. 'The only antique I own.'

'Quite a present.' From a lass who'd begged me to teach her to steal a cheap necklace free of charge.

'Thought you were in Guernsey, Lovejoy. How *is* Florida?'

No good trying to pretend. Everybody knew everybody else, except me.

'She took a friend, Lovejoy. Dook isn't it, this week?'

I never know what to say when people, especially husbands or wives, go like this. 'Aye. She's determined to bet on some antiques.'

Champion laughed. 'Uncontrollable. Still, it's her money, not mine.' He glanced shrewdly at me. 'You've taken up with Mrs Crucifex?'

'I'm the one that got away, Mr Champion.'

He chuckled, a man content with his lot. He actually looked like a retired Fuzz. 'But you have hopes? No need to answer. And it's Eddie, please. You gave us a lot of amusement, Lovejoy. We used to run a book on you at the station. I won three hundred quid once. Your Scotch scam. Remember?'

'No,' I said, cold. Like I said, I hate people who remember things, especially police, ex or extant makes no difference.

He poured himself another dram. 'You lying bastard. How can I help you?'

'What's happened about Gesso?'

'Hopped it, I heard. Why?'

'I'm worried he's been topped.'

'Sometimes *you* vanish, Lovejoy. Florida is – was? – forever hunting you.'

'But I'm alive.'

He stared into his Kothgasser beaker. The decoration on the lovely glass was St Stephen's Cathedral, which Anton used to walk past in Vienna. I like the ones with playing cards on, though collectors mostly go for his glasses showing children, views, bouquets.

'You're barking up the wrong tree, Lovejoy. Gesso's tough, worked at Albansham Priory. It's hardly the life of a harum-scarum, is it?'

Him and his Kothgasser. I wondered if I should tell Pedalo, our slinkiest cat burglar, to come night-stealing and claim commission on the theft.

'Irma Dominick's a friend of yours? I'm looking for her too.'

'Mmmh. I still think they should have taken her offer.'

'What offer?'

'For the priory. Send the monks packing, make a great hotel complex. At least it would endure, instead of falling into ruin.' He lit a pipe, puffed lazily. Nice aroma, pity about the arteries. 'Village lads'll have the lead off the roof any day. After that, rubble time.'

'To buy it? Irma?'

'Yes. Irma was grateful because I set up the meeting – Irma and Prior Metivier – in this very room. Irma offered to buy the priory, freehold, grounds and all. I used to be in Company Fraud when I was in the police. Irma wanted me to be there when she did the deal. She offered cash. Jocina found out – Metivier told her – and went berserk, called her a scheming bitch outright.'

Instead, the whole priory becomes empty as a ghost village. With a choice of money or ruin, I think I'd take the gelt. So why hadn't Prior George?

We parted amicably. I quite liked him. I noticed that the housekeeper, a pleasant lady his age more or less, looked at home. As I left, they stood together to wave me off. Well, fair's fair.

That night I stayed with Jutta, in serious training for her final assault on Reverend Dougal's hellfire morals. Next midday she drove me all the way to Weymouth. I gave her the Jersey Lily/Oscar Wilde Budge teapot. Not in payment, you understand, just for peace of mind. I knew now that Prior Metivier, alarmed at Irma's offer to buy him out – denuding him of his charity scams and gambling – had had Gesso killed. Had Gesso threatened to tell the other fundraisers, and so sealed his own fate? I was satisfied. I had the motive.

After interrogating the reception lass in the depot about Miss I. Dominick's journey – she was helpful when I explained that Irma was my diabetic sister – me and Jutta parted like fond lovers. She thanked me for showing her how to thrill Reverend Dougal, should she ever get close to him in a state of undress. I wished her luck. Jutta was on a loser, a hiding to nothing. I'd say our confidence levels were about equal.

31

AT ST PETER PORT I let everybody else get off. I chatted up the stewardesses, and asked if they knew Irma. No luck. I ambled to the Esplanade, where I sat in the gathering dusk. The show would open in two hours. Jimmy and Victoria would be demented, but I had questions.

What lass, rich as King Thingy, wanted a scruffy reprobate like me to show her how to steal from an antiques auction, and then goes and balls it up? Any dealer would have nicked it for a tenner, not batted a lid. As if Irma'd *wanted* to get caught. And what lass, so filled with antiques lore that she unerringly picks a precious – meaning violently precious – glass beaker made by an all-time Viennese great, then donates it to some ageing gent, Eddie Champion, who'd done her a favour? Last, and most ominous, what enviably rich bird, clearly an antiques expert herself, wanted a priory?

The more I thought of Irma, the more I thought of the helpless, hapless Martin Crucifex, submerged in his wife's social tide. Very like Eddie Champion, except that Florida's husband, with no allegiances – no-inherited money, passion or such impedimenta – had simply condoned Florida's county-set life and been kind when Irma had come for advice. Eddie quietly loved his housekeeper. Sauce for the gander.

The marina was busy. Which boat was Irma's? If she had one, it must be here. They all looked the business, ocean-goers, tall masts, bow railings, twice as posh as Mersea Island's and those on East Anglia's Blackwater. Had Irma got me in her telescope right now from out there? One thing, her plan was consistent. The instant she'd created maximum mayhem by her deliberately inept theft from Gimbert's Auction Rooms, she'd gone to earth. I was convinced she would try to sabotage tonight's exhibition. But who did kill Gesso? OK, I admit it was me got him captured, but was it Irma, with a little bit of help from friends? Or Metivier alone?

The light was fading on lovely, warm Guernsey. The locals speak of themselves with a soft 'G'. Which made me think all the more of Gesso. Him and his clumsy forged antiques, his reputation as a brilliant robber that had let me down so badly. I felt ashamed. Me, the loyal avenging friend, tempted by his widow, in Gesso's own cottage, as she made tea for his children. Worse, I'd even promised to make smiles with her, first chance I got. This after having lain on Gussy the previous night, just before slogging myself to a grease spot in Jutta's tender clasp. I'm a pathetic swine.

'Which boat is Irma Dominick's, please?' I asked a boatman.

'Didn't she give you a phone number?'

Nautical folk always think you'll nick their mizzen mast. 'Lost it, I'm afraid.'

'Hasn't she relatives you could ask?'

He knew Irma all right. 'I'm not sure.'

'Can't help you. Sorry.' He clunked on in his great boots, bucket clanking.

The other question was just as serious. If you were Prior Metivier and were offered cash for your sinking enterprise, namely Albansham Priory, would you turn it down? Doubt it. I wouldn't, especially with bare-fist fighters and book-makers on my tail. So why did Jocina, doyenne fund-raiser and leader of the pack, 'go berserk when she heard'? Eddie's words. The sale would have got her and Metivier off the hook.

That question stumped me. Because maybe the money from the priory sale would have had to go to some archdio-cese, or the Order itself? I was still mulling it over when I heard tyres squeal and somebody shouted, 'He's there!' and people came running. I stood, stretched, yawned. Stan, Jimmy Ozanne, two guards. They had a big Range Rover.

'Evening, lads.' I went towards their motor. 'Let's go.'

They halted, recriminations dying.

Jimmy said, reproachful, 'Jonno's show's already started, Lovejoy. It's a sell out.'

'Pleased to hear it. Thanks for coming.' I got in one of the rear seats. They looked at me. I think the word is nonplussed. 'Jimmy, Stan, come with me. You others go and scour the exhibition for electronic bugs, external wiring, plastics, anything odd. We'll be half an hour. Put an extra two men on the gate.'

'That's seen to, Lovejoy.' Stan nodded to his men to hare off.

'Well done. I'll direct you.'

Joe and Meg let us in. I liked the way they didn't ask questions or look about the Carrieres' place much. I shouted a hello through to Dove, then asked for solitude in the woodshed while they had a chat. Jimmy was nervous about the time. Alone, I did some quick work with Joe's claw hammer to check that Gussy's paintings were untouched. I removed one canvas – any would do – and strapped it between two pieces of cardboard. It was clearly a painting. I refastened the crates and shouted Stan and Jimmy to give me a hand. We carried the crates to the motor. I called ta. Stan zoomed us off.

'Look, men,' I said at one point in the reckless drive. 'There's something important I want to say.'

'What now?' Stan said through clenched teeth, eyes along his headlights.

'Guernsey's speed limit's thirty-five miles an hour. We're doing—'

'Lovejoy,' they said together, so I shut up.

Might as well talk to the wall.

The leisure centre was bulging, the world and his wife in. Anybody who could play an instrument was hard at it. Lights, colours, folk in carnival mood. Bars bulged. There was hubbub and music everywhere, a glittering procession of cartoon characters, searchlights and strobes blinding you so you couldn't see a frigging thing. Glorious. I love peace.

We screeched to a halt. Victoria rushed out with a stream of uniformed girls. Like a pit stop at Brands Hatch. Guards hurried us, until Jimmy slowed us down so we smiled our way through the crowd. We were on TV. The music hall was being broadcast.

'Is anything more maddening,' I asked Victoria, 'than hearing an audience laughing when you've missed the gag?'

'What?' She said it just like Stan, except her teeth weren't clenched. 'Where were you, Lovejoy? Everybody told me off.'

'Sorry, love.' I bussed her for forgiveness while the rest

unpacked the paintings. 'There's a number on each. See they go up in order.'

'What about your one?'

'That? It's only an extra fake. Leave it in the office, please.'

The exhibition looked really quite imposing. The stands were burgundy velvet on chrome tubing. The walls had been done in magnolia and pink. Burgundy velvet and orange curtains set off the crystal chandeliers. One thing, I thought, everybody'll remember the colour scheme if nowt else. It was quite a sight, Gussy's paintings showing to real advantage.

People in the corridors caused such a crush that the guards had to move them on. I insisted they could peer in. The TV folk were already complaining they should have priority. A comic's act ended in applause, and a singer came on. I recognized Maureen Jolly's voice. She was really good. I said this to Stan.

'I can pick 'em,' I joked. He was too preoccupied to smile. Hostesses arrived to lay out wine and nibbles in the anteroom, chattering excitedly. Victoria had to get quite stern.

'Done, Lovejoy.' Jimmy clocked the time. 'Now what?'

'Allow people in at the music hall interval. Got the bid forms?'

'Here, Lovejoy.'

Victoria had a desk by the entrance. Bonny girls in Splendid Sejour uniforms were already there. Embossed pens, modern naff crystal mobiles, television monitors showing us to ourselves, we were the height of glamour. I'd never seen so many hidden cameras. We were knee deep in security.

'Each visitor gets a card, Lovejoy.' Victoria was so

earnest. 'If they want to bid, they simply circle a number on the card and include a certified cheque.'

That didn't sound quite right. 'Standing in a crowd?'

'No, Lovejoy.' She indicated two curtained screens by the desk. 'Voting booths. Anyone wanting privacy can use those. The cabled and faxed bids have already been processed.' She said that with tight lips, meaning that she'd slaved to cope after I'd scarpered.

I cleared my throat. Everybody in the team shushed to listen. 'Look, everybody. Before the rush, I want to say thanks. You've all been . . .' I searched for some archaism '. . . tickety-boo. I'm not even half as reliable as any single one of you. Thank you.'

Victoria turned away, eyes moist, as her uniformed girls clapped, so pleased. Jimmy bounced on his heels, harrumphed, did his beam.

'Not at all, old boy. Comes with the ration gong, what?'

Stan reached for his mobile phone, snapped orders to begin a last security sweep. I heard the band crescendo, the applause for Maureen's song. I decided I'd see the second half of the music hall. Waste of time gazing at rows of forgeries. I beckoned Victoria and we stood apart.

'Here's three envelopes, love. Give one to these bidders on the sly when they come in. OK?' They were addressed 'By Hand' to Michaelis Singleton, Jocina Crucifex and Mrs Florida Champion.

'Lovejoy?' As she spoke a thunderclap made me jump. She calmed me. 'It's only Mr Ozanne's fireworks.' Through the windows came an unholy glare. Rockets and multicoloured lights shone and whizzed. My heart thundered in sympathy.

'God Almighty, love. He might have let me know.'

'Don't be frightened, Lovejoy.' Bloody nerve. As if I was

scared of a couple of bangers. She kept hold of my arm. 'Is it, well, over now?'

'What?'

'Your trick?'

'I'm not tricking anybody,' I lied. Women are quick to condemn honesty. 'Yes, it's over.'

'At ten o'clock you'll reveal which is the genuine picture?'

'Aye, love. The winner gets it. The losers go home. We keep the money.'

She was looking at her feet. The fireworks banged and whirred in the night sky. People oohed and aahed. The music hall doors parted and the clamour of a released audience began. We would soon be engulfed.

'Will I see you again?'

'Yes, love. Here. Early morning.'

'Very well.' Shyly she bussed me, toffee and lavender scent. 'Thank you.'

For what? Chattering hordes swamped the lounges and thoroughfares, rushing out to the verandah bars to see the fireworks before the interval ended. We were separated. I went and sat in the office until the two-minute showtime bell went. I took the extra canvas, and entered the darkness of the auditorium last. I stood at the back to watch the show.

There's something wrong with memories. I can remember classroom junk so meaningless there ought to be a law to protect children from having to learn it. Yet essential things go missing. I'd like to know how to keep calm, for instance. Do schools teach that? Do they heck. They teach the Church's Canon Law, which you've to learn by heart or get whacked. In the armed forces they teach you to shoot to kill, when you only want to go home. It's weird. I think God was a duckegg – who else would invent *Taenia solium*, the ugliest of ugly tapeworms, to show his cleverness? Name one thing he got right. Damned if I can.

The show was really smart, debonair, slick with repartee. Bonny girls, handsome singers, clever magicians, even two famous TV actors. I was proud. Four acts into the second half, I became conscious of somebody standing beside me in the gloaming, and whispered, 'Wotcher, Jonno. Good, eh?'

'How do, Lovejoy,' he whispered back. 'Thanks, incidentally.'

'What for?' Gratitude makes me nervous. I find it's false.

'We're sold out for weeks. I'm syndicating mainland television.'

'Oh, good.' As if I knew what it meant. 'Glad you're pleased.'

'Taking that anywhere in particular?'

'This?' The painting. 'No. We'd one decoy too many.'

'I like your friend.'

Well, I liked his. 'Er, who?'

'Maureen. She'll need time, but she'll make it.'

'Ta, Jonno.' Yet more gratitude. Of the right kind, of course. 'Was it worth your while to come?' I was serious.

'More than anything, Lovejoy.' He hesitated, then glided off as an act came to a close in a roar of applause. 'Gotter see to something.'

Me too. Prior Metivier was missing, and so was the lovely Jocina. Which proved he would be with her – maybe on her boat – making smiles. I would plant Gussy's painting on it, return to the celebrations and immediately create a fuss, claiming the prize had gone missing. I'd scream to the police, Jimmy O, Stan, the TV broadcasters, that the genuine picture had been nicked by Prior George and was probably on the *Jocina*. They would have to search for it. With Prior G. and Jocina Crucifex in custody, however temporary, I'd be able to hand the location of the cache to the highest bidder – for a fee. I'd insist on being made advisor/consultant, and live in clover for ever and ever on the proceeds.

It seemed foolproof, the thought of fools.

I left the theatre, an usherette letting me out into a startlingly bright and vacant foyer. I was glad. I made the fresh air among crowds clapping the spectacular brilliance of the fireworks. I stole one of the company's bicycles, cursing the security chains. It took me ten whole minutes to find a padlock I could open with my key ring. People get on your frigging nerves. If I'd had time, I'd have gone back and sacked Stan. I pedalled off into the night, cursing the painting clapping against my leg.

32

IT'S FUNNY WHAT thoughts come into your head. I used to know a bird who made love thinking about shopping, collecting the children from school, her sister's jealousy. For me, it's the other way about. In mid-love my mind exchanges my ordinary world for giddy excitement – in imagination. It does it without asking me. Like, I was pedalling into St Peter Port's harbour area, my brain in a fever of envy.

My scam depended solely on forgeries – if you insist, 'reproductions' – made by Augusta Quenard, a lady who copied over and over a painting she'd seen as a child in a sea cave. She turned out copies like biscuits, got laughed at. To me they looked Mondrian – from a distance. Close to? Dross. But she *had* seen something those years ago. And was any place more fortified than wartime Alderney? And the slaves had included hundreds from East Europe. The relatives of some survivors had eventually returned. Look at the fag-smoking Boris. Loot is often untraceable. These were facts.

Gussy seemed to have seen a genuine something that day. And Marie Metivier had manipulated a windfall – selling a work of art to save her brother from shoals of nasty creditors. Where had she got it? Alderney again. It was the age-old riddle: Where do you hide a tree but in a forest?

There's the famous case of the Cupid. It stood for donkey's years in plain view. A mansion house on Fifth Avenue, New York, no less. Folk wandered by the nice little statue, took no notice. They even ignored it at Sotheby's sale in 1902, which billed it as a Michelangelo. Later, an architect bought it for a song and stuck it in the courtyard. Seventy years later, one Mr Parronchi wrote in Florence that it was Michelangelo. The world yawned and said, 'Pull the other leg.' Then somebody said, 'Hey! That's by Michelangelo!' And this time publicity hit the fan. Throngs thronged. Television crews tore destructively into the courtyard. See what I mean? Pronouncements go unheeded for virtually an entire century. Sotheby's, experts wholesale, authoritative analyses were all ignored. So what changed? It was, is, the same statue. Yet not a single thief tried his hand when the statue was unguarded. Now? You'd need a regiment to wriggle within twenty yards, and still wouldn't make it.

There's no accounting for taste.

Sometimes you know because you know that something's a dud. Like that barmy 'discovery' that *A Funerall Elegie* by 'W.S.' was William Shakespeare's. It's a poem about some murdered West Country bloke. Sad, aye. Experts analysed the printing, the ink, the paper. Computers counted the words, dissected its syntax, drew histograms. Professors grappled with senile rage on faculty greenswards. But there's one truth, plain as a pike staff. It's this: the newly discovered poem is crap. My message to the discoverers? Shakespeare couldn't write junk like that if he tried. Grow up, get a real job and stop pretending you know what day it is. Fraudsters nark me. Either do it right or don't do it at all. A con trick deserves dignity.

She was waiting by the crossroads where I'd told her to be. I was so engrossed in my inner fury I almost pedalled past. I squealed to a stop.

'Wotch, Gussy.'

'Hello, darling.' She sounded so excited. Her perfume almost knocked me off my bike. 'I saw the crowds! Isn't it wonderful? All to see my art!'

Well, no, dwoorlink, but I did not say. 'You'll be famous now, love.'

'Thank you, Lovejoy. What do you want me to do?'

I alighted. The fireworks were still crackling and glittering in the sky over Splendid Sejour. Good old Jimmy, proving that advertising pays. We could hear the faint roars of the throngs.

'I want you to wait, love. I'll be twenty minutes. If any of my, our, er friends, come asking, tell them I've gone to the boat. All right?'

'Right, darling.' She hugged me. 'I'll be here.'

Trying to look heading for a genuine appointment instead of being sly, I left her the bike and legged it. Some distance along the wharfside I found three dinghies and nicked the smallest. For the gentle art of rowing you need sheer strength, and I'd not much. I hadn't much idea, either. I'm useless at that sculling business, one oar over the stern. I do it with two oars, backing forward. You have to keep pausing to see where the hell you're heading.

Down at water level on a night sea, and only the receding lights of the Esplanade to go by, you feel vulnerable. Even small yachts look massive, and the big ones seem huge liners. Worse, they don't all have lights to guide a humble seafarer, selfish swine. They all had mooring ropes straining down into the harbour waters. I was scared of getting snared. For a second, as I really warmed up and started rowing steadily, I thought I heard somebody call my name. It must have been some seagull. Do seagulls fly at night? I scanned the sky, couldn't see a one. They'd all knocked off. What was it, ten o'clock? Half past? The fireworks, now frantic and continuous, showered light. I heard a brass band distantly start up. Jimmy, bound to be him, unable to resist a parade.

I narrowly missed colliding with a long line of white craft. They nodded like tethered nags. I heard somebody singing in one. A TV reporter was bawling in that telly monotone, 'The last of the bidders is going in! Countdown to closing! Soon somebody will be a millionaire! Ten-nine-eight—' And all that.

Somebody clumped along a deck. Something poured nastily into the water. Pollution. Were they allowed? I heard rhythmic splashing. Somebody else was rowing, forgotten something maybe, or coming to a tryst on board a love ship. I felt jealous.

Then I realized I was lost. I stopped, drifting, stared about. Where had the *Jocina* been? Somewhere in the final row, I thought. Or nearer the harbour mouth? Was it like motor cars at the town hall, marked parking places? I thought of knocking on a boat's side and asking. What if nobody was at home? I'd get done for breaking and entering.

Somebody spoke gruffly, very near. I almost cried out in fear.

'You're wrong, Bessie. A lugsail only *looks* ungainly. Its surface area makes it uncommon powerful.'

'Cornwall!' from Bessie, with derision. I heard a glass

chink, a splash of soda. 'You'll have Cornish luggers at any price! Where are all the buggers now?'

Slowly I drifted past. The argument raged, dissolved. I heard a squeal, laughter, silence. Lucky end to a scrap. I resumed rowing. I was just beginning to think that I'd never find the boat, or recognize it if I did, when I saw it. It had two lights on, rose and dipped slower than the smaller boats. Its awnings were gone. I gave one long stroke for momentum and shipped the oars.

Relief's hopeless, I've always found. For maybe five minute I clung to the gangway. I could have fainted from joy, no longer drifting about the briny. I was safe. I realized how scared I'd been. I'm terrified enough on land, let alone the sea. I tied the painter, and softly went aboard, my picture under my arm.

The boat was still, silent. Except . . .

'That's it, lover.' Somebody actually cried that aloud, gave a moan. I thought, Irma? At last, I'd got her. Definitely a woman. I'd never heard her in the throes of smile-making, my tough luck, but it had to be the missing Irma. Everybody else was at the auction. I heard distant strains of Elgar's *Pomp and Circumstance*, a distant roar of crowds. Gala time tonight in Splendid Sejour. Here? Here on the *Jocina* it was gala night for two. I'd assumed Irma would be alone on her aunt's boat. I hated to interrupt, but had to.

I leant the canvas against the railings, and eeled in. I had the sense to force the door gently up to prevent squeaks. Good old Gesso taught me that.

Down five or six steps. Is it called a companionway? A light further along, the saloon. Quietly, I went towards the grunts, the exhortations. For all I knew Irma loved some gigantic oaf who'd crush me like a gnat. As long as it wasn't Dook.

The saloon door was ajar. Jocina was on her side, clutching and rocking, in ecstasy. The sofa was now a double bed. Her man was rasping, slamming into her. He too was naked, pumping as she clawed and laughed blindly over his shoulder.

My mind went, Gesso?

No, not Gesso. It couldn't be, because I'd proved that Gesso was . . .

Somebody squawked. They both stopped and gaped, eyes riveting me, mouths going ooooh. Gesso ripped away, causing Jocina to groan in anguish. He rose, stood grinning. A man of triumph, all right. Him, not me.

'Lovejoy!' He grabbed a towel, wrapped it about his waist. 'I heard your con. Great, eh? Do you actually have a real picture or not? We've checked. The real one's still with the rest.'

'Yes.' The lie took several tries. 'I've brought it.' No good explaining I'd thought to plant it on the good ship *Jocina* and swear later Prior Metivier had stolen it from the exhibition. It had been a good idea. He'd have lasted less than an hour, as the rival gambling syndicates took him apart. Jocina, deprived, was whining in grief, her stolen moment.

'You didn't die, then?' I had to ask, stupid to the last. Like he was codding, raised from the dead, some hologram trick.

'No. The pen torch was my idea.' He grimaced. 'Leaving it by the hot pool cost me emotion. But once we'd taken the decision . . .'

'Darling!' Jocina warned sharply, coming to. 'Shut *up*.'

Darling, my dull mind registered. Gesso, Jocina's darling? Had everybody else known? And decision about what? To scratch a stone, drop a tenpenny flashlight? How come such a paltry decision needed the powerful and gorgeous Jocina to warn with such alarm in her voice? Unless there was something horrid at Albansham Priory, plus the cache of war-looted antiques. I couldn't look away from the pair.

He chuckled. 'Lovejoy! You're crazy for Jocina!' He laughed so much I thought he was going to fall down. 'What's your idea? Give her the painting and take a turn with her?'

'Irma,' I said, ill. 'Where's Irma?'

They glanced at each other. Gesso smiled and lit a cigarette. I hadn't known he smoked. Jocina reclined against the pillows, pulling the duvet up. She looked exquisite. I'd have given her anything, if only she'd asked.

'Look at it this way, Lovejoy,' Gesso said, a sharper laying out cards. 'Scams come once in a lifetime. You divvied a painting for us in the priory chapel. And that Chinese face. We *had* to know if the prior's cache from Alderney was genuine or not. You were the test.'

'And the cache is hidden at the priory,' I said dully. No wonder they didn't dare sell the damned place. And no wonder Irma wanted to buy it.

'Yes, Lovejoy.' He went to a drawer. I, like a nerk, watched him take out an old blued Smith & Wesson. It would throw a thing like a carrot through any person in its path. Through me.

'And Irma realized, guessed, found out?'

'She overheard, Lovejoy.' He said it with exasperation, really annoyed. 'Then she tries to buy the priory from under us. Thinks we'd give her everything Jocina and Prior George have planned for decades. Silly bitch.'

Irma. Who'd been dragged to the hot pool, probably knocked senseless, been cast in, to sink . . . I wobbled, sat.

'Don't take it hard, Lovejoy.' He spoke so reasonably, good heavens, a fly in my soup. 'These things happen.'

'I should have realized, Gesso. You're still doing atrocious fakes, even on Guernsey. And I take it you are the non-local Mr Slevin and that little antique shop of Rita's is yours?' The oil of cloves, that bad enamel on the Berlin iron jewellery should have tipped me off. And Irma had *wanted* to get caught stealing from Gimbert's – to direct attention on to her gorgeous aunt Jocina. Too scared of her aunt's thugs – meaning Gesso – to do it any other way. Irma, poor lass, had organized the meeting at Eddie Champion's home, when she'd offered cash for the priory, hoping he, ex-policeman from the Company Fraud division, would somehow protect her. It hadn't worked. The rich get rich and the wrong get glugged into bottomless mud pools. 'And Prior George forced you to . . . ?'

They both laughed, Jocina louder, gasping herself back to breath. Laughing about Irma, how they'd killed her, and how ignorant I was.

'Prior Metivier couldn't run a booze-up in a brewery, Lovejoy,' Gesso managed at last. 'All he can do is gamble and lose. We nearly died when he conned his sister Marie into selling that antique to square his bloody stupid debts.' Gesso whistled in awe. I stared at the revolver. It was growing larger by the second. 'Those bare-fist gypos are nasty, Lovejoy, aren't they? Cross them, you're done for. No. Your Chinese bronze. We sent Marie with it to a private dealer.'

'Took a buyer's premium, the bastard,' from divine Jocina. 'Darling?'

'Yes,' from Gesso. I almost answered too. I'm pathetic.

'No use postponing this. It's time.'

Time for what? 'You can't,' I bleated, shaking.

'Don't beg, Lovejoy,' she said with faint disgust. 'You've an obligation to behave like a man.'

So rich women always say, as they ride on, radiant in wealth and beauty, leaving corpses on the kerb. Noble, manly to the last, I broke down.

'Please, Jocina. I'll do anything—'

'Goodnight, Lovejoy.' She smiled at me with one corner of her mouth, the other corner more or less ambiguous. 'Pity.'

I closed my eyes not to look. Your whole life's supposed to flash before your eyes. It doesn't. You simply hear the deafening report as the enormous revolver booms and you feel . . . Nothing?

The sound had come from behind me, the blast thumping my shoulders and shoving me forward a step. Now I couldn't hear a damned thing. Smoke funnelled and billowed to where Jocina was mouthing, seemed to be silently screaming, holding out her palms as if to fend something off.

In front of me Gesso folded, kneeling like he'd got belly wark. Except blood was swiftly spreading across the carpet, pulsing like it was still connected to him.

'No, please!' I heard a distant mosquito shriek.

I tried to ask no what, and who said it, but my voice rumbled somewhere with no noise coming out. A siren shrilled in my ears. I turned to look.

Dook was there, calm as you like. He simply nodded at me, and the weapon he was holding gave an upward nudge. The millisecond glare blinded me. I felt a sudden one-off vibration wave through my ribcage, smelled the tight stench of a double-barrelled shotgun. Something splattered on my face. My vision cleared.

Something clattered – I heard it! – on the cabin floor.

Dook, cool, had reloaded. He shot at the cabin wall. A light fixture shattered, sent shards everywhere, but I'd been ready that time and had fingers in my ears and eyes screwed up.

The cabin was an abattoir, blood all over the bed. Gorgeous Jocina was a mess, hair against the pillows mixed with brain and blood. A row of teeth, Christ's sake, lay on her bare breast. I vomited all over the dying, dead, Gesso.

Dook shook my arm, repeating the same thing over and over. I couldn't hear. It came through.

'Lovejoy. Can you swim?'

He was asking something to do with boats. Sod his boats. He dragged me out, up to the deck. Somebody was shouting, somebody hailing back calling what was the matter. A voice was insistent, get the prow battery lights on. My ears still sang.

Dook was still shaking me. He pulled me down low on the deck. He was ice cool. I'd never laugh at him admiring himself again.

'Ta, Dook,' I heard my grating voice say. 'Jesus, I was glad you came.'

'Lovejoy. Stop whimpering. Look at me. Can you swim? I'd better get rid of the dinghy you came in, or they'll blame you for the killings in there.'

'*Me?*' Then, quieter, 'Me? But you shot them.'

'To save you, Lovejoy. Here.' He pressed the shotgun stock into my hands, but kept hold of the trigger guard. 'Like that. See? If you can swim, it'd be best if you swam for it. You can say you weren't here, that you fell in.'

Good idea. It seemed so wise. 'Thanks for saving my life. Except I can't swim.'

'No?'

'Honest. I can't swim a stroke.' I shivered. 'Water gives me the willies.'

'Then here's what we'll do.' He beckoned, crawled towards the gangway. 'Those nosey bastards'll shine their prow searchlights over here any minute now.'

I swarmed along the deck after him to the bow rail. He pointed over the side.

'See that life raft on the water? I brought it. Lean out and see.'

Once a prat. I leant out. He clobbered me and lobbed me overboard. I fell like a stone, splashed in the cold, frigging *cold*, sea and kept going. There was no life raft.

The blow he'd given me was oblique. I'd suspected it. It got my cheek, and stung like hell in the salt water, but that was a bonus. Dizzy but conscious, I swam underwater until something clumped me on the nut. A boat. I was able to feel my way along it, emerge for a breath, seeing hardly anything in the dark, then dive slowly under in case Dook saw me.

Blearily I'd marked the *Jocina*, or what I thought was her, and swam to a boat three further to landward. Two deep breaths a time, going under and swimming from one boat to the next down the line of moored yachts. I'd not done the breast stroke for a long time. It's all I'm good at in water. No Dook, though, thank God. I was frightened and freezing. Twice I listened for oars, but couldn't be sure what with my ears roaring and me still dazed.

He'd got my fingerprints on the shotgun. Purdey of London, too, I'd noticed, standards falling everywhere. Poor Irma. Clinging to a mooring chain, I pondered whether to risk a shout for help, gave up the notion. In the dark you can fire a gun at noise, even with a searchlight starting to wave madly about, a laser baton conducting a mad silent black orchestra, engines and ahoys.

I must have drifted. I tried swimming for a new mooring

chain, missed it and floundered. God, I was tired. I kicked with what strength I had left, but the chain receded. So many lights were shifting about. Was this normal? Was this whole harbour normal, even? More shouts. Dook's pals, maybe, coming after me? My head banged against a boat's side. I grabbed nothing, sank, came up gasping.

Then somebody clutched me. A lifeguard! I wanted to tell the figure ta, mate. A sudden flare showed me Dook's face, his massive muscular form.

'You lying bastard,' he said, clasped me and took me down. I'd not even had the chance for a decent breath.

For a few seconds I fought, clawing and scratching, thinking why is it me that ends like this? Lights flickered on the surface. I was terrified, but something in memory lectured about fright. Drowning people feel a terminal tranquillity. It was that 'terminal' did it. I gave a knee jerk, no good. I tried to nut him, but he knew that one. He was swimming strongly, clobbering me in spite of somehow keeping me trapped. How many arms did the swine have? I felt past caring.

We surfaced. He had a hand over my mouth, shoving my nose flat. I wasn't to breathe. All this night air was for him. I felt myself go under, his hands now doing no more than press my shoulders down. I saw a haze of lights, heard a roar, saw something creamy swish up there on the surface – me looking dazedly up, wondering even as I decided it was all probably too much bother and who cared.

A clunk trembled through the water. Abruptly Dook let go. I drifted, amiably turning over, face down, not struggling. I was free, not breathing. I wasn't doing anything in particular. I still could see sod all. My arm was in the air. I flapped it. It splashed. Ought it not to be doing something?

I did it again. It splashed. I sank a bit more. I felt comfortable.

It was almost an insult when something became entangled. Part of it was me, but part was this thing with two arms, sinking past me. I found a face close to mine, bubbles streaming audibly from its mouth. I thought blandly, Hey, isn't that the sort of thing I scream at? I tried to scream, found I couldn't. I couldn't *scream*. Me, not even able to screech for help? Jesus. Fright returned with a whoosh. I reached for the surface, found none, kicked and got air.

People were shouting among lights. I bawled, vomiting. A body bobbed against my foot and I thought, sod you, pal, pressed down so he sank further. It helped me to float while I was sick enough to make room for breath, more breath.

Augusta told me later she'd held me against the side of the boat for a full ten minutes before she managed to haul me aboard. I blamed her for being slow, demanded to know why she'd taken so long. In a fury she said she'd saved my bloody life by running Dook down when he'd held me submerged. I said she'd taken her bloody time. She said what women always say when they're justly criticized. She said typical, typical, kept on saying it even at the police station.

You'd honestly think she'd have been glad, being useful for once. I think it's their minds. They do something useful and expect all sorts of praise. It narks me. The police doctor came but was no use. The police questioned me. They were no use either.

That night I slept in a cell.

33

CONVALESCENCE WAS IN a hospital ward in wicked snooty Jersey. I got my chest aspirated – sounds like bad breath. The doctor used a hell of a lot of painful needles while I felt sorry for myself. Police came and went. I got better, got up, peered out of the window down Gloucester Street. The Opera House opposite was always on the go. Jersey looked beautiful, but not a word to Guernsey that I think so.

They let me go Thursday of the following week. Police asked questions, not as many as I'd expected. Then I was returned – their phrase – to Guernsey. Face the music and dance.

Augusta met me and drove me in what looked like a new car. I was astonished that Guernsey seemed untroubled, unfeeling bastard. The stark truth was that Guernsey had taken my near death in its stride. A new pop group was due in, you see, what with dances and carnival processions. Guernsey's really big news was that a swimming competition had been won by a local St Peter Port girl. The price of garden produce was going up, or down. It was all happening. I was seriously narked. Me at death's dark portal saving civilization, and Guernsey didn't give a toss. Typical.

My companion was somehow different. Gussy had gone. In her place was this bonny bird a good ten years younger. Her hair was different. She wore lime green, genuine silk. She looked summery. I felt redundant.

'I've done nothing wrong, love,' I said, off on the right foot. 'I'm in the clear.'

'Wrong, Lovejoy. You'll see.'

She swung the motor through the gates, into the car park at Splendid Sejour. A long queue of people snaked over the grass, round a corner.

Holiday-makers roamed, bicycles weaving in and out. A band played sunny music among the greenery. Large cartoon figures wandered, patting children, dancing on paths among flowers. I could see everybody in Guernsey was really heartbroken with grief at my near fate, rotten unfeeling swine.

'What's the queue for? Tickets for Jonno's show?'

'That?' She laughed, modesty lacking. 'No. For my exhibition. Oh, Jonno's show's going well. It's been on television. He's got a BBC series.'

'So everybody benefits?'

'Every single one, Lovejoy.'

No mention of me. We parked and walked the rest of the way. Guards were much in evidence – for Augusta's clumsy replicas? My mind went off its rails. Grouville was having coffee with two girls and a woman Ploddite. He nodded affably to me, gestured me to sit. The others left.

'An informal chat, Lovejoy.' He eyed the retreating lasses, pulled himself together, concentrated on talking me into admissions of guilt. 'Your version, please.'

Augusta sat beside me. I was grateful, even though his

police eyes switched casually from her to me and back. I told them the tale, from Irma wanting to be taught how to steal an antique from Gimbert's auction, right down to Florida Champion's husband and the visit I'd paid to his – OK, his wife's – mansion house so few nights previously.

'He's an ex-policeman,' I said. 'He'll confirm they killed Irma.'

'Who?'

'Gesso and Jocina Crucifex. They told me that, on the boat.'

'And Dook?'

I told him how he'd tried to drown me, coming after me to make certain I couldn't swim, how I'd lied and survived. 'Eventually,' I added frostily, getting at Augusta.

'Lying is your natural propensity, Lovejoy, isn't it?' Grouville said. 'All for a bit of daubed colour on canvas?'

Augusta stirred, managed to keep cool. She spoke up.

'I shouted when I saw Dook take the dinghy and go after Lovejoy.' She shrugged. 'Lovejoy didn't hear. I borrowed Old Lou's outboard. I rang the police first.' She let that sink in before delivering her barb. 'They were slow coming, Ken.'

He cleared his throat, thought a minute, but managed to ignore criticism of the constabulary, not an all-time first. 'You see my problem, Lovejoy. Once you got to the boat and the shootings began, all is quite clear. But events leading up to there are definitely murky.'

'I thought I'd explained, Mr Grouville. Irma offered to buy the priory. It was in terrible difficulties, owing to Prior Metivier's gambling. His sister Marie paid off his debts, using the money from donated antiques that they had got me, unwittingly, to recognize. It's simple.'

'Why did the murdered girl want to buy an ancient priory, though?'

'She suspected some antiques were hidden there.'

'And are there?'

Somebody came and seated himself heavily between Augusta and me.

Prior George said, all sorrow, 'No, Mr Grouville. Not a single one. I've combed the place over the years, winkling out anything that can be called an antique and selling it on the open market. Funds kept running low despite all my efforts—'

'Gambling the bloody gelt, you mean.' I tried not to sound bitter. 'If you'd been honest there would have been no deaths at all! Mr Grouville, I'll give you my guess list of this holy geezer's gambling debts. I'll also provide a list of contacts. In East Anglia he's famous for it.'

'Lovejoy!' Prior George said reproachfully. 'How un-Christian!' He sighed to the Plod, 'Religion always has enemies.'

'And there are no antiques left in Albansham Priory, Prior George?'

'I give you my word,' the lying sod intoned. He almost blessed us. 'Our finances are straight, thanks to the splendid work of this leisure centre and Lovejoy's efforts. The priory is solvent again. I shall reopen next week. I invite you all to our celebratory services.'

So he was returning to East Anglia, to dismiss his security blokes and sell his cache of war-looted art with impunity.

'Excuse me, please,' I said. 'The doctor said I've to take some tablets. Be a sec.'

Augusta asked should she come with me, but I was off. I made it to Victoria's office alone. She was there, colouring up on seeing me.

'Oh, Lovejoy! You're better! But so thin!'

'No, love. I'm fine.' Like every male, I know I'm a fine figure of a man.

'There are all these forms to go over, Lovejoy—'

'Nark it, love. Quick. Where's Michaelis Singleton?'

'At the hotel. He leaves today. There's some problem over bail. He wants to see you urgently. He sounded really rather threatening.'

The death of Irma, *requiescat in pace*, would clear Michaelis. Jocina was out of it. Florida, Dook's mentor, was helping the Plod with enquiries, so delete her. But there was still the problem that Michaelis's backers, including Big John Sheehan, would hunt me down for defrauding them. After all, I'd persuaded Michaelis to bid for a fake. Victoria got him on the phone.

'Michaelis? It's Lovejoy. No, no, keep quiet and listen.' I talked him into silence, no mean feat, considering. Their legal education is always a handicap. I sent Victoria into the corridor while I spoke softly on.

'Is that true?' he asked eventually.

'It's got to be, Michaelis. Go for them. They're there somewhere in Albansham Priory. Tell Sheehan to be careful – there's a team of hired security guards. They might be in on it with Prior Metivier. Whatever, they'll need heavy persuasion to step aside while you anatomize the joint.'

'I leave today. Big John's already put two men in your cottage to wait for you, Lovejoy. If you're right about the loot, I'll see he calls them off.'

I gulped. God Almighty. 'But be sharp, Mikko. Florida will be back home soon. I can feel it. The sly cow will come the poor innocent, swear blind she knew nothing of Dook's murderous attack on Jocina when she sent him after me, wrongly supposing I was favouring Jocina by giving her a tip-off as to which of Gussy's canvases was the genuine one. My bet is, Florida'll say Dook lusted after Jocina, got jealous of Gesso, all that.'

'Will she get away with it?'

'Michaelis.' I was suddenly so tired. 'Ever know a beautiful sexy rich woman who didn't?'

'I'll pull my syndicate together and get going.'

They'd gut the priory in a night. Before Prior George hit the mainland the place would be scoured. His cache of art works that he'd found in the sea cave on Alderney and shipped to hide in Albansham Priory would be gone, wherever he'd hidden it. I tried to ingratiate myself.

'Look, Mikko,' I wheedled. 'Give me a share, eh? After all, we're pals.'

'Lovejoy.' He too sounded weary. 'We don't need you. Remember, Big John Sheehan's on *my* syndicate. We'll not use you at all, Lovejoy. We'll use experts,' he ended nastily, and rang off.

Frigging cheek. I opened the door to find Grouville nearby talking to Victoria. I coughed, swallowed hard. Had he heard?

'Thanks, Victoria, for the drink of water. Tablets are always too big for one gulp, aren't they?'

'Who were you phoning, Lovejoy?' Grouville asked.

'Trying to get Jimmy and Stan, tell them ta.'

Two hours later, I said so-long to everybody. It was hard. Jonno was wry, jokingly made me promise to stay myself and not him, haha. Jimmy came to attention, said 'Toodle pip, old sport'. I said, 'Cheerio, old chap'. Stan was laconic, graciously spared time from his electronic surveillance to say ta-ra. Victoria was tearful.

Augusta drove me to the Carrieres' bungalow. Dove was in (joke) but wouldn't be much longer. She was going to an arts course in London.

'To London? Hey, I'll come and see you!'

She smiled. 'Augusta's exhibition is funding me, Lovejoy. Thank you.' I bent to be bussed. Her mum and dad said their farewells. Dove asked worriedly, 'Do you think I'll manage all that study?'

'You'll fail, love,' I said. 'On filthy brushes. Give it up.'

'Oh, you!' She laughed, tears in her eyes. 'See you in London, then?'

'Race you,' I called, and left.

Augusta drove me to St Peter Port. At the harbour, there was half an hour to wait. I felt so happy, at ease for the first time since Irma had walked into my workshop. Christ, I'd forgotten Prince. Mind you, now I could forget him in complete safety, though Florida would expect me to have that furniture completed even if I was on my last legs.

'Hadn't we better ditch the motor and get on board?' I asked Augusta.

She stayed in the car. I thought, What now?

'I'm not coming, Lovejoy.'

'Not coming with me? I thought we . . .'

'I'm marrying Boris. I'm staying.'

Heartbreak's never easy. And the harbour seemed so peaceful, calm, not a breath of wind to ruffle the surface where I'd seen two murders and been narrowly rescued when Dook had died under the prow of Augusta's boat. I cast about for reasons. I was badly narked. I wanted to point out that I was good value.

'The Chinese say that if you save a life you're responsible for ever.'

'They're not here, are they?' She yanked me close and

plonked her mouth on mine. Then she shoved me away and drove off.

Slowly I boarded, sat staring at Guernsey.

The trouble is, you can fall in love with a place, just as you can with a woman. Escaping's never easy. What was to stop me simply walking off the ship on to St Julian's Pier and starting up in antiques? I could walk to Rita's shop in ten minutes, almost see it from the deck. Zillions of tourists would buy my antiques, and the island was exquisite.

She came and stood awkwardly against the sunlight. I squinted up.

'I came to see that you'd got everything, Lovejoy.'

'Wotcher, Victoria. Yes, ta.' Except I'd got nothing and lost Augusta.

'Ought you to be up and about quite so quickly?'

'No, love,' I said, sighing. 'I suppose kind passengers will help me to the train. If,' I put in with heartfelt sorrow, almost filling up with self-pity, 'I find money for the railway fare to East Anglia.'

The ferry slowly started to move. I realized there had been announcements that sailing was imminent. We watched the shoreline glide, the harbour slowly spin about the ship.

'Good heavens,' I said slowly, making sure. 'I think you've caught the boat.'

'It seems so, Lovejoy.' She'd got a small suitcase. She hesitated. 'I had letters and messages. Marie Metivier is waiting for you in East Anglia. A series of appeals for help from Florida, including letters. And a long letter from Mrs Rosa Vidamour. She rang several times.'

'Where's the letters?'

'I lost them all,' she said evenly, 'by accident.' She shivered as the ship moved out. 'Let me get you a shawl,

Lovejoy. And perhaps coffee.' She reached for my hand, almost made it. 'I can't have you catching cold, can I?'

'No, Victoria,' I said. I watched her go. Lovely. My heartbreak was healing. I wondered how she'd be if I got her to work the spong trick, falsely claiming insurance for some so-say destroyed or stolen antique. She had such honesty. That straight blue-eyed look was exactly what's needed, innocent and lovely. Any loss adjustor would approve any claim she made.

Thinking, I realized I'd forgotten to wave goodbye to the love of my life Augusta. Still, I could always write, if I remembered her address. How exactly did she spell her last name? Maybe it would come to me.

Victoria returned, with coffee on a small tray. She looked lovely. I thought what a terrible pity to let all that pure honesty go to waste. It was after all definitely a woman's world.

As long as I remembered that, next time I couldn't go wrong.